# THE WISHING GAME

# THE WISHING GAME

Patrick Redmond

Hodder & Stoughton

Copyright © 1999 by Patrick Redmond

First published in Great Britain in 1999 by Hodder and Stoughton
Published simultaneously in paperback by
Hodder and Stoughton
A division of Hodder Headline PLC

The right of Patrick Redmond to be identified as the Author of
the Work has been asserted by him in accordance with the Copyright,
Designs and Patents Act 1988.

10 9 8 7 6 5 4 3 2 1

British Library Cataloguing in Publication Data

A CIP catalogue record for this title is available
from the British Library.

ISBN 0 340 75016 2 Hardback
ISBN 0 340 74817 6 Paperback

Typeset by Palimpsest Book Production Limited,
Polmont, Stirlingshire
Printed and bound in Great Britain by
Mackays of Chatham plc, Chatham, Kent

Hodder and Stoughton
A division of Hodder Headline PLC
338 Euston Road
London NW1 3BH

To my Father

Peter William Dawson Redmond
(1931–1991)

with love always

# ACKNOWLEDGEMENTS

First and foremost my thanks go to my mother, Mary Redmond, for acting both as a sounding board and as a constant source of encouragement during the writing process. Her advice, especially on characterisation and pacing, was invaluable, and it is no exaggeration to say that without her support this book would never have been completed.

Secondly my thanks go to my cousin Anthony Webb, and my friends Paul Bolger, Gerard Hopkins, Iandra MacCallum, Susan McGowan, Rebecca Owen, Lesley Sims and Gillian Sproul, all of whom read this book as a work in progress and gave their comments with the great good humour I treasure so much in them.

Thirdly, my thanks to my agent Patrick Walsh for his superb work on my behalf, and for my editor Kate Lyall Grant at Hodder & Stoughton for having the courage to invest in this book.

Finally I would like to pay tribute to Jonathan Gathorne-Hardy whose marvellous work 'The Public School Phenomenon' proved invaluable when researching this novel.

'Those who have been taught from an early age to fear the displeasure of their group as the worst of misfortunes will die on the battlefield, in a war of which they understand nothing, rather than suffer the contempt of fools.

'The English public schools have carried this system to perfection and have largely sterilised intelligence by making it cringe before the herd. This is what is called making a man manly.'

Bertrand Russell, *Education and the Social Order*
reproduced by kind permission of The Bertrand Russell
Peace Foundation

# Letter Published in *The Times*, 17th October 1957

The Old Rectory
Havering
Kent

*Dear Sir,*

*I have been a loyal reader of your paper for over thirty years. I have always admired its ordered view of the world. I have, in fact, come to view it as an old friend, without whose sober companionship my day is incomplete.*

*It was therefore in shocked disbelief that I read the article by Colin Hammond: 'Prisoners of Privilege' that appeared in last Monday's edition.*

*Even now, ten days later, I am still at a loss as to how you could have printed such an article. No doubt Mr Hammond is one of those 'angry young men' one is always reading of today; an arrogant young fool whose only chance at distinction is to denigrate every institution this country holds dear. How could you have given him a platform to air his disgraceful views?*

*His article is the most offensive piece of journalism that I have ever seen. Having read it my only conclusion is that Mr Hammond is not in his right mind. Either that, or his desire for fame is so great that he will malign with impunity to achieve it.*

*How could he argue that the public school system itself was to blame for that terrible business at Kirkston Abbey? As a former public school boy myself (Ferrers College 1919–24) I must protest this slur on an institution that I have always respected. My school, like others of its kind, was a decent, happy place. It was not the brutal, fear-filled prison that Mr Hammond would have you believe.*

*The boys at the centre of the whole sordid Kirkston Abbey affair were not 'corrupted by the system'. They were not 'victims of their environment'. To portray them as such is a very grave mistake.*

*For nothing can excuse the sheer awfulness of what they did. There can be no excuses for behaviour like that. Nothing, not youth, loneliness, separation from their families, none of the numerous justifications that Mr Hammond puts forward in their defence, can begin to redeem them. Their behaviour was not that of misguided youths. It was the work of monsters.*

*It is bad enough that Mr Hammond should try and defend them. That he goes further and attempts to lay the blame on a respected institution of this country is a despicable act for which any decent person would be thoroughly ashamed.*

*I will not be reading your paper in future. I will not subscribe to a publication that prints such distortions of the truth.*

*Yours sincerely,*
*Charles Malverton*

# Prologue

## London, January 1999

A bitter wind whistled outside the window but the glow of the fire made the room seem snug. The young man in the chair stared at the clock on the mantelpiece, his cheeks warm from the heat of the flames.

Ten past twelve. He wasn't coming.

*No! He will come. He has to come! This is my life!*

He climbed to his feet and paced around the room, checking for the umpteenth time that everything was as it should be.

It was a beautiful room; lush red carpet, pale blue walls, high ceiling and large windows that looked out onto the pavement and the people who hurried by, wrapped in coats, leaning into the wind. The furnishings were expensive; reproduction Louis Quinze, and the walls were covered with watercolours of ships at sea.

Chairs stood on either side of the fire. Beside one of the chairs was a small table, holding two hardback books and a pile of photocopied newspaper articles.

The kettle was boiled, the cups and saucers set out on a tray, the biscuits laid out on a plate. Everything was ready. Everything was here.

Except for his guest.

Quarter past twelve.

He put another log on the fire. Its heat felt like burning

hands around his face. He stared into the flames, watching them dance before him. His throat was hot and dry.

The clock on the mantelpiece continued to tick away. Seconds multiplied into minutes that would eventually become hours. Time passed inexorably on, indifferent to the fact that with each passing second all his hopes and dreams faded a little more.

Half past twelve. The clock struck to mark the half-hour. There was a knock on the front door. Joy swept over him, together with a rush of adrenaline that made him feel light headed. He hurried into the corridor and down to the door at its end. He turned the lock and threw it open.

A man stood on the doorstep; a tall, gaunt, middle-aged man in a shabby coat with thinning hair and eyes that radiated suspicion; the eyes of an animal that senses that danger is near.

'Mr Webber?' The voice was deep and soft, so soft that he had to strain to hear.

'Yes. I'm Tim Webber. Come in. Come in please.'

He led the man into the room and gestured towards the chair beside the small table. 'Would you like to sit there?'

The man did as he was asked, but he kept his coat on and turned down Tim's offer of tea or coffee. He picked up one of the books and studied its cover.

Tim sat down in the other chair and watched him, happiness now giving way to a sense of anticlimax. He had expected his guest to be imposing, but the man before him had no real presence at all. He told himself that it was to be expected, the inevitable consequence of forty years spent seeking anonymity.

'Which one are you looking at?' he asked.

'The Martin Hopkins one. *A School Full of Secrets*.'

'Have you read it?'

'Of course.'

'It must be strange.'

'Strange?'

'Reading about yourself.'

The man made no reply. Silence hung in the air like mist. It made Tim feel nervous so that he rushed to end it. 'I'm glad you decided to come,' he said brightly, and at once regretted his words.

'You didn't leave me much choice.'

'I didn't mean you to feel pressured. That wasn't what I wanted. Really ...' His words petered out. He was not convincing either of them.

The wary eyes studied him closely. 'I don't believe this claim of yours. I think you're lying.' The voice was forceful, but a thread of uncertainty trembled at its core. Tim felt his confidence return.

'No you don't. If you really believe that then why are you here?'

'The Police made a full investigation. It was in all the papers. Books were written about it. You know what I did. What we did.'

Tim shook his head. 'I know what the papers said you did. I know what the Police told them you did. But the Police didn't tell them the full story did they?'

'Of course they did. They made a very thorough investigation.'

'I don't doubt that. But they didn't make all their findings public did they? Not those findings they didn't want the public to hear.'

'Rubbish! What findings?' The voice was angry but the doubt still lingered. Tim allowed a smile to play around his lips. 'You tell me.'

'This is absurd! You don't know what you're talking about!' The man made as if to rise. Tim saw that it was time.

'Have you heard of the Elmtrees residential home?'

The man stared at him blankly. 'The what?'

'The Elmtrees. It's an old people's home just outside Colchester.'

'No. Why should I?'

'I went there three months ago. I'd been commissioned to write an article for a magazine; just a filler about residential care for the elderly. I pretended to be a relative of one of the residents, used it as an excuse to get in, talk to some of them, try and find something touching to write.'

'What does this have to do with me?'

'While I was in there I met an old man called Thomas Cooper. He was very frail, but his mind was still sharp. He'd been in the home for years. His wife was long dead, his only child lived in Canada. He had no one to visit him or care about him. He was a lonely old man who just wanted somebody to take an interest in him and listen to the stories he had to tell.

'He told me all about his life. Went on and on. It was tedious stuff. I was about to make an excuse and leave. And then he started to tell me a story that made me sit up and listen.

'You see Thomas wasn't from Colchester originally. He grew up in Norfolk. His family were poor. He was in service by the time he was fourteen, in a big house out towards Yarmouth, training to become a butler. He met his wife Ellen there. She was learning how to be a cook.'

The man gave an impatient sigh. 'Where are you going with this?'

Tim ignored his question. 'After a few years, when Ellen and he had learned all that they could, they left the house near Yarmouth. Went independent you could say. They used to find employment as a live-in couple with prosperous families. She'd do the cooking and housekeeping. He'd serve at table and do odd jobs. They did very well. They spent years with a wealthy family in Norwich. Were very happy with them. Eventually the family decided to move to France. Thomas and his wife were asked to go with them, but they didn't want to live abroad. So the family found them another position. An even better one than they'd had before. With Jeremy Blakiston' – he paused, to give emphasis to what he was about to say – 'the Bishop of Norwich.'

The eyes, narrowed with suspicion now widened in alarm. A feeling of overwhelming relief swept over Tim. He had been so afraid that the story was just an old man's fantasy. Now he knew that it wasn't.

'Thomas and Ellen went to work for the Bishop in 1949. They were with him for five years. Five happy years. He was a good employer, kind, courteous, "a pleasure to serve" was how Thomas put it. He was what you might call a rather worldly cleric. Loved entertaining. Had loads of friends. Enjoyed life to the full. Until the night when everything changed.

'One afternoon, in December 1954, Thomas took a phone call from the Norwich police station. The Police were investigating some business at a school in the north of the county. A boarding school called Kirkston Abbey. It was a very bad business. Shocking. Thomas remembered that people in Norwich could talk of nothing else.

'Two boys were at the centre of the investigation. They were being questioned by the Police. The questioning had been going on for days. Now the Police wanted the Bishop to come to the station and hear the story that one of the boys was telling.

'They asked him to come at night, under the cover of darkness so that the press wouldn't find out about his meeting with the boy. That was all they would say. To all Thomas's questions they just kept answering that the Bishop had to come to the station that night.

'So the Bishop went. Before he left he made light of it. Said it was bound to be a load of nonsense and that he'd be back within an hour. Thomas and Ellen waited up. Ellen kept supper warm. But he was gone all night, and when he returned at dawn the next morning, he looked haggard, as if he'd aged ten years overnight. He wouldn't answer any of their questions. He simply told them that no one must ever know about his visit to the police station that night; made them promise that they would keep it a secret. Then he locked himself in his study and stayed there for the rest of the day.

'From that day on he was a changed man, so changed that it was as if another personality had taken possession of him. Where he'd once been cheerful and outgoing he now became solitary and withdrawn. He hardly saw anyone, experienced periods of depression when he'd sit alone in his study, for days at a time, just staring at the walls. He started having nightmares. Sometimes Thomas and Ellen would hear him crying out in his sleep. After three months he had a form of nervous breakdown. Had to resign his position. Went to live with a brother in Cornwall where he died a few years later.

'Thomas and Ellen kept their promise. They never told anyone what had happened that night. Ellen took the secret to the grave with her. But Thomas wanted to tell someone before he died. He was close to death when I met him. He died two weeks after I spoke with him and I think he wanted to get it off his chest before the end.

'I've checked with the authorities in Norwich. They confirmed that Jeremy Blakiston resigned as Bishop in April 1955 following some sort of nervous breakdown. They also confirmed that a couple called Thomas and Ellen Cooper were employed by him until his resignation. I've checked through all the press reports on Kirkston Abbey and there's no mention of the Bishop ever having met you. It never happened as far as the press and the public were concerned. But then, that's what the Police wanted, isn't it?

'I've read the press reports. I've read the books. I know what you did, or what the Police said you did. What you did was terrible. But it wasn't so terrible that it could cause a man to have a breakdown. Not unless the story you told him was far worse than the story the Police told the press.'

He paused, blowing through his teeth so that the hair rose and fell on his forehead. He could hear his heart beating. He felt intensely alive.

'I want to hear the story you told the Bishop. I want to know what really happened at Kirkston Abbey.'

The man stared at him. The anger was gone now; replaced by regret and a terrible tiredness. 'It was more than forty years ago. It's in the past.'

'Like hell it is! How many cases have caught the public imagination the way this one has? It's up there with Brady and Hindley or the Mary Bell case. It's those photographs that did it. Even now they still have the power to shock. Evil wearing the mask of childish innocence. Everyone recognises them – even people like me who were born years after it happened.'

The man shook his head. 'It's in the past. Leave it alone.'

'I can't leave it alone! This is a once-in-a-lifetime scoop! Breaking it could make me the most famous journalist in the country!'

'And that's what you want? Success? Recognition?'

'Yes! Christ yes! I've waited long enough! I've been a journalist for ten years now and I've spent all of them doing stories about old people's homes, weddings, council meetings and all the crap that no one else wants to do!'

The man gestured to the room in which they sat. 'It seems lucrative enough.'

'You think I can afford a place like this? This is the home of my girlfriend's parents. They despise me. They're away on a cruise, otherwise I'd never have made it through the front door. My home is a poky flat in Lewisham and I'm going to stay there for ever if my career carries on like this. I want to get from there to here. This story is my ticket!'

'And I'm the one who can give it to you,' said the man softly.

'I'll pay you. Half of everything I make. There'll be newspapers, magazines, a book of course, television appearances. Maybe even film rights. We're talking hundreds of thousands.'

The man stared at him. 'What good is money to me?'

'You could make a new start. A new life far away. I'd protect your anonymity as far as possible. You wouldn't have to be a part of it. Not if you didn't want to.' Privately he knew this to be untrue. But it didn't matter. What did the truth have to do with this? He would promise anything that would help him get what he wanted.

'A new life? My life ended the day the Police came to Kirkston Abbey. There can be no new life for me. All the money in the world won't change that.'

Tim's brain was whirring. Should he continue to push the money angle or move on to the threats: you tell me everything or I'll hound you until you do. You think your life is bad now; I can make it ten times worse. I won't stop until I get what I want. He decided to stick with the money; to try and keep things civilised if he possibly could. He opened his mouth to speak . . .

And heard the man say 'Very well.'

Euphoria swept over him, so intense that it was like an emotional climax. 'Do you mean it?'

The man nodded.

'You'll tell me everything you told the Bishop?'

'Yes. I haven't told anyone since that night. I've kept it a secret all that time. It will be good to tell someone. Even someone like you.'

Tim ignored the insult. 'You won't regret it I promise. We're talking a fortune. More money than you can imagine.'

'I'm not doing this for money. There will be no money. Not for either of us.'

'What do you mean? Of course there will! A bloody fortune!'

The man shook his head and for the first time he smiled. 'No money. No fame. Just the truth.' A strange light came into his eyes; a dark light that Tim could not identify and which made him feel nervous. He had a sudden feeling that somehow the balance of power between them had shifted. In his head he heard a voice whispering.

*It shouldn't be this easy.*

He pushed his confusion to one side and concentrated on the

job in hand. 'I'll have to tape what you tell me. You understand that don't you?'

The man nodded. Tim fetched a tape recorder from behind his chair. He set it up on the table beside the man. He placed a cassette in the machine. The cogs started to whir. A gentle hissing sound filled the room.

They sat facing each other in front of the fire; the young journalist, fuelled by the heat of his own ambition, and the gaunt middle-aged man with the secret eyes who had once been the most infamous schoolboy in England.

Tim moistened his lips and began the questioning.

'In his book Martin Hopkins makes the point that the events of December 9th 1954 were simply the culmination of a chain of events that had started some time earlier.'

The man nodded.

'He pinpoints the start as early November, just after the half-term break. Is that correct?'

'In a manner of speaking.'

'What do you mean?'

'To really understand what happened you have to go back further.'

'How much further?'

'A month. To a morning in early October and an event that was the real start of it all.'

'What happened that morning?'

'Something very trivial. Or so it seemed at the time.' Again the man smiled. 'In films these days beginnings are always so dramatic. An explosion, a murder. You can almost hear the drumroll as the curtain goes up. There was nothing like that at Kirkston Abbey. But there was a beginning. The incident that took place that morning was the beginning, and everything that happened afterwards stemmed from that.'

'Tell me about that morning.'

'It was just an ordinary morning at Kirkston Abbey. And it was a Monday ...'

# PART ONE

# Bonding

# Norfolk: October 1954

# Chapter One

Everything has its own beginning. The longest book begins with a single word. The longest journey begins with a single step.

At Kirkston Abbey the first step was an unexpected act of kindness; a patch of perfect blue to brighten the greyness of an October day. In time that blue would dull, turn bad, decay, and spread its infection across the sky.

The morning assembly was coming to an end. The school chapel resounded with the sound of three hundred adolescent voices denting, but not destroying the beauty of one of England's most uplifting hymns:

> 'Bring me my bow of burning gold!
> Bring me my arrows of desire!
> Bring me my spear! O Clouds, unfold!
> Bring me my chariot of fire!
> I will not cease from mental fight,
> Nor shall my sword sleep in my hand,
> Till we have built Jerusalem,
> In England's green and pleasant land.'

The voices died away, the echoes floating into the air to burst against the rafters.

'Let us pray,' intoned Mr Howard the headmaster from his seat at the front of the choirstools. The school dropped to its collective knees. The thudding sound of bottoms perched on the ends of wooden seats.

'Dear Lord, look down on we your servants, gathered here today. Grant us the strength to do your work and to obey your commandments, this and every day. In the name of Jesus Christ our Lord, Amen.'

'Amen,' echoed the school.

Thirty seconds of silence. A chance to pray, to think wistfully of the weekend that had just ended, or to panic about prep that was still unprepared.

The organ started up again; the sound of the Toccata and Fugue filled the chapel. The school returned to its feet and began to file out; house by house, row by row, each boy turning and nodding respectfully towards the altar before marching up the aisle and out into the crispness of the autumn morning.

They marched along the chapel path towards the main school building; boys in smart blue blazers emblazoned with the school crest; grey trousers with severe creases, and shiny black shoes. A mass of regulated uniformity, enlivened by splashes of colour from the prefects who were permitted to wear jackets of their own choice. The wind whistled across the flat landscape and through the branches of the beech trees that flanked the path; bitter and tinged with salt, blowing in from the sea three miles to the north.

The path divided. Same boys veered off on a path that led to the woods and to Heatherfield and Monmouth; the two boarding houses hidden in the trees. Others continued past the rugby pitches and on towards the main school building; a huge Victorian Gothic edifice which still managed to seem dwarfed by the vast Norfolk sky above.

It was in fact two buildings joined by a cloister. The building on the right contained most of the classrooms and the assembly hall. The building on the left contained two further residential houses: Abbey House, and Old School House. The boys filed into their respective houses to fetch the books they would need for the morning's lessons.

Jonathan Palmer, fourth year pupil, jostled with the other boys of Old School House as they moved through the cloister and on towards the classrooms.

He was a slim, attractive boy with light brown hair and delicate features. He was three months past his fourteenth birthday.

He walked past the assembly hall and down a long corridor with a stone floor. Boys pushed and shoved around him, exchanging news and insults, expending the last vestiges of the weekend's energy before settling down to the grind of the week ahead. The air was heavy with the smell of polish, the sound of voices and the echoes of hundreds of pairs of sensible shoes. Classrooms stood on either side. Each had a name, painted on the door in golden letters: Drake and Walpole, Pitt and Melbourne; the golden ones who had helped put the Great into Britain.

He entered Melbourne classroom; its cold white walls holding rows of battered double desks that looked like cages. The cages were filling with boys; some talking to their neighbours, others staring at their books or off into space, all waiting for the start of the first period Latin lesson. The walls reverberated with the comments they had heard for the last hundred years and would hear for the next hundred too:

'... so unfair! Everyone knows I'm better but his brother's captain so he gets picked instead ...'

'... I couldn't do any of that Maths. Can I borrow yours ...'

'... you should try sharing a study with him! ...'

'... and my father said that we can go to London and see a show ...'

Jonathan sat down at his usual desk; a particularly battered relic with a seat that threatened to collapse at any moment. A picture of the Queen hung on the wall in front of him; a display of patriotism for last year's coronation that had yet to be taken down. He had spent the day with his mother and her neighbours, all crowded into the one house in the street that had a television set. It had been the first time he had ever seen television.

The desk beside him remained empty, as did the double desk in front; waiting for Nicholas Scott and the Perriman twins to arrive from Monmouth House. Their absence made him feel isolated and vulnerable. He stared down at the scruffy piece of paper and his attempted translations of the sentences they would be studying for the next forty minutes. Most were failures but it didn't matter. Nicholas would have the answers. He always did.

The surface of the desk was pitted with names and dates scratched into the wood. He traced their outline with his slender fingers. John Forrest 1937; Peter Ashley 1912; Charles Huntley 1896. Boys who had long since grown into men and left their schooldays far behind.

Boys continued to file into the classroom. The noise level increased. Richard Rokeby strode in, books under one arm, heading for his usual double desk by the window. From the back of the classroom James Wheatley and George Turner were firing paper pellets at Colin Vale who was trying unsuccessfully to laugh it off.

Stephen Perriman entered, followed by his brother Michael. They sat down in the double desk in front of Jonathan and stared at him with their pale blue eyes.

'Where's Nick?' he asked.

Michael pretended to be violently sick.

'He started throwing up last night,' explained Stephen. 'We took him to the San. They think he's got a bug.'

Jonathan's heart sank. He was of course concerned by the poor state of Nicholas's health, but he was more concerned by the poor state of his translations.

'We tried to do the sentences,' Michael told him, 'but could hardly do any of them.'

'We?' exclaimed Stephen. Jonathan noticed that a small bruise was forming above his right eye. 'How did you get that?'

'We were raided by the fifth year last night. They were after the third year but they'd barricaded themselves in.'

'They stripped our beds,' added Michael,' and then they wanted to play dodgems with the laundry baskets. They put Julian Archer in one and they were going to put me in the other but Stephen said that he'd go in instead. There was so much noise that Mr Soper came in. The fifth years ran off through the washrooms, but Stephen and Julian were still in the baskets. Mr Soper let them out and asked Stephen what had been going on.'

'Did you tell?' asked Jonathan.

Stephen stared at him as if he were retarded. 'Oh sure! Like you'd tell if Wheatley and his gang decided to have a go at you one night.'

Jonathan turned and watched James Wheatley, his eyes flashing with excitement, continuing to fire pellets at Colin Vale. Colin was still trying to make light of it but when one of the pellets hit him in the eye he seemed close to tears. Jonathan felt a burst of anger on Colin's behalf.

And also, a small, guilty feeling.

*At least it's not me.*

'Let's compare answers,' said Stephen.

They were just about to do so when Mr Ackerley swept into the room, tall and upright, his gown flapping behind him. At once the classroom was silent.

Mr Ackerley's sharp grey eyes, set deep within his pale, patrician face, ran over the class and fixed on the empty space next to Jonathan. 'Where is Scott?'

'He's ill, sir,' explained Stephen.

'I see. I trust that everyone has done the prep.'

'Yes, sir,' chorused the class. Some with more conviction than others.

'Good.' He sat down at his desk. 'Open your text books at page 56.'

Jonathan did so and found himself staring at a diagram of intersecting triangles. Only then did he realise that he'd brought the wrong book. He felt his heart plummet to the bottom of his stomach. Of all the lessons to make this mistake! Cursing his own stupidity he stuck his hand into the air.

Mr Ackerley, on the point of starting the lesson, noticed the raised hand. He exhaled irritably. 'Well Palmer?'

'I'm sorry sir. I've forgotten my book. May I go and fetch it?'

The sharp grey eyes rolled towards heaven. 'You do know what lesson this is, don't you, Palmer?'

'Yes, sir.'

'So why have you brought the wrong book? Latin book for Latin lesson. That's easy enough isn't it, even for someone like you.'

He heard someone giggle. He felt himself flush. It was safer to say nothing but the knowledge that Mr Ackerley would not make such a fuss if it were someone else put him on the defensive. 'I brought my Maths book, sir. It's the same colour and size as the Latin book so it's an easy mistake to make.' As he spoke he was aware of his Yorkshire accent becoming more pronounced and wished that he'd said nothing.

'For God's sake, Palmer, stop whining on in that stupid voice! No one's interested!' Mr Ackerley's eyes scanned the classroom, looking for an empty seat. 'Go and share with Rokeby.'

Jonathan rose to his feet, his face still hot, hating the sensation of everyone staring at him. Michael Perriman caught his eye and flashed him a sympathetic smile.

He walked to the front of the class, to the double desk where Richard Rokeby sat alone, staring out of the window at the fields at the rear of the school.

Richard Rokeby was the school loner; a boy who treated

the rest of the school with a barely concealed scorn. He had no friends. He spoke to as few people as possible. He seemed to need no company but his own.

This behaviour had always appeared strange to Jonathan. His mother had told him that loners kept the world at a distance because they suffered from feelings of inferiority. She knew this to be true because she had read it in one of her magazines. Jonathan was sure she was right but it was hard to see what Richard Rokeby had to feel inferior about. He was extremely intelligent, supremely self-assured and, on the few occasions when he chose to show it, remarkably eloquent.

And, most noticeable of all, he was arrestingly good-looking. He was tall and athletic, with blue black hair, strong, handsome features, and deep-set eyes of piercing blue that blazed scornfully out at the world as if issuing a permanent challenge.

He sat down next to Richard, giving him an awkward smile. Richard responded with a disinterested nod, slid his text book to the centre of the double desk and continued to stare out of the window.

Mr Ackerley's eyes roamed over the classroom. 'Upton, translate sentence one.'

The lesson began. Adam Upton, bright and enthusiastic, followed the standard procedure for translation; reading out a Latin word, giving its English translation, continuing until the entire sentence was completed. The rest of the class waited apprehensively, fidgeting in their seats, hoping that they would not be picked. Jonathan, stared at his inadequate attempts, sure that he would be chosen and praying that when this happened the sentence in question would not be number five or eight.

Sentence two. Colin Vale. Another good effort. Sentence three. Michael Perriman. Not so good. Michael made mistakes and had to be prompted in whispers by Stephen. Mr Ackerley became angry. 'For God's sake Perriman, you're supposed to have prepared this! And if your brother helps you any more he'll find himself in detention. Next time do the work properly!'

Sentence four. Stuart Young. Not brilliant but better than Michael Perriman.

Sentence five. Mr Ackerley's eyes scanned the class. Jonathan, staring down at his desk, sensed them bearing in his direction. He tensed in apprehension.

'Rokeby!'

Richard Rokeby turned away from the window and towards Mr Ackerley. 'Sir?'

'Rokeby, forgive me for disturbing you. Would you do us the great honour of translating sentence five, or would you prefer to continue watching the groundsmen marking out the pitch?'

A burst of sycophantic laughter echoed round the classroom. Mr Ackerley nodded his head very slightly, as if acknowledging the applause.

'I'd rather watch the groundsmen sir,' Richard Rokeby told him.

Another burst of laughter. No longer sycophantic. Instantly suppressed.

'Pardon?' said Mr Ackerley who clearly thought that he'd misheard.

'I said I'd rather watch the groundsmen, sir.'

Mr Ackerley's eyes widened. The smile faded from his face. 'Are you trying to be funny?' he demanded. The class wriggled nervously in their desks, sensing storm clouds on the horizon.

Richard Rokeby seemed unconcerned at the prospect of bad weather. 'I'm answering your question, sir,' he replied coolly. 'I assumed that that's what you wanted me to do. Otherwise, why would you ask it?'

'You're not trying to make me look stupid are you, Rokeby?' asked Mr Ackerley. His voice had an eerie quality of calm to it.

Richard Rokeby gave the matter some thought, and then said, 'Not deliberately, sir.'

There was an audible intake of breath across the classroom. Everybody tensed, waiting for the explosion.

But it didn't happen. Instead Mr Ackerley seemed to make a monumental effort to swallow his anger. Jonathan, surprised, turned and saw that Richard was returning Mr Ackerley's glare with a composure that was not to be ruffled by an angry voice.

'Sentence five, Rokeby.' said Mr Ackerley.

'What about it, sir?' asked Richard politely.

'Translate it!'

Richard sighed, softly, but loud enough to be heard. He stared down at the text book.

Then he read the whole sentence aloud and followed it with what sounded like a perfect translation.

'Very good, Rokeby,' said Mr Ackerley in a rather forced tone.

Richard nodded graciously, then turned and continued to stare out of the window. Anger flashed across Mr Ackerley's face. He looked as if he were about to say something but then thought better of it.

The lesson continued.

Sentence six. Sean Spencer. Adequate.

Sentence seven. Henry Osborne. An excellent effort. Unsurprising. Henry had won the Latin prize last year.

Sentence eight. 'A very difficult one,' announced Mr Ackerley. 'Which brave boy shall we pick to have a go at this?'

Those who had already answered stared confidently in front of them. Everyone else looked down at their desks, trying to remain inconspicuous. Jonathan felt Mr Ackerley's eyes scanning the classroom once again like two tiny pricks of heat.

*not me, not me, please god not me, not me, not me*

'Palmer.'

'Sir?' Trying to sound confident. Feeling sick. He depended on Nicholas in these situations and now Nicholas was not here.

'Translate number eight.'

'Yes, sir.' He looked at the blank space on his piece of paper. As blank as his mind.

'Come on, Palmer. We don't have all day. You've wasted enough of our time already.'

He stared at the printed words on the page. Incomprehensible. Might as well have been in Cantonese.

'Palmer, at grammar school it may well be common practice to respond to a master's question with an open mouth and a gormless expression but it certainly isn't the practice here. Get a move on.'

A ripple of laughter. He felt himself blush again. He rubbed at his face, his cheekbone tight against his skin. He wished he didn't blush so easily.

'When we translate a sentence Palmer we start by identifying the subject. Subject, verb, object. In that order. What is the subject of this sentence?'

He stared at the words. There didn't seem to be one.

'Come on Palmer. Don't just sit there rolling your eyes like a fish.'

More ingratiating laughter. 'I'm not, sir,' he said. His heart was beating faster.

'So, what is the subject?'

'Um ...' scanning the words, trying to identify the right one.

'No Palmer, it's not Um. The word Um does not appear.'

The laughter was growing louder. He could hear James Wheatley sniggering away in the back row like a malevolent imp. He hazarded a guess.

'Come on Palmer. Even you're not that stupid. Try again.'

He stared at the page, trying to block out the laughter. The blush seemed to be spreading from his face to the rest of his body.

'Palmer! I'm waiting!'

'Yes, sir.'

'So, what is the subject? If you can't answer a simple

question like that then you've no business being at a school like this!'

He stared at the words in front of him. It could be any one. His heart was pounding. Panic was starting to make him feel dizzy.

'PALMER!! WHAT IS THE SUBJECT?! And I warn you, get it wrong and you'll find yourself on report for the rest of the term!!'

His eyes focused in on a word. He opened his mouth.

*Oh god please make this be the right one please god please god please . . .*

There was a knock on the classroom door.

'Come!' shouted Mr Ackerley.

A third former appeared, holding a piece of paper. 'Please, sir, the headmaster asked if you'd approve the timetable changes for next week.'

Mr Ackerley took the piece of paper and studied it. The third former stood placidly by his desk, oblivious to the tense atmosphere he had just entered.

Jonathan, shirt collar felt too tight. Blood seemed to be passing before his eyes so that he couldn't focus. He could hear people whispering behind him, feel their eyes upon him. Richard Rokeby, detached from it all, was doodling on a piece of paper.

He turned towards the Perrimans. Stephen was mouthing something at him. He tried to read Stephen's lips but was unable to do so. Something nudged his arm. He ignored it and tried harder. He felt the nudging again and turned.

Richard Rokeby had pushed a slip of paper in front of him. On it was written what appeared to be a complete translation of the sentence.

Their eyes met. Richard nodded.

The third former was leaving the room. Mr Ackerley turned back towards him. 'I'm still waiting, Palmer.'

He studied the piece of paper in front of him, his panic now replaced by confusion. Was this a trick? Probably, but he was a drowning man and desperate enough to grab at any straw. He read out the first word and waited for the explosion.

But there was none. He began to work his way through the rest, looking up to see Mr Ackerley nodding and saying 'Correct Palmer' in a voice that sounded disappointed.

He reached the end. Relief sweeping over him in waves so violent that he was almost trembling.

The lesson continued. He sat and stared at his book, breathing slowly and deeply, waiting for his face to cool and his heart to slow.

Sentence nine. Malcolm Usher. A rather erratic effort. Sentence ten. Timothy Watham. Fluent, finishing just as the final bell rang.

Mr Ackerley swept out of the classroom. The class moved more slowly, gathering their books, preparing to proceed on to the Geography lesson.

Jonathan turned towards Richard Rokeby, gratitude exploding out of him. 'I'd never have translated that! I'd have been on report if it wasn't for you. I'm really grateful. I'm ...'

Richard Rokeby ignored him completely. Rising to his feet he slid past him out of the double desk, and made his way towards the door. As he moved he was hailed by James Wheatley; his cunning face shining with admiration. 'Hey Rokeby, that was brilliant! The look on Wankerley's face! Do you want ...' Richard ignored him too, not even bothering to stop. James Wheatley was left standing, looking angry and embarrassed.

The Perrimans were waiting in the doorway. Jonathan hurried towards them. 'Trust Wankerley to give you the hardest one,' said Stephen as they walked out into the corridor. 'He's really got it in for you.'

Jonathan nodded, watching the crowds who milled around them; a mass of boys in blue blazers, moving between classrooms like ants moving from chamber to chamber in a great nest. The air was full of hundreds of voices, each rising into the air and merging with the others, an incoherent buzzing sound that hung over their heads like a cloud.

It was the sound of the school; an all powerful machine of many parts, operating fluently and efficiently, just as it had always done. The school of which he was a member. The school to which he was privileged to belong.

He hated it.

He followed the Perrimans towards the Geography lesson.

He visited Nicholas Scott in the half hour break between lunch and games.

Nicholas was in the school sanatorium, the sole occupant of a small ward that smelled of soup and disinfectant. He was sitting up in bed, reading a book. His small dark eyes, made even smaller by his thick glasses, lit up when he saw Jonathan. 'I was hoping you'd come.'

He sat down on the bed. 'What are you reading?'

'*Love on Ward 10.*' Nicholas grimaced. 'It's a hospital romance. Sister Clark lent it to me. It's the only book she could find.'

'I should have brought you something. I forgot. Sorry.'

'Doesn't matter. How did it go in Latin this morning?'

He told Nicholas what had happened. 'I hate Ackerley. Why does he have to pick on me all the time? What's so terrible about having been to a grammar school?'

'Nothing. None of the other masters care about it.'

'It's not as if I'm the only one. John Fisher in the third year came from a a grammar school near Yarmouth. He's got an accent you could dig potatoes with and he's even worse at Latin than me but Ackerley doesn't pick on him half as much.' He scuffed his shoes against the leg of the bed and all the feelings of humiliation came flooding back. 'I really hate him! I hate this bloody place too!'

'It's not that bad,' said Nicholas soothingly.

'Isn't it?'

'Don't let him upset you, Jon. He's not worth it.'

He didn't answer. He stared down at his shoes and found himself remembering the day when the two of them had first met.

It had been just over a year ago: his first full day at Kirkston Abbey; that nightmare day of talks and lists and tours and bells; a day of increasing misery as he struggled to make sense of this strange, regimented place that was his new home.

He remembered standing in the huge, drafty gym, wearing only his vest and underpants, waiting to be weighed and measured, shivering with the cold as stern looking men with whistles roared out instructions. He had been one of sixty new boys gathered there, but all the others had come from prep schools that seemed to have prepared them for this harsh, rule-bound world in a way that his own school had singularly failed to do. He had stood and waited, surrounded by others but feeling more alone than he had ever felt in his life.

Eventually he had begun to stare at a group of three boys who stood nearby; a small, skinny boy with a pinched face and thick glasses, and identical twins with dirty blond hair. When the skinny boy, noticing his stare, had raised an eyebrow questioningly he had become embarrassed and turned away. But when he had ventured another look he had seen that the boy was smiling and motioning for him to join them.

So, shyly, he had done so to find that he felt an instant ease with them, that he seemed to belong, so much so that by the end of that bewildering day they had become a unit, four friends who would help each other survive in this strange new world.

The memory, coming so unexpectedly, left him with a warm glow inside and a sudden burst of affection for the solemn, bespectacled boy who sat beside him. 'Hurry up and get well. It's no fun when you're not around.'

'I should be out tomorrow,' Nicholas told him.

'Just as long as you're out by Saturday.'

'Saturday?'

'There was an announcement in chapel. We're having a talk

on Saturday afternoon. General Collinson is coming to talk about the war. I'm sure it will be very interesting.'

'I'm sure it will be too. Why would we want a boring half holiday when we can spend a fascinating four hours reliving the Normandy landings with General Collinson.'

They tried to look serious but neither could maintain it for very long. Soon they both burst out laughing, saluting the other and blowing raspberries to the tune of 'Land of Hope and Glory'.

'When I was at prep school,' said Nicholas, 'an MP came to talk to us about politics. He went on for ever! He talked all afternoon and he would have talked all evening too if a first year called Peter Bowen hadn't fallen asleep.'

'What happened? God, did he start snoring?'

'No! It was much better than that. He had a nightmare! He dreamed that he was Boy, and that he was being chased through the jungle by giant spiders! The MP asked whether there were any questions and Peter Bowen started screaming "Save me Tarzan! They're eating my goolies!" '

They started laughing again, so loudly that Sister Clark put her head round the door and shouted for them to be quiet.

'Shouldn't you go?' asked Nicholas, once their laughter had finally subsided. 'Don't you have to get ready for games?'

He looked at his watch. 'No, not yet. Why? Do you want to go to sleep?'

'No. I'd like you to stay. I'm glad you're here.'

'So am I.'

They sat in silence for a couple of minutes. A warm, easy silence, comfortable as an old shoe.

Then Nicholas opened the book he was reading. 'This bit is really funny. Listen . . .'

Quarter past nine in the evening. Jonathan turned off the faucet and stepped out of the showers.

He stood, dripping hot water on to the floor, and reached

for his towel. He wrapped it round his waist and walked across the changing rooms of Old School House, pursued by the smell of dirty clothes and the noise of other boys as they too prepared themselves for bed.

He changed into his pyjamas and dressing-gown and walked down the dark corridor towards the main hall. He walked past the noticeboard, the trophy cupboard and the table where the morning mail was left and started up the stairs. His slippers, new that month and still too big for him, made a slapping sound on the cold stone floor.

He reached the top of the stairs, walked past the corridor where the prefects had their study bedrooms, and opened the door of the fourth year dormitory.

It was a long, thin room with a wooden floor. Sixteen beds, two rows of eight, each covered with regulation green blankets and with small wooden lockers by the side. It was empty, save for Colin Vale and William Abbott, already curled up in their beds, reading books.

He walked down the row of beds and through the door on the left that led into the washroom. Six sinks, a solitary toilet stall and a wooden board on the wall with mugs for toothbrushes and hooks for wash bags.

He brushed his teeth. Slowly, thoroughly. Behind him he could hear the door banging open and shut, the sound of voices, boys filing into the dormitory and on into the washroom, all in their dressing-gowns, reaching for their toothbrushes, removing flannels from wash bags, all going through the Kirkston Abbey ritual of bedtime.

He walked to his bed. He took off his dressing-gown and climbed beneath the sheets. They were clean that morning and so heavily starched that they felt like boards pressing down on him, holding him in place.

He reached for the book he kept in his bedside locker; *Silas Marner*, compulsory reading for his English class. He tried to lose himself in the text but his heart wasn't in it so instead he lay and watched the activity that was going on around him.

At the other end of the dormitory Stuart Barry sat up in bed, talking to James Wheatley. George Turner went to join them. Stuart and George. James's gang. Stuart; tall, blond, blandly handsome, limited. Very much a follower. George: huge, big boned, coarse featured, a lump of dark hair on a bullet head. Too stupid to be a leader.

And James himself; small, wiry, a clever, impish face, and shrewd, spiteful eyes. Eyes that now seemed to be roaming, slowly and deliberately, over the dormitory.

*don't make eye contact*

He dropped his eyes and pretended to read his book, feeling himself tense, wondering what amusements James and his minions might be planning for that night, and whether he would be an unwilling party to them.

He remembered a night three weeks ago when James had decided that William Abbott had insulted him. They had waited until lights out to drag William from his bed, force him into a laundry basket, fasten its lid and send it hurtling down the fire escape so that William ended up in the sanatorium for three days with bruised ribs.

Neil Archer, one of the prefects, had come storming into the dormitory, demanding to know who was responsible, reminding them that bullying was against the rules and threatening them all with a week of early morning runs unless the guilty ones confessed.

But James and his friends had said nothing. And the rest of them remained silent too, condemning themselves to a week of rising before dawn and running across muddy fields for an hour before breakfast. They had sat in silence because they could not do otherwise.

Because the only rule at Kirkston Abbey that really mattered was the unwritten one that you never told tales. No matter who did what to you, you never, ever told tales.

The door of the dormitory opened. Brian Harrington appeared. Brian, big and imposing, Captain of the House Rugby team. And now with the additional authority that came with being Head of House. An authority that had belonged to Paul Ellerson until ...

But he didn't want to think about that.

Brian's eyes scanned the dormitory, watching as those who were not already in their beds now scurried towards them. 'Right, good night, everyone.' 'Good night, Harrington,' they chorused in response. Brian flicked off the light switch and pulled the thick, wooden door closed behind him. Leaving them alone, with the darkness and each other.

At first, silence, save for the wind that battered the windows, blowing in from the sea.

Then slowly the darkness began to fill with a soft buzzing sound; whispered conversations, hissed in voices that feared detection and punishment. Jonathan, silent himself, strained to catch James Wheatley's voice, trying to gauge his intentions, eventually detecting its high, sharp timbre, focusing in on it anxiously, only to hear James yawning and saying 'good night' to Stuart. He felt himself relax. There would be no trouble that night.

He lay on his side, curled up in a ball, listening to the other voices die away as their owners drifted down into sleep. Coughs, sniffs, sneezes, the creak of bed springs as someone tried to get comfortable for the night. The occasional churning of the hot water pipe that ran along the wall. A crowded, claustrophobic black.

Thoughts of Paul Ellerson kept coming into his head. He tried to block them out, tried to think of something else. Anything else.

He thought of how much he hated the dormitory, hated the lack of privacy, hated the constant sense of being watched. He wished he had a room of his own like they had in Abbey House. Single rooms. Rooms with locks. Locks that could keep out people like James Wheatley and George Turner. Locks that allowed you to sleep easily without wondering what surprises the night might bring. He wished he was in Abbey House. Richard Rokeby was in Abbey House.

He rolled on to his back and stared up at the ceiling, remembering the events of the morning's Latin lesson. He thought back to how Richard had spoken to Mr Ackerley. He thought of how Richard had snubbed James Wheatley. He thought of how, unbidden, Richard had come to his aid.

And as he thought of it a strange new idea took root in his head. The idea of a friendship between the two of them.

Why not? The fact that Richard had snubbed him after the lesson didn't have to mean anything. He was in a hurry. That was all.

He began to plan in his head. Tomorrow he would start up a conversation with Richard. He would try to draw him out, try to find out something about him. Find a common ground between the two of them; a foundation on which he could build.

But as he planned he came to see the basic flaw in his reasoning. Richard wasn't like him. Richard didn't need friends. He was strong. All he needed was himself.

The idea vanished as quickly as it had come, pierced by the cold lance of logic, leaving nothing but a sense of emptiness and a small, aching desire.

*I want to be like that. Oh god, I'd give anything just to be like that.*

He lay on his back, staring up at the darkness, listening to the wind and the heavy silence that surrounded him and dreaming of being far, far away.

# Chapter Two

Clive Howard, headmaster of Kirkston Abbey, stared out of the window of his study.

The School Cadet Corps, resplendent in their khaki uniforms, stood outside the cloisters, waiting to provide General Collinson and his wife with an honour guard to the assembly hall. A large group of boys were approaching from Heatherfield and Monmouth House, all walking quickly, leaning into the wind. He smiled with relief. Everything was going according to plan.

He walked towards the mirror near the door and studied his appearance. A tall, burly man in his late forties with greying hair and a solid, kindly face. He decided that his tie was straight enough and that his hair did not need another combing.

He heard footsteps approaching. Light, graceful footsteps. His wife Elizabeth entered the room. She was an attractive woman, ten years younger than him, with delicate features and lively eyes, dressed in a smart blue suit that showed off her slender figure. She pirouetted in front of him. 'Will I do?'

He felt a thrill of pleasure at the sight of her. Even now, after fifteen years of marriage, he still found it hard to believe that this lovely elfin creature was his wife. 'You look very beautiful,' he told her tenderly. 'No one will be able to hold a candle to you.'

'You don't look bad yourself. But that tie needs straightening.'
She adjusted it and ran a finger through his hair. 'That's better.
Now you look almost presentable.'

He kissed her lightly on the nose. 'Not ashamed to be seen
with me then?'

'A little. But we all have our crosses to bear.'

They laughed and he kissed her again. 'Nervous?' she
asked him.

He nodded.

'Don't be. Everything will go smoothly.'

'I can't help worrying. I worry about everything since Paul
Ellerson ...'

'That's in the past,' she said quickly.

'Is it?'

'Yes!' she said forcefully. 'And you're not to go on blaming
yourself. There was nothing you could have done.'

'I was his headmaster. He was my responsibility. I let
him down.'

'You didn't let him down, Clive. He was eighteen years old.
He was an adult. He was old enough to make his own decisions.
No one forced him to do what he did.'

'I still feel I could have done more. Even afterwards. We
didn't even have a memorial service, for God's sake.'

'That was his parents' choice. It wasn't yours.' She stroked
his cheek. 'What happened was a tragedy, a terrible waste of a
life. But it wasn't your fault. You weren't responsible and I won't
have you blaming yourself. You're a good man, Clive Howard,
and Kirkston Abbey is lucky to have you as its headmaster.
Don't you ever forget that.'

He put his arms around her and kissed her cheek. 'Oh
Lizzie, what would I do without you?'

She laughed, a sweet sound, like the distant chiming of bells.
'I dread to think! And don't worry. This afternoon will be a
success. We'll make sure of it.'

✻　　✻　　✻

Jonathan walked into the assembly hall with the other boys from Old School House.

The assembly hall was a huge rectangular building with a high ceiling and oak-panelled walls covered with portraits of the school's governors and distinguished old boys. Wooden chairs filled the hall, with an aisle down the middle. The boys from Heatherfield and Monmouth were already in their places. Jonathan walked past them and saw Nicholas Scott and the Perrimans. Nicholas smiled at him and Michael stifled an imaginary yawn.

Sunlight streamed through the windows of the hall, catching motes of dust as they danced in the air. He sat near the front, feeling uncomfortable in his Sunday suit, and depressed at the thought of the dreary afternoon ahead. He wished he could be outside, away from the frigid formality of the occasion. He gazed up at the portraits that hung on the walls. Dozens of pairs of cold, flat eyes stared disapprovingly down at him, as if reprimanding him for his lack of school spirit.

Someone shouted 'Stand!' The school rose as one to its feet.

Mr Howard strode down the aisle, accompanied by a tall, white-haired man in full military uniform. Mrs Howard followed them, smiling warmly as always, escorting a plump, sour-faced woman in a polka-dot dress. The Cadet Corps marched behind, all in khaki, their boots so well polished that they seemed to glow. And behind them came the other masters, all in their gowns, walking either alone or with their wives.

The Cadet Corps and staff went to stand in the rows in front of Jonathan. The Howards and their visitors continued on to the stage where chairs stood waiting for them. Mr Howard nodded to Mr Ballantyne, the music master, who sat at a piano at the side of the stage. He started to play, and everyone joined together to sing the national anthem.

'God save our gracious Queen!
Long live our noble Queen!
God save the Queen!
Send her victorious, happy and glorious,
Long to reign over us.
God save the Queen!'

The school sat. Mr Howard walked to the front of the stage and said a few introductory words, reminding everyone how fortunate they were to have such a distinguished speaker. Jonathan, restless already, allowed his eyes to wander. Eventually they focused on Mrs Jepson, wife of the chemistry master, who sat staring in front of her with a look of intense enthusiasm ironed on to her face. He wondered if she was as bored as he was.

He noticed Mr Ackerley, staring down at his feet, a certain tightness round the mouth. The seat next to him was empty. Where was Mrs Ackerley. Was she ill?

Mr Howard had now returned to his seat. General Collinson rose to his feet and strode to the front of the stage. Applause echoed round the hall.

The General stood and acknowledged the applause for a moment but then held up a huge hand for silence. 'I'm sure,' he boomed, 'that some of you lads are sitting here today thinking "why do we have to waste a good half holiday sitting and listening to some old soldier?"' He raised an eyebrow quizzically. 'Am I right?'

There was a chorus of 'no' from the audience. Jonathan, remained silent, wishing that he had the courage to say 'yes'.

'No doubt,' continued the General, 'some of you lads are thinking that there's nothing you can learn from an old buffer like me. Well I happen to think otherwise, but I always say that one volunteer is better than ten pressed men so if any lad isn't interested and has better things to do then he's free to walk out now.'

More laughter from the audience. Spontaneous this time. Walking out indeed? Unthinkable.

In spite of his words the General clearly regarded it as unthinkable too. Hardly pausing to draw breath, he opened his mouth and continued talking. 'The first thing I want to say is ...' Jonathan, his mind already wandering sank back in his chair and noticed movement out of the corner of his eye.

He turned to look, just as everyone else was turning to look.

Richard Rokeby had risen to his feet and was moving to the end of his row.

He stepped into the aisle and began to walk towards the door. He moved lightly and confidently, head held high, shoulders back and eyes staring coolly in front of him. There was no hint of self-consciousness. No hint of attention-seeking either. He was just being himself, assured, contained, and totally unconcerned with the views of others.

A silence descended on the hall. The shocked silence of boys who are forced to sit and watch as one of their number signs his own death warrant. The only sound was the clipping of Richard's heels on the stone floor.

He reached the huge double doors at the end. He passed through and let them swing closed behind him. The sound of his footsteps continued down the corridor, growing softer and softer until they faded away into nothing.

Complete silence. A silence so heavy that it seemed to have a form of its own.

Slowly all eyes returned to the stage. Mrs Howard was whispering something to the General's wife. Mr Howard, his face as crimson as a glass of port, was staring at the floor as if willing it to open and swallow him up.

And General Collinson stood alone at the front of the stage, staring at the door through which Richard Rokeby had just passed with a look of total disbelief on his face. His mouth hung open. He could not have looked more astonished if Hitler had appeared in the assembly hall to announce that he had risen from the grave and was about to launch a new invasion.

The silence continued for about a minute. Total stunned silence.

Then one of the third years giggled.

It was a short, shrill sound, due more to nervousness than amusement. The voice was in the process of breaking, and the laughter started on a low note, shot up two octaves, and then shot down again, all in under five seconds.

The hall returned to life. Whispering broke out, together with bursts of hastily suppressed laughter. Jonathan gazed around him, studying the multitude of reactions. James Wheatley and George Turner were bent almost double with mirth. Henry Blake looked shocked – Henry's father had been killed in the war. William Abbott was shaking his head as if convinced that Richard Rokeby had gone mad. Masters whispered to their wives. The Cadet Corps stared loyally in front of them.

'SILENCE!' roared Mr Howard.

Everyone jumped. Even the General jumped. Jonathan had a sudden image of him falling off the stage. He felt a violent need to laugh and bit down on one of his fingers.

A calm. Of sorts. General Collinson composing himself. 'The first thing I want to say is . . .' The audience trying to forget what had happened and to focus on his words.

He spoke for an hour and a half. He talked about the war, of Dunkirk and D-Day, of the courage of the British soldiers, 'men of whom you should all be proud'. He talked of the importance of discipline and dedication. Eventually he came to the end. 'Hopefully I've given you some food for thought.'

Thomas Cody, head of school, leapt to his feet, crying, 'School! Three cheers for General Collinson.' Three gusty cries rang through the hall. The General was led off by Mr Howard for tea with the masters and their wives. The school filed from the hall, row by row, out into the fading sunshine and the dregs of the day.

That night nobody could talk of anything but the events of the afternoon. The General's visit had indeed provided the boys of Kirkston Abbey with considerable food for thought.

But it was not the subject matter of his talk that was acting as the main course.

Sunday morning. The church service had finished half an hour ago.

Mr Howard stood behind the desk of his study. Richard Rokeby faced him.

Mr Howard was breathing slowly and deeply. He was calm, he told himself, and he was going to remain calm.

It would have been a different story the previous evening. The shock of Richard Rokeby's behaviour, combined with the three hours he had spent trying to pacify the irate General had sent him into an absolute fury, and had Richard Rokeby stood before him five minutes after the General's departure, he would have given him the thrashing of his life.

But he'd had a chance to calm down since then. And a chance to be reminded by his wife that *technically* Richard Rokeby hadn't broken any rules.

He studied the boy who stood before him: the straight back, the proud chin, the strong, handsome features, and the cold blue eyes that regarded him with an indifference that bordered on contempt. He felt himself tense.

*This boy is trouble.*

But he had been a teacher for twenty years and had encountered his fair share of troublemakers. He knew how to deal with the likes of Richard Rokeby.

'What do you have to say for yourself?' he demanded.

The eyes observed him insolently. 'What do you mean, sir?'

'Don't be flippant, Rokeby. You know exactly what I mean.'

'As I recall sir, the General said that any boy who wasn't interested in what' – he paused, as if trying to remember something – 'some old buffer like him had to say was free to leave. I wasn't remotely interested in anything he had to say sir, so I left.'

Mr Howard breathed heavily, trying to control his temper. Anger didn't solve anything.

But the voice was so provoking; that tone of extreme politeness, laced with scorn. Like a chocolate cake dusted with salt.

'Rokeby, you know as well as I do that General Collinson didn't mean what he said.'

'Then why did he say it, sir?'

'It doesn't matter why he said it! The fact is that he didn't mean it! A fact of which you were perfectly aware!'

The eyes dropped very slightly. Mr Howard smiled inwardly. Progress.

Then they were raised again.

'Do you mean that he was lying, sir?'

'No, I do not! Don't be so damned impertinent! Don't you dare . . .' He controlled himself. He would not allow himself to be provoked.

'Rokeby, your behaviour was extremely insulting to a distinguished guest. You are, whether you like it or not, a representative of Kirkston Abbey, and you have a responsibility to behave in a way that reflects credit on the school. The General left here last night with a very poor impression of the school, an impression for which you are entirely responsible. What do you have to say about that?'

'Nothing, sir.'

He could feel his anger rising again. He tried to contain it. 'You don't feel ashamed at all?'

'No, sir.'

'Rokeby, General Collinson fought for his country. He is a very brave man and he did not deserve to be treated with the lack of respect that you displayed yesterday afternoon.'

Richard Rokeby stared back at him. The eyes unblinking. 'If you say so, sir.'

He was not going to lose his temper. He was determined not to lose his temper.

But the eyes were getting to him. The eyes that said, 'I despise you. I despise everything you stand for.'

It was too much to be endured! The boy must be made to understand that his behaviour was unacceptable.

He made it a rule not to hit below the belt: But every rule had its exception.

'Rokeby, men lost their lives defending this country! Tens of thousands died in battle! And thousands more, God help them, died in those camps! Imagine if your father had been one of them!'

'My father?' A slight jarring of the composure. A genuine note of surprise.

'Yes! Your father! In one of those places! A prisoner of those monsters! Beaten, tortured, suffering God knows what indignities, fighting to stay alive while being starved and brutalised! How would you feel about the likes of the General then? Do you think you'd be so bloody insolent towards him then?'

The eyes widened. The mouth opened slightly, but no words came out. Then the head dropped.

Mr Howard stood and watched him, feeling an uncomfortable mixture of guilt and satisfaction.

'Well?'

The head remained lowered.

'Well?!'

The head began to rise. Mr Howard opened his mouth, preparing to deliver the final part of his reprimand. He stared into the face, and at once the words died in his throat.

The eyes burned with anger, an anger that exploded out of the pupils, boring into him like drills.

And the voice that answered his question had no trace of its former composure. None at all.

'YOU WANT TO KNOW HOW I'D FEEL?! I'D FEEL PLEASED THAT HE'D SUFFERED!! I'D FEEL PLEASED THAT HE WAS DEAD!! I'D WANT TO GIVE MEDALS TO ALL THE GERMANS WHO'D HELPED KILL HIM!!'

For a moment the body shook, as if unable to contain the violent emotions that raged within. Then, as quickly as it had been lost, the composure returned. The body stilled. The eyes, cool and clear again, remained focused on him.

Mr Howard, fought against the urge to take a step backwards. Again the thought was in his head.

*This boy is trouble.*

But now it was overshadowed by a new thought. Darker. More disquieting.

*This boy is dangerous.*

He forgot about administering the rest of his reprimand. He forgot about demanding an apology for the outburst. He forgot about everything save his desire for this interview to be over.

'Rokeby you will write a letter of apology to the General which you will present to my secretary tomorrow morning. And you will never again behave with such insolence towards a guest of this school. Is that understood?'

'Yes, sir. Of course, sir.'

'That is all. You may go.'

Richard Rokeby walked out of the room. Mr Howard stood and watched him go. He took a deep breath and realised that his heart was pounding.

A minute passed and there was a knock on the door. His wife appeared. 'How did it go?'

He shook his head. 'There's something wrong with that boy.

I may have to write to his father and ask that he be taken away from this school.'

'Why? Clive, what happened?'

He told her. 'How could he say something like that about his father?'

'Try not to be too hard on him,' she said softly. 'You know his background.'

'That's no excuse. To say that!'

'That's not fair, Clive. You don't know what you might say if you were in his position.'

He shook his head. 'I tell you Lizzie, there's something wrong with that boy. There's something bad inside him. Something destructive.'

'He's just a boy, Clive. That's all. A lonely fourteen-year-old boy.'

'Lonely?!' He stared at her in amazement. 'He's hardly that! For God's sake, he's the one who treats the rest of the school as if they were lepers!'

'That doesn't mean he's not lonely. Not deep down. Everyone needs someone, Clive.'

He laughed harshly. 'Even Richard Rokeby?'

'Even Richard Rokeby. You can't go through life being an island. You die inside if you do.'

He was about to dismiss her words when suddenly he looked into her adored face and had an image of a life without her. Except that he couldn't really imagine it. There could be no life without her, just a living death. The realisation disturbed him and he put his arms around her and pulled her to him. 'I know one thing,' he said softly. 'I'd die inside if I didn't have you. I couldn't go on with my life if you weren't a part of it.'

They kissed each other tenderly, there in the stillness of his study.

Richard Rokeby sat at a desk in a deserted classroom.

He stared in front of him but saw nothing; his attention focused on a screen that hung behind his eyes.

On the screen there was but a single image. An image of his father; an image of a healthy, prosperous man, at peace with the world and himself. He focused in on the image as it blazed in front of him like a sun at the centre of his mind.

And as he did so he felt the hatred start, like a block of ice at the pit of his stomach, spreading through his system like poison, numbing any more complicated emotions that might lurk there. Washing them away in the cold, clean balm of hate.

He sat and stared in front of him. He breathed slowly and deeply, feeling his equilibrium return. The moment of weakness was over. He was himself again.

He rose to his feet and walked out of the classroom, out into the corridor, past the other classrooms and the assembly hall, towards the sounds of life. As always he moved lightly and confidently, his head high, his shoulders back and his eyes staring directly in front of him.

He came to the cloisters. Boys were gathered there in groups, waiting for the lunch bell, chatting, jostling, killing time. All turned and stared at him as he appeared. Questions and taunts bombarded him: 'what happened Rokeby, what did he do to you?', 'bet he got thrashed. That's what he deserves, uppy little prick.' He ignored them all.

He strode on towards Abbey House; a confident figure, aloof, contained, assured.

And, as always, alone.

# Chapter Three

———⟫◦◦◦⟪———

Fourth period, Tuesday morning. The lesson had just ended.

Jonathan sat at his desk, his essay in front of him, watching as the rest of the class jostled their way out of the room, off to enjoy their one free period of the week. Nicholas Scott, the last to leave, rolled his eyes at him before moving on into the corridor. The last echoes of their voices reverberated around the room before fading away into silence.

Mr Stewart, the history master, stood cleaning the blackboard, sending clouds of chalk dust billowing into the stale air of the classroom. He was a tall, athletic man in his late twenties with a strong, square face that bordered on the handsome. His arm swept over the board in easy arches, as if warming up to throw a javelin. When finished he sat down at his desk and indicated for Jonathan to approach.

'So,' he said, 'this essay of yours.'

Jonathan wriggled awkwardly, sensing what was to come.

'It was excellent, Palmer. A first-class effort.'

He felt his face grow hot. 'Thank you, sir.' His tone was a mixture of pride and embarrassment.

'Not at all. Praise where praise is due. The library has at least a dozen books on the Virgin Queen and you seem to have studied them all.'

'Not all of them, sir,' he insisted modestly.

Mr Stewart's brown eyes radiated warmth. The university blazer he wore made him look more like a senior prefect than a member of staff. He was one of the few masters who did not wear a gown. 'Is History your favourite subject?' he asked.

Jonathan nodded.

'Why?'

The question surprised him, coming from such a source. 'I just enjoy it, sir.'

'Why do you enjoy it?'

'Because it's exciting.'

'What is it that you find exciting? The wars? The feuds?'

He was tempted to say yes. But he liked Mr Stewart and wanted to be honest. 'No, sir. It's more than that. It's ...'

'It's?'

'I don't know sir. It's difficult to put it into words'.

'Try.'

He smiled, shrugged his shoulders, said nothing.

'Try, Palmer. I'd like to know.'

'Because it seems so alive.'

'Alive? How so?'

'It's the people I read about. The great people in history. When I read about their lives, what they achieved, all the dangers they had to face ...' he paused, struggling to express himself. 'They didn't just exist. They really lived their lives. It makes me feel alive just reading about them.'

Mr Stewart sat back in his chair and smiled at Jonathan. 'I know how you feel. When I was at school my friends could never understand why I might want to read a history book. To them it was a dead subject, but to me it was more alive than all the other subjects put together.'

'That's right. It's like reading a story, except it's better than a story because it actually happened.'

'You read a lot, don't you?'

He nodded eagerly. 'All the time.'

'It shows in your work. What are you reading at the moment?'

'A book about the Man in the Iron Mask.'

'Is it good?'

'Brilliant! I started reading it on Sunday. I read it all afternoon. It's the best way to spend a Sunday afternoon; losing yourself in a good book.'

'Helps you forget all about the delights of Monday morning?!'

'Helps me forget about having to be here at all!'

He stopped suddenly, realising what he'd just said. Mortified he lowered his eyes, stared down at his shoes. They were in need of a good clean. In the distance he could hear third years reciting French verbs.

'Is that what you want, Palmer? To forget that you're here?'

'No, sir.'

'Are you sure?'

'Yes, sir.'

He looked up cautiously. Mr Stewart was studying him closely but his eyes were sympathetic A question burned at their centre but Jonathan knew that it would not be asked. Certain questions were never asked at Kirkston Abbey.

He waited to be dismissed.

'It does get better,' said Mr Stewart suddenly. 'As you move up the school. The more senior you become the better it becomes. I know that's little comfort now, but it is true.'

The words, so kindly meant, struck a raw nerve within him. He said nothing.

'Don't you believe me?'

He nodded.

Mr Stewart sensed his reluctance. 'But?'

'That's what Paul Ellerson used to say, sir.'

The name, so rarely mentioned now, hung in the air like

a lead weight. He heard Mr Stewart breathe in sharply. Then silence.

'Your essay was excellent, Palmer,' said Mr Stewart eventually. 'Really excellent.' He smiled, rather weakly. 'I'm sorry I've kept you. Off you go now.'

'Yes, sir. Thank you, sir.' He turned and made for the door.

But before he left the classroom he turned and looked at Mr Stewart, sitting at his desk, staring thoughtfully into space.

Mr Stewart had liked Paul Ellerson. Everyone had liked Paul Ellerson.

Except that no one mentioned his name any more. Not after what had happened. Now it was as if Paul Ellerson had never existed at all.

He turned and walked away, moving quickly, as if running from the savage emotions that were starting to churn inside him.

The Kirkston Abbey library was a huge, oak-panelled room on the first floor of the main school building. Its windows looked out on to the rugby pitches and the chapel. It was empty save for half a dozen fifth formers, laughing as they worked at one of the tables. There was no sign of the duty prefect.

Jonathan walked past them, on towards the elephants' graveyard, otherwise known as the religious studies section; an alcove with a window seat, hidden in the far left hand corner of the room.

Until 1942 religious studies had featured prominently in the Kirkston Abbey curriculum. Reverend Johnson, the school's resident cleric, had been a graduate of the fire and brimstone school of theology. Convinced that the young were particularly vulnerable to the temptations of the devil, Reverend Johnson had devoted his lessons to the scrutiny of the ecclesiastical tomes that filled the library, together with vivid descriptions of the torments that awaited sinners in hell and exhortations to his pupils to pray that God would take mercy on their unworthy souls.

In 1942 God did take mercy on the boys of Kirkston Abbey. Reverend Johnson went to visit a brother in London and was killed in an air raid. His replacement, Reverend Potter, was less concerned with saving his pupils' souls than with enjoying a quiet life. Studies of ecclesiastical texts became a thing of the past. Lessons now consisted of summaries of the key parts of the Bible interspersed with broad hints about the end-of-year exam. Most of the books in the religious studies section hadn't felt the touch of human hands for years. It was an ideal place for people who wanted to be alone.

Jonathan moved towards the section now. Only when he reached it did he see that it was already occupied.

Richard Rokeby was sitting on the window seat. His chin rested in his hands, his elbow balanced on his knee. He was staring out of the window, his eyes following rain drops as they slid sluggishly down the glass.

The sight of him made Jonathan feel like an intruder. He turned to slip away before his presence could be detected.

And heard a voice in his head, urging him to say something.

He ignored it. Richard Rokeby would not want to talk to him.

But the voice persisted, a soft, seductive whisper.

*Say something. Anything just to start a conversation. You wanted to talk to him. Now's your chance.*

He wanted to leave. But he knew that he would despise himself if he walked away. He turned towards Richard, finding himself as nervous as if he were about to sit an important exam.

'Hello, Rokeby.'

Richard didn't seem to hear him. He tried again, louder this time. 'Hello, Rokeby'.

This time Richard heard. He started slightly, then turned

towards him. His eyes were so hostile that Jonathan was unnerved and blurted out the first thing that came into his head. 'You're not reading, are you?'

'Does it look like it?'

He gave a quick laugh, trying to mask his awkwardness.

'What do you want?' demanded Richard.

'I ...' he struggled for something to say. 'I wanted to thank you.'

'Thank me?'

'For last week. For helping with the translation.'

Richard said nothing, just sat and stared at him, making him feel as if he had to justify his presence. 'I can never do the sentences Ackerley gives me. I was really grateful for your help.'

Richard shrugged. 'Forget it.' He turned back to the rain-streaked window, the conversation clearly over as far as he was concerned.

Jonathan remained where he was, shuffling his feet, trying to think of something else to say. Richard, realising that he was still there, turned back. 'Look, what do you want?' His voice was terse, irritable.

Nothing, he said. Or would have said if the question that burned inside him hadn't burst out of his throat before he could stop it.

'Why don't you talk to anybody?'

Richard's eyes widened very slightly. 'What does that have to do with you?'

'Nothing.'

'So why are you asking?'

'Because I want to know.'

'Why?'

'Because it doesn't make any sense. Not for someone like you.'

'Someone like me?'

'You could be friends with anyone you wanted.'

'Friends?' Richard's expression was one of incredulity. 'Friends,' he repeated, his tone a mixture of scorn and amusement. He half laughed, then turned back to the window.

'Why not?'

'Go away, Palmer.'

'But why not?'

Richard breathed heavily. 'Just go away.'

'But why not?' Frustration was creeping into his voice now. 'Why do you hate everybody? What's wrong with us?!'

'You're all sheep.'

'I'm no sheep!' He was filled with sudden indignation.

Richard turned towards him. He said nothing. But his eyes were scornful. He half raised one eyebrow.

'I'm not!'

'Yes, you are.'

'No, I'm not!' He felt his face growing hot with anger.

'Of course you are. You and everyone else here. You do what the school tells you to do. You think what the school tells you to think. You're all sheep.'

'That's not true!'

'Of course it is. None of you can think for yourselves. This place is full of zombies! You've all got about as much life as Paul Ellerson!'

'DON'T YOU DARE TALK ABOUT PAUL ELLERSON!!'

The fury in his voice startled him as much as it startled Richard. His heart was racing. 'Don't you dare talk about Paul Ellerson!' he said in a more controlled voice. 'Not ever!'

'Why not?' demanded Richard. Suddenly the intense eyes were alive with interest. 'Why not? Why shouldn't I talk about him?'

'Just don't!'

'Why not?'

'Because you don't know anything about him!'

'And you do?'

'I know more than you.' He swallowed. Suddenly his throat was very dry.

'How?'

'Because he was my Head of House.'

'I know that,' said Richard impatiently. 'It doesn't mean anything.'

'I was his fag last year.' He swallowed again. He knew what the next question was going to be.

'Do you know why he did it?'

He didn't want to get into this. It was dangerous to get into this. He wanted to leave.

But the eyes were fixed on him now, hypnotising him, holding him in a stare that he couldn't break.

'I only knew him by sight,' said Richard. 'What was he like?'

'Not like the others. He was no sheep. You can say what you like about everyone else. But Paul Ellerson was different.'

'How was he different?'

Memories were filling his head: memories that he had tried to keep buried because they were too painful to remember. He fought against them now but it was like trying to stem a flood with his finger. They surged to the front of his mind like waves breaking on a beach.

And with them, finally, came the tears.

Ashamed at his grief, appalled at his weakness, he turned and rushed from the alcove.

He hurried across the library, past the fifth years who were too busy joking amongst themselves to pay any attention to him. He reached the door, threw it open, and promptly collided with two boys who were entering.

'Watch out!' exclaimed one of them, so loudly that the fifth years stopped laughing and looked to see what had happened.

He found himself being glared at by Courtney and Fisher; fourth years like himself but from a different class. He mumbled an apology and made to push past them.

54

'He's blubbing!' exclaimed Courtney.

'No, I'm not.' Again he tried to push past them.

But Courtney now stood square in front of him, blocking his way. He was a tall, thuggish boy with enormous ears that jutted out at virtual right angles from his head. 'He is blubbing!' he cried. 'Look!'

'I'm not!' he insisted. His heart was starting to race. He could sense all the fifth years staring at him; their work completely forgotten now; their eyes shining at the prospect of fourth year bloodsports. For the third time he tried to push past Courtney.

But Courtney continued to block his path, his narrow, piggy eyes studying him with a mixture of scorn and vicious amusement. He too had noticed that they had an audience and began to play to it. 'You are!' he insisted, pushing Jonathan so that he stumbled backwards, colliding into the corner of the table where the spectators sat like vultures waiting for the kill. 'What are you blubbing about, you little poof?!'

'Leave him alone,' said a voice from behind them.

Richard Rokeby had left the alcove and was watching the scene. 'Piss off, Rokeby,' said Courtney dismissively.

'I *said*, leave him alone.'

Courtney took no notice. Instead he punched Jonathan on the elbow; a savage blow, numbing his whole arm.

'LEAVE HIM ALONE, ELEPHANT BOY!'

Courtney stopped.

One of the fifth years whistled between his teeth; a soft, mischievous sound.

Courtney heard the sound. His eyes darted to the table and then back to Richard. 'WHAT DID YOU JUST CALL ME?!'

'You heard,' said Richard coolly.

Courtney took a step towards him. 'I asked you a question, Rokeby!' Jonathan, who stood between them, tensed in apprehension.

But Richard showed no sign of apprehension. He too took a step forward.

'You're not deaf, are you, Courtney?' He began to smile. 'I mean, you of all people.'

'No, I'm not!'

'That's good. Retardation must be enough of a handicap.'

Somebody sniggered.

Again Courtney's eyes darted to the table. His expression was still one of anger, but he was beginning to look uncomfortable. 'You shut your mouth, Rokeby!' he said fiercely.

'Or what?'

'Or he'll shut it for you,' answered Fisher, entering the conversation for the first time.

'God, it can talk. I thought it was just for decoration.' Richard's eyes flicked over Fisher dismissively and then turned back to Courtney. 'And how are you going to shut me up?'

'You'll see!'

'No, you tell me.' Suddenly Richard took another step forward. The smile was total now and his eyes were flashing. 'How are you going to do it? A black eye perhaps? A broken nose?' He started to laugh. 'Or would a thick ear be more appropriate?'

More sniggering. Not one person. Now it was the whole table.

The fury had faded from Courtney's face, replaced by confusion. 'You shut your mouth,' he said, as fiercely as he could manage, 'or I'll knock your teeth so far down your throat that you'll bite your own arse!'

'Don't get excited, Courtney. It makes your ears flap and if your mouth generates any more hot air you might take off.'

The sniggering had turned to full-blown laughter. Courtney, completely out of his depth now, could think of nothing to say. He opened and shut his mouth like a fish gasping for air.

The library door burst open. Mr Huntley, the Geography master came striding into the room; a pipe clenched between his tobacco-stained teeth. 'What's all this noise?!' he boomed, breathing clouds of pungent smoke into the air. 'This is the library not the junior common room. Right, fifth year, back to the classroom now.'

The fifth years climbed reluctantly to their feet, gathered their books and made for the door. Mr Huntley glared at the four boys standing by the table. 'What are you doing here?!' he barked. 'If you're not working then get out!' He gestured to the door.

Courtney, clearly grateful to have a means of retreat without disgrace, prepared to leave. 'You're dead!' he hissed at Richard.

'Oh sure!' replied Richard scornfully.

'Just wait!' said Courtney before following Fisher through the door that Mr Huntley was holding open for them.

'You two as well,' said Mr Huntley, staring sternly at Jonathan and Richard. Jonathan made as if to leave.

'But we are working, sir,' said Richard. 'We're doing a History project. It's on the gunpowder plot. Mr Stewart sent us here to find some books.'

'Really?' Mr Huntley looked suspicious.

'Ask Mr Stewart if you don't believe us,' Richard told him. 'He's in his classroom now.'

Mr Huntley shook his head. 'Get on with it then and don't make a lot of noise.' He marched out. Jonathan and Richard were left alone in the sudden stillness of the room.

Jonathan's heart was racing as hard as if he'd just run five miles. 'You shouldn't have said those things to Courtney,' he told Richard.

'Why not?'

'Because he'll get you for it.'

'No he won't.'

'He will. You heard what he said.'

'They're just words. He picks on people who are afraid of him. He'd never dare go after someone who might hit him back.'

'You still shouldn't have said it.' He paused, then awkwardly added, 'Thanks.'

Richard, who had been watching the door, now turned towards him. Suddenly Jonathan had the odd sensation that the eyes were actually seeing him as a person for the first time. His jumbled emotions crystalised into a single sensation

*connection*

which was gone as quickly as it had come, leaving him in a silence that no longer seemed uncomfortable, and with the confidence to say the things that really mattered.

'I wish I could be like you. I'd give anything to be like you.'

Richard looked at him curiously. 'Would you?'

He nodded.

'Why?'

He blushed, lowered his eyes.

'Why?'

'Because of the things you do.'

'What things?'

'Everything. Everything you do. Everything you say. The way you just spoke to Courtney. The way you spoke to Ackerley last week. The way you walked out of that talk in front of everyone. I'd give anything to have the courage to do the things you do.'

'You think I'm brave?'

'Yes! God yes! I mean I could never speak to Ackerley the way you did.'

'Yes, you could.'

He shook his head.

'You could. If you hated him enough.'

The remark took him by surprise. 'I do hate him.'

'No, you don't.'

'Of course I do.' Richard shook his head. 'I do!'

'No, you don't. You want his approval. You want him to think well of you. I don't give a damn what he thinks about me. That's the difference between us. It has nothing to do with courage.'

'But I do hate him,' he insisted. 'I hate the way he picks on me.'

'Then you have to let him see it. You have to show him that you hate him, and that nothing he can do will ever make you stop.' Richard's face darkened. 'God, if he ever made remarks about me . . .'

'But he never would,' said Jonathan quietly. 'Not about you. That's the real difference between us.'

Suddenly a light came into Richard's eyes, a warmer light than Jonathan had ever seen before. He opened his mouth to speak.

And then, abruptly he stopped himself. His face became a mask. He turned away, looking towards the windows on the other side of the library. The rain had stopped, replaced by weak autumn sunshine.

The lunch bell rang. Jonathan knew that Nicholas and the Perrimans would be waiting for him outside the dining-hall. 'I have to go. Thanks for sticking up for me.'

Richard ignored him. Hurt, he turned to go.

'Palmer'.

Eagerly he turned back. 'What?'

'You want people to like you. You want to fit in and belong. That's your weakness. That's how Ackerley and everyone else get their strength. You have to learn how to hate them and everything they stand for. That's how you're strong. That's how you win.'

He smiled ruefully. 'You make it sound so easy.'

'It is.'

# Chapter Four

Sunday afternoon, half past two. Jonathan stood in his study in Old School House, talking to Giles Harrington.

Giles was a tall, handsome fifteen-year-old with the words 'Future Head of House' stamped on his forehead. He was checking that there would be a full turn-out for his elder brother Brian's talk on the importance of House spirit.

House spirit was currently a sensitive issue for the boys of Old School. On the previous afternoon their rugby team, captained by Brian Harrington, had suffered a crushing defeat at the hands of Heatherfield House. The defeat, witnessed by the whole school, had astonished everyone; Heatherfield's reputation for sporting excellence being comparable to that of Henry the Eighth for domestic tranquillity.

But Heatherfield had one trump card in the person of new boy Basil Carter. Though only sixteen, Basil was six foot three, immensely muscular, blessed with a fluidity of movement that a ballet dancer would have envied and the ability to run like the wind. Whenever Heatherfield won the ball they fed it out to Basil who charged towards the tryline, scattering the opposition like nine pins, leading his side to victory.

The defeat, a huge dent to the collective ego of Old School, had been blamed on insufficient cheering from the touchline. Hence Brian's forthcoming talk.

'The talk starts at three o'clock,' Giles told Jonathan. 'Make sure you're on time. Brian doesn't want to have to wait around for latecomers.'

Jonathan nodded.

'Good. House spirit is important. You do see that, don't you, Palmer?'

Jonathan nodded again. Giles stared at him suspiciously. Giles was the son of Sir Richard Harrington who owned estates all over Norfolk. The Harringtons could trace their ancestors back to the Wars of the Roses. Brian and Giles were the fifth generation of the family to attend Kirkston Abbey and Giles strode about the place with the easy arrogance of one who knew that he belonged. Jonathan hated Giles.

'Of course,' he replied. 'I'm sure we would have thrashed Heatherfield if we'd all just cheered a little louder.'

He regretted the words as soon as they were spoken. Giles was sure to register the sarcasm and report it to his brother. But Giles, who possessed the sturdy, athletic type of stupidity that is so typically British, registered nothing but agreement. 'Exactly.'

'How long do you think your brother will talk for?'

'As long as he wants to!' said Giles severely. Jonathan nodded meekly, and remembered how he had once overheard Giles complaining to a friend that his father was having trouble with his tenant farmers. 'They're bone idle! They don't know the meaning of a hard day's work!' He had a sudden image of Giles, dressed in his school blazer and a pair of jackboots, goosestepping through a wheat field, beating labourers with a cricket bat. He felt the urge to laugh and bit his lip.

There was a knock on the door. 'Yes!' shouted Giles, assuming that it would be for him.

But it wasn't. The door opened to reveal Richard Rokeby.

Jonathan was taken by surprise. The two of them had not exchanged a word since their encounter in the library the previous Tuesday. Occasionally, in class, he had caught

Richard's eyes and attempted a friendly nod but had received no sign of acknowledgement.

The study was not big enough to hold three people comfortably so Richard leant against the doorframe. 'What are you doing this afternoon?' he asked Jonathan.

'He's going to a talk,' Giles informed him.

Richard ignored him. 'Well? What are you doing?' he asked again.

'I told you what he's doing!' snapped Giles who did not like being ignored. 'Now clear off, Rokeby. We don't want your sort around here.'

'Is this the Brian Harrington talk? I saw a notice on your board.'

Jonathan nodded. 'It's on House spirit.' He fought an urge to grimace.

'That's something you wouldn't know anything about,' added Giles.

'That's right,' agreed Richard affably. 'Unlike your brother of course.'

Bonhomie, coming from such a source, put Giles on his guard. 'What do you mean?' he demanded.

'What I said. Your brother's just overflowing with House spirit. We both know that he's only giving this talk because it hurts him that the junior boys don't love this House as much as he does. Personal feelings have nothing to do with it at all.'

'What personal feelings?'

'Feelings of humiliation,' suggested Richard, 'at being thrashed by a team who are a school joke.' He paused. 'Especially when that team's star player is a wog.'

A look of complete embarrassment spread across Giles's face. 'That's got nothing to do with it!' he cried

'I know it hasn't.'

'It hasn't!'

'I know that Harrington. You don't have to convince me.'

His repeated agreements only served to put Giles ever more on the defensive. 'My brother has nothing against wogs!'

'I know he doesn't.'

'He doesn't!'

'I know that.'

'It's true!'

'I know it is.'

'It is!'

'In fact,' suggested Richard, 'it would probably be true to say that he admires them.'

'He does!'

'He admires them terribly.'

'Absolutely!'

'In fact I bet he wishes he was one himself.'

'He does!' cried Giles. 'He does ... No! He bloody doesn't! He ...' He paused, realising that he had walked blindly into a trap and couldn't win with either answer. He struggled to maintain his dignity. He pulled himself up to his full height and glared at Richard. 'You're an absolute disgrace to this school Rokeby. You've no business here at all!'

Richard rolled his eyes in an imitation of Al Jolson. 'Oh lordy, Massa Harrington, don' never say dat!'

Giles tried to stare him down. But he was out of his depth. He was a Harrington after all, stock from which school heroes were made. He was used to being looked up to and admired. He had no experience of being so openly despised.

'I feel sorry for you, Rokeby,' he announced grandiosely before marching out of the study.

Richard stepped into the study and pushed the door closed behind him.

'You shouldn't have said all that,' said Jonathan.

'That's what you said last time,' Richard told him.

'I know.'

The two of them stared at each other.

Then the laughter came. They started at the same moment,

both doubled over with mirth. For over a minute they rocked back and forth, laughing like hyenas, unable to stop.

Richard composed himself first. Jonathan, managed to do the same. He straightened up and stared at Richard again.

'So what are you doing this afternoon?' Richard asked him.

The talk was forgotten. Everything was forgotten in the sudden intensity of the moment. 'Nothing,' he replied. 'Nothing at all.'

'Let's get away from here. Let's go miles away and forget all about this dump for the afternoon. Do you want to do that?'

He nodded. Excitement pulsed through him. He felt absurdly happy.

Richard turned and led the way.


Elizabeth Howard sat with Henry and Marjorie Ackerley in the drawing-room of their Bowerton home.

Bowerton was a tiny village, set on a ridge, a mile from the school gates. It consisted of half a dozen streets, all of which converged on to a well kept village green, and a sixteenth-century pub called the Fleece. The Fleece, and a tiny post office were Bowerton's only symbols of commercial activity. But its stone-clad architecture was beautiful, its atmosphere tranquil, and its comparatively high position allowed for some glorious views of the countryside as it rolled away towards the horizon. It was popular with those of the Kirkston Abbey staff who did not live in the school.

'I'm sorry i didn't come to see you last Sunday,' said Elizabeth as she accepted Marjorie's offer of a second cup of tea.

'It doesn't matter,' replied Marjorie. 'I'm sure you had enough to think about with that Randall boy walking out of the Assembly Hall.'

'His name is Rokeby,' her husband corrected her. 'Richard Rokeby.'

'So it is. You did tell me Henry. How stupid of me.' Marjorie gave her husband an apologetic smile and handed a refilled cup to Elizabeth. 'What an awful thing to happen. You and Clive must have been mortified.'

'We were,' Elizabeth told her solemnly. 'Terribly.' She tried to look solemn but the smile that was so much a part of her refused to be suppressed. 'Though not as mortified as the General.' She started to laugh. 'Poor Clive had to spend hours smoothing ruffled feathers. He looked absolutely done in at the end!'

'What will happen to Rokeby?' asked Marjorie. 'Will he be punished?'

'He should be expelled!' said Henry with sudden vehemence.

'Why do you think that?' asked Elizabeth, surprised at the passion in his voice.

'Because he's insufferable. His arrogance is beyond belief!'

'But you can't expel a boy simply because he's arrogant.'

'It's not just his arrogance. It's everything about him. You haven't had to teach him, Elizabeth. You don't know what he's like. Mark my words, that boy is trouble.'

Elizabeth shook her head. 'He's just a boy. That's all.'

'That's right, Henry,' said Marjorie gently. 'How much trouble can one boy be?'

'And what would you know about it?' he snapped.

Marjorie flushed. For a moment she stared at her husband, her eyes wide with hurt. Then she turned away and began to busy herself with the tea things.

No sooner were the harsh words spoken than Henry seemed to regret them. He turned towards his wife, seemed about to say something but then decided against. He picked up a spoon and began to stir his tea. He managed a smile for Elizabeth, but it was a tired gesture that barely stretched the muscles of his mouth and fell far short of his eyes.

Elizabeth, uncomfortable, looked away, allowing her eyes to

drift over the drawing-room. It was a beautiful room, exquisitely furnished. Marjorie had excellent taste. She wanted to admire the furnishings but instead found her gaze drawn towards the far corner of the room, to the little table and the picture of a child on a swing, a child with golden curls crying out with excitement, her eyes laughing up at the sky.

She stared at the picture until she sensed that she was being watched. Hastily she turned back to her hosts. Both were now beaming at her. The hurt was gone from Marjorie's face; buried beneath the smiling face of hospitality like dirt being concealed beneath a carpet.

'So what was the General's talk like?' asked Marjorie.

'Very dull. You were lucky to miss it, though I'm sorry that it was ill health that kept you away.'

'It was nothing, really.'

'How can you call a migraine nothing? My aunt suffers from them and you should hear her on the subject! You're clearly a good deal more stoical than she is.'

Marjorie shook her head self-deprecatingly. 'Not really. I have them so rarely. I would have come anyway. But Henry wouldn't hear of it.' She put her hand softly on her husband's in a rather nervous gesture of affection.

'I didn't want her to tire herself,' added Henry. He gave his wife a quick smile but then slid his hand from under hers. He picked up a teaspoon and began to roll it back and forth between his thin fingers. As it moved the spoon clicked against his wedding ring. Marjorie's hand hung in the air for a moment. Then it began to caress her own ring.

Elizabeth sat in awkward silence, watching them both.

There were few people she knew who merited the description 'beautiful', but Marjorie Ackerley was one of them. Though she was in her early forties, her hair still retained much of its golden colour, a colour that was enhanced by the rich hazel of her eyes, just as the regularity of her features were enhanced by the charm of her manner and the sweetness of her voice.

Elizabeth had liked Marjorie from their first meeting. It had been three years ago at a cocktail party to welcome Clive and herself to Kirkston Abbey. She could still remember standing by her husband in the doorway of a crowded room, feeling terribly out of her depth as she was confronted by the forced smiles and cold, appraising eyes of the masters' wives, all eager to disapprove of this youthful newcomer who would rank above them in the hierachy of the school. Then Marjorie had stepped out of the crowd, a smile of genuine welcome on her face, ready to introduce her to everyone, ready to make her feel accepted. Ready to be her friend.

In the years that followed she had tried to develop friendships with the other wives. But they were always shallow relationships, inhibited by her elevated position and the awkwardness and resentment that it inspired in others. The only one she felt real affection for was Marjorie.

They were close friends. They would have been inseparable were it not for Marjorie's husband.

She wanted to like Henry Ackerley. She had tried to like him. There was no clear reason not to like him. Clive described Henry as a dry stick, but then went on to say that he was a decent enough fellow. Perhaps he was right.

But there was something about Henry that troubled her. She could sense it; just as she could sometimes feel a tightening in her head and know a storm was approaching. There were times when she would stare into that cold, aristocratic face and see shadows shifting deep within the grey eyes, shadows that were all the more disturbing because their form remained a mystery to her.

Marjorie was offering her another cup of tea. She wanted to make an excuse, to leave this difficult atmosphere behind her. But Marjorie's eyes beseeched her. And Marjorie was her friend. So she smiled and held out her cup.

Thorley Park was four miles from Kirkston Abbey; a huge

expanse of woodland named after a now destroyed manor house whose grounds it had once comprised.

Richard and Jonathan wheeled their bicycles through its paths, their feet crunching over dead leaves. Eventually they left the bicycles at the foot of a huge oak tree and climbed up into its branches.

They sat facing each other on a branch, their legs dangling towards the ground, their breath condensing in front of their faces like ghosts dancing in the wind.

'I had to get out,' said Richard. 'I couldn't wait until tomorrow.'

'Tomorrow?'

'My great-aunt's funeral.'

Now he remembered Richard telling one of the masters on Friday. 'I'm sorry.'

'I'm not. All I'm losing is half a crown and a sloppy kiss at Christmas. It's a good excuse to get out for a day.'

'Why did your parents send you here?'

'Because I'm a Rokeby of course. The Rokebys come from Upchurch. It's only fifteen miles away so Kirkston Abbey is the local public school. My father came here and my uncle and grandfather. All my ancestors, right back to the dinosaurs.'

'Doesn't that feel strange?'

'Strange?'

'Sitting in class, thinking that maybe a hundred years ago your great-great-grandfather sat in the same desk having the same lesson.'

'Being taught by the same teacher probably.'

They both laughed. 'It must feel strange though,' said Jonathan.

Richard shrugged.

'I'd find it creepy if it was me.'

'I take it the Palmer family haven't been sending their sons to Kirkston Abbey since before the dawn of time.'

Jonathan shook his head. 'The dinosaurs I'm descended from couldn't afford it.'

They laughed again. 'So why are you here then?' asked Richard.

'Shouldn't I be?'

'You're not a typical Kirkston Abbey pupil.'

'Neither are you.'

'Giles Harrington is though. Perhaps we should both aspire to be like him. Is he as big a prick as his brother?'

'Worse. Our House will be a complete fascist state when he's head of it.'

More laughter. 'So why did your parents send you here?' asked Richard.

'It was my father's idea. He wants me to do well in life, to be a success. He thinks this school will help me to become one.'

Richard rolled his eyes.

Jonathan smiled. 'It's a joke, isn't it? But my father believes it. His family was very poor. My grandfather worked in a shoe factory. My uncles went into the factory too but my father was clever. He did well at school and then he went to work in a bank. He's a bank manager now. I know that's nothing compared to the fathers of most of the other people here, but it is an achievement. He's done well, and he wants me to do well too. As soon as I was born he started saving money so that one day he could send me to a school like this.'

'Does he know that you hate it here?'

Jonathan shook his head. 'I couldn't tell him. It means so much to him, having a son at public school. I don't want to spoil it for him.'

'Can't he guess? I mean when he visits you. Can't he see how miserable you are?'

'He hasn't visited me yet.'

Richard's jaw dropped. 'But you've been here over a year!'

'My father lives down in London. He says it's too long a journey.'

'Rubbish!'

'That's not the real reason. It's my stepmother. My father married her a year and a half ago. She's jealous of me. My father and I are close and she hates that. She doesn't like us seeing each other. She wants him to herself.'

'But surely your father wants to see you. Why does he put up with her?'

'Because he's mad about her. She's younger than him and very attractive. I've only met her once. The three of us went out to tea. It was awful. My father kept giving her these soppy looks and she made this big show of being nice to me but it was all false. She kept smiling at me but she didn't mean it.' He shuddered at the memory.

'What about your mother? Has she remarried?'

'No'.

'Where does she live.'

'Just outside Leeds.'

'So you spend holidays and stuff with her.'

He nodded.

'You'll be spending half-term with her?'

'No.' His face lit up. 'I'm seeing my father.'

'How come? What about your stepmother?'

'She's going to visit her parents in Devon. Dad wrote and suggested that I go and stay with him. I was going to say no at first. Mum's on her own. I know that she wants to see me too. I didn't want to hurt her feelings. But she insisted. She knows I miss dad. She said I should go. I can't wait! It's been over a year since I've seen him. There's so much I want to tell him.'

'You really love your parents, don't you?'

The question took him by surprise. 'Of course. Doesn't everyone?'

Richard didn't answer. He leant back against the trunk of the tree and stared up at the sky. A bird flew overhead, flitting through the branches, causing half a dozen dead leaves to drift down to the ground.

'Yes,' he said quietly. 'I suppose they do.'

He breathed out slowly. Questions began to form in Jonathan's mind, but some instinct told him not to ask them. Not yet.

'You can't just accept this situation,' said Richard suddenly.

'I have to. There's nothing I can do about it.'

'Yes there is. He's your father. You have to make your stepmother understand that she can't keep you apart.'

He shook his head. 'I couldn't do that. She'd never listen to me anyway.'

'Then you have to make her listen. I would. God, I'd never let anyone keep me from someone I cared about.'

'But that's you, isn't it? I'm just not like you.'

'You could be.'

'You said that last time but it's not true.'

'It is.'

'No, it's not. You make it all sound so easy but it's not. Not for me anyway. We're different. When you talk people listen. When I talk they just talk over me.'

'But if you don't do anything then she'll win. She'll take your father away from you.'

'She couldn't do that,' he said forcefully. 'My father wouldn't allow that.'

'Isn't that what's happening now?' said Richard softly.

He didn't answer. This was a question he didn't want to risk answering.

They sat in silence, listening to the birds. And when the conversation started again they talked of other things.

Quarter past five.

James Wheatley mingled with the rest of Old School House as they filed out of the Junior Common Room. As always he was flanked by George Turner and Stuart Barry.

'Bastard!' he exclaimed.

'Careful!' hissed Stuart. 'Giles'll hear you and it'll get straight back to Brian.'

James's face was suffused with fury. 'I don't care if it does! We stand around for over an hour and only then does he send a message that he's decided to go and play golf! What a prick! I wish that wog Basil Carter had nobbled him when he had the chance! I wish he'd stamped on his nuts!'

They stood facing the corridor that led to the fourth-year studies; a row of boxrooms that were known as 'the stalls' because they weren't much bigger than toilet stalls and didn't smell much better either. 'Come back to mine,' said Stuart. 'I've got lemonade and the rest of that cake my mum sent.'

'But it's supper now,' pointed out George.

'I'm not eating that shit!' James said forcefully.

'But I'm hungry.'

'Bugger off then! Stuart and I will have the cake on our own.' Stuart nodded and walked off to his study to get things ready.

George shuffled awkwardly from one foot to another, like an ape trying to pirouette. 'I didn't say I was going to go.'

'I don't care! Do what you want.'

George continued to insist that he wasn't going. James's narrow little eyes scanned over the faces of the other boys who milled around him.

Suddenly they widened.

Jonathan Palmer and Richard Rokeby were standing together by the front door of the House. Both were wearing coats, and their cheeks glowed from a combination of cold and exertion. They too were watching the others. As they watched, Richard said something to Jonathan and they both started to laugh.

'We can get bread from the kitchen,' George was saying. 'I hid half a loaf this morning.'

James ignored him, too busy watching this unexpected scene.

'So we could make some sandwiches too. I've got that beef spread. There's only a bit of mould on it.'

James indicated for him to be quiet.

George moved off. James stood where he was, watching Richard and Jonathan. Jonathan had just said something and again they both laughed.

He didn't understand it. What was Richard Rokeby doing with Jonathan? Richard who wanted nothing to do with anyone.

Richard, who wanted nothing to do with him.

It was not through lack of effort on his part. He had tried everything to attract Richard's attention. He was always the first to laugh when Richard stood up to a teacher; the first to applaud when Richard made one of them look small. And he made sure that he was always surrounded by a group of admiring friends when Richard was in earshot, cracking jokes that were guaranteed a loud laugh so that Richard would be sure to hear, and to realise what a wonderful chap James Wheatley was.

Because he wanted Richard as one of his group; had done since he had first clapped eyes on him thirteen months before. Everything about Richard marked him as someone to be pursued, cultivated, acquired. James was very concerned with the image he presented to the world. Intimacy with someone like Richard could only enhance that image.

So he had tried and tried, only to meet with the same wall of indifference. And the longer the wall remained the more desperate he was to break through it, a desperation that was now increasingly born out of secret yearnings, the nature of which he would not admit even to himself.

And now Richard was with Jonathan Palmer. Jonathan Palmer; a grammar school nobody.

Jonathan Palmer, who had succeeded where he had failed.

How could this have happened?

Richard said something to Jonathan who moved away towards the fourth-year corridor. He walked past James, removing his coat as he did so. He would leave it in his study and then he and Richard would go to supper together. The way friends did.

How could this have happened?

Richard stood alone by the door, waiting for Jonathan. James approached him, just as he had done so many times in the past.

'Hello, Rokeby. We're having some grub in Barry's study. Why don't you come?'

Richard didn't even bother to look at him. His eyes stared at some point over James's right shoulder.

'Piss off, Wheatley,' he said in a bored tone.

A couple of third years passing by heard this interchange. They sniggered and then hurried on.

James turned and walked away towards the fourth-year corridor. He felt angry and humiliated, just as he had done countless times before. But now he also felt confused.

As he entered the corridor he collided with someone who was hurrying in the other direction. Jonathan Palmer. Now without his coat, off to supper with his new friend. 'Sorry,' Jonathan cried before rushing on.

James stood and watched him go. Jonathan Palmer, off to supper with Richard Rokeby. Richard Rokeby, who still wouldn't give him the time of day.

Why? Why? Why?

Half past ten. Henry Ackerley walked into the hallway of his home.

He stood very still, listening for sounds of movement. Was Marjorie still up? Surely not. She was always in bed by ten on Sunday. He peered up the stairs but could see no lights. She was asleep. He was sure of it.

He walked into the drawing-room where earlier that day the two of them had entertained Elizabeth Howard. He turned on the light and headed for the sideboard. The Scotch stood in its decanter. He poured himself a sizeable measure and swallowed it down. It burned but it warmed. It was what he needed.

He was about to pour himself another one when he heard footsteps. Marjorie stood by the door, wearing her dressing-gown, her hair loose around her head like a golden halo. As always her eyes were wary. Once, a million years ago, they had been full of joy and laughter. But he didn't want to remember that.

'Where have you been?' she asked.

'Nowhere.'

'I was worried. I didn't know where you were.'

'I've just been walking.'

'In this weather? They said it would freeze tonight.'

'I wanted some air.'

'But your chest. Remember the cold you had last year. Doctor Pearson said you had to be careful.' Her voice was like velvet. A spoken lullaby.

'I'm all right. I'm not a child, Marjorie.'

'I know you're not. I ...' He heard the familiar note of hurt. 'I just worry about you, that's all.'

'You don't need to.'

'I worry when I don't know where you are. I start imagining things.'

'Like what?!' he cried with sudden bitterness. 'That I might have just gone off somewhere? That I might never come back?'

The words were meant to wound but this time her voice was steady. 'No, Henry,' she said quietly. 'I don't think that. I know you'll always come back.'

She turned and walked away, closing the door behind her.

He stared at the glass he held in his hand. He was filled with a violent urge to dash it against the wall.

But that wouldn't help. Nothing would help.

He put the glass down. He breathed slowly and easily.

But his hands were clenched into fists. And inside he was screaming.

✳    ✳    ✳

76

It wasn't until he left the washroom and walked towards his bed that Jonathan realised he was being watched.

James Wheatley was sitting up in his own bed, staring at him

As soon as Jonathan recognised the stare James smiled, nodded and then buried his nose in the book he was holding in his hands.

For a moment Jonathan was alarmed. Was James planning something? Was he going to be the chosen target tonight?

But then the alarm faded. Instinct told him that there would be no trouble that night. And he had spent enough months in this dormitory to know that his instinct could be relied on.

He climbed between the starched sheets of his bed and tried to find the page in his current library book.

From his own bed James Wheatley sat and watched him. He was no longer smiling.

# Chapter Five

Monday morning. Chapel had just ended. The boys of Old School House poured out of their studies, carrying the books they would need for the morning's lessons.

Jonathan stood alone in his study, a confused expression on his face.

His Latin book was missing.

For the third time he crouched down and routed through the tiny cupboard where he kept his books, searching for the hated red volume. Outside he could hear the rowdy voices of his contemporaries growing fainter as they marched off to the classrooms. He was going to be late.

He started to panic. It was Latin first period, and Mr Ackerley was the one master for whom he should never be late.

He told himself to calm down. The book had to be there. He had placed it there himself last night, following a futile hour of trying to make sense of the translation they would be discussing in class that morning.

But it was not there now. The only red volume was his Maths book — the cause of his embarrassment two weeks earlier.

So where was it?

He climbed back to his feet. His eyes scanned the little room with the decrepid desk, the battered cupboard and the shabby curtains that framed the mean window with its view of the school kitchens. There was nowhere to conceal a book here, even if he'd wanted to.

Someone must have borrowed it; must have taken it without asking and then forgotten to return it. But who?

There was no chance of finding out now. All the potential culprits would be sitting in Melbourne classroom, listening to Mr Ackerley.

Just as he should be.

It was no good. He'd have to take the Maths book for show and then surreptitiously share with Nicholas. He grabbed his books and rushed from the room.

Then he stopped.

There, lying halfway up the empty corridor, was a familiar looking red textbook.

He walked towards it, bent down and opened the cover, looking for the inscription on the fly leaf.

*Jonathan Palmer, Form IVM, September 1954.*

What was it doing here? Who had put it here?

He pushed the questions to one side. There was no time. He seized the volume and began to run towards the classrooms.

It was only as he hurried past the assembly hall that he realised the rush was unnecessary.

Ackerley was going to be fifteen minutes late. He had said so at the end of the last lesson. In his absence they were to sit in silence and work on their translations.

Fat chance.

He walked down the corridor, his solitary footsteps echoing on the stone floor. He walked past classroom after classroom, each with its own occupants and rhythm; third-year linguists reciting French verbs in a bored English drone; fifth-year mathematicians marvelling at the myriad uses of a logarithm; sixth-form philosophers contemplating Hamlet's mental state and the insights it gave on the human condition. He walked past them all, on towards the half open door of Melbourne classroom.

As he approached he could hear a multitude of voices; people talking at the same time, all in the same hushed tone.

He walked into the classroom, to be greeted by an instant silence. They had thought he was Ackerley.

He felt himself blush, smiled apologetically at no one in particular and hurried towards the double desk where Nicholas Scott sat waiting for him. He knew the voices would start up again.

But they didn't.

The classroom remained silent as he flopped down into his seat.

Surprised he turned and looked around. The rest of the class were observing him. Some looked serious. Others were smiling. All seemed expectant.

What was going on?

Unnerved, he turned back to his desk, struggling to find the right page in his book. But his hand had started to shake and he couldn't focus. The silence continued, broken only by the occasional snigger.

He could feel his face burning with the pressure of all the eyes boring into him. In desperation, he turned towards Nicholas.

Nicholas was staring at him too. There was no expectation in his face, merely a mute apology.

Jonathan said nothing. He let his eyes ask the question.

Nicholas nodded towards the blackboard.

He turned towards it. When he saw what was on it he grew cold all over.

A drawing covered the smooth, dark surface; a drawing of two boys, sketched in crisp white chalk.

One of the boys could have been anyone. He stood facing the class with his hands in his pockets, a bored expression on his face. An unremarkable figure if it weren't for the enormous phallus that bulged out of his trousers, reaching almost to his forehead.

The second boy, on the other hand, was clearly meant to be him.

He stood in profile, the delicate, almost feminine features, covered by a wide brimmed hat that a farmer might wear. A piece of straw protruded from his mouth. References to his parochial background.

The mouth was curved into a lascivious smile. The eyes were wide and eager, marvelling at the other boy's phallus which he held in his outstretched hands.

The essence of his features had been captured perfectly. The drawing was crude but it was also skilful. The standard of work one would expect of a prize winner. Last year's Art prize winner.

James Wheatley.

He turned towards James who sat in the corner of the classroom with George Turner. James was smiling at him; his small, vicious eyes shining with delight.

His mind was reeling. Why had James done this? Why did James think this of him? What had he done to allow James or anyone to think this of him?

The laughter was starting now; harsh, jagged bursts, firing at him from all sides. As he listened to it the reasons stopped mattering. All that mattered was to remove this obscenity from sight.

He ran towards the blackboard, followed by a chorus of jeers and wolf whistles, and grabbed the board rubber from its holder, wiping away the savage caricature of his own face.

The classroom door burst open and Mr Ackerley marched in.

'WHAT THE HELL IS GOING ON HERE?!'

His entrance, ten minutes earlier than expected, took everyone by surprise. The laughter and jeers ceased instantly, replaced by horrified silence. Eyes that had been focused on the spectacle now bore into the pages of textbooks. A mass abdication of responsibility.

Mr Ackerley's eyes focused on Jonathan, standing by the blackboard, as motionless as a rabbit frozen in the headlights of a car. 'Palmer, what do you think you're doing?!'

Then he saw the image on the board.

He breathed in sharply, his nostrils widening. He stared at the image for about ten seconds and then turned back to Jonathan, his expression one of disgust.

'How dare you do this?!'

It took Jonathan a moment to grasp the implications of these words.

'ME?!'

'How dare you violate school property with your filthy . . . ?!'

'But it wasn't me! I didn't draw this! I was just rubbing it off!!'

'You expect me to believe that?!'

'It wasn't him, sir!' called out a voice from the class. Nicholas.

'Silence!!'

'But, sir, it wasn't him! He's telling the truth!!'

'SILENCE!!' roared Mr Ackerley, so violently that the whole class jumped. He turned back to Jonathan, his eyes flashing. 'I would never have expected this, Palmer, not even from you!'

He ignored the insult. He was too desperate to clear his name. 'It wasn't me, sir!! Honestly it wasn't!!'

'So who was it then?!'

'It was . . .'

He stopped. He bit down on his tongue so hastily that he could taste blood. He choked down the name that had been rising in his throat.

He couldn't break the cardinal rule of Kirkston Abbey.

'Well, Palmer?! Who was it?!'

*Don't ever tell tales. No matter who does what to you, you don't ever, ever tell tales.*

'I don't know, sir.' All the force had gone out of his voice. It sounded empty, beaten.

'I thought as much. It was you, wasn't it Palmer? Who else would do something as disgusting as this?'

He shook his head.

'So who was it?!'

'I don't know, sir.'

Mr Ackerley breathed out sharply. 'Enough. You will be punished for this. At break I will see your housemaster, Mr Bryant. I will tell him what you have done and I will ask him to cancel your half-term holiday. Perhaps that will teach you to have more respect for school property.'

There was a collective intake of breath from the class. Jonathan was too shocked to say anything.

'Now go and stand in the corridor. Get out of my sight.'

He found his voice. 'You can't do that!!'

Mr Ackerley's face darkened. His eyes narrowed into slits. 'HOW DARE YOU PRESUME TO TELL ME WHAT I CAN AND CANNOT DO!!'

'But it wasn't me!' It came out as a virtual wail.

'Get out! And count yourself lucky that I don't go to the headmaster and have you expelled!'

'Sir, it wasn't me! Please, you have to believe me!'

'So who was it then?'

He didn't answer. Instead he turned, towards the far corner of the room where James Wheatley sat staring at him. His eyes flashed a silent plea for assistance.

James looked away.

'I'm waiting, Palmer? Who was it?'

'I can't say, sir.'

'Well, Palmer, I wish to be fair. If you are indeed innocent you should not be punished. So you will have until the end of prep this evening to tell Mr Bryant who was in fact responsible for this outrage. Failure to do so will ensure the cancellation of your half-term.'

He was trapped. He could never tell on James. He would have to take the punishment. But the punishment was so appalling that he couldn't bear it. He stared beseechingly into the angry face of his accuser.

And realised that Ackerley's eyes were gleaming.

Ackerley knew.

Ackerley knew that he was trapped and was glad of it. Ackerley wanted him to be the one who was punished.

'Now take your books and get out! Get out of my sight!'

He was too shaken to do anything but comply.


In the jostle of the corridor between lessons he rushed up to James Wheatley. 'You have to tell Ackerley it was you!'

'I don't *have* to do anything,' James told him. He attempted to walk on.

Jonathan grabbed hold of his arm. 'Please! You heard what he said he'd do!'

'So? It's not my problem.' James tried to shake him off and indicated for George Turner to intervene.

Nicholas Scott appeared beside them. 'You make me sick,' he told James forcefully.

'Keep out of this you four-eyed runt!'

Nicholas stood his ground. 'Why? You do make me sick! You think you're so great but you're too frightened to admit to what you've done! If I were Jonathan I'd tell Ackerley everything and to hell with you!'

Suddenly George yanked Nicholas's glasses from his face and sent them sliding across the well polished floor. Nicholas, momentarily blinded, let out a yell. He dropped to his knees, scrambling between the mass of moving legs, trying to save the lenses from being smashed.

'Bastard!' hissed Jonathan. He moved to help Nicholas.

But George grabbed hold of him, pushing him up against the wall so roughly that his head cracked on the stone. He groaned.

James walked up to him, leaning in close so their faces were almost touching. His voice was soft, little more than a whisper.

'You breathe one word to Ackerley, or Bryant, or anyone and your life won't be worth living. You tell on me and I'll make your life so miserable that you'll wish you'd never been born!'

Then he moved on, followed as always by George. Rubbing at his head, Jonathan went to help Nicholas.

One o'clock. Lunch time. The walls of the school dining-hall reverberated with the sounds of hundreds of adolescent voices, shouting, laughing, arguing, as they devoured their midday meal. The staff sat apart, at a raised table at the end of the room, talking solemnly of politics and the curriculum and trying to ignore the din. Kitchen staff in shabby blue pinafores marched between the tables, replenishing water jugs. The smell of bad food hung in the air like glue.

Jonathan sat at the corner of one of the fourth-year tables, huddled in conference with Nicholas Scott and the Perrimans.

'You can't sneak on Wheatley,' Stephen Perriman was telling him. 'You'd be mad.'

'He has to,' Nicholas told him.

'Why? They aren't going to cancel his half-term.'

'They will,' insisted Nicholas.

'Ackerley will make sure of it,' added Jonathan. He looked down at his untouched plate; mutton chops, overboiled potatoes and cabbage, all covered in gravy that had the consistency of custard. The smell made him feel sick.

'They won't cancel an exeat,' continued Stephen, trying in vain to reassure him. 'You'll just get detention or something.'

'They will!' insisted Nicholas. 'It's happened to Roger Brooke.'

'Who?'

'Roger Brooke.' Nicholas pushed his glasses up the bridge of his nose. 'He's that fifth year in Heatherfield with floppy hair and weird teeth. He had an argument with their matron last year and ended up telling her to fuck off. She complained to their housemaster and they cancelled his half-term. He had to stay here with the overseas boys.'

Stephen thought for a moment. 'Well he still can't sneak. Not on James Wheatley.'

Nicholas's pinched features were set in a determined line. 'James Wheatley deserves everything he gets!'

'Of course he does! He's a prick! But you still can't do it, Jon.'

'Everyone will hate you,' said Michael, entering the conversation for the first time.

'That's not the point!' snapped Stephen. 'The point is what are James Wheatley and his gang going to do to him if he does?!'

'They won't do anything,' Nicholas told him. 'Not if we stick up for him.'

Stephen rolled his eyes. 'That's really going to make a difference!'

'It might!' said Nicholas fiercely.

'Oh sure! What are you going to do? March up to George Turner, say "put 'em up" and hope he dies of laughter?!'

'He's done more than we have,' said Michael quietly.

'Oh shut up, Michael! You're not helping!' Stephen indicated for his brother to keep quiet.

'We've got to try,' said Nicholas determinedly. 'He's our friend.'

'They'd just laugh at us,' Stephen told him. 'You know they would. And even if they didn't we'd only be able to help him during the day.'

He leaned across the table towards Jonathan.

'We're not in your dormitory, Jon. We're not even in your House. But James Wheatley is; he and George Turner and Stuart Barry and anyone else he chooses to rustle up. You'll be on your own from the start of prep to the start of breakfast every night of the week for the rest of term. You'll have to sleep in the same room as James Wheatley. If you sneak on him how much sleep do you think you're actually going to get?'

Jonathan said nothing. He stared down at his plate. He still felt sick. But it was no longer the smell of the food that was responsible.

Twenty past eight. Ten minutes before the end of prep.

Jonathan sat alone in his study. The overhead light was off. His weak desk light sent shadows crawling over the walls.

He stared at his wristwatch, propped up on the desk in front of him. His eyes followed the second hand as it turned its slow circles, ticking away the chance to save his half-term.

But the chance was already lost. He had made his decision at lunch. Stephen's comments had simply confirmed what he already knew. This school was his world now; his life. And that life would not be worth living if he sneaked on James Wheatley.

The school authorities would contact his father tomorrow and tell him of his son's punishment. His father would accept it without protest. If the school felt it appropriate that his son missed his half-term then it must be right. It was such a wonderful school after all. His son was lucky to be a pupil there.

So his father would go to Devon with his stepmother; the woman who hated him and would know just how to turn the situation to her advantage.

He could hear her voice in his head; soft, persuasive, destructive. 'I know how much Jonathan means to you. I know how much you mean to each other. But now he's spoiled it for you both. Perhaps he didn't really want to see you. Perhaps you don't mean so much to him after all.'

She would say these things and his father would believe her because he wasn't there to tell the truth.

She would win. Just as James Wheatley would win. Just as Ackerley would win.

He was beaten, and there was nothing he could do about it.

Twenty-five past eight.

He picked up the watch, his fingers scraping against the engraving on the back. He turned it over to read it.

*To Jonathan. Love Dad. Xmas 1951.*

And then, suddenly, an unexpected anger filled him; rising up from the pit of his stomach; a burning, churning ball of black rage.

He was not going to accept this! He was not going to be robbed of the chance of seeing his father; a chance he had been dreaming of for over a year. He was not going to suffer in silence because the system decreed that it was the proper thing to do. If that was how the system worked then it was all wrong.

And he was not going to be cowed by it.

He rose to his feet.

He left his study, marching up the corridor, towards the central hall and the poorly lit passageway with the red carpet that led to Mr Bryant's study.

The corridor was deserted save for Henry Blake who stood in the doorway of William Abbott's study; the two of them whispering to each other for fear of being heard by a prefect.

Henry watched Jonathan's progress with an open mouth. At first he was too astonished to do anything.

Then he moved away from William's study, hurrying down the corridor, knocking on doors, wanting to be the first to spread the word.

Twenty to nine. Jonathan walked out of Mr Bryant's study.

Mr Bryant; traditional, decent, limited, had listened gravely to what Jonathan had to say. When James Wheatley's name was mentioned he sighed and shook his head. He did not approve of one boy letting another take the blame for his actions. But then, as a typical product of the public-school system, he did not approve of sneaking either.

Now he was ushering Jonathan out. James Wheatley was standing at the end of the passageway, shuffling his feet expectantly. Mr Bryant saw him. 'Come here please, Wheatley. You may go now, Palmer.' His voice was cold, static. It was hard to tell which boy he disapproved of more.

They passed each other in the corridor; James slowing for a moment to stare at Jonathan. He said nothing. There was no need. The venom in his eyes was eloquent enough.

Half past nine.

Jonathan, dressed in his pyjamas and dressing-gown, sat on a bench in the corner of the changing rooms, breathing slowly and deeply.

The changing rooms were empty. The fifth year did not go to bed until quarter to ten, and the fourth years had already changed and made their way up to the dormitory. He should have been with them. But instead he had held back in his study, waiting until the coast was clear. He did not feel ready to face them.

He had done the right thing. They could not expect him to suffer in silence and lose the chance of seeing his father. He had been right. He knew it.

Only now that it was done he was not so sure.

For he would have to face them soon. Face them, and whatever retribution was coming.

He rose to his feet and walked out of the changing rooms, down the corridor to the main hall. He crossed the hall, passing the noticeboard and trophy cupboard, and began to make his way up the stone stairs to the dormitory. His legs felt like lead weights. As always his too large slippers made a slapping sound as he passed. But today it seemed as if the sound was drowned out by the pounding of his own heart.

He came to the door of his dormitory. Behind it he could hear the sound of voices. Were they talking about him? Discussing what they were going to do to him? His balls crawled up into his groin. The urge to turn and run was overpowering. But it was hopeless. There was nowhere to go.

He had done the right thing. He would see his father in four days. He was not afraid.

He opened the door and walked into the lions' den.

To be faced by a scene he had witnessed countless times over the last year. Boys curled up in their beds, reading or trying to sleep, while others wandered too and fro, talking to friends. All looked up when he entered. The conversations stopped. Then, almost instantaneously they started up again. Everyone continued to go about their business. It could be any night.

He walked along the corridor of beds to the empty wash-room. In the still of the room he brushed his teeth and washed his face with his flannel. As he splashed cold water on to his skin he stared out of the window, looking at the moon, almost full, rising high in the clear late autumn sky. One of the Abbey House prefects was walking past, whistling, sending clouds of white mist rolling up into the air. He wondered if it would freeze that night. He could see his reflection in the panes of glass. His eyes were wide and watchful; almost too big for his face.

He was not afraid.

He turned off the tap and walked back into the dormitory, towards his bed. He took off his dressing-gown and climbed between the sheets. He removed the current book from his locker; a collection of ghost stories. He found his page. The owners of the monkey's paw were about to make the first of their three wishes. He wondered what they would wish for and whether it would turn out all right.

He was not afraid.

His eyes left the words on the page, flitting nervously about the room. James Wheatley was sitting on Stuart Barry's bed. Stuart kept running his hands through his thick blond hair. Stuart was vain about his looks. James was always teasing him about it, though in truth they could not compare with those of Richard Rokeby. He wondered how the funeral for

Richard's great-aunt had gone. He hoped Richard hadn't been too upset.

He was not afraid.

George Turner went to join James and Stuart. The three of them started laughing about something. Him? He kept expecting them to turn and stare at him but they didn't. Perhaps James had decided to let it go; had accepted that he was in the wrong; that he should have come forward at the time and stopped the situation from escalating. Perhaps it would be all right after all.

The door opened. Brian Harrington strode in, just as he did every night, to turn out the light. 'Right, into bed everyone.'

James, the last to move, rose from Stuart's bed. Slowly he began to make his way towards his own.

As he did so he turned towards Jonathan and winked at him.

Brian turned out the light, and pulled the door shut behind him. As always, they were left to the darkness and each other.

Jonathan lay in his bed, staring up at the ceiling, up into the blackness that engulfed him.

He waited for the voices; for the whispers; for the sounds of movement as they came for him.

But there was nothing. Just darkness, and an expectant silence that hung over him like a storm cloud.

He had done the right thing. He was not afraid.

He could hear his heart beating like a clock inside him, ticking away the seconds that turned into minutes, quarter of an hour, half an hour. And still there was nothing but silence.

He lay motionless in his bed. Waiting. And in his head the same thought was hammering against his brain like a bird trapped in a cage.

*I am afraid, I am afraid, oh god I am so afraid . . .*

He woke with a start.

He was still lying on his back. Darkness still enveloped him. How long had he been asleep?

It didn't matter. He was totally awake now. Every nerve ending in his body, every instinct screamed a warning. It was about to begin.

He heard noises, a sound of movement; a creaking floorboard, muted laughter. He strained to hear what was going on but the darkness had a muffling effect, like a blanket over his ears. It was all a blur.

Sweat was breaking out on his forehead. He felt he could be sick and soil himself at the same time. His hands crept over the blankets that covered him. His hands began to knead the top sheet, so heavily starched that his fingers made a scratching sound against the fabric.

Then suddenly the sheets and blankets were gone. Torn from the bed, leaving him exposed and shivering in the cold of the room. He sat up, preparing to defend himself and heard a whistling sound in the air. A pillow thudded into the side of his head. The shock of the blow disorientated him so that at first he did not struggle as he was seized in a neck lock and dragged from the bed. Around him the rest of the dormitory slept, or pretended to sleep.

The door of the washroom opened. The light went on. James Wheatley stood in the doorway. Another, smaller figure stood behind him. He was marched towards the door; his leg thudding into a bed end as he went. He was pushed into the washroom, falling heavily on to the stone floor, twisting his ankle and nearly hitting his head on one of the basins. He heard the door shut behind him. He climbed to his feet, wincing at the pain from his ankle, and turned to face his attackers.

James Wheatley stood in front of him, flanked by George Turner and Stuart Barry. The trio he had expected.

And next to Stuart stood William Abbott; meek, inoffensive William Abbott. What was William doing here? Was he going to be a part of this too?

As if to answer his question James turned towards William. 'Go and stand in the corridor. If you hear anything come and tell us.'

William hesitated. His eyes darted towards Jonathan and then back to James. 'What are you going to do to him?' he asked. His voice was little more than a whisper.

'The same as we'll do to you if you don't fucking move!'

William did as he was told. But before he did his eyes met Jonathan's again. I'm sorry they said. I don't want to be a part of this. But you see how it is. I don't have any choice.

'Your face is dirty, Palmer,' said James once the door had closed behind William. 'We don't like dirty little oiks at this school. So we're going to give you a wash.'

He knew then what they were going to do. The panic that had been bubbling beneath the surface now took over. He tried to dash past them, to make for the door, but George blocked his path, his eyes shining at the prospect of what was to come. He tried to struggle but was no match for someone who was six inches taller and two stone heavier. Once again he was held in a neck lock, his left hand forced behind his back, and was marched towards the toilet stall.

Stuart held the door open. George pushed him through the door and then forced him down into a kneeling position while Stuart and James crowded in behind. His face was slammed into the bowl, his forehead thudding into the enamel surface as he went. He cried out in pain. Blood rushed to his head, his nose and mouth were thrust up against the inner surface that stank of bleach and urine so that he felt as if he would vomit.

He heard the sound of the chain being pulled and then water exploded all around his head, streaming into his eyes, his ears, his nose and his mouth, almost choking him. The suction effect made him feel as if he were about to be dragged down into the pipe and trapped there for ever.

The chain was pulled again. This time the only response was a metallic thud. 'Useless thing!' he heard Stuart exclaim.

'Doesn't matter,' he heard James answer. 'I know another way to wash his face.' The three of them started to laugh. There was a hissing sound and then the smell of ammonia as he felt his face growing wet. James was urinating on his head.

He tried to struggle but both his arms were pinned behind his back. He shut his eyes to protect them, choking back tears of humiliation.

The chain was pulled again. For the second time the bowl filled with water, blocking all his facial orifices, making him feel as if he would surely drown.

His head was yanked out of the bowl. He was dragged to his feet and marched out of the stall.

He was pinned up against the wall; George holding one of his arms, Stuart the other. Water from his hair was dripping into his eyes so that he was half blinded. Slowly, deliberately, James approached him.

'I warned you,' he said softly, 'but you didn't listen. You were too stupid to listen. Ackerley's right about you. You are stupid and you don't belong here. You should have stayed at your stupid grammar school.' He started to laugh. 'I bet you'd give anything to be back there now!'

James pulled back his fist ready to land a blow. Jonathan, helpless to defend himself, flinched. But James's fist stopped, inches away from his face. A finger reached out and flicked him sharply on the nose. George and Stuart were laughing.

'Are you frightened, Palmer? Are you?'

He was shaking as if he had a fever, but some last remnants of pride made him shake his head.

James smiled at him; a slow, vicious smile. 'You should be. No one sneaks on me.' His eyes began to flash. 'No one! You think this is bad? This is nothing! You're going to be sorrier than you can imagine for what you've done. You're going to be having nightmares about me for the rest of your life!'

He took a step back and went through the same ritual again; pulling back his fist only to flick him on the nose.

'Are you frightened now, Palmer?' he asked softly. 'Are you scared?'

He was scared. Terrified. Every instinct was telling him to nod in agreement, do anything just to have it end.

But somewhere, buried deep within his fear, was a tiny spark of fury at the injustice of it all. Now, as he was confronted with James's taunting smile that spark blazed into life, wiping away the fear, destroying it in a burst of absolute rage.

Suddenly he didn't care what they did to him. Let them do their worst. At that moment only one thing mattered; to wipe the smile from James Wheatley's face.

'I HATE YOU!' he cried, 'YOU'RE A COWARD!! YOU SHOULD HAVE TOLD ACKERLEY!! YOU SHOULD HAVE TOLD HIM BUT YOU WERE TOO SCARED!! JUST LIKE YOU'RE TOO SCARED TO FIGHT ME ON YOUR OWN! WELL GO AHEAD AND HURT ME THEN BUT IT WON'T CHANGE ANYTHING! YOU'LL STILL BE A PATHETIC LITTLE COWARD AND I BLOODY HATE YOU!!'

The smile did fade. His words had hit home. It was madness but inside a part of him was laughing.

James kicked him in the balls.

The pain was unbelievable. Fire roared up from his groin into his stomach. He screamed, his legs collapsing beneath him. He would have fallen to the ground had Stuart and George not been there to support him.

James stepped towards him. His eyes were merciless, like an animal consumed by bloodlust.

'Hold him steady,' he said and moved in for the kill.

The second bell had rung ten minutes earlier. The dormitory was empty now; its occupants either dressing in the changing rooms or making their way to breakfast. The curtains were still drawn but crisp autumn sunshine shone through them, sending blocks of cold light to decorate the floor and the nearby beds.

Jonathan stood in the empty washrooms, in front of the mirror next to the sinks, inspecting the damage.

His body was a mass of bruises; the pink of his skin decorated with a patchwork of blues and purples, blending into each other like a piece of abstract art. He turned right and left in front of the mirror, using its limited scope to inspect himself as best he could. He moved slowly. Too sharp a motion sent pain rushing through him. His breathing was as shallow as he could manage. Each breath hurt too.

There was a bruise on his forehead where he had hit the toilet bowl. But apart from that his face was unmarked. They had been careful. Savage but careful. All the tell-tale signs would be covered by his uniform.

He stared at his face in the mirror; the eyes heavy with pain and lack of sleep. He told himself that he had done the right thing. Only four days and he would be with his father. No time at all.

If he survived that long.

He left the dormitory, heading downstairs to the changing rooms. He moved as gingerly as he could. The changing rooms were virtually empty too. Just a couple of fifth years who had decided to miss breakfast, too busy wishing they were back in their beds to pay any attention to him. He dressed quickly, anxious lest someone should see the bruising. It made him feel ashamed, as if he had been branded. His clothes rubbed against his skin, aggravating the pain he already felt. He tried to ignore it. They were just bruises. They would fade. No permanent damage.

Not yet.

He left the changing rooms, heading for his study, to gather together the books for the morning's lessons. The central hallway was empty. The others were still at breakfast but would be returning soon. The thought made him quicken his step.

He passed the table by the stairs. The morning post had already arrived. He saw a white envelope addressed to himself.

His father's handwriting. Travel arrangements for half-term. He had been expecting them. He opened the envelope and began to read the enclosed letter as he walked down the deserted corridor towards his study:

*My dear Jonathan,*

*I have bad news. Your stepmother is unwell. She caught flu a couple of weeks ago. She seemed to make a full recovery but the bug has made a sudden reappearance. She will not allow me to call a doctor but has confined herself to bed and seems very under the weather.*

*Naturally I have insisted that she cancel her trip to Devon. She insists that you and I should not alter our own plans because of her, but every time I see her she is shivering and coughing and I know that she is not up to having a visitor in the house.*

*This means, I'm afraid that you will not be able to spend half-term with us. I'm sure this will be as much of a disappointment to you as it is to me but obviously your stepmother's health must come first. I know that you will understand.*

*I will contact your mother and let her know the situation. I'm sure she will be delighted to be seeing you instead.*

*Thank you for your last letter. I am pleased to hear that the term continues to go well. Your stepmother sends her love. Be sure to write and tell us if you need anything.*

*Love as always,*

*Dad*

He had reached the door of his study. He opened the door and walked inside.

The room was in disarray. His desk lay on its side. His lamp was on the floor; the bulb smashed. The door of his locker stood open. The contents were strewn everywhere; books with their covers ripped off; letters torn into pieces; a small framed photograph of his parents with the glass smashed.

The curtains had been drawn. A piece of paper was affixed to the tiny window. On it was scrawled a single sentence:

*This is just the start.*

He closed the door behind him. His back resting against the wall, he slid down into a sitting position, his knees pressed up against his chest. Outside he could hear the voices of his neighbours as they returned from breakfast and prepared for morning chapel. His tears fell slowly and silently. In his mouth he could taste salt. His fist crushed his father's letter into a ball.

He sat like that for what seemed like an age. He didn't bother to wipe the tears from his face. He didn't care if the whole world saw them.

There was a soft knock on his door. He ignored it.

'Palmer, it's me, Rokeby.'

He didn't say anything. The door opened anyway. Richard stepped inside and surveyed the destruction.

'Jesus!'

He pushed the door closed behind him and crouched down in front of Jonathan; his feet sliding over the books and torn paper that covered the floor. 'Are you all right?'

Jonathan nodded.

'I heard people talking at breakfast. Why didn't you tell me? The funeral was at lunchtime. I was back by half past six. I was around. You should have told me.'

'What difference would that have made?'

'I could have protected you.'

'How?'

'I would have found a way.'

'Why did he draw that picture? Why does he think that about me? I don't understand.'

'I do,' said Richard quietly.

A bell rang. Outside he could hear the sound of footsteps hurrying away up the corridor. It was time for morning chapel. The prospect made him feel physically sick. The tears came again. He hid his face in his knees, ashamed of his weakness.

'It's all right,' said Richard gently. 'Cry if you want to. I don't care.'

He wiped at his eyes. 'What's happened to Wheatley? Has his half-term been cancelled?'

'For now.'

He looked up. 'For now?'

'He's James Wheatley remember. His parents are on the Board of Governors. They're forking out thousands of pounds to have that deathtrap of a gym refurbished. He'll phone his mother and tell her what an injustice the whole thing is and then his mother will phone your housemaster and hint that her patronage of the school just might stop if darling James isn't allowed home for his half-term break.'

'You think that'll work?'

Richard raised an eyebrow. 'Trust me. He'll be packing his suitcase on Friday just like the rest of us.'

The words, so innocently uttered, hurt him more than any blow. He held out the ball of paper that had been clenched in his fist. Richard uncrumpled it and read. He whistled softly between his teeth.

'What will you do? Go to your mother's?'

'Where else?'

'You could come and stay with me.'

'With you?!'

Richard nodded. 'If you'd like to.' Jonathan didn't say anything. 'Would you?'

He didn't know what to say. He found the prospect exciting and yet somehow alarming.

'Would you?' asked Richard again.

'I couldn't.'

'Why not? Would you rather see your mother?'

He shook his head.

'I'd understand if you would rather see her. It's not like we get that many exeats is it?'

'It's not that. It's just that it's only three days away. It's too short notice for your family.'

'No it's not.'

'It would be inconvenient. I don't want to put them out.' He knew that he was trying to talk himself out of going, yet was relieved when Richard persevered. 'It'll be fine. Don't worry. I'll call them at lunchtime and arrange it. Will you come?'

He nodded. 'Yes.'

Richard smiled. 'Good.' The intense eyes studied him, making him feel self-conscious. He lowered his head and stared at the paper Richard held in his hand. 'She's going to win, isn't she? Just like you said.'

'She hasn't won yet.'

'She will though.'

'Not if you don't let her.'

'You think it's so easy, don't you?'

'It is easy.'

'You keep saying that, but it's not true. I didn't want Ackerley to win. He knew I hadn't drawn that picture but he didn't care. He wanted me to be punished. And Wheatley was just going to sit there and let it happen. I told on Wheatley because I wasn't going to let him get away with it. But Wheatley gets off scot-free and Ackerley has the satisfaction of knowing what happens to people who tell tales. So they win after all.'

'And you just accept it,' said Richard calmly.

The words stung. 'I'm not just accepting it!'

'Yes you are. Just like you always do.'

Frustration swept over him. 'Well, what else am I supposed to do?! They have all the power. It's the way the system is. You can't fight it.'

'Yes you can. I do. I do it all the time.'

'But that's you!'

'It could be you too.'

'No it couldn't. I'm not like you.'

'No,' said Richard softly. 'But you want to be.'

'Wanting it won't make any difference.'

'It will. You just have to want it enough. If you don't then accept things as they are and let them keep on winning. It's up to you.'

They stared at each other. 'So what do you want?' Richard asked him. 'What do you really want?'

The eyes bored into him. Their intensity was hypnotic. He stared deep into them, feeling the power they generated.

'I want to be like you,' he answered. 'I'd give anything to be like you.'

'Then I'll help you. I'll show you how to win. And then no one, not Ackerley or Wheatley or your stepmother or anyone will be able to hurt you again.'

The eyes were shining; alive with light. Jonathan looked deep into the light and suddenly they made him feel afraid.

Then Richard smiled at him; a smile that said that everything would be all right. And because he trusted Richard he pushed the fear aside and smiled back.

# Chapter Six

Upchurch Hall had been the home of the Rokeby family for over three hundred years.

It was a Jacobean house, a slab of grey stone with huge bay windows and clusters of chimneys that stretched up to the sky like fingers. The stone, battered and worn after centuries of exposure to the elements, gave the house an air of faded grandeur. At its front, well-tended lawns ran parallel to the drive. At its rear, woodland grew wild and tall, shielding the house from the harsh wind that whistled in from the North Sea.

Jonathan sat at the window of Richard's bedroom. Richard lay sprawled on the bed, reading a book. Mr Rokeby was in his study, pitting his wits against the *Times* crossword. Down below, Mrs Rokeby, well wrapped up against the rain, stopped to speak to the gardener before climbing into her car and heading off down the drive. Life went on as normal at Upchurch Hall.

Except that there was nothing normal about life at Upchurch Hall.

They had arrived on a wet evening two days ago. Jonathan had stood on the steps of Abbey House, suitcase in hand, waiting with a subdued Richard. Boys jostled around them, shouting and laughing, waiting for their parents to arrive. Out of the corner of his eye he saw the boys whose parents were overseas and who had not been invited to stay with friends, walking towards the dining-hall to eat a lonely supper. The sight of them made him feel guilty, as if he were somehow responsible for their plight.

Richard nudged his arm, gesturing towards a Bentley that had joined the line of cars circling the front drive. A middle-aged man sat at the wheel of the car. Richard introduced him simply as Jessop. Jessop explained that Mrs Rokeby had planned to come herself, but that the wife of the local JP had arrived unexpectedly and she could not get away. They had climbed into the back of the car and set off.

They drove for half an hour, through the darkness and the rain. Eventually Jessop steered the car through a pair of iron gates and up a stone drive. Jonathan stared in astonishment at the huge outline of the house that Richard called home. It was worlds apart from the nondescript semi in a Leeds suburb where he lived with his mother. He began to panic. He did not belong in a place like this. Richard's family would laugh at him. He had been a fool to accept the invitation.

Mr and Mrs Rokeby waited on the front porch. Mr Rokeby was tall and athletic and carried himself with a military stiffness. He shook Richard by the hand. Mrs Rokeby, smaller and rounder, kissed him on the cheek. They were not as grand as Jonathan had feared and he began to relax.

Mrs Rokeby led them up a staircase and along a corridor. 'You must change out of those wet things before dinner,' she told them. Richard vanished through a door while Mrs Rokeby led Jonathan into a huge room with a four poster bed, a fire blazing in the open grate and a door in the right wall. 'That's a passage to Richard's room,' she told him. 'I thought the two of you would like that.' Jonathan, overwhelmed by the splendour of his surroundings, just nodded.

The four of them ate dinner at a long dining table with family portraits gazing down at them. Mrs Jessop served the food and then left them to eat. They ate beef off china plates and drank wine from crystal glasses. Jonathan ate slowly and carefully, terrified that he would use the wrong fork or spill something. Mr and Mrs Rokeby asked him questions about himself which he answered as fully as he could while feeling painfully aware of his accent. He sensed that Mr Rokeby's questions were prompted by politeness but Mrs Rokeby seemed genuinely interested in him. She smiled frequently as if sensing his awkwardness and wishing to put him at his ease. Richard said nothing, picking unenthusiastically at his food and acting as if he would rather be somewhere else. Occasionally, as if prompted by telepathy, Mr and Mrs Rokeby would look at him, then at each other, before turning their attention back to their guest.

Later, as Jonathan undressed in the quiet of his bedroom he heard a noise behind him. Richard had made use of the passage between their rooms. He squatted down in front of the fire, prodding at the coals with a poker. Jonathan stood and watched him.

'I like your parents,' he said awkwardly.

'They're not my parents.'

'Not?! But . . .'

'My aunt and uncle.'

'Oh.'

'My uncle is my father's elder brother.'

'Where are your parents?'

'Dead.'

He could not stop the question. 'How?'

Richard stared into the fire. He spoke quickly and easily, as if reciting words he had spoken many times before and now knew by heart. 'My father was in the RAF. He was killed in the war. My mother died when I was nine. Of cancer.'

Jonathan tried to think of something positive to say, but he had a sudden image of how desolate his world would be if his own parents were to die and knew that there were no words for this. 'I'm sorry, Richard,' he said awkwardly. 'Really.'

Richard continued to stare into the fire. 'It doesn't matter,' he said eventually. He rose to his feet. 'I'm sorry about the grilling tonight.'

'I didn't mind.'

'You're the first person from school I've brought here. They're bound to be curious.'

He smiled. 'At least I didn't break anything.'

'They wouldn't have cared if you had. I'm tired. I'm going to bed. Tomorrow will be better. I'm glad you're here.'

'So am I.' The words came automatically. But as soon as they were spoken he realised they were true.

And the next day was better. The Richard who collected him for breakfast seemed more relaxed than the one of the previous night. Mrs Rokeby urged them to eat their fill. 'I know what the food is like at that school,' she said as she pressed another kipper on Jonathan. 'Richard's cousin Edward went there too and he was always thin as a rake when he came home in the holidays.'

'He's made up for it since,' observed her husband.

'Well, who can blame him after all that dreadful rationing. What plans do the two of you have for today?'

'We haven't decided,' Richard told her.

'What about a day out? We could go into Norwich.' She smiled at Jonathan. 'Would you like that?'

He swallowed his mouthful and looked to Richard for guidance. But Richard was staring into space so he had to make the decision himself. 'Very much,' he said politely.

'Good.' She beamed at him. 'We'll go at eleven. That will leave plenty of time for a nice lunch and then a film. When you've finished eating why don't you call your parents. Let them know you've arrived safely. Richard will show you the phone . . .'

He called his mother first. He tried to tell her about the splendours of Upchurch Hall but she was worried about him wasting the Rokeby's phone bill and would stay on only long enough to remind him to say please and thank you at every opportunity and to eat everything that was put in front of him.

Then he phoned his father's office. He spoke to the secretary who told him that his father was not there today. 'He's taken your stepmother to Devon to see her parents.'

'To Devon?! But she's ill!'

'She looked fine when I saw her.'

He put down the receiver. He told himself that he had no business being surprised. But still he felt betrayed, as if someone had punched him in the solar plexus.

Richard watched him from the corner of the room. 'I take it she's recovered.'

'Dad's taken her to Devon.'

'Round one to her then.'

He shrugged, tried to act unconcerned. 'I don't care.'

'Yes you do.'

He didn't want to get into this. Not when he was feeling vulnerable. 'I'm going to get ready.' He hurried from the room before Richard could question him further.


Mr Rokeby drove them to Norwich. Jonathan stared out of the window, across the fields that rolled away towards the horizon. The huge Norfolk sky was filling with dark clouds. There would be rain before the day was out. A sharp wind whistled around them. Mr Rokeby smoked a pipe, filling the car with the pungent smell of tobacco. At one point his wife opened a window to clear the smoke, sending a cold draught into Jonathan's face. He didn't mind. Its freshness acted as a reminder that he had escaped, if only temporarily, from the prison he called school.

They had lunch at a restaurant in a square behind Norwich Cathedral. The restaurant was discreet but exclusive. Waiters buzzed attentively round them as they ate. When they had finished they drank coffee from tiny white cups.

'I've found the key,' Mr Rokeby told his wife as he prepared to relight his pipe.

'Where was it?'

'In that box of old coins.'

'Did you open it?'

'Briefly.' Mr Rokeby dug out the used tobacco with a pocket knife and prepared to insert a fresh batch. 'Packed with junk from what I could see. I'll have a sort through tomorrow.'

'Perhaps the boys could do that. It might be fun for them.'

'Do what?' asked Richard. He had been gazing out of the window and only now realised that he and Jonathan were the objects of the conversation.

'Have a look through that chest of Aunt Eleanor's.'

Richard shrugged. 'Maybe.' He turned his attention back to the window. Mrs Rokeby smiled at Jonathan. Mr Rokeby called for the bill.

It was an hour until the next showing of *The Dambusters*. Mrs Rokeby had some shopping to do. She dragged her husband off to help her and left the boys to wander the city on their own.

They walked through the crowded streets, stopping to look into the occasional shop window. Eventually they found themselves in Cathedral Square. The rain had started now. They sought shelter in the Cathedral itself.

The choir stood in the stalls at the end of the long nave, rehearsing a Gregorian chant. Soprano, alto, tenor and bass voices rolled over each other like strands of thread, spun to produce a sound that was both beautiful and eerie. Two dozen people were dotted around the aisles, all listening in respectful silence as the voices blended together and floated up into the high vaulted roof.

They walked across the nave towards the door that led to the cloisters. The clatter of their sensible school shoes echoed on the stone floor. Richard moved away to inspect the engravings that adorned the wall. Jonathan walked out into the cloisters and began to make his way round them. The rain was falling heavily now, blown by the wind so that drops sprayed through the pillars and on to the walkway itself.

The cloisters seemed empty save for an elderly couple in front of him. The woman was reading from a guidebook in a jarring voice. He hurried past them, rounding a corner and coming across a young couple sitting on a stone seat which looked out on to the grass square at the centre of the cloisters. They sat facing each other, both wearing heavy coats and long scarves that hung from their necks like robes.

They were kissing; there in the wind and the rain. Their bodies bent towards each other, their faces touching as their lips brushed together; an act that had less to do with passion than with intimacy, an intimacy that enabled them to forget all about the outside world. A closeness. A connection.

The sight of them made him feel intrusive. He stopped, stood still, watching. But the watching made him feel embarrassed. He lowered his eyes, stared down at his feet, and realised that he was standing on a grave. The floor was a mass of stones, all bearing the names and dates of those who had died and been buried there. Beneath his feet lay the remains of Robert Medlicott who had died on the 15th October 1819. He had been the son of Thomas Medlicott and his wife Catherine. He had been sixteen. Now he was just dust under a stone beneath Jonathan's feet.

The elderly couple were approaching. The woman's voice rang out, disturbing the boy and girl. They looked up and saw Jonathan. He felt himself blushing. The two of them smiled at him. The girl's hair was wet from the rain. Both looked immeasurably happy. He hurried past them, rushing back to the Cathedral and Richard.

Richard was studying an engraving. He beckoned Jonathan over. A woman and a girl of about thirteen were approaching from the other direction. The woman was pointing things out to the girl who looked completely bored. As they passed Richard her eyes focused on him, coming suddenly alive with interest.

The sight made Jonathan feel uncomfortable. The girl realised he was watching him. She dropped her eyes and passed by. He stood and watched her go. Then he walked towards Richard.

The engraving stood in a tiny alcove in the wall, flanked by pillars. It was a memorial tablet. A skeleton stood behind a stone; its fingers resting on the top, joined together as if in prayer. On the stone was engraved a rhyme:

*Thomas Gooding here do Staye*
*Wayting for Gods Judgement Daye*
*All you that do this place pass bye*
*Remember death for you must dye*
*As you are now even so was I*
*And as I am so shall you be*

Jonathan read the words slowly, absorbing their meaning. 'I wonder what he did,' he said softly.

'Did?'

'It sounds like he's being punished. For something he did when he was alive.'

They stared at the skeleton. Its mouth was curled into a smile that mocked the praying hands below. The pillars on either side were like the bars of a prison cell, keeping him confined until judgement day.

Richard breathed out slowly. 'Whatever it was, I bet he regrets it now.'

The choir were silent now, save for a solo soprano. The voice rose and fell like waves on a beach. The tone was plaintive, like a lament.

'I don't like it here,' said Jonathan suddenly. 'Let's go.'

They walked towards the door. As they reached it the soloist finished. A smattering of applause came from the aisles.

That night, in his dreams, Jonathan walked again through the Cathedral. It was empty now; a huge, tomb like place full of shadows, with silence lying heavily against its stone walls.

He came to the alcove that held Thomas Gooding's memorial tablet. The skeleton was gone now, replaced by a portrait of a pale boy with mournful eyes, only a little older than himself, dressed in regency costume. He knew the boy to be Robert Medlicott.

'Why are you here?' he asked. 'This isn't your place.'

The boy in the painting just stared at him, watching him with those sad eyes. They were the eyes of a boy of sixteen but they seemed centuries old and filled with an intense longing that made Jonathan feel afraid. He turned and hurried towards the door that led outside, and to the sound of laughter that he could hear behind it.

But when he reached the door he found it locked. He beat against the wood, calling out for someone to help him. But the laughter faded away and there was no one to hear. He was alone, trapped inside the silent Cathedral. It was still dark. But it was no longer empty. The shadows were starting to move . . .

He woke with a start. He lay in his bed, his heart pounding. His room was dark and cold, like the Cathedral.

He rose quickly, needing to see the light. He pulled back the heavy curtains and stared out at the early morning. The sky was already darkening. It was going to be another wet day.

He dressed and descended the stairs. The dining-room was empty. No one else was up yet.

The dining-room led into a corridor of rooms, each running into the other. Family portraits covered their walls. Restoration rakes, bewigged Georgians, Regency dandies, sober Victorians. Generations of Rokebys stared down at him. He stared back, searching for Richard's likeness in their faces but finding none he could recognise.

He came to a corner room; its walls lined with red damask. A writing desk stood in its centre, covered in framed photographs. He picked up one; a wedding photograph, taken about twenty years ago. The bride and groom stood outside the church, flanked by immediate family. The couple next to the groom were Mr and Mrs Rokeby. He realised that the bridal couple must be Richard's parents.

They were an attractive pair. The man was dark; tall and sturdy like his brother but far more handsome. The woman was fair and delicate, with the same elegant features and deep-set eyes that she had passed on to her son. A middle-aged man who resembled her strongly – her father presumably – stood beside her.

He picked up another photograph. Richard's mother was sitting in a garden on a summer's day, next to the man he assumed was her father. On her knee sat Richard; four or five, no older. Her arms were wrapped protectively round him. The three of them ignored the camera, all laughing at some private joke. Their happiness made him feel uncomfortable, as if he were intruding into corners of Richard's life where he had no business.

There was a noise behind him. He replaced the photograph and turned to face Mrs Rokeby.

'I was just looking,' he said defensively.

'I saw the door was open. I thought it must be you.'

'I was just looking. That's all.'

'That's all right.' She smiled reassuringly. 'Do you like them?'

'Them?'

She gestured to the portraits on the wall.

'Oh. Yes. Very much.'

'I think they're morbid. Being watched over by long dead relatives, all with the same chins and noses.' She laughed. 'Give me a dozen landscapes any day!'

'I'm sorry. I should have asked.'

'It doesn't matter. I'm sorry I wasn't up sooner.'

Her apology made him feel even more awkward. He said nothing.

'You like Richard very much don't you?'

'Yes.'

'I'm glad. I worry about him sometimes. About his being so solitary. Everyone should have a friend.'

'What was his mother like?'

Mrs Rokeby's eyes widened. 'His mother? Has he talked about her? Has ...' Her eyes focused on the table with the photographs and then came understanding. She smiled again, but a guarded look had come into her eyes. 'She was lovely. A lovely person.'

'She looks it.'

'Has Richard told you anything about her?'

'No. Except to tell me she was dead. I didn't like to ask questions after that.'

'Best not.'

He nodded.

They heard the sound of voices. Richard and his uncle must be up. Mrs Rokeby made as if to leave, but then turned back towards him.

'I'm glad you're here, Jonathan. I really am. Richard's needed a friend for a long time and I'm glad that friend is you.'

Her words embarrassed and pleased him at the same time. He smiled shyly. 'So am I.'

They left the room together and went to join the others.

Ten past eleven. Mrs Rokeby had just driven off to see a friend. Jonathan sat on the window ledge in Richard's room. Richard lay on the bed, reading a book.

There was a knock on the door. Mr Rokeby entered. 'What are you two up to?'

'Waiting for the rain to stop,' Richard told him.

'Why not look through that chest of Aunt Eleanor's. It might be fun.'

Richard looked sceptical.

'Blame your aunt. It was her idea. There's the key.' He tossed it on to the bed. 'The chest's in the junk room.'

Richard pushed his book to one side. He picked up the key and indicated for Jonathan to follow him.

The junk room looked out on to the woods at the rear of the Hall. The chest stood at its centre; made of oak and engraved with images of ships. Richard turned the key in the lock and lifted the lid, releasing a musty smell into the room. He pulled out a pile of newspapers, tied together with string. He handed them to Jonathan who looked at the front page. 'WAR IS OVER!' proclaimed the headline. The year was 1918. 'Why did your aunt keep these?'

Richard shrugged. 'Why do people keep anything?' He began lifting out piles of dusty books. Jonathan picked one up and studied the cover. '*A Tempest of the Heart*'. A historical romance; the sort his grandmother was always borrowing from the library. He gazed out of the window, hoping for an easing in the rain.

'Look.'

Richard was holding a wooden board; one foot by two, covered in letters written in gothic script. An antique ouija board.

'God, imagine Aunt Eleanor having one of these.'

Jonathan took the board from Richard. 'Why shouldn't she have one? The Victorians were always using them.'

'Aunt Eleanor was hardly a Victorian. She only died two weeks ago!'

'Maybe it was her mother's then. The Victorians loved seances. They used to have them after dinner parties as a sort of entertainment.'

'I thought they just played bridge.'

'Seances were really popular. I read about them in a library book on the history of the supernatural.' Jonathan turned the board over in his hands, trying to see some sign of when it was made. He had never seen a genuine board before. 'Have you ever used one of these?'

'No.'

'I have.'

'When?'

'Two years ago. At the house of a friend. A group of us used to do it every afternoon after school. We didn't have a proper board. We made a circle out of bits of paper and put a glass in the middle.'

'Did anything happen?'

'Yes, but only because a boy called Mark Peters was pushing. When we'd worked out it was him we used to ask questions like "which one of us will be the most successful?" and then watch the end of Mark's finger turn red as he tried to push the glass towards the letter M!'

'Do you want to try now?'

He remembered the fun he'd had with his friends the last time. 'Yes. But we don't have a glass.'

'There's one on my bedside table. I'll get it.'

Richard left the room. Jonathan stared down at the board. His fingers traced the wood. It was dull but still smooth. How old was it? How many years had it spent buried away in this chest? It might not have been used for decades. When was the last time a glass had moved across its surface? What secrets had it revealed to its users? What ghosts had it conjured up for them?

And were they watching him now?

Suddenly he had a sense of foreboding; an urge to put the board back in the chest and lock it shut.

Richard returned with a small glass. He placed it on the board. 'Perhaps we shouldn't do this,' Jonathan said hesitantly.

'Why not?'

'We don't know what might happen.'

'Nothing's going to happen. It's just a game. It's not as if we'll go to hell for it.'

Jonathan looked out of the window. The sky was still black. He wished the rain would stop.

This apprehension was ridiculous. He hadn't felt frightened last time he'd done this. He gestured to the board. 'This is what we do . . .'

But when the rain did finally stop his dread was long gone, replaced by frustration. The glass had not moved an inch. Neither had any tables started to rattle or doors to close of their own accord. Nothing out of the ordinary had happened at all.

Richard took his finger off the glass and yawned.

'It might still work,' said Jonathan encouragingly.

Richard did not look convinced. In the distance they heard a car pulling up in the drive; Mrs Rokeby returning from seeing her friend.

'It might,' he said again.

He found himself remembering a passage from the book he had read on the supernatural. Something about the mortal world being linked to the spirit world by a succession of doorways. But the doorways would not simply open on request. The emotional balance of those who sought to open them had to be just right.

Something like that.

He wondered whether to tell Richard.

Mrs Rokeby was calling for them to come downstairs. 'Go on,' Richard told him. 'I'll put the board in my room. Maybe we'll try again later.'

Jonathan walked down the stairs. He assumed that they were being called for lunch and made his way to the dining-room. But the room was empty, save for Mrs Jessop, methodically laying the table. Voices were coming from the drawing-room where he had phoned his parents. He knocked on the door and heard Mrs Rokeby call 'come in'.

She was sitting on a sofa, smoking a cigarette. He had never seen her smoke before. Another woman sat beside her; a much younger woman, pretty and well dressed. Mrs Rokeby rose to her feet when he entered, her smile fading slightly when she saw he was alone. She seemed nervous. 'Richard's just coming,' he explained. She nodded, sat down again.

Mr Rokeby was standing by the window, a glass of Scotch in his hand. Another man stood with him, also cradling a Scotch; a handsome, dark-haired man in his early forties, wearing a blue blazer. Richard's father.

But it couldn't be Richard's father. Richard's father was dead.

Mr Rokeby made the introductions. 'Malcolm, Catherine, this is Richard's friend Jonathan Palmer. Jonathan, this is Richard's father and his wife. They've come up from London.'

Jonathan, completely bewildered, did his best to conceal it. He smiled shyly at Catherine and then offered his hand to Malcolm who shook it firmly. He had a scar on his palm like a misshapen star. 'I understand you're a pupil at my old school. How are you liking it?'

'Very much,' he replied automatically.

Malcolm laughed. 'Liar!' His eyes were kind but he seemed preoccupied. 'How long have you and Dick been friends?'

'Dick?'

'Richard.'

'Um ... not very long.' He could feel everyone staring at him and felt a need to explain. 'We sat next to each other in a Latin lesson. I couldn't translate the sentence I was given. Richard helped me.'

'How are you enjoying your half-term?' asked Catherine.

'Very much. Thank you.' His mother's training in gracious behaviour came to the fore. 'It's very kind of Mr and Mrs Rokeby to have me.'

'We're very pleased to have you,' said Mr Rokeby kindly. 'We hope you'll come again.'

'I'd like that,' he replied awkwardly.

The door opened. Richard walked into the room. 'Why are you in here? Mrs Jessop's serving up ...'

He saw his father.

The colour drained out of his face. Mrs Rokeby rose to her feet and hurried towards him. 'Richard darling, look who's here.'

Richard continued to stare at his father. His mouth opened slightly, as if he wanted to say something but had forgotten how to use his tongue.

Malcolm stepped towards his son. 'Hello Dick. It's good to see you.'

Richard turned to his aunt. 'What is he doing here?!' he demanded.

'Your father and stepmother have come up from London to see you,' explained Mrs Rokeby. 'They've taken us by surprise. I thought we could have lunch together.' She smiled encouragingly at him, tried to put her arm around his shoulder, but he pulled away from her, his eyes flashing with anger.

'YOU KNEW!'

'Now Richard ...' she started soothingly.

'YOU'RE A LIAR! A BLOODY LIAR! YOU KNEW THEY WERE COMING!!'

'RICHARD, HOW DARE YOU SPEAK TO YOUR AUNT LIKE THAT!' roared Mr Rokeby. His voice was intended to intimidate but had completely the opposite effect. His nephew now turned his anger on him. 'You knew too! You both knew! You promised me!'

'But Richard!' cried his aunt. 'He's your father!'

'Not any more!'

'He just wants to see you. He's come all this way. Why must you be like this?'

He stared at her in disbelief. 'You know why!'

'But this isn't right!' she cried, her voice wobbling slightly. She was close to tears. 'Oh Richard, please, this has to stop!'

'Why?!'

'BECAUSE I CAN'T STAND ANY MORE OF IT!' cried Malcolm suddenly.

For a moment his face was dark with anger but when his brother laid a soothing hand on his arm he made an effort to calm himself. 'Richard this cannot go on. You're making everyone wretched. You're going to make yourself ill. I know how you must feel but you have to see ...'

Richard turned towards his father, acknowledging him for the first time. 'You have no idea how I feel!'

'Of course I do. We both lost ...'

'We?! You didn't lose anything!'

Mrs Rokeby gasped. 'Richard, how can you say that?!'

'Because it's true! I know it! We all do!'

'THAT'S ENOUGH!'

For the second time Malcolm made a monumental effort to control his anger. He took a series of deep breaths and when he began to speak the words came slowly.

'Richard, we cannot go on like this. We have to put this behind us. We have to stop being enemies. You're my son. I love you. I want you to be a part of my life. Especially now.'

Richard's eyes narrowed. 'Now? Why now?'

'Because I'm going to have a baby,' said Catherine softly.

She rose from her feet and walked towards her stepson. 'I'm pregnant, Richard. Your father and I are going to have a child. Nobody knows yet. We wanted to tell you first.'

She stood in front of him; her tone gentle, her smile pleading. 'The baby will be your brother or sister, Richard. Someone to love you as your father does. And he does love you, so much. You have to try and let go of the past, for your own sake. We're going to have a family and we want you to be a part of it.'

Richard spat in her face.

Catherine cried out, stumbling backwards, wiping at her face. The others stood, frozen with shock.

Richard took a step towards Catherine. 'I hope your baby's deformed,' he told her. 'I hope it's a freak with two heads and no eyes. I hope it screams all the time because it's in pain. I hope you have to sit there and listen to it screaming and know that it's in pain and that there's nothing you can do. I hope the screaming drives you mad. I hope that one day you pick up a knife and cut your own baby's throat ...'

Malcolm struck him. A stinging blow to the head that knocked him to the ground. 'No don't!' cried Mrs Rokeby, trying to shield him. But Richard thrust her aside. He climbed to his feet and turned towards his father; his face red from the blow, his eyes blazing with hate. 'THIS IS NEVER GOING TO BE OVER!' he screamed. 'THIS WILL NEVER BE OVER UNTIL I'M DEAD!!'

He turned and ran out of the room.

Catherine was in tears. So was Mrs Rokeby. 'This is all my fault' she sobbed.

Her husband put his arm around her. 'No it's not,' he insisted.

'But it is! I thought it would be better this time. I really did.'

Malcolm, now comforting his own wife, shook his head. 'You're not to blame.'

'But I am. I told you to come. I thought it would be better. He seemed happier this time, less angry. And having Jonathan here. It just seemed ...'

Suddenly the four of them remembered that Jonathan was still in the room. Mrs Rokeby made a huge effort to compose herself. 'Jonathan, dear. I'm sorry you had to see that.'

'Could you go after him?' asked Mr Rokeby. 'Check that he's all right.'

He was only too glad to have the chance to leave. He rushed from the room. In the distance he heard footsteps and then a door slamming. He followed the sound. It led him to the back of the house, and on to the woods outside. Soon he saw Richard ahead of him, striding through the trees, kicking at the dead leaves that lined his path. He called his name. Richard ignored him. He ran after him. 'Richard, wait!'

'Go away!'

'Wait!'

'Piss off!'

'Your stepmother's crying! Your aunt too! You made them cry!'

Richard spun round to face him, his eyes still blazing. 'Clear off! Leave me alone!!'

'But you told me your father was dead.'

'I WISH HE WAS!'

He was shocked. 'How can you say that?!'

Richard stared at him scornfully. 'And what would you know about it?!'

'I know that he's your father! And I know I could never say that about my father! Do you think there haven't been times when I haven't hated him for leaving my mother and me?! But I'd *never* wish that he was dead! No matter what he'd done!'

The moment the words were spoken he regretted them. A look of such fury came into Richard's face that it made him grow cold all over. Richard took a step towards him. He was shaking with rage. 'HOW DARE YOU PREACH TO ME! YOU'RE JUST LIKE THEM! YOU UNDERSTAND NOTHING!!' Jonathan was afraid. His instinct was to turn and run. But something, a spark of frustration, made him stand his ground.

'OF COURSE I DON'T UNDERSTAND!' he shouted back. 'I WANT TO BUT I CAN'T!! HOW CAN I WHEN YOU WON'T TELL ME ANYTHING?!'

His words had an odd effect on Richard. They seemed to calm him, to dissipate his anger. They stared at each other. Then Richard turned away, went to sit in front of an oak tree.

Tentatively Jonathan approached and crouched down beside him. The ground was cold and wet from the morning's rain; the air heavy with the scent of decaying leaves and damp wood.

'Why do you hate him so much?' he asked softly.

Richard didn't answer. He picked up a stick and began to scratch at the wet ground. Nervous energy poured out of him like electrical waves. Jonathan watched him, waiting. In the distance he could see a squirrel moving between the trees.

'What did he do?' he asked. 'What did he do that was so bad?'

The stick continued to dig into the earth.

'I want to understand. I really do. Can't you just tell me? Is it to do with your stepmother?'

'My stepmother?'

'That he married again. After your mother was dead. Did you hate him for that? I know I'd hate my father if my mother was dead and he remarried. I'd feel it was disloyal. It isn't really but I'd feel that it was. I suppose I'd want to hate him because I'd need someone to blame for her not being there any more ...'

'Don't!' Richard told him. There was a tremor in his voice. 'Don't. Please.'

'I'm sorry. I just want to understand, that's all. I will understand. I promise. If you just tell me.'

'I CAN'T TALK ABOUT THIS!'

Richard hung his head. He made a gulping sound, as if trying to swallow down grief. Jonathan felt ashamed. He wanted to show sympathy and knew that mere words would not be enough. Tentatively he put his hand on Richard's shoulder. Richard raised his head, stared straight at him.

And all at once Jonathan's churning emotions crystallised into one intense sensation. Just as they had done when the two of them had been alone in the school library.

But this time the feeling was ten times stronger. A hundred times stronger.

*connection*

At that moment it all became clear. He was with Richard. Being with Richard was the only thing that mattered.

'I'm sorry about what I said. About my father. I shouldn't have said anything. You're right, I don't understand.'

Richard's eyes bore into him, as if trying to see into his soul. 'Do you want to understand?'

He nodded. 'You can trust me with anything. I'll always try and understand.'

Richard continued to stare at him. Jonathan stared back. Each of them entirely focused on the other.

'I know you will,' said Richard softly.

They hugged each other, there on the wet ground beneath the trees.

When they returned to the house Malcolm and Catherine were long gone.

They ate supper in the dining-room. Mr Rokeby was conspicuously absent. Mrs Rokeby sat with them but did not eat. Her eyes were still red from crying. She kept staring at her nephew.

'Oh Richard,' she cried, 'how could you behave like that?'

Richard said nothing.

'You have to stop this Richard. For your own sake. You can't go on hating for ever. You'll destroy yourself if you do.'

This time Richard spoke.

'I can,' he told her. 'And I will.'

Tears filled her eyes. She rose from the table and ran from the room.

That night, as the rest of the house sank into sleep, they tried the board again.

They sat huddled together in the darkness of Richard's bedroom, their bodies touching, the only light coming from the dying fire in the grate.

They put their fingers on the cool surface of the glass. Jonathan felt a sudden shock run up his arm, like electricity. He wondered if Richard had felt it too.

He looked down at the board. It was just a piece of wood. Just a game. That was all.

He moved closer to Richard. In the still of the room their shadows merged to become one.

☆     ☆     ☆

With a rush Stephen Perriman came out of sleep.

Michael was having a nightmare.

He rose from his bed and made his way to Michael's room. The thunderous snores of his father echoed behind him as he moved.

He entered the room and turned on the bedside light. Michael was lying on his side, his body hunched up into a ball beneath the sheets. His forehead was covered in perspiration, his eyelids flickering, his mouth forming unspoken words.

He shook his brother. 'Mike, wake up.'

Michael's eyes flew open. He stared around him in bewilderment, half blinded by the light.

'You were having a bad dream,' Stephen told him. 'That's all.' He sat down on the bed. 'Are you all right?'

Michael nodded, rubbing his eyes.

'What were you dreaming about?'

'Us.'

'Us? What about us?'

Michael didn't answer. 'Tell me,' prompted Stephen.

'We were in a room.'

'What room.'

'A beautiful room. It was all white. There was a window and all I could see out of it was blue. We were talking about something. I can't remember what.'

'And?'

'It went dark. So dark I couldn't see anything. When the light came back you weren't there any more. Richard Rokeby was there instead.'

'Richard Rokeby?'

Michael nodded. 'I asked him where you were. He said that you'd gone away. I asked him where you'd gone but ...' He paused, staring down at the floor. 'He just said that I was never going to see you again. And then he was gone too, and I was alone.'

'It was just a dream, Mike. That was all.'

Michael nodded. 'I know. You wouldn't just go away and not come back.' Suddenly he looked up at his brother. 'Would you?'

'No. Of course not. We'll always be together. You know that.' Stephen smiled affectionately at him. 'Who else would put up with you?'

Michael smiled too. Stephen climbed into bed beside him and switched off the light. The two of them lay together in the darkness.

'What will happen to Nicholas?' asked Michael.

'Nicholas?'

'Jonathan is his best friend. What if Richard Rokeby spoils that?'

'That won't happen,' Stephen told him.

'It might.'

'It won't,' Stephen insisted. 'And even if it does it won't affect us. There's no way Richard Rokeby could come between us.'

'Promise?'

'Promise.'

'I love you'.

'Love you too, you idiot. Go to sleep.'


Dawn. The harsh winter sun climbed above the horizon, sending rays of crisp light across the cold earth.

The Perriman twins slept together in Michael's bed. They slept peacefully now; no nightmares disturbing their rest. Their arms were draped around each other, their bodies wrapped together as if fusing back into the single egg that had created them.

Jonathan and Richard lay together on Richard's bed. Richard's arm was around Jonathan. Jonathan's head rested against Richard's shoulder. They too slept peacefully.

Nicholas Scott lay in his bed, staring at the curtains of his room. He had been awake for hours. He had slept badly, his rest disturbed by an unease he could not explain.

He watched the first rays of light creep under the curtains and into his room.

He wondered what the new day would bring.

# PART TWO

# Wishing

# Chapter One

Eight o'clock on Monday evening. A cold, wet November evening.

Elizabeth Howard stood at the window of her bedroom, watching a procession of cars make their way up the school drive.

Boy after boy took leave of his parents. Displays of affection were conspicuous by their absence. Fathers shook their sons by the hand. Mothers kissed them lightly on the cheek. All three parties acted out a well rehearsed tableau designed to give the impression that the forthcoming separation was of little consequence to any of them.

Elizabeth was no stranger to sights such as this. She had been a teacher's wife for fifteen years now, and throughout her own childhood she had often waved her younger brother off to school. Her father had been a product of the boarding tradition and was all in favour of it – for boys at least. 'He can't stay tied to your apron strings all his life,' he would tell her less enthusiastic mother. 'School will teach him independence. It will make a man of him.' Perhaps he had been right.

But it all seemed pointless to her. The younger boys were still children for all their attempts to act otherwise. Why force them to act like men? They would have the whole of their adult lives to do that.

She remained by the window, watching the leavetakings.

Quarter past nine. The third years of Old School House were already in their dormitory, waiting for lights out.

James Wheatley stood in the changing rooms. The other fourth years milled around him; walking to and from the showers, towelling themselves down, putting on pyjamas and dressing gowns. Steam filled the room.

There was less conversation than usual. Michael Coates was talking about a show he'd seen in London but otherwise people said little. Most wished themselves back home, though all would have died rather than admit this.

James was one of the few who did not dream of a return to the bosom of his family. His half-term had been grim. His father had taken him to task for the drawing on the blackboard. 'It's about time you bucked up your ideas! If it weren't for your mother's pleas I would have let them cancel your half-term. I'm not wasting my money for you to play silly buggers!' James, stung by his father's criticism, had retorted that as most of the family money belonged to his mother, it was really none of his father's business whether it was wasted or not. At this point things had turned very nasty indeed and it had taken all of Mrs Wheatley's powers of persuasion to defuse the situation.

James had been grateful to his mother, but her intervention had its price. He was expected to accompany her on boring visits to elderly relatives, to help out at a church fête she was running, and to organise the games at his odious little sister's birthday party. Soon he felt as if he were trapped in the pages of an Enid Blyton novel, and it was something of a relief to escape back to school.

He took his dressing-gown off the peg and stared down the row. William Abbott, just out of the shower, was drying himself slowly. The corners of his mouth sagged. He looked close to tears. James considered having some fun with William that night but decided against. He was not in the mood. There would be other nights. William was always good sport and he wasn't going anywhere.

His eyes moved over William, past Michael Coates who was still going on about his stupid show, past Christopher Deedes and Henry Livings. On to the end of the row and Jonathan Palmer.

Jonathan sat on the wooden bench, towelling himself down. He stared into space, lost in thought. Probably wishing himself back home. He had good cause.

The bruises around his ribs had dulled, but faint traces remained, like shadows on his skin. The sight of them excited James; reminded him of the other things he planned to do to Jonathan. Things he had dreamed up at home, lying in his bed at night, when his imagination was at its most active.

He hadn't finished with Jonathan yet. He hadn't even started.

But for now Jonathan would wait. James enjoyed inflicting pain. But even more delicious was watching the dread caused by its prospect. Jonathan's half-term would have been ruined by fear at what awaited him upon his return to school. And now that Jonathan had returned he could wait a little longer.

He put on his dressing-gown and walked down the row. He stopped in front of Jonathan who sat on the bench, naked except for his towel.

'How was your half-term?' asked James.

'Fine,' Jonathan told him.

'Good.'

Jonathan said nothing. 'Tell me,' asked James. 'Was it worth it?'

Jonathan lowered his eyes, stared down at the floor. 'Well?' prompted James.

'Yes,' said Jonathan quietly. 'I think it was.'

James laughed softly. 'We'll see,' he said, and headed for the door.

*   *   *

Morning chapel had just ended. Hundreds of boys, books clasped under arms, marched down the corridor towards the first lesson of the day.

Henry Ackerley strode towards his lower sixth Latin class; groups of boys parting before him like the Red Sea before Moses. His expression was severe. The din of voices was insufferable first thing in the morning. If he had his way, talking would be prohibited in the vicinity of the classrooms.

A group of third years walked in front of him, laughing and clowning about. One pushed the arm of another and a collection of books fell in Henry's path. The owner, giggling with his friends, stopped instantly when he saw who had nearly fallen over them.

Henry snorted. 'Don't just stand there, Churcher. Pick them up!'

'Yes, sir. Sorry, sir.' Churcher did as he was told. The spine of one of the books had broken, sending pages drifting across the floor. 'For God's sake, Churcher, get a move on!' Groups of boys hurried by, lowering their voices as they approached then raising them again once they had passed. Out of the corner of his eye Henry saw that one boy had stopped to watch the scene. Irritation flared into anger. This was not a public entertainment! He turned and saw that it was Richard Rokeby.

Richard was leaning against the wall, books under one arm, his free hand in his back pocket. His casual posture only heightened Henry's fury. 'Don't lounge around Rokeby!' he snapped. 'Get to your lesson!'

It was only as he spoke that he realised that Richard was not watching the scene.

The blue eyes were focused upon him.

The intensity of the stare made Henry uncomfortable. 'Rokeby!' he blustered. 'Get a move on!'

No acknowledgement. The eyes bored into him. There was a heat at their centre but they remained ice cold.

'Rokeby! Didn't you hear what I said?!'

The eyes didn't flicker. Fascination mixed with detachment; studying him as if he were a rare exhibit in a science museum.

Then suddenly they looked away. Richard turned and moved on, strolling down the corridor towards his first class.

Henry watched him go. A shiver ran through him as if someone had walked on his grave.

Churcher had finished gathering up the pages from the floor. Henry waved him away, the desire to reprimand extinguished by a sudden sense of unease.

He pushed the feeling from his mind. He moved on towards the first class of the day.


As Monmouth House was furthest from the main school building the boys who lived there were always the last to arrive for class. The corridor was fast emptying as Nicholas Scott and the Perrimans walked towards their English lesson.

Michael was telling Nicholas about a ghost story he had heard on the wireless during half-term. Something about a grandmother who had gone insane and haunted an old attic. It sounded good, or would have done if Michael hadn't kept jumbling the plot and needing to start all over again. 'So guess what happened next?' he asked Nicholas as they walked into the classroom.

'What?' asked Nicholas, studying his surroundings. It seemed they were the last to arrive. Two dozen boys already filled the room, sitting in their appointed desks or standing, talking to friends. Bursts of conversation interlaced with shouted insults. A typical first period; everyone dispelling energy as they waited for the lesson to begin.

A double desk stood empty, waiting for the Perrimans. Behind it was another double desk where Jonathan sat alone, waiting for him.

Except that this morning Jonathan was not alone.

Richard Rokeby sat perched on Jonathan's desk. They were talking quietly.

Nicholas stood and watched them. Richard said something to Jonathan and they both started to laugh.

Nicholas thought back to the Tuesday before half-term. Of Jonathan appearing for lessons, bearing the bruises of James Wheatley's retribution. He remembered his own anger, his intense but hopeless longing to inflict on James Wheatley the pain he so regularly inflicted on others. His anger had been so great that at first he had not registered what Jonathan was telling him.

'Richard Rokeby! But you don't even know him!'

'I've spoken to him a few times.'

'But he's not a friend of yours. He's not friends with anyone.'

Jonathan had shrugged awkwardly. 'He asked. I couldn't say no. It wasn't like I had anywhere else to go.'

'But you did! You could have come to my house. You still could. I'll phone my parents and ask them. They'll say yes. They really like you.'

Jonathan had shaken his head. 'It's too late. He's phoned his family. Told them I'm coming. I can't change my mind now.'

So he had let it go. Told himself that it didn't really matter. Which it didn't. There was no chance of Jonathan and Richard actually becoming friends. Richard was so aloof he might as well be on Mars. Jonathan was in for a miserable half-term; ignored by Richard and the rest of the Rokeby family who were bound to be as stand-offish as Richard himself. He would spend his time going for lonely walks or hiding away in his room with a book, wishing he had accepted Nicholas's invitation instead. Nicholas was sure Jonathan's half-term would be like that.

He hoped it would be like that.

So why were they laughing? Like friends sharing a secret observation.

He experienced a sinking feeling in the pit of his stomach.

The Perrimans sat down at their double desk. Jonathan looked up and saw Nicholas. He smiled in welcome. Nicholas smiled back. He walked towards his seat. Richard said something to Jonathan and then climbed off the desk. His eyes met Nicholas's. He nodded as if in greeting. Nicholas gave no acknowledgement. Richard moved away to the double desk by the window where he sat alone. Nicholas watched him go. Inside his head a voice screamed that he should have acknowledged him.

He slid into his seat. 'How was your half-term?'

'Great.'

'Oh. Good.' He struggled to keep the disappointment out of his voice. 'Rokeby actually spoke to you then?'

Jonathan smiled. 'Sometimes.'

A thousand questions buzzed in Nicholas's head. He reached for one at random. 'Where does he live?'

'Upchurch. It's a village, out towards Yarmouth.'

'What's his house like?'

Jonathan rolled his eyes.

'So you felt you had to be on best behaviour the whole time?'

Jonathan nodded. Nicholas felt pleased. 'What about his family? Were they awful?'

'Awful?'

'Stuck up.'

'No.'

Again he felt disappointment. 'Not at all?'

Jonathan shook his head. 'He lives with his aunt and uncle. They were really kind.'

'What about his parents?'

'They're dead.'

Nicholas had a sudden image of his own dependable parents and wondered how he would feel if they were dead. 'God, that's awful. Poor Rokeby.'

He looked at the figure who sat alone by the window. An orphan. He tried to feel sympathy for him. It should have been automatic. He was a compassionate boy, easily moved by the pain of others. But today the sympathy refused to come.

Mr Curtis, the English master, walked into the room, a pipe clamped between his teeth. The noise level dropped but only slightly. Mr Curtis was as mellow as his tobacco. There was the rustle of pages as people tried to find their places in *Oliver Twist*. Mr Curtis set his books out on his desk whilst breathing clouds of thick smoke into the air. The room would smell like a tobacconist's shop by the end of the period.

'Come back to our study at break,' said Nicholas. 'My mother went mad in the kitchen. She's sent me back with enough to feed the five thousand.'

Jonathan made a face. 'I'm not eating loaves and fishes!'

Nicholas smiled. 'I've got other stuff too.'

'Cake?'

'Yes. The chocolate one you like. It'll taste great with croissants and pilchards.'

As he spoke, Nicholas studied Jonathan's face, looking for something he couldn't identify. 'You will come won't you?'

Jonathan didn't say anything. His eyes drifted across the room, towards the figure who sat alone by the window.

And then back. He smiled at Nicholas. The old, familiar smile. 'Try and keep me away!'

The classroom was quietening now. Their voices dropped to whispers. Nicholas opened his battered copy of *Oliver Twist*. 'This is a hundred times better than *A Christmas Carol*.'

'That was all right.'

'It was awful! Every time Tiny Tim opened his mouth I wanted to puke!'

'That's a wicked thing to say. Tiny Tim is a classic figure in British literature.'

'Is that right, Professor?'

'Indeed it is. His cheerfulness in the face of suffering is an inspiration to us all. He's a Victorian Shirley Temple.'

'If I were Dickens I would have turned the Cratchitts into

cannibals. Then they wouldn't have needed to plague Scrooge for money. They could have eaten Tiny Tim for their Christmas roast and made millions of readers very very happy.'

They burst out laughing, shattering the silence. 'Simmer down you two!' said Mr Curtis. Nicholas looked up to see that everyone was staring at them. Normally he hated to have attention focused upon him. But today he almost relished it.

Out of the corner of his eye he saw that Richard too was staring. Well let him. Jonathan and he were best friends. One half-term was not going to change that.

He didn't feel threatened. Richard posed no threat to him.

He damped down his laughter and turned to the right page in his book.

Tuesday was a half holiday at Kirkston Abbey. Pupils were free to find their own amusement in the two hours between the end of afternoon games and the start of supper. As they were only permitted to leave the premises at weekends all such amusements had to be confined to the school grounds. Small groups of boys were scattered across the playing fields, ignoring the drizzle, playing haphazard games of rugby. Others congregated in their studies, working, reading, listening to the wireless, or complaining about the prefects, the teachers and the dozens of rules that governed their lives.

The art room was a small outhouse behind the main school building. A collection of tables covered in paint blotches, and easels which supported assorted works in progress. The air was filled with the smell of turpentine.

James Wheatley sat at one of the easels, working on a drawing he had started before half-term. A carriage rushed through the snow, its occupants ignoring the pleas of the rag clad girl who knelt by the side of the road, her hands outstretched, begging for money. The occupants were just faces but the destitute girl was a dead ringer for James's little sister. James considered making her a cripple but decided against. He had not forgotten the row when he had drawn his father in the guise of Quasimodo. He started work on the horses instead.

Stuart Barry sat on a table, watching him. They were alone. George Turner was playing British Bulldogs with a group of fifth years. Stuart was eating an apple. 'It stinks in here,' he announced.

'Clear off then,' James responded, his eyes fixed on the piece of paper in front of him.

'I don't mind.'

'Why say it then?'

'I don't know. Something to say.' Stuart took a final bite of his apple and threw the core at the dustbin in the corner of the room. He missed. 'Damn.' He wiped his mouth with his hand. 'So why not tonight?'

'Because I say so.'

'He's only had one kicking. You can't just leave it.'

'I'm not going to.'

'So why not tonight?'

'Because I want him to sweat. He knows it's coming but he doesn't know when. That's almost worse than the kicking itself.'

Stuart drummed his knuckles on the table. 'I'm still hungry. I'm off to tuck shop. Want anything?'

'Wine gums.' James reached into his pocket for some money. 'Give it to me later,' Stuart told him. He climbed off the table and walked out of the room. James continued to work on the head of one of the horses. He drew the eyes: huge, wide saucers, glazed with sweat and bulging from exertion. He began to shade around them, accentuating them with dashes from his pencil. He lent back in his seat and decided that the shading needed to be darker. In the background he heard the door open and close as Stuart resumed his position on the table. 'That was quick.' He held out a hand without looking up. 'Where's my stuff?'

'What stuff?'

Richard Rokeby sat on the table, watching him.

James began to feel uncomfortable. Unsure of himself. The way he always felt around Richard. In his head he heard the questions he had asked himself a hundred times already.

*Why doesn't he like me? What do I have to do to make him like me?*

But now the old questions jostled with newer ones. Darker ones.

*What has Jonathan Palmer said about me? What does he think about me now?*

*And what is he doing here?*

He felt his face growing hot. Over Richard's right shoulder he could see the door. No sign of Stuart. The two of them were alone in the room.

'What stuff?' asked Richard again. His eyes were fixed on James.

'Wine gums. Stuart Barry's getting them.' James fought an urge to blink. 'He'll be back soon.' The last sentence came out almost aggressively.

'No, he won't.' Richard reached into the pocket of his jacket, pulled out a piece of fudge and put it his mouth. He kept staring at James. 'There's a massive queue. That Indian kid in Heatherfield is waving a five-pound note around, buying up the whole shop. Probably the first time Mrs Noakes has had to change anything bigger than half a crown.'

'Probably.'

Richard pulled a small white bag out of his pocket and offered it to James. 'Want some?' James shook his head.

'Go on. Have one.'

James took a piece. He put it in his mouth and bit down. A soft, rich sweetness filled his mouth. Too sweet almost.

'Thanks.'

Richard ate another piece. 'Better than that muck we had for lunch. I hate liver.'

James felt compelled to say something. 'Mine wasn't cooked properly.'

'That's dangerous. You can get food poisoning like that.'

'I've had food poisoning.' He stared over Richard's shoulder, willing Stuart to hurry.

'When?'

'At prep school. They gave us mince that had gone bad. People complained but they made us eat it anyway. We were sick for days.'

'That happened at my prep school too,' Richard told him. 'Something was off. The whole school had the squits. The queue for the bogs was a mile long. In the end we ran out of toilet paper and had to use old library books.'

James laughed nervously. Richard's eyes continued to bore into him. Where the hell was Stuart?

'The bogs all got blocked in the end. The smell was disgusting.' Richard offered James more fudge. 'How was your half-term?'

James felt trapped. 'Fine.'

'Good.'

The eyes were making him dizzy. He wasn't hungry but he reached for another piece of fudge. Any excuse to look away.

'Mine was interesting,' Richard told him.

A question hung in the air. James didn't want to ask it but felt compelled to do so. 'Why was that?'

'Because I learned things I didn't know before.'

James put the fudge into his mouth. His throat was dry. 'Like what?'

'Like just how vicious you really are.'

He bit down. Once again sweetness filled his mouth. He felt sick.

'Jonathan told me all about you,' Richard told him. 'About the things you and your minions do to people. He told me how you pissed in a tooth mug and made Christopher Deedes drink it. He told me how you locked William Abbott in a laundry basket, put it in a cupboard in the wall and left it there all night. William's claustrophobic. He had nightmares for weeks afterwards. But that was the fun wasn't it?

'And then there was Henry Blake's photograph. Of him and his father. Henry's father was killed in the war. Henry had only one picture of the two of them together. He kept it in his locker but you and your gang broke in and stole it. You let Henry sweat for a week and then you told him he could have it back if he gave you a pound. It was near the end of the term. He only had eight shillings. He gave it all to you but you told him it wasn't enough. You burnt the picture and you made him stand and watch you do it.'

Richard's eyes continued to hold James. James saw himself reflected in their centres like two tiny mirrors. It was the most familiar image in the world. But this time there was no feeling of recognition. The image seemed like that of a stranger. An image of himself as the world saw him. He stared at the stranger in Richard's eyes and found him repulsive.

He could not admit to the repulsion, even to himself. In its place came defensive anger. He lashed out.

'Well what if I did?! They deserved it! Christopher Deedes wets his bed!! He's fourteen and he still wets his bed!! And William Abbott's a baby!! You just tap him and he starts crying!! And Henry Blake talks about his father like he was the biggest hero who ever lived!! He talks about him like he won the Battle of Britain single-handed!!'

'And what about Jonathan?' asked Richard coolly. 'What did he do?'

'You know what he did!! He sneaked on me!! He tried to lose me my half-term!!'

'But that's not the real reason is it?'

James, in mid-rant, was thrown by the question. 'Of course it is!' he insisted.

'You're a liar.'

'I'm not!'

'You're jealous.'

'Jealous?! Why would I be jealous of someone like him?!'

'Because he's got something that you'll never have.'

'And what's that?'

'My friendship.'

James swallowed.

'You've wanted to be my friend since the first day we got here. You try and try but you get nowhere. And you can't stand it, can you? Everyone has to like you. Or be afraid of you. One or the other.'

'SHUT UP!'

'But it doesn't work with me, does it? I don't like you and I'm not afraid of you. I just despise you. And deep down you know it. So you try harder and harder and it just makes me despise you even more.'

'SHUT UP!!' screamed James. He was starting to tremble.

'Or what?' asked Richard.

'Or you'll be sorry!!'

'I'm sure I will. But don't start with me. Start with Jonathan.' Richard began to smile. 'You should have heard the things he said about you over half-term. The names he called you. I'd kill anyone who talked that way about me. You should teach him a lesson. The last one didn't do any good. Why not do it tonight? No one's going to stop you. Wait until the lights go out and then make him suffer. Make him scream for mercy.'

'I bloody will!' James told him. He was trembling all over.

'Good. You do your worst to him. And you enjoy it while you can.'

Suddenly Richard leant towards James. Their faces were inches apart.

'Because whatever you do to him is nothing compared to what I'm going to do to you. You can't even imagine what I'm going to do to you.'

They remained like that for almost a minute, their faces almost touching, their eyes locked together. Like lovers poised on the edge of a kiss.

Then Richard looked away. 'I have to go,' he said in a tone so neutral that they might have spent the last five minutes discussing the weather. He climbed down from the table and gestured towards the unfinished drawing. 'That's good.' He reached inside his pocket and placed a piece of fudge on the easel. 'In case you get hungry.' He turned and walked out of the room.

James watched him go. His heart was pounding. He turned back to the drawing. He reached for his pencil but his hand was shaking. He put it down again.

He picked up the fudge. He put it in his mouth. The taste made him want to vomit. He spat it on to the floor.

That evening, as the fourth years of Old School House brushed their teeth in the washroom, James sat in his bed. George Turner and Stuart Barry were perched on the edge. The three of them were deep in conversation.

'Stuart's right,' George was saying. 'We should do it tonight.'

'You can't leave it too long,' added Stuart. 'Otherwise people will think you've just let it go. It might give them ideas.'

'It won't,' James told him.

'It might,' Stuart insisted. 'You don't want to take the risk'.

James stared into space, preoccupied. He had seen Richard and Jonathan sitting together at supper on a table near his own. And after prep he had seen Jonathan hurry off down the corridor that led to Abbey House. Richard's house. Jonathan had been late for bed too. He was now washing hastily in the few moments of light that still remained.

What had the two of them been talking about? Had they been discussing him?

It didn't matter. He had waited long enough. Tonight Jonathan would get what was coming to him. And tomorrow night. And every night for the rest of term if he felt like it. There was no one to stop him except Richard Rokeby. And though Richard was far tougher than Jonathan he would still get poor odds in a fight with George Turner.

Yes, it would be tonight. He had made up his mind.

The door of the washrooms opened. Jonathan walked into the dormitory. His hair was still damp from the showers. It curled slightly around his ears. His slippers were too big. They dragged along the floor as he moved. He realised he was being stared at and flushed slightly. He looked delicate and very vulnerable. James opened his mouth to tell the others of his decision . . .

And heard Richard Rokeby's voice in his head.

*. . . whatever you do to him is nothing compared to what I'm going to do to you. You can't even imagine what I'm going to do to you.*

In his head he saw cold blue eyes that bored into him as if they could read his thoughts.

He tried to push the image from his mind. George would murder Richard. It wouldn't even be a contest.

Jonathan reached his bed. He took off his dressing-gown and laid it across his bed. He looked across the room at James. In his eyes was the clear light of fear.

But there was something else too. Something that James couldn't identify; something that made him uneasy.

'We'll leave it tonight,' he told the others. 'Tomorrow instead. That should be long enough.'

Their protests were cut off by the appearance of the duty prefect. 'Right, into bed everyone. That means you too, Turner. Get a move on.'

People shuffled towards their beds. The lights went out.

James stared up at the ceiling; angry with himself. Why had he pulled back? Richard's words were just that; words. He would not allow himself to be intimidated. If any intimidating was to be done it would be done by him.

He lay in the darkness, berating himself. It helped him ignore the fact that underneath the anger was a core of fear.

# Chapter Two

George Turner hated the Wednesday morning Maths period.

This was not to say that he enjoyed the rest of the week's lessons. Lacking both intelligence and application, he promised nothing but heartache to even the most enthusiastic teacher. The staff at Kirkston Abbey had long given up trying; content to let him sit in sullen silence at the back of the classroom on the tacit understanding that he would not disrupt the lesson.

But every rule has its exception and for George Turner the exception was Mr Cleever. Mr Cleever, the Maths master, was nudging sixty. In spite of being a teacher all his life he had managed to keep the delusion that even the most unpromising boy possesses a deep seated desire to learn. In George Turner the desire was so deep rooted that no one else, George least of all, had the slightest awareness that it existed. But Mr Cleever knew the rest to be wrong and he continued to persevere with the intense enthusiasm of the profoundly misguided.

This unwarranted faith did not generally cause George problems. Though the chances of his answering complex mathematical problems were on a par with the chances of his giving birth, he was fortunate to share a desk with James Wheatley. James was good at Maths, and though his malicious streak encouraged him to let George flounder initially, eventually he could be relied on to provide the correct answer.

The drawback to this arrangement was that James's weekly piano lesson clashed with Wednesday's Maths period, leaving George to sink or swim unaided. And for George this invariably meant sinking like a stone whilst Mr Cleever uttered words of encouragement and the rest of the class tried to stifle their sniggers.

So he hated the Wednesday lesson; knowing that humiliation was inevitable. The knowledge made him angry and with the anger came aggression, so that on this particular Wednesday morning, sitting at his desk, waiting for the arrival of Mr Cleever, he was looking for a victim on whom it could be vented.

His eyes came to rest on the double desk where Jonathan Palmer sat with Nicholas Scott. The two of them were poring over their books, talking quietly to each other; no doubt comparing answers to the problems they would be studying that morning.

In just a few hours Jonathan would receive the second instalment of James Wheatley's vengeance, but suddenly a few hours seemed an awfully long time to wait.

George rose to his feet and walked towards the pair, using his great bulk to push past the few who had yet to settle at their desks. Jonathan saw him approach. His expression became apprehensive which he tried to conceal by turning back to his book. The sight excited George. He stared down at Jonathan. 'You die tonight.'

Jonathan said nothing. 'You think last time was bad,' continued George. 'It was nothing compared to what you've got coming.'

'Oh sure,' said Jonathan, attempting nonchalance. His eyes remained focused on his book. The room was quieting as everyone listened to the exchange. The silence made George feel powerful. He reached across the desk and flicked Jonathan's book shut. 'I don't like sneaks. Do you know what I'm going to do to you?'

'He didn't sneak on you!' cried Nicholas Scott suddenly. 'Why don't you just leave him alone?'

'Keep out of it you four-eyed runt!' said George contemptuously.

'Better that than being a two-eyed moron!' retorted Nicholas.

Considering the setting, this was not the right thing to say. 'Little prick!' shouted George. He grabbed Nicholas in a neck hold and began to bend his arm behind his back. Nicholas yelled in pain while Jonathan tried to loosen the hold. 'Leave him alone! You'll break it!' George shook him off. The classroom was completely silent now except for someone calling his name. He ignored it and bent Nicholas's arm even further back.

'Turner, has anyone ever told you that you've got beautiful eyes?'

George stopped.

Shocked, he released his grip on Nicholas and turned towards the source of the voice.

'WHAT?!'

Richard Rokeby sat alone at a double desk by the window; his feet up on the seat, his back resting against the wall. He raised an eyebrow quizzically at George. 'Well?'

George stared at Richard as if he were mad. 'What are you talking about?!'

'I'm asking you a question. Did you know you've got beautiful eyes?'

George, thrown completely, beat a retreat to familiar ground. 'Fuck off, Rokeby!' he snarled and turned back to Nicholas.

'I'm only asking.'

George ignored him. He made to grab Nicholas.

But Richard was not going to be ignored. 'You don't have to get upset, Turner. It's meant to be a compliment.'

George had had enough of this. He turned back. 'Shut your mouth!'

'It's all right, Turner. You don't have to answer if you don't want to. Let's have a vote.' Richard turned to the rest of the class. 'Does anybody here *not* think that Turner's got beautiful eyes?'

Silence. Richard smiled at George. 'Seems unanimous to me.'

Still nobody spoke, but slowly the silence was breaking. Around him George could hear soft bursts of laughter. He glared at Richard. He would wipe the smile off his face! He was really angry now.

But his cheeks were growing hot. He stood awkwardly in the middle of the classroom while twenty pairs of eyes bored into him. Anger faded, replaced with embarrassment.

'You're blushing,' Richard told him.

'Am not!'

'You are.'

'Bloody not!'

'You are. Look everyone. He is, isn't he?'

'I AM NOT!' shouted George. He couldn't stand this scrutiny. His face felt as if it were on fire.

'You shouldn't be ashamed,' Richard told him. 'A lot of people think blushing is very attractive. Just like your eyes really.' Again he turned to the rest of the class. 'Does anybody here *not* think Turner's blushing is attractive?'

'YOU SHUT YOUR MOUTH ROKEBY!' roared George.

Richard continued to smile at him; his face alive with mischief. George wanted to ram a fist into that face but he felt as if he were paralysed; his limbs turned to stone by the weight of the collective scrutiny. It was with almost ridiculous relief that he heard a noise behind him and Mr Cleever's voice boom, 'Turner, to your desk please. We've a lot to get through today.'

He went to sit down. His eyes scanned the room. A few boys were still staring at him but all looked away hastily when he made eye contact. His face was still burning.

'I hope,' continued Mr Cleever, 'that everyone has attempted all the questions. Quadratic equations may not be the easiest of concepts but it's one that is hugely popular with the examiners. Who will have a go at number one?'

Silence.

'Nobody feeling suitably brave?'

Still silence.

And then Richard Rokeby spoke up. 'I think you should ask Turner sir. He looks like a chap with a lot of spunk.'

The room erupted into laughter. Mr Cleever looked surprised. 'What's this noise? Rokeby, as you seem so opinionated perhaps you would try question one yourself.'

The class quietened as Richard did as he was bid. George, his face burning again, willed him to fail. But of course he didn't.

'That's very good, Rokeby.'

'Thank you sir, but I'm sure Turner would have made a much better fist of it.'

Once again laughter resounded through the room. 'That's enough Rokeby!' exclaimed Mr Cleever. 'Now, question two. Stephen Perriman, perhaps you'd like to have a go at that.'

Slowly the lesson assumed its normal tempo. Stephen started well but came unstuck halfway through. Mr Cleever tried to guide him while the rest of the class shuffled in their seats, staring at their books or at the clock on the wall, wondering whether they would be picked on today. From the back of the classroom George watched Richard Rokeby. His moment in the spotlight now over, Richard stared out of the window with the easy confidence of one who knew that he would be able to answer any question put to him, and was not much concerned at the consequences even if he couldn't.

Richard had made a big mistake in trying to humiliate him. One that he was going to regret.

Sensing that he was being observed, Richard turned to stare at George. Coolly he studied George's face and read its message of hate. His mouth opened slightly, his tongue rolled round the corners of his mouth. Slowly, erotically.

Then, smiling, he winked at him.

The two of them continued to stare at each other. George was the first to look away.

James Wheatley was out of breath. He had run all the way from the music school but had still been drenched by the rain.

Muttering, he walked down the corridor towards his second period Divinity lesson.

The rest of the school poured out of the classrooms around him. In the distance he saw his classmates filing out of Gladstone. Jonathan Palmer emerged, flanked by Nicholas Scott and the Perrimans. The Perrimans walked on but Jonathan stood still, waiting for someone. Nicholas waited with him. Richard Rokeby appeared and made his way towards them. Nicholas stood close to Jonathan but somehow Richard managed to slide between them. The three of them began to walk up the corridor; Richard bending his head to talk to Jonathan.

There was a commotion behind them. A raised voice. George Turner was pushing through the crowds. Richard turned to face him. Others in the class gathered round, watching.

George's face was flushed with anger. He was speaking fast, jabbing a huge hand menacingly at Richard. But Richard just laughed, reached out his own hand and tried to stroke George's cheek. George backed away; the anger in his face replaced by confusion. Laughter rang out around him. James found his pace slowing.

Mr Cleever, now leaving the classroom himself, saw the group gathered by the doorway. He gestured for them to move on. Reluctantly they began to do so. Jonathan saw James. He nudged Richard.

'What's going on?' demanded James.

'What's it got to do with you?' replied Richard.

James turned towards George. 'Well?'

George didn't say anything, just stared at the ground, as if ashamed.

'Well?!'

'Turner's a bit upset' Richard told him. 'I've paid him a compliment but he's taken it very badly.'

'You shut your mouth!' cried George. The tone was meant to be threatening but it failed to convince.

'Or what? You'll kick my head in? Don't you need permission from Wheatley here before making threats like that?'

'I told you to shut up!' bellowed George.

'It's all right, Turner. I don't hate you. I may despise you but I don't hate you. Even if you did beat my friend up, I don't hate you for that. I know you were just obeying orders.'

'You'd better do what he says,' James told Richard.

'Why? Because you'll get him to beat me up?' For the second time Richard reached out a hand to touch George's cheek. Once again George backed away. Richard laughed. 'Look at him. He's not going to lay a finger on me. So take your threats and stick them.'

The corridor was emptying. Nicholas Scott, who had been watching the scene anxiously now nudged Jonathan's arm. 'We'll be late. We'd better go.' Jonathan hesitated, looking at Richard. But Richard smiled and nodded. The two of them moved away, leaving Richard with James and George. 'So,' said Richard to George, 'teach me a lesson then.'

James stared at George, willing him to do something. But George just looked at the ground, his face crimson. Again Richard laughed. The sound stung James. 'Why would we waste our time on you? It's Palmer we want. We're going to have him too, tonight, and there's nothing you can do about it.'

Richard eyed James contemptuously. 'We we we. You make the threats but it's your minions who carry them out. You depend on them completely. You'd be nothing on your own.'

A smile began to spread across his face. 'Wouldn't it be awful if something happened to them. Imagine if they weren't around any more? Wouldn't you feel exposed then.' He shuddered in fake horror. 'God, it doesn't bear thinking about it, does it?'

He turned and began to walk up the corridor, following Jonathan and Nicholas.

James watched him go. 'Why did you just stand there?' he demanded of George. 'You should have hit him.'

'I wanted to.'

'So why didn't you?'

No answer. 'So why didn't you?!' demanded James again. George shrugged. 'Well?!'

'It's not that easy.'

'Of course it is!'

'You don't understand.'

'Understand what?!'

'You weren't there. You didn't hear what he said.'

'Said?! That's just words. He's all talk and talk means nothing. You'd wipe the ground with him! You know you would.'

'It wasn't just the things he said. It was the look in his eyes when he said them.'

'What look?!'

'The one that says he's a freak.'

James swallowed.

He reached for some words but could find none. In silence the two of them walked up the empty corridor towards their next lesson.

Nicholas Scott did not have his own study. Like the other fourth years in Monmouth House, he was obliged to share. He and the Perrimans occupied a room at the back of the house, looking out on to the woods.

There were times when Nicholas longed for privacy. The room was too small for three, and though Stephen and Michael spent much of their time arguing there was still an intimacy in their relationship that sometimes made him feel excluded. But for the most part he was happy with the arrangement and the companionship it provided.

He was also grateful to be in Monmouth itself. Buried deep in the woods that covered the eastern part of the grounds, it was renowned as the most relaxed of the four school houses; less competitive in school sports and less rigid in its enforcement of school traditions. Though he had experienced his share of bullying, even this was somehow less regimented than in other houses, and for the most part a spirit of live and let live prevailed.

His only regret was that Jonathan was not also a Monmouth resident. Jonathan was his best friend, and for a serious, thoughtful boy who had never made friends easily, this meant a great deal. Over the last year he had acted as a safety valve for Jonathan; listening in sympathetic silence for hours at a time as Jonathan poured out his distress about his parents' divorce; his loathing of his stepmother and terror of losing his father; his hatred for the school and his pain at the death of Paul Ellerson.

And in return he had confided in Jonathan, telling him personal things that he would not share with others; of his fear that he was a disappointment to his military, athletic father; of his pain as he watched his beloved grandmother sliding into senility while his mother buried her head in the sand and refused to acknowledge what was happening; of how he still cried for his handsome, gregarious elder brother who had died of tuberculosis five years ago, leaving him with grief and a terrible sense that his parents, however much they loved him, might have chosen that he be the child they were forced to lose.

Both had revealed themselves to the other; exposing their inner demons; knowing that they could trust the other to keep their secrets safe.

Jonathan often spent his midmorning breaks in Nicholas's study rather than his own. Together with the Perrimans the two of them would devour whatever food they had and complain at length about whatever aspect of school life was bothering them at the moment. It had become something of a ritual, greatly enjoyed by all.

On this particular morning Nicholas returned alone with the twins. Jonathan had promised to follow later. Nicholas rummaged through his tuckbox, digging out the last of the chocolate cake and an unopened packet of biscuits. Stephen produced a bottle of lemonade and began to pour it into chipped mugs. In the distance they could hear Ruby Murray warbling over a cheap phonogram. 'I wish we had a gramophone,' said Michael.

'No chance,' Stephen told him.

'We could try Dad again.'

'Don't be a dick. You know what happened last time.'

'That was only because you told him the truth. You know how he feels about Alma Cogan. If it was up to him all we'd ever listen to would be Beethoven and choral music.'

'I like Beethoven,' said Nicholas.

'You would.' Stephen handed him a mug of lemonade. 'As far as Dad's concerned, anything recorded in the last hundred years is an abomination.'

'Except Elgar,' Michael reminded him.

'God I hate Elgar! Him and his bloody pomp and circumstance! Dad's mad about Elgar! If Elgar rose from the grave and played at the Royal Albert Hall, Dad would be in the front row screaming for him like the bobbysoxers do at Frank Sinatra! He always listens to Elgar when he writes his sermons.'

'And Holst.'

'I hate him too! You can always tell the tone of the sermon by the music Dad listens to when he writes it. If loads of women are screeching "Land of Hope and Glory" then God is love and it's wonderful to be alive, but if Mars the Giver of War is doing his stuff then God's in a foul mood and we're all headed for the eternal flames!'

They all laughed. There was a knock on the door. Jonathan entered the room. Stephen held out a chipped mug. 'Who do you hate more? Elgar or Holst?'

Richard Rokeby followed Jonathan into the room.

The laughter stopped. There was an awkward silence, as if the three of them had been caught doing something they shouldn't.

'I brought Richard,' said Jonathan quickly. 'That was OK, wasn't it?'

'Um ... yes, of course,' said Stephen. 'Come in if you can find some space. Do you want a drink?'

Richard nodded. Stephen offered him a glass. 'It may be a bit flat. Our aunt gave us the bottle and she hoards stuff for months.'

'It's fine,' Richard told him. 'Thanks.' He smiled but remained standing by the door. Jonathan, who would normally have thrown himself down on the battered sofa, stood beside him.

'We've got cake too.' Nicholas handed Jonathan a piece. 'There should be enough for all of us.'

'Don't worry about me,' Richard told him.

'It's no problem.'

'No, really. I'm fine.'

'I thought what you did was brilliant,' Michael told Richard. 'Making George Turner look like a complete dick.'

'That wasn't difficult. He is a complete dick.'

'It was still brilliant though. I've never seen anyone go so red. Thought we'd all get third degree burns!' He started to laugh, joined by Stephen and Jonathan.

'You shouldn't have done it though,' said Nicholas.

'Why not?' Richard asked him. 'It stopped him hitting you.'

'That's not the point.'

'What is the point?'

'You made him look a fool. That's not something he's just going to forget.'

'George Turner isn't going to lay a finger on me.'

'It's not you I'm thinking about.'

'Jonathan doesn't have anything to worry about.'

'Doesn't he? In case you'd forgotten, he shares a room with George Turner and James Wheatley. They had it in for him before this morning. What do you think is going to happen to him now?'

'Nothing,' replied Richard calmly.

'Nothing! How can you say that?! You're not in Jon's dormitory. None of us are. He's on his own in there and you saw what they did to him before half-term! Now you've gone and made it ten times worse! It was a stupid thing to do!'

Nicholas stopped. His face felt hot. Richard and Jonathan were both staring at him; Richard coolly, Jonathan anxiously. 'I'll be all right Nick,' Jonathan told him. 'Don't worry.'

'You don't know that.'

'Yes, he does,' Richard told him. He continued to stare at Nicholas.

Nicholas was forced to lower his eyes. He told himself that he was being a fool. Richard was trying to help and he shouldn't be so antagonistic. 'I'm sorry. I didn't mean it to sound like that. I am grateful you stepped in. I just don't want Jon to get any more hassle, that's all.'

'I understand,' Richard told him. 'Forget it.' He looked about him. 'This is nice,' he told Jonathan. 'Better than that toilet you've got.'

'Not as good as having your own room though. I'd love to have my own room like you.'

'You could,' Richard told him, 'if you moved House.'

'How could I do that?'

'Easy. Guy Wilson is leaving at Christmas. His room will be free.'

'You'd never get his room though,' Nicholas told Jonathan. 'Everyone wants to be in Abbey House.'

'Not everyone,' said Jonathan. 'Giles Harrington would never leave Old School. He'd never survive the move!'

'It would be like leaving the womb,' added Richard. The two of them started to laugh.

'But loads of people would move if they got the chance. What if James Wheatley wanted to move? He could get his parents to pull strings.'

'Wheatley isn't the only one with influential parents,' Richard told him.

'Jon's parents don't have any sway.'

'Mine do.'

'Yours?'

'My aunt and uncle actually. They could pull enough strings to put the Wheatleys to shame.'

Jonathan's face lit up. 'Do you think they would?!'

'Of course. They really liked you. Shall I ask them?'

'God, yes!'

'But you wouldn't want to move,' said Nicholas suddenly. 'Not to Abbey House. I mean, if you were going to move House then you should come to Monmouth.'

'But there aren't any spaces,' Jonathan reminded him.

'There might be one day. And if you'd moved once they wouldn't let you move again. This is the House you should move too. All your friends are here.'

'All but one,' Richard told him.

Again Nicholas told himself that he should not antagonise Richard. He was just being selfish. Anything that enabled Jonathan to move out of Old School House had to be a good thing.

Jonathan had finished his cake. 'We should go,' Richard told him. Jonathan caught Nicholas's eye and smiled. 'Thanks for the food.'

Nicholas smiled back but said nothing. Jonathan followed Richard out of the door.

'What's up with you?' demanded Stephen once they'd gone.

'Up?'

'You were in a right mood.'

'I wasn't.'

'You were. Rokeby saved you from getting thumped. You should be thanking him rather than disagreeing with everything he said.'

'I did thank him.'

'Eventually.'

'Leave him alone' said Michael.

'I'm just saying.'

'Well don't. It's nothing to do with you. Stop sticking your nose in.'

'Me?! That's rich coming from you!'

Stephen and Michael started to argue. Nicholas sat and listened, saying nothing.

Half past eleven. Old School House was in darkness. The only light came from the washroom next to the fourth-year dormitory.

James stood in front of the door, flanked by George and Stuart.

Jonathan stood alone beside the washbasins. His pyjama top, torn in the scuffle that had brought him here, hung from his shoulders. His eyes were wary. His arms were crossed in front of him. His hands rubbed at his sides while he lifted his bare feet alternately from the cold stone floor. He looked defenceless and apprehensive. Just as he had the last time.

But this time something was different.

James steeled himself to give the order. He had it all planned. Last time would be as nothing compared to tonight. In one hand he held a candle; its surface growing sticky in the heat of his grasp. In the other he held the cord from his dressing gown to be used as a gag.

Jonathan's eyes kept darting to the candle. James could tell Jonathan knew what was coming. He let the cord slip to the floor. He began to toss the candle from hand to hand.

'Where's your faggot friend now?' he asked slowly. 'Nowhere to be seen. Not now we're going to show you how we treat faggots at this school.'

He waited for the familiar rush of exhilaration. But it would not come.

'I hate you,' said Jonathan. His voice was so soft that it came out as a sigh. A weak, submissive sound. James took a step towards him. 'You make me sick, faggot,' he said.

'We both hate you.'

James stopped. He remembered the smell of the art room. He exhaled. 'And I'm supposed to care.'

'You should.'

James laughed, but made no move towards him.

'What are we waiting for?' demanded Stuart. 'Someone will hear us in a minute. We can't just hang around.' He picked up the cord.

'Don't do this,' Jonathan told him.

'Why not? Who's going to stop me?'

'You're just making it worse for yourself.'

'Fuck off!' Stuart turned to George. 'Come on, let's do it.'

'Wheatley's the one that Richard really hates. He doesn't have it in for you or Turner, but he will if you carry on with this.'

'Oh sure!' sneered Stuart. He made a move towards Jonathan but realised that George and James remained where they were. 'What is this?' he demanded. 'I'm not frightened of that poof Rokeby.' He nudged George. 'Are you?'

George shook his head.

'So let's stop wanking around then.' Stuart turned to James. 'Come on. This was what you wanted. What are you scared of?'

'Nothing,' said James, a little too quickly.

'You're a liar,' Jonathan told him. 'You are scared. And you've got good reason.'

'You shut your mouth!' hissed James. He remained rooted to the spot.

'For God's sake!' Stuart held the cord out to George. It swung in the air. James saw that Jonathan's eyes widened as they followed its motion. He began to feel himself again. Richard Rokeby was no threat. He was just talk.

But George just stared at the ground. 'We shouldn't be doing this,' he said.

'What's wrong with you?!' exclaimed Stuart. 'You can't be scared of Rokeby?!'

'No, of course not. I just ... I ... I don't want to be a part of this. We should leave this alone now.' He turned to go.

Stuart grabbed hold of his arm. 'What are you talking about? This is stupid!' George shrugged him off and barged out of the room.

'Well, that's it then,' said Stuart. 'I can't hold him down on my own. We'd better get out of here before someone comes.'

James took the cord from Stuart and pointed a finger at Jonathan. 'You're still going to get it faggot! We haven't finished with you.' He turned towards the door. He felt an unpleasant mixture of frustration and relief.

'It's all starting to fall apart isn't it?' said Jonathan quietly.

James gestured for Stuart to leave. He stood, facing the door.

'Can't you feel it?' continued Jonathan. 'It's all starting to change. Just like Richard said it would.'

'Shut up,' said James. But he did not turn round.

'Richard was right. You're nothing without your henchmen. All your power comes from them. If they won't obey you then that power fades away. And who's going to fear you then?'

James turned to face him. 'I told you to shut up.'

'I hate you,' Jonathan told him. 'I hate you for what you've done to me and to everyone else. And one day soon when all your power's gone you're going to find out just how many other people hate you too.'

He took a step towards James, a smile spreading across his face. 'It's like you said on that note you left when you trashed my study. This is just the start.'

The two of them stared at each other. Then James turned and left, pulling the light cord as he went, plunging the room into darkness.

✻    ✻    ✻

Jonathan, alone at last, felt as if he would vomit. He hurried through the darkness to the toilet stall, on legs that threatened to collapse beneath him, and crouched beside the bowl. When the sensation had passed he sat and stared up at the ceiling.

He was shaking all over. His heart was pounding with the force of a bass drum. But still he felt elated. He had done what Richard had told him. And it had all come right.

He wished his father was here. He wanted to tell him of what he had done and receive his approval. But when he shut his eyes and tried to visualise his father, Richard's was the face that he saw.

# Chapter Three

As she poured the tea Elizabeth Howard watched Alan Stewart admire a Norfolk landscape that hung on the drawing-room wall. 'Two sugars?'

'One please.'

'Of course. I always forget.'

He gave her the boyish smile that made her think of Arthur. She felt the old pain, dulled by the years but always present. She sat down beside him. 'Sorry to have waylaid you. I know how precious free periods are and I'm sure you have far more interesting things to do.'

He nodded. 'A pile of third-year essays on the War of Italian Unification to wade through. Given the choice of that or havng tea with you I'm sure you can guess which wins hands down!'

'That was Garibaldi wasn't it?' She laughed. 'Isn't it awful? I spent God knows how long studying nineteenth-century history at school and remember next to nothing of it now.'

'Neither do the third years and they only studied it last week! Luckily for them the textbook has a very good four-page summary of events and I expect to find it reproduced in ninety per cent of cases!'

'Not verbatim, surely?'

'Oh no. They'll move the odd paragraph and change the odd word. Otherwise I might suspect!'

They both laughed. 'You shouldn't put yourself down,' she told him. 'The fact that the number of sixth formers taking History has doubled since you joined us is a glowing testament to the job you're doing. And those projects you had the fourth years do! The one on the Princes in the Tower was wonderful! That was the Perrimans wasn't it?'

'Yes, technically. I think they helped sticking the pages together and drawing family trees. Jonathan Palmer and Nicholas Scott were the driving forces. Jonathan especially.'

'With some assistance from his teacher I'm sure.'

He shook his head. 'Jonathan chose the subject, did most of the research and wrote most of the text. He read every relevant book in the library, together with a couple of extra ones I lent him.'

'And all his hard work paid off. It was an excellent piece of work.'

Alan smiled. 'He's a very bright boy. Probably the best student I've got. A few years from now he could be a successful Oxbridge candidate. He certainly has the ability, and the application. All he really lacks is confidence.'

'You could give him that.'

'I'll try. I want to see him succeed. I hate to see potential wasted and I think he has a great deal. You should see him in class; the way his eyes light up as I start on a new subject. A reaction like that is so rewarding. Reminds me of why I wanted to do this job.'

His own face became animated as he spoke and as she watched him she again found herself thinking of Arthur, her beloved younger brother; always so full of energy and enthusiasm before his life was cut short by a German bullet twelve years ago. She had lost him for ever on that day, but there were still times when she saw his ghost in the idealistic young man who now sat beside her.

She smiled at him affectionately, fighting an urge to stroke his untidy mop of dark hair. 'He's lucky to have a teacher like you.'

He lowered his eyes. 'Not really,' he murmured.

'So, let me tell you why I invited you here.'

He looked hurt. 'You mean it wasn't for the pleasure of my company?'

'Of course! You didn't think . . .' She realised he was teasing her. 'Very funny! Actually I have a favour to ask.'

He smiled expectantly.

'Would you come to dinner on Saturday? I know it's short notice so please say if you have other plans.'

'No, nothing.'

'We'll be having lamb.'

His eyes lit up.

'I thought it would make a change from the delights of school food.' Alan, who lived in Abbey House as deputy housemaster and had no wife to cook for him, nodded eagerly. 'What's the occasion?'

'My cousin Jennifer has been visiting friends in Lincolnshire and is coming to see us on her way back to London.'

'And you want me to meet her?'

'Don't worry. I'm not trying to matchmake. Jennifer's four years older than me anyway so she'd hardly be suitable for you.'

She stopped, feeling suddenly embarrassed. He stared at her quizically. 'Unlike Charlotte?'

Alan had met Charlotte at a party in Norwich a year ago, and the two of them had seen a great deal of each other since. Charlotte had been a regular visitor to the school, and Elizabeth, keen to promote the romance, had invited the young couple to dinner more than once. Both she and Clive had taken to Charlotte whose lively personality complemented Alan's. The two of them had made an attractive couple and Elizabeth was already speculating on whom the children would take after when Alan returned at the start of term and told her that they had decided to stop seeing each other. Charlotte was now involved with a prosperous but dull banker and when Elizabeth bumped into her in Norwich she had seemed uncomfortable and would do no more than exchange the briefest of pleasantries.

'I wasn't thinking that.'

'Weren't you?'

He wasn't smiling, but his eyes were kind. 'Well perhaps I was,' she admitted. 'Is there really no chance?'

He shook his head.

'I'm sorry.'

'So am I.'

She put her hand on his. 'Someone else will come along. You wait and see.'

'I don't think so,' he said quietly, and suddenly his eyes were full of pain and a desperate need to confide. She squeezed his hand. 'The fact that I haven't asked dozens of questions doesn't mean that I don't care. I just didn't want to pry.'

He nodded.

'You know you can unburden yourself to me. That anything you tell me will be in confidence.'

He lowered his head. 'I know that,' he told her. 'I want to tell you. More than you can imagine.'

They sat in silence, she waiting patiently for him to speak. But in the distance they heard the bell ring for the next lesson and she knew that for now at least the moment was lost.

A strange formality descended on them both. He gathered his possessions together while she lit a cigarette and went to stand by the window, watching a class of fourth years leaving the main school building and walking in small groups towards the Science laboratory.

One group caught her eye. Richard Rokeby and Jonathan Palmer were walking together. The Perriman twins walked behind them with Nicholas Scott buzzing between the two pairs as if not quite sure where he belonged.

Alan came and stood beside her. The two of them watched

together. 'Palmer spent his half term with Rokeby,' she told him. 'Did you know that?'

'Yes.'

'I was surprised when I heard. But pleased too. Rokeby needs a friend. In spite of all his attempts to show that he doesn't.'

'It's a pity he had to pick Palmer.'

She turned towards him. 'Why do you say that?'

He looked startled, as if his words had surprised him as much as they had her. 'I don't know,' he told her honestly. 'I just wish he'd chosen someone else.'

'You sound like Clive. He doesn't like Rokeby either.'

'I didn't say that.'

'Not in so many words.'

'I don't dislike him. I have nothing against him.'

'Clive thinks he's destructive. Perhaps he is. People often are when they're as deeply unhappy as he is. But that's why this friendship is a good thing. Making a connection with another boy will stop him feeling so alone.'

'We're all alone,' he told her. 'It's safer that way. When you make that connection you become vulnerable. You start to need it. It becomes the centre of your life and then one day it's taken away from you and all the joy in your life goes with it.'

The bitterness in his voice alarmed her. 'Oh Alan . . .'

He shook his head. 'I'm sorry. I shouldn't have said that. Forgive me. I must go. I'll be late. I'm glad that Rokeby's found a friend. You're right. We all need human contact. That's what makes us human, isn't it?'

She kissed his cheek. As he reached the door she called his name. He turned.

'I'm always here if you want to talk. I value our friendship. I'd never damage it by betraying a trust.'

He gave her the boyish smile again. 'I know you wouldn't,' he told her. 'And I love you for it.'

He left the room. Again she found herself thinking of Arthur and tears came to her eyes.

\*　　\*　　\*

'Told you it would be all right,' said Richard as they hurried towards the Science lab.

Jonathan nodded. The wind whistled around them. He shivered with the cold.

'So you don't have to be afraid of them. Not any more.'

'I was afraid last night.'

'Why?'

'Because you weren't there. It was just me.'

'There was no need. I told you nothing would happen if you did as I said.'

'Wheatley was afraid too. He tried to hide it but I could tell.'

'He's got reason. He's going to be sorry for what he's done to you.'

'I think he is already.'

'Not enough. We've hardly started with him yet. Or Ackerley.'

'Ackerley? What can we do to him?'

'I know what to do. Leave it to me.'

And Richard did know. Jonathan was sure of it. Just as he had known what to do about Wheatley.

Nicholas appeared by his side, saying something he couldn't catch, trying to involve himself in their conversation. For a moment he felt angry at the intrusion.

Then he felt ashamed. Nicholas was his best friend. He had every right to be a part of things. How could he think otherwise?

It wasn't until they had finished their evening meal that Marjorie Ackerley told her husband about the dinner invitation.

He was sitting at the living-room, smoking a cigarette and staring into space. She hovered in the doorway like an anxious butterfly, fearful of disturbing him, knowing what his reaction would be. He realised that she was there and fixed her with his cold grey eyes. 'Well?'

'Elizabeth Howard telephoned this morning.'

'What did she want?'

'Nothing.'

'She must have wanted something. Why tell me otherwise?'

She swallowed nervously. 'She's invited us to dinner on Saturday. Her cousin is visiting and Elizabeth wants her to meet some of their friends.'

'And you've accepted?'

'Of course not. I said that I'd have to check with you. That we might have other plans.'

'Which we do.'

She looked confused.

'You think I'm going to suffer an evening of that condescending little bitch playing lady of the manor?!'

'Henry!'

'While her buffoon of a husband pontificates on things he knows nothing about. Expecting us all to be interested in his tedious opinions because of the supposed grandeur of his position.'

'That's not true!'

'Isn't it?'

'They're our friends!'

'Open your eyes woman! The Howards are no friends of yours. They despise you. Always have. You can see it in their eyes every time they speak to you.'

'How can you say that . . . ?!'

'Almost as much as they despise me.'

He took hold of his wedding ring, twisting it round and round his long, slender finger. Over the years she had come to know all of his gestures intimately, and this had always been the one that frightened her the most. She stood and watched him, her mouth dry. Silence hung like a fog between them.

'I'm sorry,' he said eventually.

'It doesn't matter.'

'I know how much Elizabeth and Clive think of you.'

'And of you.'

He laughed.

'They don't despise you, Henry.'

'Don't they?'

'No.'

'They should.'

'Don't say that.'

'Why not? It's true. No one knows that more than you.'

'We won't go. I'll say that we have plans. Elizabeth will understand.'

'And what will we do instead? Spend another evening like tonight.'

Again she swallowed.

'Well?'

'It doesn't have to be like this.'

'Doesn't it?' His eyes, still heavy, looked at her blankly. 'How else can it be between us?'

She turned to leave. Needing to leave.

'I had the dream again last night.'

She stopped, wanting to run but feeling his eyes upon her.

'We were back in London. At the house in Frith Street. She was hiding from me. I couldn't see her but I could hear her laugh. It was so clear. The way it dropped and then lifted at the end. I only ever hear it clearly in my dreams.'

'Henry, don't ...'

'I was running from room to room. I was making a great show of looking, but I knew that she'd be in the boxroom at the top of the stairs. All the time I was pretending to look I could hear her laugh. It was buzzing around my head like a moth. As I ran up the stairs it grew louder and louder and I knew that it had all been a bad dream and that when I opened the door she'd be waiting there for me.'

Her lip was starting to tremble. 'Henry, please ...'

'But when I reached the door the laughter stopped. And it wasn't the boxroom any more. It was her bedroom. You were all standing round the bed, and Doctor Adams was walking towards me, saying that there was nothing that anyone could have done and that we would have to help each other through it.'

Tears came into her eyes. 'I tried. I really did.'

'But he was a fool. What did he know about my loss?'

'It was our loss Henry. Not just yours.'

'Was it?' he asked her.

She turned to face him. 'You know it was. You don't have a monopoly on grief, much as you'd like to believe that you do.'

He snorted. The sound stung her.

'After all' she added, 'I wasn't the one who wanted her dead.'

As soon as the words were spoken she regretted them. The pain that came into his face was as raw as it had been in that bedroom in Frith Street sixteen years earlier. He lowered his head. 'Yes I did,' he whispered. 'I have to live with that every day of my life. Isn't that enough without you having to throw it in my face?'

'I'm sorry' she said softly. 'I shouldn't have said that.'

She waited, hoping for a reply, but there was none. His head remained bowed. 'I'm sorry' she said again. She left the room.

He remained where he was. His eyes came to rest on the table in the corner, and the picture of the little girl in the swing. He wanted to cry but there were no tears. The heat of the rage inside him had burned them away.

Evening prep had finished fifteen minutes ago. The corridors of Old School House echoed with the sound of voices. Nicholas Scott, wearing his coat and feeling out of place, stood in the doorway of Jonathan's study. William Abbott stood beside him. There was no sign of Jonathan.

'You haven't seen him then?'

William shook his head. 'Not since before prep. Did he know you were coming?'

'No.'

'Well then,' said William brightly.

'I was just going for a walk. I came in to say hello.'

'What are you doing here?' demanded a voice.

James Wheatley was standing nearby with Stuart Barry. 'Mind your own business,' Nicholas told them.

'He's looking for that faggot Palmer,' said Stuart. 'But he's not here. He's probably visiting his fag boyfriend.'

Nicholas was not going to stand by and hear Jonathan insulted. 'You're the faggots! You're the ones who can't go anywhere without holding hands!'

Instantly he regretted his show of courage. A look of complete disbelief spread across Stuart's face. 'What did you say?!'

Nicholas's first instinct was to run for it, but they were blocking his path.

He looked across at William whose eyes were wide with fear. He remembered everything Jonathan had told him about the bullying William suffered. This made him think of what they had done to Jonathan before half-term and suddenly his panic was replaced by an unexpected feeling of defiance. He glared at them. 'You heard. What are you going to do? Beat me up? That'll really make you look tough!!'

'Probably not,' Stuart told him. 'But it will make us feel better.' He took a step towards him.

'Go ahead then. You both make me sick. You make everyone else sick too and one of these days you're both going to be sorry for everything you've done to people like him' – he pointed to William – 'and Palmer.' As he spoke he reached for his glasses, preparing to hand them to William for fear they would be broken.

But at the mention of Jonathan's name a look of something

like alarm came into James's eyes. He put a restraining hand on Stuart's shoulder. 'Leave him alone.'

'You're joking?! After what he said?!'

'Just leave him. He's not worth the effort.'

'What is all this?!' demanded Stuart. 'First you go soft on Palmer and now you do the same with this prick!'

'Just leave it!! Come on. Let's go.'

Stuart pointed a finger at Nicholas. 'I'm going to have you!' The two of them turned and walked away.

Nicholas watched them go, puzzled. 'Sorry about that,' he said to William.

William said nothing; just stared at Nicholas with something like awe. Nicholas felt embarrassed. 'Tell Palmer I was here all right?' William nodded.

He walked across the main hallway, towards the front door. A group of third years appeared from the changing rooms, wrapped in dressing-gowns, making their way to bed. He stood and let them pass.

On his right was the poorly lit corridor that connected Old School with Abbey House. It was empty. In the distance he could hear laughter. The sound was harsh and shrill. He thought of Richard and Jonathan. Did they laugh when they were together? What did they laugh at? Did they laugh at him?

He shivered. Wrapping his coat around himself he headed for the door.

# Chapter Four

Though Melbourne classroom was silent a sense of anticipation hung in the air. It was Saturday morning after all and only a few hours separated the boys in the room from the comparative liberty of the weekend.

Henry Ackerley sat at the front of the room, lighting a cigarette and trying to decide who should translate the first sentence. It was a difficult sentence, though not as difficult as the fourth, which, in his head, had already been assigned to Jonathan Palmer.

As he studied the rows of desks he noticed something unusual. Richard Rokeby, sitting in his customary isolation, was not staring out of the window. Instead he was staring at his teacher. No doubt wondering whether he would be picked. Henry's eyes skimmed over him and came to rest on a double desk on the other side of the room. 'Spencer.'

Sean Spencer, alert and prepared, started well but then ran into difficulties. Not unexpectedly – this was still a new concept for the class. 'What is the sentence construction Spencer?' Spencer thought for a moment. 'Past imperfect, sir.' Henry shook his head. 'Close, but not correct.' He drew on his cigarette, sucking the rich smoke down into his lungs and then exhaling through his nose. 'Perhaps someone can enlighten him?'

One hand rose in the air. Henry felt a familiar burst of

irritation. 'Is that all? We only studied this last week.' He saw recognition dawn around the room and a further half dozen hands rose into the air. 'That's better.' He allowed himself a little joke. 'I'm glad that at least some of you pay attention in my lessons.' Sycophantic laughter rippled across the room. Richard Rokeby was still staring at him.

'Well, Osborne?'

'It's a gerundive, sir.'

'Correct. Ring any bells, Spencer?'

Spencer flushed slightly. 'Yes, sir. Sorry, sir.'

'Proceed.'

Spencer, now enlightened, finished smoothly enough. 'Good. Next time remember to identify the constuction before you start. You won't have Osborne to help you in the exam.' More laughter. Henry flicked ash into the tray by his side and considered who to pick next. As the sentence was an easy one most of the class returned his stare.

So did Richard Rokeby.

This constant scrutiny was starting to make him uncomfortable. Normally Rokeby's habit of gazing out of the window annoyed him. But now, as the intense blue eyes remained fixed and unblinking upon him, he began to wish that old habits would die less easily.

He took a slow drag on his cigarette. A boy near the front began to cough. Bothered by the smoke perhaps. Too bad. It was his classroom. He exhaled. 'Stephen Perriman.' The Perrimans looked briefly at each other – they always did this when one was asked a question.

Stephen began to translate, slowly but accurately. Behind him, Jonathan Palmer and Nicholas Scott stared at their books. He suspected that all four were relying on answers that Nicholas had prepared. Not that it mattered. Even Nicholas Scott, for all his ability, would have problems with sentence four.

He wished that Richard Rokeby would stop staring.

Stephen Perriman made a mistake. Or had he? Though

Henry's eyes remained fixed on Stephen, his attention kept wandering towards the desk by the window. 'Repeat that last part, Perriman.' Stephen did so. Correctly. No mistakes after all. He felt embarrassed. 'Keep your head up, Perriman, and open your mouth more. You're swallowing your words.' Stephen, relieved to have reached the end without mishap, nodded meekly.

Sentence three. Not so easy. Those who had formerly returned his gaze now stared hard at their desks. But not Richard Rokeby. The eyes remained fixed on him. Unblinking. Concentrated.

It was cold in the classroom but the air was starting to seem close. He stubbed out his cigarette. 'Rokeby. Translate number three.'

He expected the eyes to drop. But they didn't. They continued to study him. Detached but hostile.

'Rokeby, did you hear me?'

'Yes, sir.'

'Concentrate on your text then. The answer's not hanging in the air. And be quick. We don't have all day.'

*Look away, look away, look away.*

The mouth began to move, but Henry found it difficult to concentrate. The eyes remained focused upon him. He tried to keep the words in his head, turning towards his own text, checking the accuracy. Perfect. 'Well done.' He turned back to the rest of the class who continued to study their desks. 'Now who shall we pick for number four.' He paused, watching shoulders tense. 'Palmer, I think.'

A loud sigh rose from the desk by the window, echoing round the room. The eyes were still fixed on him. He lit another cigarette and realised that his hand was shaking.

Jonathan Palmer's head remained bowed. He began slowly, translating the first word, then the second. Then silence. Henry began to feel more confident. 'Continue.'

'I can't, sir'.

'We don't want to hear that, Palmer. We are all depending

on your expertise.' Again a soft burst of laughter. Familiar ground. 'What word comes next?'

'I don't know, sir'.

He allowed an edge to creep into his voice. 'Palmer, I've warned you. Don't keep us waiting. What word comes next?' He waited for the flushing, the stammering, the panic.

Jonathan Palmer raised his head and stared at his teacher. His face was pale, his eyes clear. 'I told you, sir. I don't know.'

Henry felt his stomach lurch. This was not supposed to happen. 'Palmer, I'm warning you . . .'

'Perhaps someone else could enlighten him, sir?'

Richard Rokeby was repeating his own words back to him! But what had Rokeby to do with this? 'No one will help him. I have asked Palmer to translate the sentence and we will all have to sit here until he does so.'

He kept his eyes on Palmer, looking for the familiar signs of humiliation. But still there were none.

'I am *still* waiting, Palmer.'

'And I *still* don't know, sir.'

'Perhaps someone could help him, sir? Just as you let Osborne help Spencer?'

'Rokeby, if I want your opinion . . .'

'Just trying to be helpful, sir. If he doesn't know the answer now he never will. And as you said yourself sir, we don't have all day.'

He felt hypnotised by the eyes. Weakly he nodded. 'Very well then. Who is going to help Palmer?'

'Perhaps you could ask Turner, sir.'

Laughter erupted across the room. George Turner turned crimson and stared at the floor. Henry sensed a hidden meaning in the words and feared that he was losing control. 'SILENCE!' Several boys jumped. 'Rokeby, as you're so eager, perhaps you could enlighten Palmer.'

The eyes bore into him. 'Yes sir. Perhaps I could.' More laughter.

'DO IT!'

Nonchalantly Richard Rokeby gave the right answer. 'Correct,' said Henry reluctantly. 'Now carry on, Palmer.'

Palmer turned his attention back to his book. But Rokeby continued to stare at him. Henry's heart was pounding. The cigarette, forgotten in his hand, burned down until it scorched his hand. He winced, scattering ash across his desk. He tried to concentrate on what Palmer was saying, praying for a mistake. At last one came.

'Repeat that, Palmer.'

'What, sir?'

'What you just said! Quickly!'

'The frightened citizens had forgotten to . . .'

'Tense! What is the tense?!'

'Had forgotten . . .'

'Wrong! Wrong! Wrong!' Jubilation swept over him. 'How many times do I have to tell you?! How stupid are you?! Can't you do anything right?! Why . . .'

'I think you'll find he's not wrong, sir,' said Richard Rokeby.

'What do you mean? Of course he is! Look at the text!'

'I am, sir.'

'Well not hard enough obviously.' Henry looked at his own text.

And his heart fell through his stomach.

Jonathan Palmer had been correct.

How could he have made such a basic mistake? How, if not for the confusion that Rokeby's unbroken stare had caused him. He swallowed.

'It appears I am mistaken, Palmer. I apologise.' He kept his eyes on his text. In the background he could hear whispering. 'Continue.'

Palmer completed the sentence. No mistakes. 'Good. Now we must press on. Time is passing. Next sentence . . . Young.'

Stuart Young began to speak. Henry looked up. The

whole class was watching him. All were quick to lower their head.

All except two.

He breathed slowly, directing his attention towards Young, trying to concentrate on what he was saying. But the words were just noise, bursts of sound drowned out by the power of the eyes.

Then, suddenly Rokeby leant back in his seat and turned his gaze to the window. Just as he always did. Palmer sensed the change. He glanced across at Rokeby to confirm it, and then looked down at his book. Normality was restored.

Henry's face felt hot. His heart was still pounding, and there was a tightness in his skull that warned of an impending headache. He breathed slowly and deeply. Young finished and was replaced by Stephenson, then Osborne. He lit a cigarette and inhaled. His hand was no longer shaking. He began to feel calmer, more in control. And angry. Both Rokeby and Palmer had been extremely insolent. He would have words with both of them at the end of the period.

But when the bell rang he did nothing except watch them leave.

'Terrible. You could have heard it for miles.'

'Did you see it close up?'

'No. Did you?'

'No, but Stephen Forrester did. He said it was a right mess.'

The two third years, muddy and sweating from the rugby pitch, stopped to look at the Old School noticeboard. James Wheatley, who had feigned an upset stomach and spent the games period reading in his study, caught the thread of their conversation. 'What was a mess?'

'Haven't you heard?'

'Heard what?'

'About the accident?'

'What accident?'

'The Under Sixteens were having a practice game. We could see them from our pitch,' chorused the third years, both eager to be the first to tell. 'The ball was fed down the line to Giles Harrington who charged straight into the other side's scrum . . .'

'. . . there was a ruck. His own scrum started to pile in after him and then he dropped the ball so Mr Evans blew his whistle so they could have a proper scrum . . .'

'. . . but then it got really strange. Everybody ignored him. He kept blowing his whistle but no one took any notice . . .'

'. . . people were shouting. It was like they were so excited they couldn't hear him . . .'

'. . . it was really out of control. All the other games had stopped and were watching . . .'

'. . . the shouting just got louder and louder. People were jumping on top of each other. Not just the scrums any more. Some of the back line were getting involved too. Climbing up on each other's shoulders . . .'

'. . . until the whole thing collapsed and there was this terrible cracking sound . . .'

'. . . it was really loud. We could hear it from our pitch . . .'

'. . . and then this screaming started. No one could see who it was. It was coming from this great pile of people . . .'

'. . . Mr Evans kept blowing his whistle, trying to get everybody off but people were all tangled up in each other and some of them couldn't move. It took ages to get everybody off and the screaming just went on and on . . .'

'. . . and then when everyone had got up we could see that it was George Turner. He was lying on the ground. Some people tried to help him up and then we saw his leg . . .'

'. . . God it was awful! It was all bent out of shape. Someone went charging off to the main school to phone for an ambulance. People were just standing around. No one knew what to do.

Turner just kept screaming. Eventually someone put a shinpad in his mouth, just to stop that noise . . .

'. . . when the ambulance came they took him to Norwich General. But he may have to go to London. He'll need all sorts of operations on his leg. He may never be able to walk properly on it again. Well that's what Rokeby said anyway. Apparently the ambulance man . . .'

'Rokeby?!' James, who had been listening to the unfolding drama with increasing alarm, now felt something close to panic. 'What was Rokeby doing there?!'

'Of course he was there. He's in the Under Sixteens too. He was in the back line on the other side but he wasn't involved in the ruck . . .'

'. . . he was one of the people who helped George Turner off the pitch and he heard Mr Evans talking to the ambulance man . . .'

'. . . and Mr Collins was supervising our game and when the ambulance had gone he went to speak to Mr Evans. Stephen Forrester heard Mr Evans say that it was the strangest thing because they'd just been having an ordinary practice game, nobody was even taking it that seriously, and then suddenly they all became hysterical, piling in like that . . .'

'. . . and then they all stood around looking shocked, like they couldn't really believe what had happened . . .'

'. . . it was really odd. I'm going for a shower. Come on.'

The two third years raced off to the changing rooms.

James watched them go. George Turner would be in Norwich now. Perhaps even on his way to London. Who knew when he would return, or what state he'd be in.

And Richard Rokeby had been there.

But of course he'd been there. He was in the Under Sixteens after all. And he had played no part in the ruck. In fact, when it was over, he'd tried to help. It was just a terrible accident.

He couldn't be responsible. Could he?

The hall was filling with others returning from the sports

fields. The sound of studs on stone filled the air. James remained by the noticeboard, his head spinning with thoughts that made no sense.

Nicholas peered round the door of Jonathan's study. Empty, just as he'd feared. He knew where Jonathan would be.

It didn't matter. It was good that Jonathan had found another friend. He was pleased for him. Really he was . . .

'Hello. What are you doing here?'

Jonathan was walking down the corridor, holding a mug of tea. The sight of him made Nicholas feel absurdly happy. 'Going for a walk. Thought I'd see if you wanted to come.'

'No chance. Still trying to do this bloody Maths. Bet you've done it already.'

'Naturally.'

They sat down: Jonathan at his desk, Nicholas in the battered chair that stood in the corner of the tiny room. 'Do you need help?' asked Nicholas.

Jonathan shook his head. He seemed subdued.

'Are you all right?' asked Nicholas.

'Fine.'

'Did you hear about the accident?'

'Yes.'

'Bet you were pleased.'

Jonathan looked alarmed. 'What do you mean?'

'After what he and Wheatley did to you before half term. I was pleased.'

'Oh. I see. Yes of course.'

Nicholas noticed that Jonathan looked pale. 'Sure you're all right?' he asked.

'Just a headache.' Jonathan breathed out slowly. 'They've taken George to Norwich General. He'll need loads of operations apparently. They reckon his leg may never be the same again.'

Nicholas, who hadn't heard the full prognosis, was shocked. 'That's awful!'

'But you said you were pleased.'

'I was pleased he got hurt. But I thought he'd just broken his leg. I didn't realise it was that serious.'

'It's not that serious.'

'This could affect the rest of his life. I call that pretty serious. I might hate him but I wouldn't wish that on him.'

A strange look came into Jonathan's eyes. He stared at Nicholas. He seemed on the point of saying something but then changed his mind. He lowered his head.

'Would you?' demanded Nicholas. No answer. 'Well, would you?'

'No, of course not.'

'Well, that's all right then.' Nicholas climbed to his feet. 'Is your headache bad?'

Jonathan looked up. He managed a smile. 'It's OK.'

Nicholas gestured towards the open maths book. 'Sure you don't want any help?'

'No. Honestly.'

'Come over after tea.'

'I can't.'

'Why not? The prep doesn't have to be in until Monday.'

'It's not that. I'm going to see Rokeby'

Nicholas told himself that it didn't matter. But still he felt hurt. 'Alright then.'

'It's not that I don't want to come,' said Jonathan quickly. 'It's just that we've made plans.'

'To do what?'

'Do?'

'You said you'd made plans. It sounds formal.'

'No. I'm just going to his room. To talk, you know.'

'So why can't I come too?'

Jonathan's eyes widened.

'Why not?'

'Well . . .'

'He's been to my study.'

'I know. It's just . . .'

Nicholas decided that he was not taking no for an answer. 'So it's not like we don't know each other. And you're not ashamed of me, are you?'

'Of course not. It's just . . .'

'So I'll come then.'

Jonathan nodded. Nicholas could tell he was not pleased. It didn't matter. He was not going to be sidelined by Richard Rokeby. He stood up. 'See you at supper?'

'Course.'

'Bye then.'

'Bye.'

He was pleased at his assertiveness. He was smiling as he walked up the corridor.

Elizabeth Howard's heart lifted when she heard a knock at the door. Pre-empting the maid she rushed to answer it.

Alan Stewart stood outside, wrapped up against the rain. 'Am I late?'

'Not at all.'

'Thank God! You did say a time but I forgot it! How's it going?'

'Dreadful. Henry Ackerley's hardly said two words since he got through the door, and though Marjorie's trying to start up a conversation with Jennifer, my cousin is far more interested in teasing Clive.'

'And how does Clive like that?'

'Not excessively. I love Jennifer dearly but she does have this knack of rubbing Clive the wrong way. I had to take her to Norwich this afternoon, just to keep her out of his hair.'

'Did you have a nice time?'

'Yes. We had tea and wandered round the shops.' She hesitated, before deciding to continue. 'We bumped into Charlotte.'

His face became a mask. 'How was she?'

'We only spoke briefly. She was in a rush. She seemed well.'

'Good.' He paused. 'Was she ...'

She shook her head. 'I rather got the impression that's over now.'

'I see.'

'She asked after you.'

'That was decent of her.'

'You could call her, you know. I'm sure she'd be pleased to hear from you.'

'No,' he said quietly. 'I don't think she would.'

'Alan ...'

He kissed her cheek. 'Let's not keep the others waiting.'

Frustrated, she led the way into the drawing-room.


Nicholas made his way to Richard Rokeby's study.

The Perrimans were with him. Both had insisted on coming. At the time Nicholas had resented the intrusion, but now, growing nervous as they approached their destination, he was glad of their presence.

He had never been inside Abbey House before. He had no friends here and so had no cause to visit. The fact that all but the third years had their own rooms meant that it was the most sought after of the four school Houses. But to Nicholas it seemed a depressing place. The rooms were packed into corridors, one on top of the other, like shelves. As they climbed the staircase they passed the prefect's corridor, then the lower sixth then the fifth year, all with their own tribal sounds and smells, intimidating to a visitor. Each was bleaker than the one before, the ceilings lower, the light poorer. The need for privacy had been catered for, but the result was an atmosphere that was more oppressive than intimate.

The fourth-year corridor was at the top of the House, wedged into the roof. The noise from the other floors rose through the stairwell, providing a constant background hum.

The ceiling was so low that Nicholas could touch it with his hand. There were no windows visible so a row of bare light bulbs lit the way. He had asked directions and knew that Richard's study was the third door on the left. The air was stale and heavy with the smell of sweat and dirty sheets. The doors around them were closed but many at the other end of the corridor were open and a group of boys were gathered in a doorway, talking. A boy in his class raised a hand in recognition. He knocked on Richard's door and was told to enter.

It was a small, square room with an arch-shaped window in the middle of the far wall, rising from the floor to a height of about three feet. It was sparsely furnished: iron framed bed, battered desk, wardrobe. Jonathan was draped over the chair by the desk. Richard was on the bed, leaning against the wall. Both stared at Nicholas as he entered. He felt embarrassed and blurted out, 'Bet you thought we'd got lost!'

'It's not that difficult to find' said Stephen, following him into the room. Jonathan, now smiling, rose to his feet. 'Did you bring any food?' Michael handed over a bag of buns. Jonathan put them on the desk, beside a box of biscuits and a bottle of lemonade. Michael looked around him. 'It's a nice room,' he said politely.

'It's a dump,' replied Richard. The air in the room was fresher and colder than in the corridor. The window was open a fraction. 'Sit down,' Jonathan told them.

Stephen sat on a battered chair by the window. Michael perched on one of its arms. Nicholas took off his coat and sat down on the bed. Jonathan took a swig from the lemonade bottle and offered it round. Nicholas passed it to Richard who smiled at him, his eyes deep pools of hostility. From the next room they could hear an opera singer warbling away on a battered gramophone. 'The walls are thin, aren't they?' said Michael.

Richard nodded.

'Doesn't the noise bother you?'

'Sometimes.'

'I wish we had a gramophone.'

'Don't start that again,' Stephen told him.

'I was just saying . . .'

'Well don't. It's boring. Is there any more news about Turner?'

'I think he's still at Norwich General,' said Jonathan. 'Richard helped him off the pitch.'

'So you must have seen his leg then. Was it gross?'

Richard nodded.

'Do you think it'll ever be right again?'

Richard shrugged. 'Who cares?'

Nicholas was shocked. 'That's a bit callous!'

'Better that than a hypocrite.'

'I'm not a hypocrite!'

'Aren't you? George Turner was a friend of yours was he?'

'No, of course not. I thought he was a shit. But he didn't deserve that!'

'But he did deserve a broken leg? Forgive me if I find your compassion unconvincing.'

Nicholas turned towards Jonathan, stunned by the perceived betrayal. Jonathan looked at the floor, refusing to meet his eyes. Stephen, sensing the tension though not understanding its history, attempted to diffuse the situation. 'You were great in Wankerley's lesson,' he told Richard.

'Was I?' Richard sounded bored.

'Yes. It was brilliant the way you spoke to him.'

'I didn't say much.'

'But it's the way you said it. You know how to make him feel uncomfortable.'

Richard allowed himself a smile, one that was directed at Jonathan. 'Yes, I suppose I do.'

'I wish I could do that. I'd love to be like you.'

The compliment hung in the air, ignored by Richard, leaving Stephen looking embarrassed. 'Hand round the buns, Jon,' he said quickly. Jonathan smiled at Nicholas as he did so. Nicholas smiled back and sensed Richard's eyes upon him. He took a bite and found that he had lost his appetite.

Silence, broken only by the strangled warblings coming through the wall.

'Well,' said Richard, 'isn't this nice?'

Michael giggled nervously.

'What shall we talk about now?'

No one answered. Richard turned towards Nicholas. 'Well?'

'I don't know. What do you and Jon usually talk about?'

'What does that matter? You're the one who wanted to come. What do you want to talk about?'

Nicholas lowered his eyes. 'Nothing.'

'So we'll just sit here all evening then. Fine.'

Nicholas struggled for something to say. Jonathan came to his rescue. 'So you like this room then?'

'It's all right.'

'Better than all right. It must be great not to have to share with other people.' He gestured towards the wall. 'Provided you don't mind Wagner!'

Nicholas wanted to keep the conversation going, but he could feel Richard's eyes upon him and felt inhibited. He nodded.

Silence.

Richard yawned.

'Sorry we're boring you,' said Stephen with an edge to his voice. 'Perhaps we should go.' He nudged Michael and stared at Nicholas.

'If you must,' said Richard.

'No, don't,' said Jonathan quickly. 'It's good that you're here. Stay.'

'Yes, do.' Richard looked at his watch. 'It's only two hours till bed.'

'We don't have to do anything,' Jonathan told Richard. 'We can just sit here and chat.'

Richard raised an eyebrow. 'Like we're doing now I suppose?'

'We could do something else then.'

'What?'

'I don't know.'

'Why don't we play a game?' suggested Richard

'No, not that.'

Something in this last exchange caught Nicholas's attention. 'What sort of game?'

'No sort,' said Jonathan hastily.

'So maybe they should go then,' said Richard meaningfully.

'But they can't go yet. They've only just arrived.'

'What sort of game?'

'Nothing. He didn't mean anything.'

'Didn't I?'

A strange light had come into Richard's eyes, replacing the boredom. Nicholas was alarmed. 'What's going on?' he demanded.

'Nothing,' Jonathan told him.

Richard stared at Jonathan. 'Why not? They might enjoy it.'

Nicholas and Stephen exchanged looks. 'What would we enjoy?' asked Stephen.

'Ignore him,' Jonathan told them. 'He's just joking.'

'No, I'm not.'

'Yes, you are. Just leave it. Who wants more food?'

'Yes, let's have more food. We can enjoy the silence as we eat.'

'Or maybe we should just piss off,' said Stephen.

'Yes, maybe you should,' Richard told him.

'Yes, maybe you should,' added Jonathan quickly.

Nicholas decided that he was not leaving until he understood what was going on. 'No,' he said forcefully. 'We're staying.' He glared at Stephen. '*Aren't* we?' For a moment Stephen seemed uncertain, but then he nodded. 'So' continued Nicholas. 'Let's play this game of yours.'

Richard stared at him. 'Are you sure?'

'Richard!' exclaimed Jonathan. 'Just leave it. Please.'

Richard smiled reassuringly at him and gestured to the door. 'Can you take care of that?' Jonathan remained where he was; his face lined with anxiety. 'It's all right, Jon,' said Richard soothingly. 'Don't worry.' For a moment Jonathan hesitated, but then he rose to his feet and pulled the bolt on the door.

Richard reached under his bed and pulled out a tuckbox. He produced a set of keys from his pocket and opened it up. He removed an old ouija board and a glass and set them down in the middle of the floor.

Nicholas stared at the board. 'Is this your game?'

Jonathan nodded.

'Do you want to play?' asked Richard.

'You shouldn't be playing with that,' Michael told him.

'Why not?'

'Because it's rubbish. That's why.'

'So what's the harm in playing with it?'

'You just shouldn't. That's all.'

'But why not?'

'Because you don't know what you're getting into.'

'We're not getting into anything. It's just a game.'

'You don't know that.'

'You do though. You've just told me it's rubbish.'

'It is rubbish.'

'So what are you afraid of?'

Michael flushed. 'I'm not afraid!'

'Of course you're not. It's just that the way to hell is paved with ouija boards. Is that what Daddy told you?'

'You keep our father out of this!' said Stephen forcefully.

'Look, if he doesn't want to . . .' began Jonathan.

'Of course,' said Richard. 'If it's too frightening for him.'

'I am *not* frightened!'

'Prove it.'

'He doesn't have to prove anything to you,' said Stephen. He rose to his feet. 'Come on Mike, we're leaving.'

'I'm staying!' Michael told him.

'Mike!'

'I'm not afraid.'

'I know you're not.'

'So stop telling me what to do!'

'Michael! This is stupid!'

'You go if you want to! I'm staying!' Michael shook off Stephen's arm and crouched down beside the board.

Stephen remained standing, glaring at Richard. Then he knelt down beside his brother.

Richard turned to Nicholas. 'And what about you?' The tone was provocative. Nicholas refused to rise to it. He sat down between Michael and Jonathan. 'I'm ready.'

'Good.'

Richard moved the glass to the centre of the board and placed a finger on it. Michael did likewise. Then Stephen. Then Nicholas. The surface of the glass was surprisingly cold. 'Come on, Jon,' said Richard encouragingly. Jonathan shook his head.

'Looks like someone else is afraid,' said Michael sarcastically.

'You shut your mouth,' Richard told him. 'Jon come on.'

Again Jonathan shook his head.

'I can't do this without you.'

'I know,' said Jonathan quietly.

Richard sighed. 'All right then. Shut your eyes everyone, and concentrate.'

Nicholas did as he was told. In the self-created darkness he felt a breeze from the window on the back of his neck. His heart was pounding.

They sat in silence for a minute. The glass remained motionless. 'You see,' said Stephen. 'It is rubbish.'

Nicholas felt movement beside him. He opened his eyes. Richard had draped an arm over Jonathan's shoulder. The anxiety was fading from Jonathan's face, replaced by something like tranquillity. Richard brushed Jonathan's cheek gently with his fingers. Jonathan leant against Richard. Reaching out an arm, he placed his finger on the glass. Nicholas felt a momentary tingling in his own finger like a tiny electric shock.

The glass began to move.

Slowly at first, but then faster, rotating in circles that grew larger as its speed increased. Nicholas saw that Stephen had also opened his eyes. The two of them stared at each other.

'We shouldn't be doing this,' whispered Stephen.

The glass stopped.

'We have company,' said Richard softly.

'WE SHOULD NOT BE DOING THIS!'

Stephen jumped to his feet. 'This is mad! You don't know what you're doing!'

'It's a game,' Richard told him. 'That's all.'

'That's shit! You know that's shit! Well, do what you want, but leave us out of it! Mike, we're leaving!'

'But Stephen ...'

Stephen grabbed Michael by the arm, pulling him to his feet. 'NO ARGUMENTS! We're leaving now!'

'Shut the door on the way out,' Richard told him.

'But I don't want to go ...'

'Shut up!' Stephen dragged Michael to the door and undid the bolt. He turned to Nicholas. 'Come on!'

'Yes, run along,' said Richard.

'Come on!' said Stephen again.

Every instinct Nicholas possessed was telling him to leave. Richard was smiling at him; his eyes alive with dark light. He knew he should go with the twins. He was frightened to be here alone.

Except that he wouldn't be alone.

Richard's arm was still around Jonathan's shoulder. Protectively.

Possessively.

Jonathan was staring at him too. His eyes were sad. But he did not ask him to stay.

And if he left now he risked losing Jonathan for ever.

'Come on!' cried Stephen.

*Oh Jonathan, what is happening to you?*

'Nick, come on!'

He shook his head. It was just a game. Just as Richard had said.

'Well, sod you then!' hissed Stephen. He pulled Michael from the room, slamming the door behind him.

'You're staying?' Richard asked him.

He nodded. The hatred in the eyes made him feel sick.

'Are you sure?'

'Yes.'

'Bolt the door then.'

He did as he was told and stood for a moment, watching the two of them. Jonathan was still leaning against Richard; the two of them locked together like two halves of a single whole.

He was afraid of Richard. He was afraid of all this.

But Jonathan was the best friend he had ever had and he was going to fight for him.

He went to join them.


In the interlude between dessert and coffee Jennifer lit a cigarette. 'Have you heard any more from his parents?'

Elizabeth Howard shook her head. 'We didn't really expect to.'

Jennifer exhaled. She was a tall, angular woman, a harsh version of her cousin. 'Poor people. It must be terrible to lose a child.'

Marjorie Ackerley paled slightly. 'It is,' she said quietly, her voice as sweet as always. She began to fiddle with a lock of her hair.

Elizabeth winced. She had asked Jennifer not to talk about the Paul Ellerson business, explained its sensitivity, and Jennifer had promised faithfully not to say a word. But that was before the wine had loosened her tongue.

'So what was he like? This boy?'

'A very fine young man,' said Clive Howard gravely.

Jennifer laughed. 'For God's sake Clive, you're not giving his funeral oration. If I want the official version I can read the obituaries. What was he actually like?'

Clive's heavy features darkened. Elizabeth, eager to keep the peace, gave her husband a sympathetic smile but he ignored her. 'I'm sorry if it sounds boring, Jennifer,' he said sharply, 'but it happens to be true. He was a very promising young man.'

'Who just happened to take an overdose?' Jennifer snorted. 'I don't think so. Mark my words, there will be any number of skeletons buried in the family cupboards.'

'All families have skeletons,' Elizabeth told her.

'Don't they just.' Jennifer drew deeply on her cigarette. 'Wouldn't you agree, Clive?'

'Perhaps there were skeletons,' said Clive, 'but we never saw them.'

'You can always find them if you look hard enough. What are his parents like?'

'A very charming couple,' Clive told her.

'What does the father do?'

'He retired last year,' said Elizabeth. 'They bought a house just outside Norwich. Before that they were in Singapore.'

'And Paul spent his holidays there?'

'The summer holidays, yes. The rest he spent with relatives.'

'Well, that's a start then.'

Elizabeth was confused. 'What do you mean?'

'Being passed around the relatives while his parents enjoyed the good life in the colonies. That must have caused resentment. Did he have siblings? Did they go to school in this country too?'

'JESUS CHRIST!' roared Alan Stewart.

Everybody jumped. Alan's normally affable expression was now one of fury. 'The boy's dead! He was a fine young man. He was everything that Clive said and more and his death is not a bloody party game!'

'Here here,' said Clive under his breath.

'Well excuse me!' said Jennifer indignantly.

'I'm sure Jennifer didn't mean to make light of it,' said Elizabeth, hastily trying to diffuse the situation.

'Well it sounded like it.' Alan breathed deeply, trying to compose himself. 'I'm sorry. I didn't mean to be rude. It's just that his death is not a subject for speculation. It was a tragedy. Let's just leave it at that.'

Henry Ackerley started to laugh.

He had been silent for most of the meal. He had eaten little, concentrating most of his energies on the wine bottle. He was now very drunk and his voice had a dangerous edge.

'It's always a tragedy isn't it? That's what people say when a young person dies. That's what they said when our daughter died. What a tragedy. She had the whole of her life in front of her. Just think what she could have done with it.'

Marjorie flinched. Her beautiful face, already pale, took on a ghostly hue. 'Henry . . .' she began.

'But it's all shit isn't it? What do they know? What do they *really* know? They would have said the same in Austria sixty years ago if Hitler had died as a child. The doctor would have patted his parents on the back and said, "It's a tragedy Mr and Mrs Hitler. Little Adolf had so much promise. Imagine what he could have done if he'd only lived. Why, he could have grown up to start a world war and kill millions. Why, he could have been the biggest mass murderer in history if only the pneumonia hadn't come along and stamped out all his wonderful potential."

'Our daughter would be twenty-one if she'd lived. Three years older than Paul Ellerson. Imagine if it had been her instead of him. What would people have said? Would it still be a tragedy? Poor little Sophie Ackerley. What a terrible waste of a life. Or would it be too late for that? Would all of her wonderful potential have come shining through so that people would have just shrugged and said good riddance, she was a poisonous little bitch but with parents like that what could one expect?!'

Marjorie sobbed; a short sharp burst of pain.

Elizabeth forgot all about trying to keep the peace. Her eyes were flashing. 'For God's sake! You may despise your own loss but can't you at least respect your wife's?!'

Henry stared back at her. 'Don't ever presume to talk to me about loss. You couldn't begin to comprehend how great my loss has been.'

Marjorie ran from the room. Elizabeth hurried after her. Henry watched them go. 'It appears I've ruined the evening,' he said matter of factly. He reached for the wine bottle and filled his glass.

Stephen rushed into his study, breathing hard. The rain was coming down in sheets and he had not thought to take a coat. Michael followed. They stood facing each other in the middle of the room, dripping water on to the floor, steam rolling off their bodies.

'Richard was pushing,' said Stephen forcefully.

'No, he wasn't.'

'Of course he was! He was trying to scare you.'

'So why did we have to leave?'

'We just did.'

'But why?'

'Because he *was* scaring you. Soon you'd have shown that you were afraid and then he would have laughed at you.'

Michael stared at his brother. 'I wasn't the only one, was I?'

'What's that supposed to mean?'

'You know what it means.'

'I wasn't scared! The whole thing is a big con trick! Anyone with a brain can see that!'

'So why were you afraid?'

'I was not afraid! You were afraid! We only left because of you!'

'All right then! I was afraid! But so were you! Why won't you admit it?!'

'Because it's not true!'

'It is!'

'It's not! The whole thing is rubbish just like Dad says!'

Michael lowered his eyes, stared down at the pool of water that was collecting round his shoes. 'But if it is rubbish,' he said softly, 'then why did he make us promise that we would never try it?'

Stephen didn't answer.

'He's afraid too, isn't he? He says it's rubbish but he doesn't believe that. He thinks it's dangerous. And you think he's right.'

Stephen remained silent. Michael raised his head. 'You do, don't you?'

'I don't know what I think,' replied Stephen truthfully.

The two of them stared at each other. 'If it is dangerous,' said Michael slowly, 'then we should stop them.'

'I didn't say it was dangerous.'

'You didn't have to.'

'Well what if it is?!' cried Stephen. 'It's their choice. It's nothing to do with us.'

Michael was shocked. 'How can you say that?'

'Because it's true.'

'But Nick and Jon are our friends!'

'Jon isn't our friend. Not now he's got Rokeby.'

'But Nick is!'

'Not any more.'

'He is!'

'No he's not! He could have left with us but he didn't. He's made his choice.'

'But Stephen . . .'

'But nothing! It's not our problem!'

'You selfish pig!'

'Yeah, maybe I am. So what? I've told you what we're going to do. I don't want to talk about it any more.'

'You can't tell me what to do all the time! I'm sick of it! It's my life!'

Stephen screamed.

Rage burst out of him like a bullet. He threw himself at his brother, a mass of fists and feet. Michael, crying out in panic, tried to shield himself from the onslaught. The blood pounded in Stephen's head. Each blow represented years of resentment at knowing that his parents expected him to be the responsible one: years of anger at knowing that they would blame him if something happened to Michael in a way that they would never blame Michael if something happened to him; years of fear that they might never be able to forgive him if something did happen.

Years of knowing that he would never be able to live with himself if it did.

The rage subsided as quickly as it had come. He stopped, stepped back. Michael was curled up into a ball, whimpering. As he watched him Stephen found himself remembering how the two of them had stood and watched their parents drive away on their first day at boarding school. Michael, frightened at what lay ahead, had been crying. For Stephen there had been no tears; just the knowledge that his brother needed him and that he would kill anyone who tried to hurt him.

It had all been so simple then. It was simple now.

He put his arms around him, making soothing noises as if to a small child. Michael resisted at first, but then allowed himself to be held.

The Ackerleys had left already and Elizabeth was showing Alan Stewart to the door. Clive stood by the window of the drawing-room, watching Jennifer pour herself another drink. She raised her glass to him. 'Here's to a successful evening.'

'All credit to you.'

'Me?'

'Harping on about Paul Ellerson. After Lizzie has asked you specifically to avoid the subject.'

'Oh yes. Poor Lizzie. We mustn't upset her, must we?'

'She goes out of her way for you.'

'I know. She's an angel. I can't think why she puts up with me.'

'She wouldn't if it was up to me,' he snapped before he could control himself.

Jennifer put down her glass and stared at him. 'Is that so?' she said coldly.

Clive flushed. He turned to stare out of the window.

'But as we both know, that would be a very bad idea.'

He made no acknowledgement. In the distance they heard Elizabeth approaching.

'What's the matter Clive?' asked Jennifer softly. 'Worried the skeletons are starting to rattle? Frightened that she'll hear them?'

He ignored her and went to greet his wife.


It was almost time for bed by the time Nicholas returned to his study.

Stephen and Michael sat together at Stephen's desk, studying a textbook. The two of them looked up briefly as he entered. Michael's eyes were red. Nicholas's first instinct was to ask why but then he thought better of it.

'What are you doing?' he asked nervously.

'Maths,' replied Stephen without looking up.

'Do you need any help?'

'No.'

'I've done it already. You can borrow mine if you want.'

'It's all right.'

'It's there if you change your mind.'

'We won't.'

Stephen shut the book and punched Michael lightly on the arm. 'Let's grab a shower, before it gets crowded.' He walked past Nicholas to the door. Michael followed. As he passed Nicholas's desk their eyes met. Michael gave him a small smile.

'Mike, come on.'

The two of them left the room. Nicholas stayed where he was. There was a lump in his throat. He swallowed it down. It wouldn't do any good. Not now.

The bell was ringing. He rose and made his way to bed.

# Chapter Five

Alan Stewart studied the fourth year class before him.

They sat in silence, heads down over their books, or staring at the blackboard and the test he had set. The only sounds were the occasional sigh and the scratchings of pens on paper.

He glanced at the empty space at the back of the classroom. George Turner's seat. There was still no news of George; no word on when he would return to school or what state he'd be in when he did. Before the accident Alan had never cared for George but now he found himself saying a silent prayer for his full and speedy recovery.

The space seemed bigger than was necessary for a single boy. A reflection on George's build perhaps. His absence left James Wheatley looking both exposed and isolated. Alan had enough familiarity with fourth-year politics to know how important George was to James. He wondered if James, who had probably taken George's presence for granted, was only now starting to realise it too.

Two boys were whispering. 'Southcott! Priestly! Your own work please.' Two pairs of eyes looked at him guiltily and then returned to the blackboard. He noticed that someone else was turning round. Richard Rokeby was staring at someone. The paper in front of him was covered in writing. He had probably finished long ago and was bored. Alan checked his watch. 'Time's up gentlemen.' A chorus of groans. 'Finish the question you're on and make sure your name is on the top. Except for you Upton. Nobody could forge your handwriting.' The groans were replaced with good-natured laughter. 'Stop writing now. Pass your answers to the front. Vale, can you collect them please.'

With the test over the classroom filled with noise. People swivelled in their desks, turning to talk to friends. The lesson was about to end so Alan did not call for silence. Judging by the reactions Osborne was confident, Spencer was not and Thomas was telling Upton that he couldn't have copied his answers because his bloody elbow was in the way. Alan smiled. He had seen it all before.

But there was something he hadn't seen. Or rather, something he would have expected to see but didn't.

The Perrimans sat whispering to each other. Behind them, Jonathan Palmer and Nicholas Scott did the same. But there was no interaction between the two pairs. Which was most unusual.

Perhaps there had been some sort of falling out; an argument which would be forgotten in a week. Friends were always falling out.

Jonathan turned away from Nicholas, looking across the room, towards Richard Rokeby. The two of them smiled at each other. Some form of silent exchange appeared to be taking place. Nicholas said something to Jonathan but Jonathan ignored him.

'Here are the answers, sir.'

A strange look came into Nicholas's eyes; part hurt, part something that Alan couldn't identify. Was it wariness?

'I've got the answers, sir.'

Something wasn't right here. Something troubled him.

'Sir?'

Vale was standing by the desk. 'Of course. Thank you, Vale.' The bell rang. 'Right, class dismissed.' The noise level increased. 'Quietly please! Other classes may not have finished yet.' 'Sorry, sir. Goodbye, sir. See you on Thursday, sir.' Boys filed past his desk. The Perrimans moved quickly; Nicholas and Jonathan more slowly; stopping by the door, waiting for Richard.

Richard walked past Alan's desk. His walk was distinct; graceful and purposeful. It was all part of the Rokeby aura; strong, confident, contained, needing nothing from anyone. The aura was admired by the other boys. Alan had often admired it himself. Now he found himself asking what forces had led to its creation, and what demons it concealed.

Richard reached Jonathan and Nicholas. The three of them remained in the doorway. James Wheatley walked past them. Richard said something to Jonathan and the two of them laughed. Nicholas was watching Richard. The same look was in his eyes, but stronger than before. Wariness that seemed more like fear.

Richard gestured to Jonathan. The two of them moved away with Nicholas following. An unlikely trio that Alan suspected would soon become a duet. Old friendships replaced by new. It was none of his business.

But he didn't like what he had seen. Clive Howard considered Richard destructive. That seemed an extreme reaction. But he was certainly charismatic, and charisma itself could be destructive; seducing others into behaviour that was both alien and damaging to them.

He was fond of Jonathan. He believed in Jonathan's potential and wanted to see him succeed. He would not stand by if he felt that potential was in danger.

He decided to monitor the situation.


Mid-morning break. James Wheatley and Stuart Barry sat in Stuart's study.

'I'll phone them again tonight,' said James.

'I wouldn't. Bryant said not to. He'll let us know when there's news.'

'I'm not waiting for an announcement. I want to know what's happening now.'

'I just don't think it's a good idea, that's all.'

'Why not? Don't you care how he is?'

'Of course I do. But his parents aren't going to be pleased if you keep phoning. They won't want to be bothered.'

'But we're his friends. We've a right to know.'

'Try telling my parents that! When my sister fell down the stairs her friends kept phoning and my mother went mad. She ended up shouting at them. She and my father were worried enough. They didn't want to have to keep making progress reports. So phone if you want to, but don't be surprised if you get screamed at.'

James scratched his head.

'Your sister was all right though, wasn't she?' he asked quietly.

'Of course. Though she still pretends she isn't when Mum asks her to do something she doesn't want to do. George will be all right too. Just you wait and see.'

James stared into space. Stuart saw that he was rocking backwards and forwards in his seat. The motion was barely perceptible and almost certainly involuntary. 'Are you OK?' he asked hesitantly.

'Why shouldn't I be?' The tone was defensive.

'No reason.'

'I'm fine.'

'Good.'

'Rokeby kept staring at me in History.'

'Was he?'

'We were doing a test. He kept turning round.'

'Ignore him. He's a prick.'

'I know.'

'So don't let him get to you.'

'I didn't!' Again the tone was defensive. 'But he put me off. I made a right mess of it.'

'Don't worry. We'll sort him out.'

'We?'

'Us and George.'

'But George isn't here.'

'He'll be back soon.'

'What if he's not?'

'He will be.'

'But what if he's not? What if he doesn't come back for ages?'

'Then we'll just have to wait.'

'You could sort him.'

Stuart didn't answer.

'You don't need George. You could do it on your own.'

Stuart stared at the floor. James watched him. 'You're not afraid of him, are you?' No answer. 'Are you?!'

'No.'

'You don't sound very sure. You were confident enough last week.'

Stuart hung his head; his thick blond hair falling over his eyes. 'George was here then, wasn't he?'

'You bloody coward! You're pathetic! You act so tough when George is around and the moment he's gone you turn to butter!'

'And what about you!' cried Stuart. 'When did you get your hands dirty?! Oh yes, I remember. When you beat up Palmer. Except that you didn't do a bloody thing! George and I had to hold him for you. Palmer could probably sort you out on his own. And Rokeby would fucking kill you!'

'I know,' said James in a small voice.

'So don't have a go at me! Just don't! George will be back soon. We'll sort it then.'

Tension hung in the air like static.

'Why does he frighten you?' asked James.

Stuart shrugged.

'Last term you had a fight with Courtney. He's as big as you are but you didn't need George then.'

Stuart said nothing.

'Rokeby's no bigger than Courtney.'

'It's different though.'

'Why is it different?'

'It just is.'

'But why?'

'Because I knew what Courtney was going to do. He'd try and beat the shit out of me and I'd do the same to him. It would just be a fight, and we'd both know when to stop. It wouldn't be like that with Rokeby. I couldn't predict him like that. I don't know what he'd do. I don't know how far he'd go. That's why he frightens me.'

'Me too,' said James quietly.

The bell rang. It was time to start gathering their books together. In the corridor outside they heard footsteps, then a knock on the door. 'Who is it?' called out Stuart.

The door opened. Mr Bryant the housemaster stood in the doorway. James and Stuart jumped to their feet. A well dressed woman stood beside him. Stuart's eyes widened. 'Mum!'

She smiled at him. 'Hello, darling. Hello, James.'

'Hello, Mrs Barry.'

'Mum, what are you doing here?!' Panic crept into Stuart's voice. 'Has something happened?!'

'Everything is fine, Stuart,' said Mr Bryant. 'No need to worry. Your mother has some news for you, that's all.'

'What news?' demanded Stuart.

Mr Bryant and Mrs Barry exchanged glances. 'Why don't we go to my study?' suggested Mr Bryant.

'But I've got lessons now, sir.'

'I think you can forget about them for the moment,' Mr Bryant told him. 'But James, you should run along.'

James remained where he was. Alarm bells were ringing in his head. 'What's this news?' he demanded.

'That's none of your business,' Mr Bryant told him. 'Now off you go or you'll be late.'

James had no choice. Reluctantly he went to collect his books for the next lesson.

Jennifer had only left the previous day but had already phoned Elizabeth twice, to thank her for the hospitality and then to ask her to forward some scent that she had left behind. Elizabeth had wrapped it and was just finishing the accompanying letter when the maid came and told her that Mrs Ackerley was here.

Marjorie stood in the doorway, smiling hesitantly. 'Is this a good time?'

'Absolutely!'

'I don't want to disturb you.'

'You're not! It's lovely to see you. Come in.' They sat together on a sofa in front of the fire. 'Can I get you anything?'

'No, nothing. I won't stop. I just wanted to apologise properly for Saturday night.'

'But Marjorie please, there's no ...'

'Need?' Marjorie sighed. 'Oh but there is. It was inexcusable, subjecting you to a scene like that.'

'You don't need to do this. I'm the one that should be apologising. I should have come to see you before but I couldn't. Jennifer only left yesterday evening.' She paused. 'I should have come then.'

'But you were worried Henry might be there?'

Elizabeth blushed. 'A little.'

'I understand.'

'I wish I did,' said Elizabeth quietly.

Marjorie shook her head. 'You shouldn't judge him too harshly.'

'Why not?' Elizabeth knew that she was venturing on to dangerous ground but felt suddenly reckless.

'We all have our own way of dealing with things.'

'That's no justification. It was a vicious thing to say.'

Marjorie smiled. 'I've heard worse.'

'That's what bothers me.'

'He loved her very much you know. And then, suddenly she was gone. It's the only way he knows to cope with her loss.' Marjorie's eyes filled with tears. She wiped them away. 'I'm sorry. How stupid.'

Elizabeth put her hand on Marjorie's and was alarmed at how cold it felt. She rubbed it gently between her own. 'She was your daughter too,' she said softly.

'I know.'

'He should respect your grief.'

'He does.'

'That's not how it appears.'

'Appearances can be deceptive.'

'I worry about you.'

'You don't need to.'

'But I do. He has so much anger trapped inside him. What if he were to hurt you?'

A coolness crept into Marjorie's voice. 'He wouldn't.'

'But he might. You don't deserve to be treated like this.'

'Don't I?'

'No!'

'How dare you presume to talk to me like this!'

Elizabeth's jaw dropped. 'What?'

'You know nothing about Henry and me! What gives you the right to moralise about our relationship?!'

Elizabeth realised that she had overstepped the mark. 'I'm sorry. It's none of my business.'

'That's right. It's not. And in future I'd be grateful if you would remember that.'

Elizabeth was still holding Marjorie's hand. It was warm now. She released it, expecting Marjorie to leave.

But she didn't. Instead she took Elizabeth's hand and squeezed it gently. 'I'm sorry. I didn't mean that. You're my best friend, Elizabeth. I know you care about me and I love you for it. But Henry and I have been married for over twenty years and there are things between us that only the two of us could understand. We're not like you and Clive. God knows we're a long long way from that. But he's all that I have, and if you condemn him then our friendship would have to end. And I wouldn't want that.'

'Neither would I. Forgive me, please.'

Marjorie kissed her cheek. 'There's nothing to forgive. I must go. It's cold outside. Stay by the fire. I'll see you soon, yes?'

'Of course.'

Marjorie left the room. Elizabeth stayed where she was. Her fears for Marjorie remained.

She was still there when Clive returned. 'Sally says that Marjorie was here'.

She nodded.

'How was she?'

'Fine,' she said and then started to cry.

He hurried to sit beside her. 'Sweetheart, what is it?'

'Nothing.'

'You don't cry for nothing.' He pulled her towards him, cradling her in his arms. 'What is it? Tell me?'

She told him what had happened. 'It's silly I know. It just upset me, that's all.'

'Of course it did. You were just trying to help.'

'I hate to see her unhappy. And she is, Clive. Desperately. But she won't hear a word against him.'

'Just as I wouldn't hear a word against you.'

'It's not the same.'

'Yes, it is. You're my wife. He's her husband. It seems the same to me.'

She stared at him. 'How can you compare their marriage to ours?'

'I'm not. But if those are her wishes then you have to respect them.'

'I just wanted her to know that I'm here if she needs me.'

'She does know that. She's lucky to have a friend like you.'

'Is she?'

'Of course she is. You know she is.'

She did not look convinced. Tenderly he stroked her cheek. 'I love you,' he told her.

'I love you too.'

'Always?'

'Always.'

'That's all right then.' He pulled her closer, kissing her neck and breathing in the scent of her hair. Contentedly they sat and watched the fire. He saw that she had started to smile. 'What is it?' he asked.

'Jennifer phoned. She'd forgotten something.'

He smiled too. 'True to form.'

'It was just some scent. I'll send it back. She said she'd enjoyed the dinner party.'

'In spite of all her efforts to wreck it.'

She slapped his arm. 'That wasn't her fault.'

'I know.'

'She asked if she could come again. The week after next.'

'Oh God! Lizzie, you didn't say yes, did you?' No answer. 'Did you?'

'Just for a few days. That's all.'

'She's only just left.'

'I know. But she sounded depressed on the phone. I couldn't say no.'

'Surely there are other friends she can visit.'

'I think she's rather outworn her welcome there.'

'Which could never be said of us.'

'Clive!'

'I'm sick of these constant visits. We're not a bloody hotel!'

'She is my cousin.'

'I have cousins too. None of them have taken up residence.'

She stroked his face with her hand. 'I'm sorry. I should have asked you first. I know she can be difficult. But we are important to her, and it's not as if she has much in her life.'

The flames sent shadows dancing across her face. She looked very beautiful. He kissed her cheek. 'Not like us.'

She kissed him back. 'No, not like us.'

She snuggled against him, the two of them sitting in companionable silence. She felt him sigh. 'What is it?'

'Nothing.'

'Tell me.'

'I was just thinking of what we have. It's so precious to me, you know. I don't know what I'd do if something were to spoil it.'

'Nothing will.'

'I know.'

He pulled her closer still, kissing the top of her head, caressing the nape of her neck. He was no longer smiling.


Afternoon lessons had just finished. The boys of Old School House stowed their books in their studies before making their way to the dining-hall. James Wheatley heard a rap on his study door. 'Come in.'

Stuart Barry entered. 'Where have you been?' demanded James. 'I thought you'd be back ages ago.'

'Mum took me out for lunch. We went to that restaurant on the Uxley road. You know, the one that looks like a farmhouse.'

'And you spent all afternoon there?'

'No. We went to Cromer. We had a walk along the beach. We had stuff to talk about.'

'What stuff?'

Stuart didn't answer. He had an odd expression on his face; half excitement, half shock. 'What stuff?' demanded James.

'Dad's been offered a new job.'

This was hardly news. Mr Barry was a very successful

London banker. Stuart was always boasting of how rival banks were trying to poach him. 'What job?'

'In another bank.'

'So?'

'It's fantastic money. Double what he's on now.'

'Is he going to take it?'

'Yes'.

'So what's the big deal.'

'It's on Wall Street.'

For a moment the implications were lost on James. But only for a moment.

'NEW YORK?!'

Stuart nodded.

Panic swept over him. 'You're leaving?!'

'Yes.'

'When?! At the end of term?!'

Stuart shook his head. James's alarm began to subside. 'Next summer then I suppose.'

'The day after tomorrow.'

James felt as if he had been kicked in the chest. For a moment he was unable to draw breath. His legs threatened to collapse beneath him. The room seemed to be spinning.

'Dad has to be out there in a fortnight,' continued Stuart. 'That's the deal. They've already found us a house and they're going to help with schools.'

'But you don't have to go then! You could go later!'

'I can't. Mum's nervous about leaving England so she's decided that the whole family's to go out there together. She's going to see my sister tomorrow. She'll have to leave St Felix. We've got to pack up all our stuff and say goodbye to the relatives.' Stuart was growing increasingly excited. 'We leave on the 29th. We're going to fly. I've never been on an aeroplane before.'

James sat down at his desk. His heart was pounding.

'Goodbye Kirkston Abbey. No more nazi prefects and crap

food. I'll be going to a day school in the city. Mum says that if we're living in a strange place then she's not having us all at schools miles from home.'

'But you can't leave!' It came out as a virtual wail.

'I have to.'

'But you can't!'

'Don't be like this. We'll keep in contact. You can come and visit.'

'That makes me feel a lot better!'

'What's the matter? I thought you'd be pleased for me.'

'Pleased?! Stuff that! What about me?! I'm the one that's stuck here!'

'Well sod you then!' shouted Stuart. He turned to leave.

'Don't go!' cried James.

'Why not?'

'I'm sorry. I am pleased for you.' He swallowed. 'It's just ...'

Stuart turned back to face him. James didn't finish the sentence. He didn't need to. Both knew exactly what he meant.

It was past midnight. All was still in the Ackerley house.

Henry stood at the foot of his wife's bed, watching her sleep. Rest had smoothed away the anxiety in her features. She looked as beautiful as she had done the first time he saw her.

The window was half open. It was cold in the room but he didn't notice it. Hate and the whisky he had consumed helped keep him warm.

The silence was dangerous. It allowed him to hear the voices; the dark, seductive voices that lived inside his brain, like sirens singing from the very depths of his mind. Their songs were of destruction but still he flirted with them, as if willing them to lure him to his doom.

They sang to him now, like unseen ghosts. And floating above them, like a solo soprano in a choir of baritones, was the laughter of a child. It was the sweetest sound in the world to him and yet the most painful; a lament for the loss of love and hope and everything that could give his life meaning.

He remained where he was, watching his wife sleep; the moan of his sobs mingling with the gentle hiss of her breathing.

# Chapter Six

Thursday afternoon; dreary and wet. Games had finished and the half holiday begun; two hours of freedom before the drill of supper and evening prep began.

The door of Richard Rokeby's study was bolted. Richard and Jonathan lay on the bed, staring up at the ceiling. Richard's arm was draped around Jonathan. Jonathan's head rested on Richard's shoulder. A companionable silence existed between them. In the corridor outside they could hear the voices of the other fourth years flitting from each other's rooms, looking for entertainment. The boy in the next room had forsaken opera and was now playing Frank Sinatra on his battered gramophone. One song finished and was replaced by another. 'Paul Ellerson loved that song,' said Jonathan.

'Did he?'

'He played it all the time. Guy Perry had the study next door and he got so sick of it that one day he sat on the record while making it look like an accident. But then he felt so guilty that he confessed and bought Paul another copy and Paul promised that he'd only listen to it on alternate days.'

'Where is Guy now?'

'Sandhurst. His family were military. Both his brothers went there too.'

'Did you like him?'

'He was all right. A bit full of himself but all right. He came back when it happened. He was in tears, which was strange. He wasn't the sort of person you imagine crying. But Paul was his best friend. I envied his being able to cry.'

'You could have cried too.'

'No, I couldn't. Not even in front of Nick. If I'd started I wouldn't have been able to stop and then everyone would have seen. That was the first thing Paul told me, that you should never let anyone here see you cry.'

'You can cry in front of me. You know that, don't you?'

Jonathan smiled. 'Course I do.'

'You never talk about him.'

'You never talk about your mother.'

'No,' said Richard slowly, his eyes remaining fixed on the ceiling. 'I don't.'

'Don't you want to?'

'What's the point? I loved her when she was alive. I miss her now she's dead. I could talk for hours but that's all I'd be saying.'

Silence. But as comfortable as before, and Jonathan realised that he did want to talk about Paul after all.

'I met him at the start of my second week here. It was a really awful time; grace period was over and the fourth years were making up for lost time. Duties had just been allocated. William Abbott and I got the changing rooms. It used to take hours. People left all their crap lying around because they knew we were the ones who'd get it in the neck if there was a mess.

'And then the fag list went up. When I saw I'd got Paul Ellerson I felt sick. I'd heard enough to know that your fag master could make your life complete hell for twelve months and with Paul being Head of House he was bound to be worse than anyone.

'I reported to him. He was standing outside his study, talking to Guy. I'd only ever seen him from a distance before. He seemed incredibly glamorous. Like a film star. He was tall and good-looking and clever and athletic and everything you could ever want to be. I told him I was his fag. He didn't even look at me; just told me to go and wait in his room. As I waited I kept telling myself that I would cope with whatever he put me through.'

He paused. A lump had formed in his throat. 'Go on,' said Richard encouragingly.

'He came in. He shut the door and stood there. I expected him to start ordering me around but he didn't. He just smiled and told me that I didn't have to look so scared; that the person he'd fagged for had made his life a complete misery and that he had no intention of putting someone else through that.

'It sounds stupid now but that really upset me. I was homesick and scared and I just wasn't expecting someone like him to be nice to me. It threw me off balance and I started to cry. I thought he'd despise me but he didn't. He guessed it was my first time away from home. He told me that there was nothing to be ashamed of; that he'd been homesick too when he first came here. He said that I should never let any of the others see me cry because they'd view it as a sign of weakness and they'd make my life hell because of it. But I could cry in front of him and he wouldn't think any the worse of me.

'Things didn't seem so bad after that. It was like having an elder brother. I saw him every day. I'd go and empty his bin and wash the cups up and he'd ask what I'd been up to and how I was getting on. I didn't tell him everything of course. Not what happened in the dormitory; that sort of thing. You don't tell people stuff like that. But he understood. I always acted happy around him but he could tell when I was miserable and he'd always try and do something to cheer me up.'

'Like what?'

'Like sending me to buy him some sweets and then saying he didn't want them after all and giving them to me. Or reading me soppy bits from letters he used to get from a girl he'd met on holiday.' He started to laugh. 'Or playing his records so loudly that Guy would bang on the wall and shout that Frank Sinatra was the devil. Or just telling me that the more senior I became the better things would get.'

In his head he could hear Paul Ellerson's voice saying the words.

'I believed him then. But not now. Not after it happened. Now I know it's all lies.'

The lump was back; bigger this time, like a boulder in his throat, blocking the words.

Richard turned towards him. 'Don't be embarrassed. I understand.'

'Well I don't!' he cried. 'I want to but it just doesn't make sense. He had *everything* going for him. Why couldn't that be enough?'

'I don't know.'

'He was clever. He was popular. Everyone liked him. Everyone wanted to be his friend. You couldn't hate him if you tried.'

'Perhaps he hated himself.'

'He couldn't have done. There was nothing to hate.'

'You don't know that.'

'I do.' Jonathan became defensive. 'I know more about him than you.'

'I'm not saying he should have hated himself. But that doesn't mean that he didn't.'

Jonathan shook his head. 'He was a happy person. Guy used to call him the eternal optimist. It was infectious too. Just being around him made you feel better about things. That was why everyone liked him so much. He was happy all the time.'

'Except at the end.'

His eyes were filling with tears. Angrily he wiped at them. Richard moved closer to him. 'Sorry. I shouldn't have said that. We don't have to talk about it any more.'

He breathed deeply, struggling for composure. 'No. I want

to tell you. It's hard, that's all. I just want to understand. It would be easier if I could understand.'

'When was the last time you saw him?'

'The last day of last term. That was the last time I saw him properly anyway. I went to say goodbye. I'd bought him a present; a book about Peter the Great. History was his favourite subject too. He was brilliant at it. He would have walked Oxbridge.'

Richard smiled. 'Just like you will.'

Jonathan smiled too. 'He was much better than me. The book was to say thank you for everything he'd done for me that year. He was really pleased. I remember him sitting at his desk by the window with the sun shining in. He seemed happier than ever that day. He'd just arranged a holiday to Whitby. He loved Whitby. His grandparents used to live there and he'd spent all his summers there before his parents went abroad. He told me to have a good summer and said that he'd see me next term.'

'And that was it?'

'Almost. He sent me a postcard from Whitby. He said that a local artist had drawn a cartoon of him dressed as a vampire. Whitby was where Dracula's ship was wrecked.' Richard nodded. 'He said it was good to have a break before he started revising for Oxbridge. I was really happy he'd remembered me but Paul was like that.'

'What about this term? Did you see him at all?'

'Not properly. I was late back the first day. I saw him walking off somewhere with a pile of books. Going to the library probably. I called out to him and he waved and smiled. I unpacked, went to bed, got up the next morning, went to breakfast, and by the time I got back Brian Harrington had gone to knock for him and seen what had happened and there was all this commotion and the police were there and ...'

'And it was all over,' said Richard, finishing the sentence for him.

'Do you know what the worst thing is?'

Richard stared at him expectantly.

'Nobody talks about him any more. The prefects never mention his name and they make sure that nobody else does either. When Brian Harrington heard two third years talking about it he went mad. They all act like it's bad luck to say his name.'

'People always act that way around a suicide,' Richard told him.

'But it's not right. He was a wonderful person, not some dirty secret. If we don't talk about him then it's like he never existed at all.'

'A suicide is always a dirty secret. All the people who knew them feel guilty. They feel as if they should have done something and the feeling is so awful that the only way to deal with it is to pretend that the person never lived at all. That's what happened with my mother.'

'Your mother?!'

Richard nodded.

'But you told me she died of cancer!'

'I lied.'

'But when?! How?!'

'When I was nine. People told me she took an overdose.'

'You weren't there?'

'No. I was staying with my aunt and uncle.'

'Well that's something I suppose.'

Richard gave a hollow laugh. 'Yes, I suppose it is.'

Jonathan willed the ground to swallow him. 'I'm sorry. It wasn't supposed to come out like that. It's just that ... well imagine if you'd been the one to find her.'

'Yes,' said Richard quietly. 'Imagine.'

They continued to lie side by side. Richard's arm was still around Jonathan's shoulder. A question burned inside Jonathan's head but he felt he couldn't ask it. In the end he didn't need to.

'Don't you want to know why?'

'Yes.'

'You should have asked him then, when you had the chance.'

'Who?'

'My father.'

'You think it was his fault?'

'I don't *think* it.'

At last all that he had witnessed between Richard and his father made perfect sense. And yet, knowing what he now did about Richard's mother, such animosity seemed terribly wrong. Richard, noting his silence, and sensing the unease that lay behind it, turned towards him. 'What is it?'

'Nothing.'

'Tell me.'

'It doesn't seem right, that's all.'

'What doesn't?'

Jonathan swallowed. In the corridor outside he could hear a scuffle and raised voices; a fight was breaking out.

'That you should hate him so much.'

Richard's eyes widened. 'How can you say that?'

'Because he's the only parent you've got.'

'So what?'

'Well ...' Jonathan struggled for the right words. 'What happened to your mother was terrible but hating him isn't going to bring her back.'

'Do you think I don't know that?! What the hell does that have to do with anything?! If someone killed the only person in the world who mattered to you wouldn't you hate them too?!'

'But he didn't kill her,' said Jonathan awkwardly.

'He did!'

'She killed herself.'

'He's responsible though! He made her do it!'

'But ...'

'But NOTHING!! Understand?! You don't EVER lecture me about this!'

Suddenly Richard sat up and leant over Jonathan. His features were twisted with fury; his eyes blazing with rage. Fear paralysed Jonathan. He struggled for words but could only nod weakly. Outside the commotion had turned into chanting; harsh and excited, baying for blood.

'You're just a liar! Like everyone else! You told me you'd always understand! That's what you said! But that was all lies wasn't it?!'

'But Richard . . .'

'You're so pathetic! You can't do anything for yourself! Wheatley and his mob would still be kicking ten types of hell out of you if I hadn't sorted them! I do everything for you and then when I try and tell you about the most terrible thing that's ever happened to me you act like everyone else and start preaching forgiveness! Well I don't need you to preach! I need you to understand! I NEED SOMEONE TO UNDERSTAND!'

Richard clenched his fist and pulled his arm back. Jonathan cried out and tried to shield his face. But Richard drove his fist into the pillow beside him.

They remained on the bed. Richard was breathing hard. Jonathan's heart was pounding. Outside an adult voice was bellowing over the adolescent ones, calling for order: a prefect trying to break up the fight. Jonathan wondered who was involved and if anyone had been hurt.

'I'm sorry,' he whispered.

Richard ignored him. He stared into space. His body was rigid. He gave off energy like electric waves.

'I'm sorry, Richard. Really I am.'

'It's not your fault,' said Richard abruptly. 'How could I expect you to understand? It hasn't happened to you. I hope you never do have to understand.' His tone, so savage a moment ago, was now flat and empty. He looked down at Jonathan. All the fury had left his face. Now it was smooth and easy, like a mask covering the turmoil that raged beneath. Jonathan stared up at him and remembered an expression he had read in a storybook years ago. Here be demons.

In his head was an image of George Turner, lying in a hospital bed in London, his leg smashed, perhaps beyond repair. It had been what they had asked for. It had been what he had wanted.

Or what Richard had told him that he wanted.

He wasn't in control anymore. When Richard stared at him he felt dazzled. He couldn't think clearly. He needed to be with his old friends. They would make him feel himself again.

But Richard made him feel alive.

He reached out a hand and touched Richard's face. Richard smiled down at him. It was a beautiful smile. It made him feel safe. Paul Ellerson had made him feel safe too but Paul had gone and left him and he knew that Richard would never do that.

'You can tell me,' he said gently. 'I will understand. I promise I will.'

There was a knock on the door. 'Ignore it,' whispered Richard. 'Whoever it is will go away.'

But they didn't. There was another knock and then someone tried the door, only to find it bolted. 'Jon, Richard, are you in there?' It was Nicholas. Richard cursed under his breath.

'You'd better let him in,' said Jonathan. 'He's not going to leave.' Richard remained where he was. 'Go on.'

'We don't need him.'

'He's my friend.'

'*I'm* your friend. You don't need him any more.'

'I know.'

'Tell him then.'

'I will.'

'When?'

'I don't know. But I will.'

'You'd better. Or maybe I'll do it for you.'

Jonathan felt a surge of protectiveness towards Nicholas. 'Don't. Please don't.'

Richard smiled. 'I'm only teasing you.'

'Promise.'

'Of course. I won't say anything.' Richard rose from the bed. 'I'm coming,' he called out. Before he reached the door he turned and stared at Jonathan; his expression a mixture of possessiveness and predation. Its intensity was frightening. But it was also exciting.

Twenty minutes later Jonathan and Nicholas walked down the corridor that led to Old School House. It was still an hour until supper but Richard had seemed out of sorts and the two of them had thought it better to leave.

They reached the main hallway. Jonathan seemed on the verge of saying goodbye. 'Can I come back to your study?' asked Nicholas. Jonathan nodded awkwardly. Both knew that a month ago such an exchange would have been unnecessary.

They sat in the study. Jonathan produced an expensive-looking box of biscuits. 'Where did you get these?' asked Nicholas.

'Richard's aunt sent them to me.'

'That was nice of her.'

'You don't have to sound so surprised.'

'I'm not.'

'Just because she's his aunt doesn't mean you have to hate her too.'

'I don't hate him.' Jonathan looked unconvinced. 'I don't.'

'If you say so.'

'He hates me though, doesn't he?'

Now it was Jonathan's turn to look uncomfortable. 'No.'

'Yes he does. Deny it all you want to but we both know it's true.'

'If he hates you so much then how come he includes you in everything?'

'Because I'm not like the twins. I'm not going to let myself get pushed out.'

'The twins weren't pushed out.'

'Of course they were.'

'They chose to go.'

'That's right,' said Nicholas sarcastically. 'Richard had nothing to do with it whatsoever.'

'He didn't!'

'You were there. You saw what happened. Why won't you admit it?'

'Because there's nothing to admit. So we don't go around with the twins any more. Big deal. We may have been friends with them last year but that doesn't mean we have to stay friends for ever.'

'There speaks Saint Richard of Rokeby. All hail Saint Richard.'

'Don't talk about him like that!'

'Why not? You'd say black was white if he told you to. And when he persuades you to dump me he'll tell you it's all my fault and you'll believe him too.'

'I'm not going to dump you. You're my friend.'

'And that really counts for a lot! The twins were your friends too except that now you don't talk to them any more because Saint Richard wouldn't like it.'

'You don't talk to them either!'

'Wrong! They don't talk to me! And we all know whose fault that is!'

'If Richard's so terrible then why don't you piss off! Nobody's making you stick around!'

Nicholas paled slightly. 'Is that what you want?'

Jonathan shook his head.

'Isn't it?'

'Of course not.'

'But it's what Richard wants though,' said Nicholas quietly. 'Isn't it?'

Jonathan said nothing; just stared at the ground. 'This isn't right, Jon,' said Nicholas. 'This isn't you talking.'

'Don't . . .' began Jonathan.

'Why not? It's true.'

'No it's not.'

'You have to break with him. Before you get in too deep.'

'You don't understand.'

'Don't I?'

The two of them stared at each other.

'Of course I understand,' said Nicholas. 'He's good-looking. He's confident. He's not scared of anyone. Everybody would like to have him as a friend and he's picked you. And you're so flattered that you'll go along with whatever he wants.'

'It's not like that.'

'Isn't it?'

Jonathan rubbed the back of his neck. 'Maybe it was at first. But not now.'

'So how is it now?'

'He makes me feel safe. Ever since I came here I've been afraid of something. Of Wheatley. Of Ackerley. Of losing my father. Of everything. I feel powerless here. It's like being in a prison. Richard makes me feel powerful.'

'He's the powerful one! You're just doing what he tells you to!'

'Well what if I am?!' cried Jonathan. 'He makes the fear go away. Just like Paul Ellerson used to, except that with him it's a hundred times better.'

'How can you compare Richard to Paul Ellerson?! Paul Ellerson didn't enjoy hurting people! He didn't try and separate people from their friends!'

'You see,' said Jonathan quietly. 'You don't understand.'

Silence. Nicholas stared at a blue stone resting on the window ledge. Jonathan had found it on Southwold beach last summer when Nicholas's parents had taken them to Suffolk for a day. On a hill above the beach there was a row of Napoleonic cannons. His father had taken a picture of the two of them sitting on one of them, making faces for the camera. He still had the picture somewhere. It was a memory of good times, just like the stone.

He didn't want it to be like this. He wanted to turn the clock back to that summer.

'My parents are coming to see me next Sunday. They're taking me out to lunch.'

'Lucky you. Say hello from me.'

'You could do that yourself if you came too.'

Jonathan shook his head.

'They'd love to see you. They always ask after you.'

'It's not that.' Jonathan lowered his eyes. 'Richard's aunt and uncle are coming that day. I'm going out with them. I'm sorry.'

Suddenly Nicholas felt terribly tired. He was not defeated yet. He was not going to give up. But he knew that if he was to have any chance of winning he would need far stronger weapons than those he currently possesed. And where those would come from he did not know.

He rose to his feet. 'I've got work to do. I'll see you at supper.'

He didn't wait for Jonathan's reply. Quickly he left the room.


After supper James Wheatley helped Stuart lift his trunk into the boot of the car.

Mrs Barry stood with Mr Bryant. She wore a headscarf as protection against the wind and was smoking a cigarette. When James caught her eye she smiled at him but her expression was tense. She still had to drive to Suffolk to collect Stuart's sister before making the long trek back to London.

'Is that everything?' she asked Stuart. He nodded. 'Are you sure? I don't want to have to come back.'

Stuart rolled his eyes at James. 'I'm sure Mum.'

'We'll be on our way then.' She offered her hand to Mr Bryant. 'Thank you again. Ralph and I are very grateful for everything you've done for Stuart.'

'Not at all. We're just sorry he's leaving. He'll be a great loss to the House.'

Stuart smirked at James. Both despised Mr Bryant and were sure that the feeling was mutual. Normally James would have smirked back. But not now.

Mr Bryant shook hands with Stuart. 'Good luck, Barry. Come and visit us when you're back in this country.'

'I'll be sure to, sir,' said Stuart. He was still smirking. Mr Bryant nodded to Mrs Barry and then made his way back into the House. 'Well goodbye, James,' said Mrs Barry. 'Stuart, say goodbye.'

So this was it. Awkwardly Stuart held out his hand to James. 'Bye then.'

'Yeah, bye.' James tried to sound nonchalant.

'It'll be all right.'

'Expect so.'

'George will be back any day.'

'That's not what Bryant said.'

'What does he know. You'll see.'

'Sure.'

Silence. There was so much James wanted to say but he could tell that Mrs Barry was growing impatient. 'You'd better go.'

'Yes, come on, Stuart,' said Mrs Barry, rather sharply. 'Katie will be waiting. James, you be sure to come and visit us.' James started to thank her for the offer but Mrs Barry was already climbing into the car, eager to beat the traffic.

He watched the car move away. A part of him wanted to run after it, begging Stuart to stay. But it wasn't up to Stuart and there was nothing that could be done.

He stared up at the school building. It towered above him like a stone colossus. He felt dwarfed by it; exposed, and vulnerable.

Slowly he walked back into Old School House.

That night he sat in the dormitory, trying to read a book.

Two of the beds had been stripped bare. Stuart would be in London now, making plans with his family. George was in London too, seeing a specialist. Mr Bryant had said that it was unlikely George would return until the start of next term.

Around him the other fourth years prepared for bed. The air was full of voices. William Abbott emerged from the washrooms and walked towards his bed. Little William, so often the victim of his bullying who usually slunk around as if begging to be ignored. Tonight William moved with new confidence. There was no need to be frightened any more.

He wished George was here. Next term seemed awfully far away.

Christopher Deedes was sitting on Henry Blake's bed. Both were staring at him. He stared back. Quickly they looked away. But not as quickly as they would have done two weeks ago. And a smile passed between them as they did so. Past victims both. What did they have to fear now?

Were they going to try something? Well let them. They would be sorry if they did. Next term. When George came back.

He wished George was here now.

The door opened. Brian Harrington looked in. 'Hurry up. You should all be in bed by now.' The stragglers emerged from the washroom. Jonathan Palmer was one of them. He walked towards his own bed. As he passed James he stopped and smiled at him. 'Sweet dreams,' he said softly.

'Palmer!' bellowed Brian. 'Hurry up!' Jonathan climbed into his own bed. 'Good night everyone.' 'Good night Harrington.' The lights went out.

James lay very still, peering into the darkness. All around him was silence. There was no sound except the pounding of his own heart.

He was not afraid. No one would try anything. They wouldn't dare. They wouldn't bloody dare!!

He wished he was in London. He wished he was anywhere but here.

He pulled the sheets up around him. He curled himself into the foetal position. He tried to ignore the fact that he was shaking.

He exploded out of sleep like a bullet from a gun. He was sitting bolt upright in bed. He was drenched in sweat. The air was full of the sighs and snores of those who continued to sleep around him.

His eyes scanned the shadows, trying to focus, searching for movement.

But there was nothing. It had just been a bad dream.

All of this was a bad dream.

Alone in the darkness, surrounded by those who hated him, he began to cry.

# Chapter Seven

Henry Ackerley could barely contain his relief when the bell rang at the end of the period.

'Right. Class dismissed. And quietly please.' The fourth years rose to their feet and began to make their way out of the room, preparing for the mid-morning break. Henry sat and watched them go. James Wheatley looked drawn. Perhaps he had slept badly. It was of no matter. The object of his attention was approaching. For a moment he hesitated but then resolved to see it through.

'Rokeby!'

Richard Rokeby turned towards him. 'Sir?'

'A word please.'

Richard Rokeby stood and waited while the rest of the class filed out around him. Henry saw Jonathan Palmer and Nicholas Scott hovering in the doorway. 'What are you two waiting for? Off you go. And shut the door after you.'

Scott did as he was told. Palmer remained where he was. 'Palmer, are you deaf?' Still no reaction until Richard Rokeby turned and nodded at him. Henry swallowed down his anger and turned to the matter in hand.

'So Rokeby. What is going on?'

The blue eyes stared levelly at him. 'What do you mean, sir?'

'Don't play ignorant with me. You know exactly what I mean.'

'Do I, sir?'

'How long do you think I'm going to put up with this behaviour?'

'What behaviour, sir?'

Henry breathed deeply. 'Rokeby, I do not like being provoked.'

'I'm sure you don't, sir. But it would help tremendously if I knew what you were talking about.'

'You consider yourself very clever don't you, Rokeby?'

Richard shrugged.

'Don't you?'

'I think that's a question for my teachers, sir. Do you consider me clever, sir?'

'Don't try and turn this, Rokeby.'

'Turn what, sir?'

'Other members of staff may be willing to tolerate your insolence but I most certainly am not.'

'Am I insolent, sir?'

'You know damn well you are!'

'I don't sir. I'm sure I always try to be polite. But if you'd like to explain what aspect of my behaviour you consider insolent then I'm sure I could try and change it.'

Henry realised that he had boxed himself into a corner. What Rokeby said was true. His behaviour always wore the mask of perfect politeness. It was what lay behind the mask that troubled him.

Like the staring.

It was getting worse and worse. Those eyes, intense and unblinking, now remained focused on him from the moment the lesson began to the moment it ended. He had tried to ignore it. But it was difficult, for in those rare moments when he looked into the eyes he saw all the venom they contained and it made him feel afraid.

Just as he was now.

They held him as surely as if there was a clamp around his head. They bored into him like drills, making him feel that they could see into his soul and the darkness that dwelt there.

It was a confrontation and he was losing. He struggled to regain control.

'I've said all I'm going to, Rokeby. Take this as a warning. If this behaviour continues I will take steps to have it stopped. I am the master here and as such I hold the power. You would be wise to remember that.'

Strong words. Instantly regretted. Almost imperceptibly Richard Rokeby straightened his back.

'You're not threatening me are you, sir?'

The tone was still courteous. The eyes were glacial.

Henry swallowed.

'Are you, sir?'

'No.'

'I'm glad, sir. It would seem very unfair when I try so hard to be polite.'

Richard took a step forward. Henry fought against an urge to lean back in his chair.

'In fact, sir, it might provoke me into showing you just how insolent I can be.' A smile began to play around the corner of his mouth. 'Let's hope things don't come to that, sir.'

Henry tried to speak but his throat was dry. All he could do was nod.

'Was there anything else you wanted to say to me?'

Henry shook his head.

'May I go then, sir?'

'Yes.'

'Thank you, sir.' Richard turned and made for the door. When he reached it he turned back, smiling. 'See you tomorrow, sir. Second period.' Then he was gone.

Henry remained where he was. He reached for a cigarette. His hand was shaking so hard that he had trouble lighting it.

*　　*　　*

Last period had just ended. As the top French set trooped out of Walpole classroom Nicholas heard someone call his name. He turned and saw Richard Rokeby walking towards him.

'Coming then?' asked Richard.

Nicholas stared at him warily. 'Where?'

'Didn't Jonathan tell you?'

'Tell me what?'

Momentarily Richard looked surprised. 'Obviously not.' He shrugged and moved away.

'Tell me what?' Nicholas called after him.

'Nothing,' said Richard without stopping.

Nicholas rushed after him. 'Must have been something or why would you have asked me?'

'They're serving up that mince muck tonight. My aunt sent me a big parcel yesterday. I thought we could work through that instead. I did tell Jon.'

'He didn't say anything to me.'

'Must have forgotten. It's up to you. I expect you'd rather have supper with the rest of them.'

You'd love that thought Nicholas. 'I'll come,' he said forcefully. 'Thanks.'

Richard made no attempt to hide his displeasure. 'All right then,' he said grudgingly. 'Let's go. Jon will meet us there.'

They climbed the stairs of Abbey House. Neither spoke. The two of them had never been alone together and this unexpected intimacy made Nicholas uncomfortable. He wondered if Richard felt the same way.

They reached Richard's room. Nicholas hoped that Jonathan would be there already but the room was empty. Richard sprawled on the bed and gestured to the chair by the desk. Nicholas sat down. 'I expect Jon will be here soon,' he announced.

'Should be.'

'Mr Fleming always runs over. Jon's always complaining about it.'

'Yeah.'

In the distance Nicholas could hear voices, but all was silent on the fourth year floor. Richard was staring at him. The unblinking gaze unsettled him. He struggled for something else to say. 'It's really stupid, isn't it? Having sets for French.'

'Why? Some people are better than others.'

'You could say that about any subject. Look at Jon; brilliant at History, lousy at Latin. And what about George Turner? If they had a Maths class for morons he'd still find it a struggle to keep up.'

'So?'

'So it's stupid.'

'Do something about it then. Write a letter to the Governors.'

Nicholas laughed nervously. 'That's a bit extreme.'

'Not if you feel strongly about it.'

'I don't feel that strongly.'

'Why mention it then?'

Nicholas shrugged. 'Something to say I suppose.' He wished Jonathan would hurry.

'Why say something for the sake of it?'

'I don't know.'

'Does silence frighten you?'

'No.'

'Do I frighten you?'

Nicholas could feel his cheeks growing hot. 'No. Of course not.'

'Then why are you so nervous?'

'I'm not.'

'You do this with everyone do you? Go bright red, stare at the floor and wriggle like you're going to wet yourself.'

'No.'

'No, of course not. Only with me. If being in the same

room as me is such torture why don't you go and wait for Jon downstairs.'

It was very tempting. Every instinct screamed at him to do so.

'Or, better still, just piss off back to your old friends and leave us alone.'

Suddenly the steel in Nicholas rose to the surface. Deep down he had known that a confrontation like this was inevitable. Now the moment had come and he was not going down without a fight.

He raised his head and stared at Richard. 'You'd like that, wouldn't you?'

'What do you think?'

'I think it's what you've wanted all along. But it's not going to happen.'

'Really?'

'No. I won't let it.'

Richard smiled at him. 'Do you want to bet on that?'

'Jonathan's not coming is he? There was no parcel from your aunt. Jonathan doesn't know anything about this.'

'That's right. He doesn't. This is about you and me.'

'No it's not. It's about Jonathan and me. You've tried to turn him against me but you've failed, so now you have to resort to threats to scare me off.'

'Why don't you just face it? Jonathan doesn't want you around any more than I do. The only thing that's stopping him from telling you is worry over how you'll react. He doesn't like you. He just pities you. Who can blame him? You're so pathetic. I'd kill myself if I was as pathetic as you.'

'You really hate me don't you?'

'Yes,' said Richard. He was still smiling. 'I really do.'

Slowly Nicholas rose to his feet. His breathing was smooth and easy. His face was cool. He was amazed at how calm he felt.

'Hate me all you want to, but you're not going to drive

me away. You don't frighten me. Jonathan may think you're wonderful at the moment but soon he's going to see you for what you are. And when he does he'll dump you like a piece of shit and I'll be there to laugh in your face!'

He turned and walked slowly to the door, determined to keep his dignity. What came next threw him completely.

'How's the family?' asked Richard.

He stopped. Turned back. 'What?'

'Your family? How are they?'

'None of your business.'

'Things can't be easy for your mother. Is she coping any better now?'

'My mother? What are you talking about?'

'It can't be easy for her; knowing that your grandmother's just going to get worse and worse. Always worrying about what's going to happen next. Like that time your grandmother went to town in her nightgown and had to be brought home by the police. Have there been any other incidents like that?'

Nicholas's jaw dropped. 'How do . . .'

'No wonder she tries to pretend it's not happening. Who wouldn't choose to bury their head in the sand rather than actually do something? It's so much easier to fuss over your husband and bake cakes for your son and tell yourself that everything's fine and that when your mother leaves the gas on or falls in front of a bus it will just be a terrible accident and nothing to feel guilty about.'

The blood drained out of Nicholas's face.

'You're fond of your grandmother, aren't you? I'm sure she's fond of you too. When she actually remembers who you are. Or is she? Perhaps she preferred your brother, like your parents did.'

Nicholas felt as if someone had stripped away his skin and was scraping away at the exposed flesh with a razor. All his most painful secrets being paraded before him. Secrets that he had told to no one. No one except Jonathan.

'Do you think your grandmother wished that you'd been the one to die? I'd want to know if I were you. Pity you'll never be able to ask. Not with her the way she is now.'

His eyes were filling with tears. He tried to contain them but it was no good.

'Your father's military isn't he? Quite an outdoors sort I gather. Like your brother was. But not like you. He sounds a nice chap though. Not the sort who'd ever let you see that he was disappointed.'

The tears were rolling down his cheeks. He stared mutely at Richard, his tortured expression a silent plea for mercy. But the eyes were devoid of compassion. They burned with hunger for the kill.

'I suppose Jonathan and I are lucky being only children. We never have to worry about whether our parents love us as much as our siblings. And when a sibling dies we never have to worry about whether our parents would have wished it was us instead. It must be terrible, having to carry that knowledge around inside you. But try not to let it upset you. I'm sure your parents are fond of you.' A pause. 'In their own way.'

He couldn't stand any more. Letting out a sob he ran from the room.


Quarter to eight. Alan Stewart walked down the darkened corridor towards his classroom. He had left his cigarettes in his desk and wanted to retrieve them before he started the evening's marking.

During the day the corridor was full of noise but now all was silent; the only sound the clicking of his heels on the well polished floor. But as he approached his destination he realised that he could hear a muffled whimpering sound.

He slowed his pace, trying to identify the source. No one should be here at this hour. Masters were supposed to keep their classrooms locked outside school hours. But inevitably there was always someone who forgot.

He saw that one door was open a fraction. He walked through it and turned on the light. Nicholas Scott was sitting at one of the desks. His head was buried in his hands; his glasses perched on the desk in front of him. He was sobbing as if his heart would break. He was so distressed that he didn't seem to realise that the light had been turned on.

Alan was horrified. His first thought was that one of Nicholas's parents must have died. 'Scott, what is it?!'

Nicholas started violently. He looked up, his reddened eyes widening with alarm. 'It's all right, Scott,' said Alan gently. 'It's just me, no one else.' He closed the door behind him. 'What's happened?'

Nicholas struggled to regain his composure. 'Nothing sir,' he gulped, wiping at his eyes.

'It doesn't look like nothing to me,' said Alan kindly. He sat down at the desk beside Nicholas. 'What's this all about? Have you had bad news from home?'

'No, sir.'

'What is it then?'

Nicholas reached for his glasses. Alan smiled reassuringly. 'Why don't you tell me? Has someone done something to hurt you?'

Nicholas shook his head.

'They have, haven't they? What's happened?'

'I can't tell you, sir.'

Alan was about to make promises about confidentiality when suddenly it came to him.

'This is to do with Palmer and Rokeby, isn't it?'

He saw Nicholas tense. He knew he was right.

'No, sir.'

'What did they do to you?'

'Nothing, sir.'

'Scott, this is important.'

'Nothing's happened, sir.'

Alan took a deep breath. 'Scott, listen to me. I'm not a fool.

I have eyes. I see what goes on. I know how close you and Palmer are. Only now Rokeby's got in the way hasn't he?'

Nicholas stared down at the desk, saying nothing.

'I'd expect you to be jealous of Rokeby,' said Alan, making his voice as soothing as possible. 'It's a natural reaction. I know I've felt it as a boy. But it's more than that, isn't it? I've seen the way you look at Rokeby. He frightens you, doesn't he?'

Nicholas didn't answer, but Alan sensed he was close to a breakthrough. 'Doesn't he?' he asked gently.

Slowly Nicholas nodded.

'Why Scott? Has he been violent towards you?'

'No, sir.'

'Has he threatened you in some way?'

'No, sir.'

'Why then? Is it yourself you're frightened for, or someone else?' No answer. 'Is it Palmer?'

'Yes.'

'Why Scott? You must tell me? What is going on between those two?'

Nicholas began to cry again. Alan put an arm around him. 'I'm sorry, Scott. I don't want to upset you, but I have to know. Is Palmer in some sort of danger?'

'He swore to me,' whispered Nicholas.

'Who did?'

'He promised me! It was the most painful thing in the world to me! And then the two of them sit there and laugh about it like it's a big joke! How could he do that to me? After I went along with everything? I didn't want to but I was scared for him and I didn't have any choice.'

Alan was confused. 'Scott, what are you saying? What did you go along with?'

'Well damn him! Damn them both! They're welcome to each other! I wish they were both bloody dead!'

Sobbing, Nicholas jumped to his feet and ran from the room.

✳     ✳     ✳

Prep had finished an hour ago but Stephen and Michael still sat at Stephen's desk poring over a Maths book.

'Do you understand now?' asked Stephen.

Michael nodded.

'Explain it to me then.'

'Can't be bothered.'

Stephen sighed with exasperation. 'You don't understand at all.'

'I do!'

'Mike, you've got to make more of an effort. I won't be there in the exam.'

'I know,' said Michael irritably.

'So pay attention then. Don't just sit there and daydream. You can't rely on me all the time.'

'I don't. I'm not that desperate.'

'You are. They'd have kept you down a year if it wasn't for me.'

'And don't I know it! Don't you ever get tired of being perfect?!'

'There's no need to be like that.'

'Why not?! I'm sick of you always acting like you're better than me.'

'I'm not doing that! I just don't want you to fail your exams. If you did we could end up in different classes and you'd hate that.'

'So would you.'

'Yes I would. So try and make an effort, OK? For both our sakes.'

The two of them had been so busy arguing that only now did they realise that Nicholas had entered the room.

He sat at his desk, his shoulders hunched, his eyes red and swollen.

'You'd better wash your face,' said Stephen after a long silence. 'You don't want people to see you've been crying.'

'The bell will be going in a few minutes,' added Michael, 'You'd better go now.'

Nicholas remained where he was. Michael stared expectantly at Stephen. For a moment Stephen did nothing. Then he nodded. The two of them rose to their feet.

'We'll come with you if you like. Make sure no one sees.'

They walked up to Nicholas. 'What happened?' asked Michael. Stephen shook his head. He put his hand on Nicholas's shoulder. 'Forget about them Nick. They're not worth it.'

'I know,' said Nicholas slowly. 'I know.'

'Come on then. We'd better go now.'

Together the three of them left the study.

# Chapter Eight

Last period on Saturday morning. Alan Stewart had finished discussing the causes of the Civil War with the fourth-year class. Now, in the dying minutes of the lesson, the class sat in supposed silence, studying the summary of the War that was set out in their textbooks.

In truth little reading was taking place. The air was full of the soft buzz of whispered conversation. Alan always tried to finish a little early on Saturday. He knew the boys were excited about their weekend and did not think it fair to demand that they concentrate until the final bell.

But on this particular morning he had his own reasons for not demanding silence. There was a situation which called for his intervention, but he needed to check the current state of its dynamics before taking any action.

There had been a change in the seating arrangements. Jonathan Palmer had moved from the desk he shared with Nicholas Scott and now sat with Richard Rokeby. Their heads were bent together, the attention of each completely focused on the other. They had about them an aura of apartness, as if they were present in body but not in spirit.

Nicholas Scott now sat alone. Stephen and Michael Perriman were whispering to each other and Alan was pleased to see that Nicholas was once again included in their exchanges. But

Nicholas himself did not seem pleased. Frequently he cast his eyes towards the desk by the window where Jonathan now sat with Richard, and his face was a mask of pain and . . .

And what?

Alan didn't know. He couldn't figure it out.

What had gone on between the three of them? He needed to get to the bottom of it, but if Scott's reaction was anything to go by he wondered if he ever would.

These were the boys he was interested in. The ones he wanted to observe. But, unexpectedly, another boy also attracted his attention.

James Wheatley sat alone at the back of the classroom. He talked to no one but was not looking at his book. He stared blankly in front of him. His face was grey, his features strained. There were huge bags under his eyes. He looked exhausted, as if he could drop at any minute, but he was not still. Almost imperceptively he was shaking in his seat, as if his body was charged with static.

Alan sensed movement at the front of the class. Jonathan and Richard had turned and were studying Wheatley. Richard whispered something to Jonathan who whispered a response. Then they turned back to face the front. Both were smiling.

Wheatley looked as if he belonged on his deathbed, not in a classroom. What on earth was wrong with him?

And did Richard and Jonathan have something to do with it?

No, of course not. How could they? He was letting his imagination run away with him.

But it didn't seem like imagination.

The bell rang for the end of the lesson. Wheatley, almost jumping out of his skin, let out a faint cry of alarm. Many of the boys turned to stare at him. Alan saw Richard whisper something to Jonathan. Both were trying to suppress laughter.

This couldn't go on. He had to do something. And quick.

'Wheatley, you look terrible. Forget about games this afternoon. Get yourself down to the sanatorium.'

Wheatley looked uncertain.

'It's not a suggestion. It's an order. Get yourself down there now.'

Wheatley nodded. He began to gather his books together. The rest of the class were filing out. Jonathan and Richard walked by Alan's desk. 'Palmer?'

Jonathan turned towards him. So did Richard. 'Sir?'

'I need to talk to you, about your last essay.'

Jonathan looked surprised. 'You said it was fine, sir.'

'It was. But there are a few things I think we should discuss.'

Jonathan nodded. Richard's eyes were suspicious. 'What things, sir?' he asked.

'None of your business, Rokeby. Palmer, perhaps you'd come to my study at four o'clock. Is that convenient?'

'Yes, sir.'

'Good. See you then.'

The two of them walked off together. Richard glanced back over his shoulder, his eyes still distrustful. Alan hoped he was doing the right thing.


Five past four. Alan sat in his study in Abbey House. It was a sizeable room, comfortably furnished and with a fire burning in the grate. There was a knock on the door.

'Come in.'

Jonathan entered, breathing hard as if he'd been running. 'Sorry I'm late, sir. We only finished games ten minutes ago.'

'Don't worry. Have a seat. Would you like tea?'

'Yes please, sir.'

Alan handed him a steaming cup. They sat on either side of the fire, staring at each other. A strong wind was blowing, rattling the windows. Jonathan smiled politely. His face was masklike, his manner guarded. He seemed altogether different from the boy Alan had watched and encouraged for the last twelve months.

'Thank you for coming, Palmer. I'm sorry to interrupt your half-holiday.'

'That's all right sir.'

'I thought we should have a talk.'

'About my essay, sir?'

'Actually no. About something else.'

The eyes did not register surprise. Richard must have guessed exactly what was coming and briefed Jonathan accordingly. 'What about then, sir?'

'About Richard Rokeby.'

A polite smile.

'The two of you seem to have become very intimate recently.'

'Intimate?'

'Close.'

'We're friends sir, if that's what you mean.'

'Good friends, judging by the fact that you're now sharing a desk. You should have checked with me before changing your seating arrangements.'

'I'm sorry, sir. I didn't think you'd mind.'

'I'm not saying that I mind . . .'

'So it's all right then.'

'Well, yes. It is all right. It's just that I would have expected you to ask. It seems out of character to just go ahead like that.'

'We didn't think it would matter, sir.'

Alan leant forward. 'We?'

'Rokeby and me, sir.'

Alan sipped his tea. 'You seem to have cut your ties with Scott and the Perrimans. What's happened to cause that?'

'Nothing, sir.'

'You've just stopped being friends.'

'Yes, sir.'

'And that was what you wanted?'

Jonathan nodded.

'Are you sure?'

'Yes, sir. Things change. I don't have to keep the same friends for ever.'

'Not if you don't want to. But Palmer it should be what *you* want. Not what somebody else wants.'

'I don't know what you mean, sir.' The face was still a mask but a defensive note had crept into the voice.

'I think you do.'

'No, sir.'

'It was what Rokeby wanted, wasn't it?'

'No, sir.'

'So it's just coincidence that as soon as you become friendly with Rokeby you drop everyone else.'

'It wasn't like that, sir.'

'So what was it like?'

Jonathan shrugged.

'Perhaps you and Rokeby just have more in common than the others?'

Jonathan nodded.

'I see.' Alan smiled in understanding. 'You just like doing different things?'

Jonathan smiled back. 'Yes, sir.'

'What things?'

The smile faltered. A slight pause. 'Nothing in particular, sir.'

'But you've just said that you and Rokeby like doing different things to the others. What things are those?'

Another shrug. 'Just stuff.'

'What sort of stuff?'

'I don't know. Talking.'

'You couldn't talk to the others?'

'Not like I can talk to Rokeby, sir.'

'Not even Scott?'

Jonathan said nothing. The mask remained in place but a new emotion was starting to creep into the eyes. Shame. Alan sensed he was making progress. 'Not even Scott?' he said again.

'No, sir.'

'He was your best friend, wasn't he?'

'Yes, sir'.

'The two of you were inseparable.'

'I suppose so'.

'Until Rokeby came along.'

Another shrug. Not as convincing as the last one. 'Like I said sir, things change.'

'That's right, they do. You've chummed up with Rokeby.'

A nod.

'And Scott's left to cry alone.'

The eyes widened. 'What do you mean?'

Now it was Alan's turn to shrug.

'When was he crying?'

'Last night. I found him in one of the classrooms.'

Jonathan looked appalled. 'Was he all right?!'

'What do you care? He's no friend of yours.'

'That doesn't mean I want him to be unhappy. Why was he crying?'

'You tell me.'

'I don't know!'

'Don't you?'

'No!'

'I think you do, Palmer. I think you know very well.'

Jonathan swallowed. 'All right. He'd had an argument with Richard. But I didn't think he'd be that upset about it.'

'What was the argument about?'

'I don't know! I wasn't there. It was just an argument. People have arguments all the time.'

'It must have been a savage one to leave him that upset.'

Jonathan shook his head.

'How do you know? You've just said you weren't there?'

'Richard told me what happened.'

'Did he tell you what he'd said to upset Scott so much?'

'He didn't say anything!'

'Yes he did. He just chose not to tell you. Just as you're choosing not to believe it.'

'It's not true! Richard's not like that!'

'Isn't he?'

'NO!'

'Then why does he frighten Scott so much?'

'Because he's stupid!! Richard wouldn't do anything to hurt him!'

'Perhaps not,' said Alan slowly. 'But you see, Palmer, that's not what Scott's afraid of.'

Jonathan looked confused. 'What do you mean?'

'He's afraid of what Rokeby might do to you.'

'Me?!'

Alan nodded.

'But that's rubbish!'

'Is it? Scott doesn't strike me as stupid. Far from it in fact.'

'Richard wouldn't hurt me!'

'So why is Scott afraid for you?'

'I don't know!'

'What is going on between you and Rokeby to make him so afraid?'

'I don't know!'

'No, of course you don't. Just like you don't know what's wrong with James Wheatley.'

Jonathan paled. Beads of sweat began to appear on his forehead.

Alan felt his heart sink as he realised that what he had tried to dismiss as imagination was all too true.

'Oh Jonathan,' he whispered, more to himself than to his companion, 'what on earth have you got yourself into?'

Jonathan stared back at him. He was shaking. His eyes were fearful. He looked like what he was; a young, vulnerable boy. Alan knelt down beside him and rubbed his arm with his hand; his inquisitorial tone replaced by one that was as soothing as he could manage.

'Jonathan, listen to me. I'm trying to help you. Do you think I don't understand how you feel? I went to a school like this. I know how powerless you feel. I know how wonderful . . .' – he struggled for the right word – 'how magnetic, someone like Rokeby must seem. But Jonathan that sort of magnetism is dangerous. It's seductive. It can make you do things that normally you wouldn't dream of doing.

'When I see you with Rokeby I don't see the boy I've known and liked for the last twelve months. I see someone else. Someone I don't like at all. Someone who has nothing to do with the real Jonathan Palmer.

'I don't know what's going on between the two of you. Perhaps it's none of my business. But you have to believe me when I say that this friendship is harmful to you. It's leaving you isolated and if you're isolated then you become dependent. For your own sake you need to break it. You know that don't you?'

Jonathan's lip was trembling. His eyes were filling with tears. Alan knew that he had achieved a breakthrough. He put an arm around Jonathan's shoulders. 'Why don't you tell me what's been going on, eh? Let's see if we can sort it out before things get messy.'

Jonathan nodded. He opened his mouth to speak.

There was a knock on the door.

Alan cursed under his breath. 'Go on,' he told Jonathan encouragingly. 'Whoever it is will go away.'

But they didn't. There was another knock. 'I'm busy!' called out Alan. 'Come back later.'

'I'm sorry, sir, but I really need to speak to you.' It was Patrick Marsh, a house prefect.

'Stay where you are,' whispered Alan to Jonathan. 'I'll be as quick as I can.'

Alan stood in the doorway, talking with Patrick. Jonathan sat, staring at the ground. His head was spinning. He wished Patrick would go away. He needed to talk. There were things he needed to tell.

He knew he shouldn't. Richard would think it madness and Richard was always right. He trusted Richard implicitly. But he couldn't stop thinking of Nicholas who had always stood by him only to be abandoned and left to cry in the dark. Richard was to blame for that. But he had played his part too, and now that Richard wasn't here he could see what he was becoming, and the reality frightened him.

He rubbed at his temples. He wanted to think clearly but his thoughts were like pieces of string that kept tangling with each other, forming knots that he could not unravel. He was rocking back and forth in his seat. His feet scuffed the carpet, nudging a pile of books by his chair, sending them toppling over. He bent down to rearrange them. A piece of paper had slipped from one of them. A drawing of some sort. He picked it up and stared at it.

It was a cartoon. In the background was a harbour, full of fishing boats. In the foreground stood a figure, wrapped in a cape so that only the face was exposed. The mouth was set in a grin revealing two fangs. The features were crude but the artist was skilled. It was clearly Paul Ellerson.

An aching started in his head. An idea had come to him, so huge that it felt as if his mind was being bent out of shape trying to accommodate it. Automatically he returned the cartoon to its place and rearranged the pile. The blood was pounding behind his eyes. He felt dizzy. He took a deep breath, then another, trying to steady himself.

The door closed. Once again Alan crouched down before Jonathan. 'I'm sorry, Palmer. We shouldn't be interrupted now.'

Jonathan looked blankly at him. He seemed dazed. Alan was concerned. 'Palmer, are you all right?'

Slowly Jonathan nodded.

'So then, why don't you tell me what's been going on.'

Jonathan stared at his teacher. A moment ago he had wanted to tell him everything. But that was before . . .

Before what?

The need to talk had left him. He needed to think about what he had seen. There were pieces that had to be put in place but could he arrange them himself? Perhaps, but he wanted Richard. He needed Richard.

'Well, Palmer?' said Alan gently.

'Well what, sir?'

'You were going to tell me what's been happening.'

'I've changed my mind,' said Jonathan slowly.

Alan was thrown. 'But I don't understand . . .'

'There's nothing to understand, sir. I've changed my mind. As you said yourself sir, what goes on between Rokeby and myself is none of your business.'

As he spoke Jonathan listened to his own voice. It sounded very far away, as if the words were being spoken by someone else. Richard perhaps. It was the sort of thing that Richard would say. He liked that.

'I have to go, sir. I have some work to do. Is that all right sir?'

Alan nodded weakly. Jonathan rose to go.

'Palmer.'

'Sir?'

'I'm always here if you need to talk. You know that, don't you?'

Jonathan nodded. Slowly he walked out of the room.

Alan remained where he was, kneeling in front of the fire, wondering what on earth had gone wrong. Outside, Jonathan raced towards Richard's room.

✻　　✻　　✻

James Wheatley sat in a bed in the school sanatorium. His pyjama top was open. Doctor Tasker and Sister Clark stared down at him.

'Where did the bruising come from?' asked Doctor Tasker.

'Got it in rugby.'

'It looks painful,' said Sister Clark.

'I got stamped on in the scrum. It happens all the time. It's no big deal.'

'Well apart from that,' announced Doctor Tasker solemnly, 'there's nothing wrong with your stomach.'

James glared at him. 'I told you, I feel sick.'

'Have you been sick?'

'Yes.'

'When?'

'This morning. After breakfast.' Doctor Tasker looked sceptical. 'It's true!'

Doctor Tasker shook his head. 'You don't look nauseous. What you do look is exhausted. When was the last time you had a good night's sleep?'

'Last night.' Doctor Tasker raised a bushy eyebrow. 'I did!'

'Judging by your appearance you haven't slept for days.'

Sister Clark nodded her agreement. 'It's nothing to worry about,' she said kindly. 'Everybody suffers from insomnia at some point.'

'I'm not sleeping badly!' cried James. 'I feel sick, that's all! I've probably got food poisoning. Hardly surprising when you think of the muck we get to eat here.'

'That's enough,' said Doctor Tasker sharply. 'I'm tired of you boys going on about the food. If it was really as disgusting as you'd have us believe then you'd all have starved to death years ago.'

'We would have done,' James told him, 'if God hadn't given us toasters.'

Doctor Tasker turned to Sister Clark. 'I prescribe three days' bed rest with as much sleep as possible.' James opened his mouth to protest. 'No arguments,' Doctor Tasker told him forcefully. 'Now lie down.' James ignored him. Angrily he began to knead the starched sheets with his hands. In the corridor someone dropped a tray with a harsh clang. The noise made James jump. Sister Clark and Doctor Tasker exchanged glances. 'James,' said Sister Clark slowly, 'is something troubling you?'

He stared at her suspiciously. 'No. Why should there be?'

'Because you're a bundle of nerves,' Doctor Tasker told him. 'Are you sure there's nothing worrying you? That could explain why you're not sleeping.'

'I *am* sleeping! I'm sleeping fine! Why won't you believe me?!'

Sister Clark sighed. Outside it was growing dark. She turned on the light and went to draw the curtains. Doctor Tasker shook his head. 'Have it your own way. The verdict still stands. Now I've got other boys to see.' He left the room. Frustrated, James rubbed at his neck. 'Why don't I fetch you a nice mug of cocoa?' said Sister Clark encouragingly. 'It might help you relax.'

The last thing James wanted was a soothing hot drink. He was on the point of telling Sister Clark where she could stick her nice mug when suddenly he understood what was happening. He saw the helplessness of his position. He was completely at her mercy. If he were to survive he would have to be crafty. He forced a smile. 'That would be nice. Thank you.'

She went to make it. He stared around him. There were five more beds in the room, all of which were empty. He wasn't sure whether that was a good thing or not. It was cold in the room. In spite of the wind outside, the window was half open. Doctor Tasker was obsessed with the beneficial qualities of fresh air. The road to hell is paved with good intentions and people always joked that the path to Doctor Tasker's surgery was paved with frozen corpses. At this moment in time James was glad of this obsession. When you were shivering it was harder to fall asleep.

Sister Clark returned with a steaming mug. He took a tiny

sip. The sweet taste made him feel sick. She watched him expectantly. He made his opening gambit. 'It's very hot. I'll wait until it cools.' It didn't work. She remained where she was. More extreme measures were needed. He lay down in his bed. 'I'm sorry if I was rude before. You're right. I haven't been sleeping. I just felt stupid saying so. Insomnia's the sort of thing my mother would go to the doctor for.' He faked a yawn that quickly became one that was all too real.

It worked. She softened. 'Very well. You finish that. I'll be back in ten minutes to collect the mug and turn the light out.'

As soon as she had left he hurried to the window and disposed of the contents of the mug. As he'd suspected there were telltale traces of residue at the bottom. A trick to aid his slumbers. Stupid cow.

Ten minutes later he was curled up into a ball, his eyes tight shut, breathing deeply and easily. Sister Clark nodded approvingly. She straightened the sheets around him, picked up the empty mug and turned out the light.

As her footsteps died away he sat up in bed, kicked away the sheets and removed his pyjama top. The cold swept over him. His skin erupted in goosebumps. He stared into the darkness that engulfed him. In his head he made a list of all the songs he knew and began to mouth the words to each, one after another. His hands were clenched into fists. When he felt his eyes closing he jabbed them into his bruised ribs.


As soon as she entered the house Marjorie Ackerley knew that something was wrong.

It was half past four. Henry's coat and umbrella hung in the hallway. The morning post was stacked neatly on the hall table waiting for her attention. In the distance she could hear the gramophone playing a Mozart concerto. Everything was as it should be. But something was wrong.

She sensed it with an instinct honed over more than twenty

years of marriage. She took a deep breath and steeled herself for what was to come.

She walked into the drawing-room. Henry sat in his usual chair by the fireplace. A bottle of scotch, half full this morning but now empty stood on the table by his chair. He was cradling a glass in his hands, rolling the last drops round and round, staring at them as if hypnotised. He didn't realise she was there. She called his name softly. He looked up. His eyes were glazed but hostile. She felt afraid. She was always frightened when he was drunk.

'What do you want?' he demanded. His voice was clear. He never slurred his words, however intoxicated.

'I just wondered how you were?'

'Checking I'm still here more like.' He laughed. The sound made her flinch.

'Don't say that.'

'Why not? It's true. Even now you're scared I'll run off. Christ knows why. You're the one holding the chain. You'll always be able to haul me back wherever I go.'

'Henry ...'

'What? We both know it's true.' He pointed to the empty bottle. 'I told you to get another.'

'Haven't you had enough?'

'I'll have as much as I want. I pay the rent. Not you.'

'I know that. It's just that it's not good for you.'

'Makes me less easy to control. Is that what you mean?'

She shook her head.

'Good. You don't control me.' He paused, stared down at the glass. 'No one controls me.'

'Has something happened?' He ignored her. 'Tell me,' she said encouragingly. He muttered something under his breath. She thought she heard the word bastard. 'Henry, what is it?'

'Wants to make me sweat. Thinks he can make me dance to his tune.'

'Who does?'

'Thinks he's so clever. Staring at me with those eyes. Trying to intimidate me. Well it won't work! He's going to rue the day he crossed swords with me.'

'Henry, I don't understand ...'

'Him *and* his bastard friend. His bastard friend with his bastard accent. Little bastard! Little whining Yorkshire bastard!'

She flinched. He turned towards her. The hostility in his eyes had now become outright malevolence. 'You bitch! You come in here and ask about my problems!'

'Now Henry ...'

He rose to his feet. The glass was still clasped in his hand. 'Pretending to care! Pretending to be concerned when every problem I've had in my fucking life is because of you!'

He took a step towards her. Involuntarily she took one back. 'Henry, for God's sake ...'

'IT'S ALL YOUR FAULT! ALL OF IT!!'

He hurled the glass at the wall behind her head. Splinters showered the room. She screamed and covered her eyes. He was shaking with rage. 'YOU DON'T CONTROL ME!! YOU DON'T CONTROL MY LIFE!!'

She was afraid. But the words struck a nerve deep within her. She stood and faced him. 'Oh but I do Henry. And do you know why? Because you're too weak to control it yourself.'

His jaw dropped. His mouth lolled open as if he were retarded. 'What do you mean?'

'You're weak Henry. You always have been. I knew it as soon as I met you.'

'You're lying!'

'No I'm not. I do control you. You're easy to control. You act as if you're strong and decisive but it's all a sham. Underneath you're a man of straw.'

'SHUT UP!! SHUT UP!!'

'So go ahead and blame me if it makes you feel better. Scream at me. Do whatever it takes to stop you having to face up to how weak you really are!'

He punched her in the face.

She staggered back, one hand raised to cover the spot where he had hit her, the other held out in a feeble attempt to ward him off. He struck her again. She fell to the floor. He kicked her in the stomach. She screamed and tried to curl herself into a ball. His fist was pulled back, ready to strike the next blow.

Ten past seven. Evening prep had started. Alan Stewart sat at the desk in his study. A pile of papers lay in front of him. Twenty-five descriptions of the causes of the French Revolution. The evening's marking.

But the papers remained untouched. His mind was far away; reliving a scene that he had witnessed as a thirteen-year-old at his school in Surrey and had spent the rest of his life trying to forget.

The school had been in a state of uproar. One of the fifth years in Alan's House had been caught engaging in mutual masturbation with one of the gardeners. Reprisals had been swift and terrible. The gardener had been dismissed on the spot. The boy had been marched into a packed assembly hall, thrashed by the headmaster, branded a pervert and told that he was to leave the school on the first train the next morning.

That night Alan and his classmates had been roused from their beds. They had been marched downstairs to the changing rooms where the other boys in the House were already assembled. They had stood in the darkness, waiting in expectant silence until the door burst open. The prefects marched in dragging the culprit behind them. He was gagged: his face bruised and bleeding; his expression one of blind terror. A laundry basket was positioned in the middle of the room and the culprit was forced to bend over it. His pyjama bottoms were torn off and he was given an enema; a mixture of treacle, water and salt, administered with a bicycle pump. The whole thing had been carried out in virtual silence; the only sounds the muffled howls of the culprit. Shock caused him to lose control of himself. As the prefects went about their work the stench of urine and excrement filled the room.

When it was over the head of house announced that the same punishment would be suffered by all perverts. He then ordered everyone back to bed. They had filed out as quietly as they had come, leaving the culprit curled up in a ball, whimpering with pain and humiliation.

The next morning the culprit had carried his suitcase to the station. Boys had lined his route to the school gate, pelting him with eggs, fruit and whatever else they could get their hands on, shouting abuse as they did so. The air had been thick with the sound of hate: the howl of the many as they rejoiced in the destruction of the one. The culprit had been a pitiful figure; shuffling, head bent, eyes swollen from crying; suit plastered with filth. Alan had stood and jeered along with the rest. And as he did so he had wanted to cry with fear because this was the punishment for desires that he was starting to recognise in himself.

At that moment something had shut down inside himself. A door in his mind had been bricked up so that the room behind it could never again be entered. No one need know that it had ever existed. He might even forget its existence himself.

In the fifteen years since that day he had largely succeeded. He had progressed smoothly through the school, distinguishing himself both academically and athletically. He had read History at Cambridge with equal success. He was popular with his elders and his peers. He enjoyed his studies and had a gift for communicating that enjoyment to others; making even the driest areas seem fertile with life. He was a born teacher. And when he saw his friends leaving university and stumbling from one unsatisfying job to another he was grateful for having found his vocation before his working life had even begun.

He could have stayed at Cambridge and become a lecturer.

Instead he had taken a position at a public school in Hampshire. In his mind he was already formulating his life plan. His own schooldays had been a mass of ritual and savagery, dictated by a system that he considered flawed and wanted to help change. He would progress through the ranks, become a headmaster and mould the school in question to the shape of his own personality. It would be an example to other schools; his gift to those who came after him.

Kirkston Abbey was only his second school. Already he was an assistant housemaster and head of his department. His power was increasing, he was starting to make his mark, and when he felt he had achieved all he could here he would move on to another school and achieve even more. He expected to be a headmaster in ten years and then the serious work could begin. It would be challenging but it would also be rewarding and he was grateful to have a purpose into which he could pour all his energies. It helped him to ignore the emptiness that gaped like an open wound in another part of his life.

There had been women in his life. One at college. Two since. He had cared for them with an affection that had everything to do with tenderness and nothing to do with passion. He had taught himself to think that this was how it should be; that companionship and shared ambitions were the necessary building blocks from which to construct desire.

It had been that way with Charlotte. She had seemed the perfect life partner in every way. All their interests had been mutual. They had liked the same books, the same films, laughed at the same jokes, shared the same dreams. He had told her of his ambitions and she had applauded and encouraged them; had shown him in a hundred different ways that she wanted to be a part of them. When the two of them had been guests of Clive and Elizabeth she had sparkled at the table. She was attractive, animated and entertaining. She had charmed them both and as she did so she would catch his eye and give him a shy, secret smile that said look how people respond to me; look at how much they like me; look how much help I can be to you if you just let me into your life. And as he smiled back he told himself that this was all that he could ever want, and that the gentle warmth in his heart when he stared into her eyes marked the dawning of a genuine passion that would fill the emptiness in his life and make it complete.

Perhaps he had been right. Perhaps it could have worked between them if he had just given it more time. But it was not to be. From that moment six months ago, when Paul Ellerson came into his life, there had been no room for anyone else.

Even now, after all the misery, there were still aspects of the relationship that seemed wonderful. It was as if he'd spent the whole of his life sleepwalking underground before suddenly awaking in the full heat of the sun. He had tried to fight against it, had told himself that it was wrong, but it had been no good. The sheer fact that it was possible to feel this way about another human being, and to have that feeling reciprocated, had blinded him to all the dangers.

Over the summer the two of them had spent a week together in a rented cottage in Whitby. The days had been spent exploring the surroundings together, talking about everything and nothing, always laughing, luxuriating in the intimacy permitted them in a place where they were known by no one and ran no risk of censure. The nights had been spent in another form of intimacy, one that was new and wonderful to both of them, and when it was over and they had lain peacefully together in the darkness he had felt as if he had been lost but had now, at last, found his way home. It had been the happiest time in his life.

Until the last night, when his dreams had led him back to the school changing rooms, alone this time, shivering with cold and fear. The door had burst open, the prefects marched in with their victim and proceeded to administer the punishment. Horrified, he had tried to run, but found himself paralysed, unable to do anything but stand by and watch. Behind him, in the darkness, he could feel the stirrings of life. The jeering began;

one voice after another, building to a crescendo like a symphony of hate. And as he watched the victim turned his head towards him and he recognised his thirteen-year-old self. The terrified eyes begged him for assistance but all he could do was shake his head, his pity eclipsed by terror that someone would realise that the two of them were one and turn upon him too.

At last he found the strength to turn, only to find his path blocked by all the people he had ever known in his life, each nodding in approval as they watched the punishment; their mouths twisted with the obscenities they were screaming, their features contorted with revulsion, their eyes glazed with hate . . .

He had woken with a cry, his heart pounding, his body bathed in sweat. Paul had tried to soothe him, telling him that it was just a dream. He had allowed himself to be comforted. But for the rest of the night he had lain awake beside his lover, crying softly, knowing that the last week had been a beautiful illusion that would never be repeated. There could be no future for them in a world that would never accept them. The most wonderful thing that had happened to him was over almost as soon as it had begun.

For the rest of the summer he had wrestled with his conscience. He had tried to convince himself that there was hope; that the two of them could go away together and try and build a life far away. But he knew that he was lying to himself; that for all the misery that separation would cause him he lacked the courage to see it through.

On the first evening of the new term Paul had come to see him. He had explained, as gently as he could, that for both their sakes it had to end. Paul had hung his head and wept; the tears like drops of acid on his heart. 'Don't,' he had said gently, starting to cry himself. 'Please don't.'

'Why not?'

'Because I can't bear it.'

'Then don't do this.'

'I have to. Can't you understand that?'

'How can I understand it? We love each other. What else matters but that?'

'Everything. You talk about love. You make it sound beautiful. But to the world what we feel is an abomination. People would never accept us. We'd always be outcasts. You're only eighteen. I can't ask you to live the rest of your life like that.'

Paul had raised his head and stared at him. 'Why not? It's my life and it's my choice. You're everything to me. I don't want a life without you. Let people hate us if they're stupid enough to do so. I'm not afraid of the ignorance of others.'

Now it was his turn to hang his head. 'No,' he replied softly, 'but I am.'

For a time they had sat in silence. Then Paul had sighed; a sound full of loss and regret.

'I'm sorry,' Alan had whispered. 'It has to be this way.'

'Then there's nothing for it,' said Paul sadly, rising to his feet and walking away, leaving him to cry alone.

The next morning, when he heard the news, he had wanted to die. He had stood in his bathroom with a razor to his wrist and had willed himself to carry out the act. But he couldn't see it through. Though he was afraid of the world's scorn, he was also afraid to leave it.

So he had continued with his life. More than ever he had poured himself into his work. He told himself that it was important; that there was much good that he could achieve. But he was lying to himself. It was nothing more than a hole in which he could bury himself and try to escape from the pain of his loss. And his guilt.

Now he sat in his study, reliving the scene of fifteen years ago. This time the victim was his adult self, and all those who stood and watched his punishment wore Paul Ellerson's face. All were nodding in approval. As he pictured the scene he was nodding too.

\*     \*     \*

Richard and Jonathan sat facing each other on Richard's bed. They had been talking for hours.

'It all fits together,' announced Richard. 'Don't you see?'

Jonathan shook his head.

'Deny it all you want to, but we both know it's true.'

'We don't know for sure.'

'Of course we do. How else do you explain it?'

'I don't know.'

'Exactly. There is no other explanation. Paul's put forward as an Oxbridge candidate. He gets personal tuition, just like all the candidates do. His special subject is History so he gets Mr Stewart. They're on their own together a couple of times a week. They get to know each other and something starts.'

Once again Jonathan shook his head. Richard looked cynical.

'I would have known!'

'How?'

'I just would.'

'Rubbish! They weren't going to walk around holding hands. Paul was never going to call you in one day and say, "Palmer, thanks for keeping my study so clean and, by the way, I'm having a thing with Mr Stewart and thought you should know." The *last* thing they'd want would be for someone to find out. They would have done everything to make sure that never happened. No one would have known if you hadn't seen that drawing.'

Jonathan stared at the floor. Deep down he knew Richard was right. He just didn't want to believe it.

'Once you know about the holiday,' continued Richard, 'all the little things start to add up. You said that sometimes, towards the end of last term, Paul seemed preoccupied. You thought he was just anxious about the exams. But that was when the tuition started wasn't it? You said that one day you bumped into Guy Perry coming out of Paul's study and Guy said, "Perhaps he'll tell you her name because he won't tell me." You said that Paul was always winding Guy up by pretending to have fallen in love with some girl or other. You didn't think anything of it. But this time he wasn't pretending and Guy knew it. You said he seemed really excited about his holiday. You said it was because he was going somewhere he'd loved as a child. But that was crap. It didn't matter where he was going. What mattered was who he was going with. And then there was the last day. You saw him rushing off with some books. You thought he was going to the library but that was crap too. We both know where he was going . . .'

'Stop!' cried Jonathan. 'Please!'

'I will, if you just admit that I'm right.'

'All right. I admit it.' He rubbed at his head. 'I just don't believe it.'

'Incredible isn't it? Imagine what would have happened if the police had found out?'

Jonathan was still too shocked to think clearly. 'The police?'

'It's a criminal offence. They could have sent Mr Stewart to prison. They still could.'

'How? There's no proof.'

'We worked it out.'

'But that's based on assumptions. There's no actual proof. Like you said, they made sure that no one saw anything.'

'What about the drawing?'

'What about it? Mr Stewart could say Paul gave him the drawing as a joke. The police couldn't prove anything.'

'No, I suppose they couldn't.' Richard stretched his arms and then rested his back against the wall. He stared at Jonathan.

'But Mr Stewart doesn't know that does he?'

'What do you mean?'

'What do you think I mean?'

Understanding came in a rush, together with alarm. 'No way!'

'It should be what you want. You were so close to Paul. Now he's dead and it's all because of Mr Stewart.'

'Mr Stewart didn't kill him!'

'Not with his own hands. But he was responsible.'

'We don't know that! We don't know what happened at the end!'

'We can make a good guess. Trust me, Mr Stewart is as responsible for the death of Paul Ellerson as my father is for the death of my mother.'

Jonathan struggled for words but could find none. Richard's eyes were shining. He felt as if he were sinking in quicksand. In vain he shook his head.

'You don't care that Paul's dead?'

'Of course I do! You know I do!'

'But you don't want to do anything about it. You go on and on about wanting to understand what happened. Now you do know and you just sit there and act like you don't care.'

'Of course I care!'

'Good. You know what you have to do then.'

Richard's eyes transfixed him. He managed to look away. 'No! I don't want to do this! This isn't right!'

'Of course it's right! He deserves everything he gets. If you don't do it then I will!'

'You can't! It's nothing to do with you! You didn't even know Paul!'

'Do you think I give a damn about Paul Ellerson! That pig Stewart tried to come between us! He tried to separate us! If it was up to me I'd fucking kill him!'

Suddenly Jonathan understood, and with understanding came a lifeline.

'But he didn't succeed did he?' he said, making his voice as soothing as possible. 'No one will. You'll always be my friend. No one could ever turn me against you.'

The eyes seemed to soften. He persevered.

'Of course I hate him. I'd like to see him suffer. But Paul wasn't like that. Paul never hated anyone and I know he wouldn't want us to do anything. So we won't.' He paused nervously. 'OK?'

The eyes continued to bore into him. They made him feel dizzy. 'OK?' he asked again.

'Promise me,' said Richard.

'Promise what?'

'You know what.'

Jonathan swallowed. 'I promise. No one will ever break us up.'

'No they won't,' said Richard slowly. 'Because I won't let them. That's a promise too.'

As James Wheatley tripped he twisted his ankle. The pain woke him from sleep.

He lay in a heap on a floor of a corridor in the sanatorium. Everything was in darkness. All was still.

At first he didn't register the transition from sleep to waking. His mind remained locked within the dream. He scrambled to his feet, knowing that he had to keep going. He was lost if he stayed still. His eyes struggled to focus, to make sense of the shadows that enveloped him. They were moving. A pounding sound crept into his ears. But as the fog inside his head began to lift he realised that the movement was simply a curtain stirred by a draft and the noise just the beating of his own heart.

There was nothing. Just an empty corridor, as silent as the grave.

A scream was rising in his throat. He stifled it. Instead came tears that were a mixture of exhaustion and frustration. He needed to sleep. His body was screaming for sleep. But it was too dangerous. He had to keep awake.

The battle was growing harder and harder. Even now he could feel his eyes struggling to close. He jabbed his fist into his side, wincing as he hit the bruises that covered his skin like a patchwork quilt. Full consciousness was restored again but for how long? He couldn't fight against nature however hard he tried.

He told himself that they were just dreams. They couldn't hurt him however frightening they seemed. The rational part of his mind knew this to be the truth. He knew that were he to confide in adults they would tell him that too.

But another part; one that was all instinct, screamed otherwise.

For it was seeking him out. Each time he slept it drew closer, drawn to the smell of his fear like a predator drawn by the scent of blood. Sometimes he thought he heard it whisper his name and the sound had a hunger that made his blood run cold. His eyes would search for the source but find nothing. How could they see something that was not meant to be seen?

Sleep was his enemy, but a beautiful one. It was like a siren seducing him into her arms only to turn savage when she caught him in her embrace.

He made his way back to his room and sat on his bed. He was shivering with cold and exhaustion. More than anything he wanted to sink beneath the sheets and rest. But that was the one thing he could not do.

There was no one he could talk to. No one who would understand. He was alone and he was afraid.

He curled himself into a ball. Softly he began to whisper the words of the Lord's prayer.

# Chapter Nine

Sunday morning. Elizabeth Howard rang the doorbell for the second time. She stared up at the front of the house. All the curtains were drawn. There was no sign of life but she sensed that she was being watched. She considered ringing again but decided against it. If Marjorie didn't want to see her then so be it. She still had a dozen things to do before Jennifer arrived. She turned to go.

She heard movement behind her. The door opened a crack. 'Elizabeth, hurry!'

Confused she did as she was bid. She pushed the door closed behind her then stood and stared, too shocked to say anything.

Marjorie beckoned her into the drawing-room which looked out on to the walled garden at the back. The two of them sat together on a sofa. Elizabeth was close to tears. 'Oh my God ...'

Marjorie managed a tiny smile. 'It's not as bad as it looks.'

'But when? ... How? ...'

'Yesterday afternoon. I'm sure you don't need to ask how.'

'But why?'

'He was drunk. I provoked him.'

'Provoked him?!' What could you have done to deserve this?!'

'Told him things he didn't want to hear.'

'What things?'

'The truth.' Marjorie raised her hand and pressed gingerly at her swollen eye. Then she began to cry. Gently Elizabeth put an arm around her, holding her. The two of them sat like that for some time.

'I'm sorry' said Marjorie eventually. 'I shouldn't have called you in. But I feel so alone and you're the only person I'd trust to tell.'

'Of course you can trust me. You know that. Has he . . .'

'No,' said Marjorie quickly.

Elizabeth looked sceptical.

'There have been times when he's come close. Always when he's drunk. But he's never done this before. It was like he was mad. When his head cleared he didn't know what to do.'

'I know what to do,' said Elizabeth determinedly. 'You must go to the police.'

'The police?!' Marjorie's eyes widened. 'I can't do that!'

'Yes you can. You have to. What if he does it again?'

'He won't!'

'He might. You can't take the chance.'

Marjorie shook her head.

'Look at you! You should be in hospital! This isn't just some domestic argument. You have to report this!'

'I can't!' A note of panic had crept into Marjorie's voice.

'You don't have to be afraid. I'll come with you.'

'No!'

'You have to leave him! The man is dangerous! You can come to us. We're your friends. We'll help you.'

'No!' Marjorie's face was flushed. 'You don't understand! I can't go to the police! I can't!'

'For God's sake why not?!'

'BECAUSE . . .'

Marjorie stopped. Elizabeth stared at her. 'Because of what?' No answer. 'Because of what?!'

'Because of things I can't tell you or anyone else ever! Elizabeth you have to promise me you won't tell anyone about how you've found me. If anyone asks about me then say I've got the flu and I'll stay in the house until the bruises have gone. Do you promise?'

'But ...'

'Promise!'

'But this is madness! You ...'

'PROMISE!'

'All right! I promise! I won't tell anyone.'

'Thank you,' whispered Marjorie. She lowered her head and again touched the bruises on her face. Elizabeth sat and watched her, her stomach churning with a mixture of distress and confusion.

'It's getting worse,' said Marjorie softly. 'Every day it gets worse. I knew it would.' Her speech had a strange, trancelike quality, as if she were talking to herself. Elizabeth reached out and squeezed Marjorie's hand. Marjorie squeezed it back. 'I knew what I was getting into,' she continued. 'I only have myself to blame. I thought I knew it all. But oh God, Elizabeth, I never expected it to be like this.'

She rested her head on Elizabeth's shoulder. Once again she began to cry.

Clive Howard was reading the paper in his study when the maid came to tell him that Miss Sinclair had arrived. Cursing under his breath he made his way towards the drawing-room. Where the hell was Lizzie? She should be back from the Ackerleys by now.

Jennifer was standing by the window, wearing the dark blue suit she always wore when travelling. She smiled as he entered; her mouth a crimson slash of lipstick. Dutifully he went to kiss her. Her skin smelt of cheap scent heavily applied. He fought an urge to wipe his mouth. 'Drink?'

'Scotch.'

'A bit early isn't it?'

'Perhaps. So what?'

'Nothing.' He poured them both a drink. She sat down and lit a cigarette. 'Where's Lizzie?'

'Visiting friends. We didn't expect you until after lunch.'

'Caught an earlier train. Thought I'd surprise you. Why are you here anyway? Shouldn't you still be at church?'

'There's no service this morning. Evensong.'

'I see. So I have that delight to look forward to.' She took a long drag on her cigarette and blew smoke at him. 'Lucky me.'

'You don't have to attend.'

'Oh but I do. It's such fun to participate in these quaint rituals that you consider so important.'

'I'm sorry you find us so parochial. You didn't have to come.'

'Oh but I did. Dear Lizzie insisted.'

'And so you came. Turning down God knows how many other invitations just to grace us with your presence.'

He saw her tense. He knew the barb had hit home. She took another drag on her cigarette and stared at him coolly. 'Now Clive. Anyone would think I wasn't welcome here.' Her gaze made him feel uncomfortable. He stared down at his glass.

'That would upset me,' she continued, 'and you don't want to do that, do you Clive?'

He raised his head. 'Is that a threat?'

She smiled at him. Her gaze was like that of a cat studying its prey. 'You're such a decent man aren't you? Dear, kind, decent Clive. A prince among men. That's how Lizzie describes you.' She laughed softly. 'I wonder what words she'd use to describe you if she knew.'

Now it was his turn to tense. 'There's nothing to know.'

'I beg to differ.'

'It meant nothing. You know that.'

'To you perhaps. But what about me?'

'What about you? We both know what motivates you.'

Her eyes narrowed. She sipped at her drink. 'And what about Lizzie? What would it mean to her?'

'You know what it would mean to her!'

A smile began to play around the corner of her lips. 'Yes I do.'

Loathing rose in him like vomit. 'You bitch!'

'Dear Clive. Dear, kind, faithful Clive. And what does that make you?' She laughed and then downed the rest of her drink. She held out the glass to him. 'Be an angel and fetch me a refill.'

'Haven't you had enough?'

Again she laughed. 'Worried about my health, Clive? Or just worried that alcohol will loosen my tongue?'

'You wouldn't dare!'

'Wouldn't I?' She leant forward in her chair. She was still smiling. Her eyes were pools of venom. She gestured to their surroundings. 'This is a beautiful room. You have a beautiful home and a beautiful wife. You have a beautiful life in fact. And I can take it all away from you whenever I choose. I hold the power here, not you, and don't you ever forget it. Now get me another fucking drink!'

His hand tightened on the glass he held. It smashed between his fingers. He let the pieces fall to the floor. 'Get your own drink! I hope it chokes you!' He rose to his feet and marched from the room.


Half an hour later Alan Stewart was shown into Clive's study. 'Sorry to disturb you. Is now a good time?'

'Of course.' Clive gestured towards a seat. Alan noticed that a bandage was wrapped loosely round his hand. 'Accident?'

'Cut myself,' Clive told him. His tone was brusque.

'Are you sure this is a good time?' asked Alan.

'I just said so didn't I?!'

The uncharacteristic outburst took Alan by surprise. 'Of course,' he said awkwardly. 'I'm sorry.'

'No, I'm sorry,' said Clive quickly. 'That was uncalled for. Lizzie's cousin Jennifer has come to stay again and I've already managed to have a row with her.'

Alan smiled. 'She struck me as the sort of woman it would be easy to row with.'

'She is. Bloody woman! Why can't she just stay away?' Clive seemed on the point of saying more but then remembered himself. 'Anyway, I apologise. Let's start again. It's good to see you. Is this a social call?'

'Work related I'm afraid. It's about Jonathan Palmer.'

Clive thought for a moment. 'Isn't he the one who's chummed up with Richard Rokeby?'

Alan nodded. 'That friendship is the reason I'm here.'

'You have reservations?'

'I do.'

'Lizzie's no end bucked about it. She says it's just what Rokeby needs; thinks it will do him no end of good.'

'Perhaps it will. My concern is what it's doing to Palmer.'

Clive looked at him quizzically.

'I don't think this friendship is doing him any good. Quite the reverse in fact.'

'Why?' A look of alarm flashed across Clive's face. 'Christ, you don't think they're messing around with each other do you?!'

'No,' said Alan quickly. He flushed.

'Sorry. It's just the first thing that springs to mind.'

Alan shook his head.

'Thank God. After the Paul Ellerson business the last thing we need is some scandal over a couple of perverts.'

'No, of course not,' said Alan quietly.

'What is it then?'

'Do you know Palmer at all?'

'Not really. I've spoken to him once or twice. He seems a nice enough lad.'

'He is. That's the point.'

'Meaning?'

'I know him well. I've always liked him. He's good-natured. He's polite and enthusiastic. He has a close group of good friends. He works hard. He always tries his best and he wants to do well. I'd have described him as a sensible boy with his feet on the ground. At least he was until Rokeby came along.'

He stopped. Clive nodded encouragingly. 'Go on.'

'Since the friendship started there's been a huge change in Palmer. His work has started to suffer. He's cut himself off from his other friends. It's like he and Rokeby are in their own little world. And there's an edge to him. A' – he struggled for the right word – 'a malicious streak that wasn't there before and which I don't like at all.'

'I see.'

'I know it's none of my business. Friendships do change. It's a fact of life. But I'm worried about Palmer. I know his background. I know it's a struggle for his parents to send him here. He's always had the potential to do very well but now I think that potential is being damaged.'

'And you think Rokeby's responsible?'

'Yes I do. I'm sorry to come to you, Clive. Perhaps I should have gone to Palmer's housemaster, or Rokeby's. But I thought you'd understand. Lizzie told me once that you considered Rokeby destructive. At the time I thought that an extreme view. But now, when I see the change that's taking place in Palmer I don't think it's so extreme after all.'

Clive sighed. He sat back in his chair and stared up at the ceiling. Alan watched him anxiously. 'Well?'

'You're right to be worried. I do think he's destructive. I'd go so far as to say that he's the most destructive boy I've ever met.

'When he first arrived here I thought his whole persona was a sham. I've seen it so many times before: boys who pose as loners because they think it gives them charisma; boys who pretend they don't care what the world thinks when in truth their whole life is a performance designed to gain applause. At first I dismissed Rokeby as just another of those. But I was wrong.

'Because it's not an act. None of it. He really doesn't care. He doesn't want approval. He doesn't want to feel special or important. He doesn't want to connect at all. There's an anger at the centre of his being which is so powerful that it's destroyed any other emotion he might have had. Most of the time he keeps the anger hidden, but occasionally he lets it out and believe me when you see it you don't forget it. I've been a teacher for twenty years and he is the only boy I've ever encountered who's had the ability to frighten me.'

As he listened Alan shivered.

'What do you want me to do?' asked Clive. 'Speak to Palmer?'

'I've tried. It didn't do any good. He's too enthralled by Rokeby. I think he'd do anything Rokeby told him to.'

'So you want me to speak to Rokeby?'

'I did. Now I'm not sure. Do you think he'd listen?'

'Probably not.'

'What then? We can't just leave it.'

'I'm not suggesting that. For Palmer's sake we should do something.'

'But what?'

'I don't know, Alan. I really don't know.'


Sister Clark was on the way to her office when she heard a whimpering sound.

It was coming from the room where James Wheatley slept. She stopped and put her head round the door. Two rows of beds faced each other like rugby scrums. There was no sign of James.

She must have imagined it. She turned to go and heard the sound again.

'James? Are you there?'

She entered the room. The cold made her shiver. Silently she cursed Doctor Tasker and his mania for fresh air.

The sound was coming from behind the last bed on the right. She walked towards it. 'James? Is that you?'

Then she saw him. She let out a cry of alarm.

He was in the corner of the room, curled up in a foetal position, his face pressed against the wall. His skin glistened with sweat. His whole body was shaking.

She knelt down beside him. Softly she whispered his name. He continued to whimper. She tried again; louder this time. Still no response. Gently she placed a hand on his shoulder. He screamed and lashed out at her with his fists. She tried to grab hold of his arms. His eyes were wide with fear. He looked straight through her, staring at some point in the distance. 'James wake up! WAKE UP!'

At last his eyes focused on her. The blows stopped. The terror faded from his eyes, replaced by shock. His lip began to tremble. He burst into tears.

She stroked his head, making soothing noises. 'It was nothing James. Just a bad dream. That's all.'

'NO!'

'But James . . .'

'It's not a dream! It's happening!'

'Nothing's happening. You just imagined it. Is that what all this has been about? Bad dreams?' She smiled at him. 'Silly. They're nothing to be ashamed of. We all get them from time to time.'

'They're not dreams!'

'Of course they are. Now come on. Let's get you back to bed. You're going to make yourself ill if you don't get some rest.'

'Rest?!'

He started to laugh. There was a wildness in the sound that alarmed her. 'James, that's enough. It was just a dream. Nothing more. Now back to bed.'

'I won't sleep. I won't! You can't make me!'

'You have to sleep. I'll give you some pills to take. They're very good. I promise you won't dream.'

'NO!'

'Now James ...'

'I'M NOT TAKING YOUR FUCKING PILLS!'

Her jaw dropped. She stared at him.

'I'm not taking them! do you understand?'

She rose to her feet. 'Now listen here James Wheatley, I may not be one of your teachers but that doesn't give you the right to talk to me like that!'

'You're just like all the rest!!'

'James, I'm trying to help you!'

'NO YOU'RE NOT!! YOU'RE MAKING IT WORSE!! YOU'RE USELESS, JUST LIKE EVERYONE ELSE!! WHY DON'T YOU JUST FUCK OFF AND LEAVE ME ALONE!!'

Shaken she turned to go. 'I'll come back later when you've calmed down.' As she left the room she heard him sobbing.

After lunch Alan Stewart returned to his study.

He was feeling depressed. As he had eaten his overcooked beef and badly boiled vegetables he had watched Richard Rokeby and Jonathan Palmer sitting together on the corner of one of the fourth-year tables. Their heads had been bent together as if plotting. Other boys had sat near them but they still managed to give the impression that they were somehow separate from the rest. Splendid isolation. Just how Richard wanted it.

He sat down at his desk. In front of him was an unfinished letter to his sister. He picked it up. The camera in his mind was replaying the conversation with Clive. He was glad Clive appreciated the need for action. But now, after hearing what Clive had to say, a small part of him wondered whether intervention would make things worse rather than better.

Distracted as he was, it took him a moment to realise that

there was a piece of paper hidden under the letter. A sheet of expensive writing paper marked with one neatly printed sentence.

*Paul Ellerson's blood is on your hands.*

For a moment he feared he would lose control of himself. His hand began to shake. In his head was a single thought, battering the inside of his brain like a bird trapped in a cage.

*someone knows someone knows someone knows someone knows someone knows someone knows . . .*

Quarter past seven. Evensong had finished. The boys filed out of the school chapel into the cold night air; row by row, house by house. Most were silent; depressed by the end of the weekend and the prospect of another school week ahead.

Richard stood on the path, waiting for Jonathan. The wind whistled around him. He wrapped his arms around himself for warmth. It was a clear night. The vast Norfolk sky was filling with stars. As he stared up at them he thought of a night years ago when he had stood in the garden of his home with his mother kneeling beside him, teaching him to recognise the constellations. He tried to recognise them now but the act made him feel sad so he began to watch the people around him instead.

Nicholas Scott walked by with one of the Perrimans. He stared at Richard; his expression one of hostility laced with fear. Richard's instinct was to stare back but he decided against. There was no need. He had what he wanted. Nicholas was no longer a threat and it would just be a waste of energy.

Close by, Mr and Mrs Howard stood talking to Reverend Potter, all sharing a joke. Another woman stood with them, laughing along. He had seen her before. Mrs Howard's cousin. As he watched she tapped Mr Howard's arm. Mr Howard turned towards her. He was still smiling but a tension came into his face. Briefly her hand lingered on his arm. She said something to him.

He replied a little too quickly and then turned back to his wife. For a moment she looked hurt, but when the laughter started up again she was quick to join in. The four of them moved away. In the distance Richard saw Jonathan. 'At last! I thought you'd taken holy orders!'

'Sorry. Brian Harrington made us stay and tidy up the hymnbooks.'

'Let's go back to mine.'

As they walked he grabbed Jonathan affectionately in a neck lock. He heard Sam Green mutter something about poofs. 'None of that Sammy boy,' he said loudly, 'or we'll have to stick you in a gas oven.' Around him he could hear gasps of shocked laughter. Sam scowled and marched off.

'You shouldn't have said that,' Jonathan told him.

'Why not? Because it's not nice? I know it's not. But it is funny.'

'Not to Sam.'

'Good. It'll teach him to mind his own business.'

'You don't care what anyone thinks, do you?'

'I care what you think. But sod the rest of them. Stuff them all in gas ovens. I'll even supply the matches.'

Jonathan grimaced. 'Don't say things like that.'

'Why not?'

'Because sometimes you sound like you mean them.'

'I do.'

The two of them stared at each other. 'Don't you ever get tired of hating?' asked Jonathan.

'No. It's what I'm good at.'

'It just scares me, that's all. What if you decided you hated me?'

'You?' Richard laughed. 'I'd never do that. You don't need to be scared.'

'Promise?'

'Promise. You're my friend. Keep being my friend and I'll never hate you. Now come on, I'm freezing.'

Together they moved through the crowds towards Abbey House.

Half past nine. After an uneasy dinner Jennifer had gone to have a bath. Clive poured two drinks and handed one to Elizabeth. She stared at him reproachfully. 'You might make more of an effort.'

'I am.'

'You've been like a bear with a sore head all evening.'

'Hardly that.'

'Has she said something to offend you? You know she doesn't mean it. Sometimes she just speaks without thinking.'

'And sometimes she doesn't.'

She frowned at him. 'What's that supposed to mean?'

'Nothing. Forget I said it.'

The phone rang. She went to answer it. 'I wish you'd tell me,' she said before picking up the receiver. 'Hello, Elizabeth Howard speaking.' He sat and watched her. He wished he could too.

'No, of course not Mrs Rokeby. How are you?'

Clive leaned forward in his chair, to hear what his wife said next.

But she said nothing. Instead she just listened. As she did so her hand covered her mouth and the blood drained from her face.

It was nearly midnight. Sister Clark sat in her office, dozing over her latest novel. Would Nurse Cooper find true love with Doctor Garson or would she go and fight disease in the Congo? It was a compelling dilemma but one that she was too tired to resolve tonight. She rubbed at her eyes and prepared to make her way to bed.

In the distance she heard a creaking sound; a door being opened. One of the boys on his way to the bathroom. She put the book down and leaned back in her chair, feeling too lazy to move. Outside her door someone ran down the corridor.

Startled, she sat bolt upright. 'Who's there?!' she cried. She hurried to the door, pulled it open and stared out into the darkness. Suddenly she knew who she had heard.

But it couldn't be. She had locked the door to his room; fearful that something like this might happen.

'James?'

Nothing. Only silence.

She *had* locked his door. She was sure she had.

'James? Where are you?'

In the distance she heard a sharp clicking sound; as if someone was drawing a bolt.

Panic swept over her. She rushed down the corridor towards the front door. As she ran she offered up a silent prayer that she would make it in time. But when she entered the hall she felt a sharp gust of wind and saw the front door standing open. She ran towards it and looked outside. At first she could see nothing. Then she saw a figure running into the distance.

'JAMES!!'

He didn't hear her. He kept on running as if the devil were behind him.

She stood in the doorway, crying for help that would come too late.

Midnight. Jason Burchill put his foot down on the accelerator and cursed under his breath. It had taken all his powers of persuasion to get Sally's father to agree to his taking her to a dance at Cromer, and that was on the express understanding that he would have her home an hour ago.

She smiled at him from the passenger seat. 'Don't worry.'

'Easy for you to say. Your dad'll kill me.'

She started to laugh. 'Worth it though, weren't it?'

He laughed too. 'Damn right!' She touched his hand with her own. He felt a warmth inside him. This was the girl for him. Let her father do his worst.

On the left he could see the gates of Kirkston Abbey. The

best school in the area so his mother claimed, rather bitterly as the fees were well beyond their reach. Jason didn't care. It had always seemed a sad place to him; somewhere for rich people to dump their kids and forget about them. No, they could keep all their privilege. He had everything he wanted right here.

He turned towards her. 'I love you,' he told her.

Her expression was like that of a child on Christmas morning. 'Do you mean it?'

'Course I do. D'you love me?'

'Course I do.'

'Well that's all right then.'

She squeezed his hand and then turned to watch the road. For a moment he kept his eyes on her. She was beautiful. He didn't know what he had done to deserve her.

Suddenly her eyes widened with alarm. 'JASON! LOOK OUT!'

He turned. He opened his mouth to scream.

A boy had appeared in the road. He was wearing nothing but a pair of pyjama bottoms.

And he was running straight towards them.

He slammed his foot on the brake but it was too late. The boy's face came into focus; a pale white mask in the headlights. He knew what was going to happen and couldn't bear to see. He shut his eyes. His ears rang with the sound of Sally's screams merging with his own and then the dull thud of hard metal hitting soft flesh.


In his dream Jonathan walked through Upchurch Hall towards the corner room with the red damask walls and the photographs of Richard's parents. As he walked he gazed up at the Rokeby family portraits which decorated the walls. His mother and father walked beside him, flanked by other relatives and friends. All the people, except Richard, who had ever mattered in his life.

They entered the room before the corner room. It was large

and square, just like the others they had passed through. A portrait of Richard hung above a roaring fire. Jonathan pointed it out to his companions, explaining that Richard was his best friend. All exclaimed at his having made so impressive a social connection, and his father patted him approvingly on the back. He smiled, happy to bask in their praise.

As they admired the portrait it began to sag. The strings that held it were weakening, eventually snapping altogether. The portrait fell into the fire. Jonathan tried to rescue it but the flames were too hot and the portrait too heavy. When he turned to call for help he saw that his companions were walking back up the corridor in the direction from which they had come. He turned back to the portrait. The heat was causing the paint to bubble and crack, and as he watched it dissolve he saw that the likeness was no longer of Richard but of himself.

Terrified he tried to run after the others, calling for them to wait. But as he reached the door it slammed shut in his face. Pounding on it, he heard noises behind him, coming from the room with the red damask walls. It was the sound of voices, shrill and twisted with madness, all chanting his name ...

When he woke and continued to hear voices he thought it was just the dying echoes of his dream. But as his senses cleared he realised that the sounds were all too real.

He sat up in bed. The dormitory was alive with activity; everyone else was awake and clambering out of bed, rushing towards the windows through which he could see a faint light flashing. He went to join them.

Below them was a police car. Mr Bryant and his wife stood on the steps of Old School House, both wrapped in dressing-gowns, talking to two police officers. Sister Clark was there too. Another police car arrived. He didn't understand what it all meant.

The door of the dormitory burst open. Keith Pringle rushed in and was met by a chorus of excited voices. 'What took you so long?!' 'What did you find out?!' 'What's going on?!'

'It's Wheatley! He's been hit by a car!'

A gasp ran round the dormitory. 'A car?!' exclaimed some-one. 'But how?!'

'He was on the road outside the gates.'

'But he was in the San!' cried someone else.

'Sister Clark said he was sleepwalking.'

'Sleepwalking! . . .'

'Bloody hell! . . .'

'Is he in hospital?!'

'No point,' announced Keith. 'He's dead.'

Momentarily the listeners were too stunned to speak. Then they burst into a chorus of voices.

'Dead! . . .'

'Jesus! . . .'

'Has the driver been arrested? . . .'

'I don't believe it! . . .'

'Believe it!' Keith told them. 'It's true.'

He pushed his way towards one of the windows. 'What's going on now?' People continued to fire questions at him. Jonathan didn't wait to hear his answers. His stomach was heaving. He ran into the washrooms and vomited.

# PART THREE

# Paying

# Chapter One

Dawn.

In Old School House the fourth-year dormitory was still. Its occupants, who had sat up half the night talking, now tried to snatch some sleep in the brief moments before the sounding of the morning bell.

Jonathan sat alone on the window ledge in the washrooms. A huge, red sun was rising on the horizon, sending shafts of clear light across the frozen earth. The start of another day at Kirkston Abbey. A day of bells and routine. A day like hundreds of others with nothing to distinguish it except the fact that James Wheatley was dead.

His eyes roamed over the room. Here he had been urinated on; his head flushed down the toilet. He had been kicked in the balls and beaten while his hands were held so he couldn't defend himself. James Wheatley had done that to him. James Wheatley had enjoyed hurting him, just as he had enjoyed hurting others. He had been a vicious bully with no redeeming features. The world was a better place without him.

But the old indignation refused to come. Instead was an image of a boy who was alone and frightened, running to his death on a dark road. A boy his own age. A boy whose life he had helped destroy almost before it had even begun.

*Oh God, I didn't mean it! I didn't want it to be like this!*

He buried his head in his hands. Silently he began to cry.

Ten past eight. He sat in his study. He had missed breakfast.

There was a knock on the door. He didn't answer. He knew who the visitor would be, and that he would enter with or without an invitation.

The door opened. Richard walked in. 'You've heard?'

He nodded.

'At breakfast people couldn't talk about anything else. Mr Howard made a brief appearance. He looked sick and who can blame him? After the Paul Ellerson business he needs this like he needs a hole in the head.'

Jonathan said nothing. Richard stared at him. 'You've been crying.'

'Maybe.'

'Why?'

'Why?! God, how can you ask that?!'

'You're upset about Wheatley?! You're joking, right?'

'No.'

'Yes you are. What's the matter? Has somebody had a go at you? Tell me who it was. I'll sort them out for you.'

'No one's had a go at me.'

'So why are you upset?'

'Richard, he's dead!'

'So?'

'SO?!'

'Yeah. So?' Richard snorted. 'Oh right, let me guess. Now that he's dead you've realised that though he spent every waking moment acting like a complete cunt he was really a gentle soul who loved his mother and was kind to animals. Well spare me that crap! We'll get enough of it at the memorial service.'

'He's dead and it's our fault!'

'Good. He got what he deserved.'

'How can you say that?!'

'Because it's true.'

'And what about his family? Did they deserve this?'

'Who cares about his family?' Richard exhaled irritably. 'This is getting boring. They've cancelled lessons today as a sign of respect. Let's go over to my room.'

'I don't want to.'

'OK. We'll stay here then.'

Jonathan shook his head. He stared at the ground. 'What's that supposed to mean?' demanded Richard.

'Nothing.'

'Are you sure?'

'Yes.'

'You're not trying to drop me are you?'

There was an edge to Richard's voice. Jonathan looked up. Richard's eyes were cold. They frightened him. He swallowed. 'No, of course not.'

'You'd better not be.'

'I'm not, I promise.'

'Good. We're in this together, remember. You're just as responsible as I am.'

'I know.'

'You knew what we were getting into. It's too late to back out now.'

'I'm not trying to back out.' He struggled for words. 'It's just ...'

Suddenly the tears were back. The sight of them seemed to soften Richard. He came and crouched down beside Jonathan and put an arm around his shoulder. 'Hey, I'm sorry. I didn't mean to upset you.'

He wiped at his eyes. 'You didn't.'

'What is it then?'

'I'm just frightened. That's all.'

'Of what?'

'Of all this.'

'Why? Nothing bad is going to happen to you.'

'Isn't it?'

'No. I won't let it. You know that, don't you?'

'Yes.'

Richard began to stroke his hair. 'You don't have to be frightened. I'll always protect you. You know your problem. You're too soft-hearted. You shouldn't let it get to you. Wheatley got what he deserved. We both know it. You just need some time to get your head round it.'

He nodded.

'I'll leave you alone for a bit, OK? You come and find me when you're ready.'

Again he nodded. Richard kissed his cheek, then walked towards the door. When he reached it he turned and smiled. 'You don't ever have to be scared. You're the only person in this world who matters to me and no one is ever going to hurt you. I'll kill anyone who tries.'

He managed to smile back. Inside he wanted to scream.

Clive Howard stood and watched the police drive away. Elizabeth stood beside him, holding his hand.

'Why did this have to happen?' he asked her.

She sighed. 'Why does any tragedy happen? He was only fourteen. Just a child. God, what his poor parents must be going through.'

'They'll be in shock.'

She nodded.

'A pity it has to wear off.'

She stared at him. 'What do you mean?'

'When it does they'll start looking for someone to blame.'

She squeezed his hand. 'Well they won't find anyone here.'

'Won't they?'

'No. You heard what the police said. There's no question of negligence. The sanatorium door was bolted. He let himself out.'

'He was on the road for God's sake.'

'The school gates were locked.'

'He must have climbed over them. How could he do that in his sleep? God, what was going on in his head?'

'Some people do extraordinary things in their sleep. I knew a boy who once walked out of his parents' house and was found by the police eight miles away, marching along the side of the road, muttering to himself. His feet were bleeding but he never woke up.'

He frowned. 'And that makes it all right, does it?'

'I'm just saying that it's happened and it's a tragedy, but it's no one's fault. I know you, Clive. You'll start blaming yourself just as you did over Paul Ellerson and that wasn't your fault either.'

'They're both dead though, aren't they? Two boys from the same school in the same term. How many people will want to send their sons here now?'

'I don't know. We'll cross that bridge when we come to it. Let's just be thankful that it wasn't us receiving an early morning visit from the police to say that a loved one was dead.'

'We must speak to his parents. I should have called them already. I just couldn't face it. I . . .'

'It's all right' she said soothingly. 'We'll do it together.'

He bent down and kissed her, and as he did so he thought of something else they had to do that day. 'We should send for Rokeby.'

She shook her head. 'Leave it until tonight.'

'We'll do that together too, yes?'

She stroked his hair. 'Of course.'

He pulled her close to him, cradling her in his arms. 'Oh Lizzie, don't ever leave me.'

She rested her head against his chest. The two of them remained like that for some time. He heard a noise and looked up. Jennifer was standing in the doorway, watching them. Her eyes were cold. He stared back at her. Instinctively his arms tightened around his wife.

\*     \*     \*

Reverend Potter was climbing into his car when he remembered that he had left his copy of *The Times* in the vestry.

He dared not leave it there. A renowned chef was sharing the secrets of good pastry with the readership and Mrs Potter was collecting them in the hope that some of his culinary genius would rub off on her. Wearily he climbed out again and made his way towards the school chapel.

He entered by the side door. He didn't switch the lights on. He could find his way blindfolded. He walked to the vestry, collected the paper and was on his way out when he heard a whimpering sound.

He stopped, looked about him. The moon was rising but it did not provide enough light for him to see clearly. It was cold in the chapel. He shivered as his eyes scanned the pews. He thought he saw movement in one. 'Hello.' There was no answer. He tried again. 'Hello. Is someone there?'

At first nothing. Then a boy's voice whispered, 'Yes.'

He began to walk towards the voice. 'Who is it?'

'Palmer, sir. Jonathan Palmer.'

Jonathan was sitting in one of the pews near the back, his legs hunched under him, his arms wrapped around his chest. Reverend Potter sat beside him. 'What's all this then Jonathan?' he asked.

Jonathan rubbed at his eyes. 'Nothing, sir.'

'It must be something,' said Reverend Potter kindly. 'You don't sit alone in the dark for nothing. Why not tell me?'

'I can't.'

'You can trust me, you know.'

Jonathan turned towards him. Even in the poor light Reverend Potter could see that his eyes were swollen from crying. 'Can I?'

'Of course you can. Come on now. You'll feel better if you tell me.'

Jonathan lowered his head and began to sob.

Reverend Potter had few illusions about himself. He knew that if he put half as much effort into spreading the word of God as he did into pursuing an easy life then the boys of Kirkston Abbey would be amongst the most enlightened in the country. But he was a compassionate man who hated to see distress in others. Gently he put his arm around Jonathan. 'Hush now. It can't be that terrible, can it?'

In response Jonathan buried his head in Reverend Potter's chest. Touched, Reverend Potter sat quietly, holding him in his arms, waiting for him to calm down. When he sensed the tears were easing he tried again. 'What is it Jonathan? What are you doing here?'

Jonathan whispered something that Reverend Potter couldn't hear. 'What did you say?'

'I was praying.'

'Praying? Why?'

'Because of Wheatley.'

'I see.' Reverend Potter sighed. 'Yes, that's a terrible thing. Poor boy. I didn't know he was a friend of yours.'

'I hated him.'

'Oh.' Reverend Potter was taken aback. 'Then why . . .'

'Because it's my fault.'

'Your fault? How?'

'I wanted something bad to happen to him.'

'It's not a sin to hate someone,' said Reverend Potter. Then he hurried to correct himself. 'Well yes, technically it's a sin. Turn the other cheek and all that. But it's not a great sin. You'd have to be perfect to like everyone and I've yet to meet anyone who can claim to be that.'

Jonathan shook his head. 'You don't understand. I made it happen. I willed it to happen.'

'Willed it?' Reverend Potter smiled. 'I don't think so.'

'I did! You have to believe me!'

Reverend Potter took Jonathan's chin in his hand and stared into his eyes.

'Jonathan, listen to me. This is important. When someone dies unexpectedly there's always guilt. People who knew them always feel they're responsible in some way. Do you think you're the only person who feels guilty about James? Think how Sister Clark must be feeling. And what of his parents?'

'His parents?' Jonathan stared at him. 'What do they have to feel guilty about?'

Reverend Potter sighed. 'I talked to Mrs Howard this afternoon. She and her husband had just spoken to Mrs Wheatley. The poor woman kept blaming herself. She said that if only she'd told someone about James then perhaps this could have been avoided.'

'What do you mean? What should she have told?'

'That James had a history of sleepwalking.'

Jonathan's eyes widened. 'He's done it before?!'

'Yes. All the time when he was a small child apparently. Once he dreamed that he could fly and threw himself out of an upstairs window. After that his parents used to watch him like hawks, terrified that something awful would happen to him. Then, when he was about eight, he stopped doing it and his parents told themselves that the problem was over. Now we know it wasn't.'

'So it wasn't my fault?!'

'No, of course not. How could it have been? Bad things happen because that's the way it is. But you can't will them to happen Jonathan. You're not God.'

Jonathan started to laugh. A shrill, hysterical sound. Reverend Potter kept his arm around him. 'You had got yourself into a state, hadn't you?'

Jonathan nodded.

'Didn't I say you'd feel better if you told me? You see, there's nothing for you to feel guilty about. Now I have to go. My wife will be expecting me. Walk with me to my car. Have you had supper?'

'No.'

'Well if we hurry you'll still be in time.'

They walked towards the side door. 'Thank you,' said Jonathan awkwardly.

Reverend Potter smiled at him. 'You don't need to thank me. I was pleased to help.'

'Yes, I do. You can't imagine what I've been thinking. I wish there was something I could do for you.'

Reverend Potter thought for a moment. 'Perhaps there is.'

Jonathan smiled eagerly.

'You're friends with Rokeby aren't you?'

'Yes.'

They reached the side door. Reverend Potter stopped. 'I'm glad. He's going to need a friend.'

The smile faltered slightly.

'He's got some rather bad news coming. It seems there's been an accident at home. Mr and Mrs Howard should be speaking to him now.'

Jonathan stared at Reverend Potter. His lips began to move but no sounds came out.

'He's going to have to be very brave. And that's how you can help me. Will you keep an eye on him for me and the Howards? You see, what's happened is . . .'

'NO!'

It came out as a scream.

'No! You said we hadn't willed anything! You said we couldn't!'

'Jonathan, I don't understand. What are you talking about?'

Jonathan stared wildly into space, running his hands through his hair. His breath was short and ragged. Reverend Potter put a hand on his shoulder. 'Jonathan, what is it?!'

'OH GOD!'

'Jonathan . . .'

'I didn't mean it! Oh God I didn't mean it! It wasn't supposed to be like this!'

He turned and ran from the chapel. Baffled, Reverend

Potter stood and watched him go. In the pew his newspaper lay forgotten.

Henry Ackerley was just pouring himself a drink when he heard the phone ring. He listened for Marjorie's footsteps. Let her answer it. He sat down beside the fire.

He heard her lift the receiver, say something, then put it down again. She entered the room. The bruising on her face was fading but still visible. He looked away. 'Who was it?'

'No one.'

'Must have been someone.'

'Wrong number. As soon as they heard my voice they hung up.'

He continued to avoid her eyes. She remained where she was. 'You can't bear to look at me, can you?'

He turned towards her. Then looked away again.

'There was a time once when you couldn't stop looking at me.'

'Don't . . .' he began.

'Why not? What else do we have but the past? That and each other.'

'If that's all we have,' he said softly, 'then there's no hope for either of us.'

She turned and left the room. He downed his drink and reached for another.

There was a knock on Clive's study door. Elizabeth squeezed his hand in encouragement. 'Come in,' he called out.

Richard Rokeby entered. He stood by the door without offering a greeting. 'Sorry I'm late, sir. I had to make a phone call.'

'A call?' Clive was alarmed. 'Who to?'

'A friend. Why?'

'Um . . . no reason. Just curious.' He shuffled awkwardly, trying to think of something to say. Elizabeth, so much better in this type of situation, quickly came to his aid. She smiled at Richard and gestured to the sofa. 'Why don't you come and sit down.'

He did as she asked. She sat down beside him and Clive sat across from them in an armchair. Richard eyed them both suspiciously. 'Why did you want to see me, sir?' he asked Clive.

Clive took a deep breath. 'Richard, there's something we have to tell you.'

'We've had a phone call from your aunt,' said Elizabeth. She moved closer to Richard and put an arm around him. 'I'm afraid there's been some bad news.'

'What news?'

'There's been an accident.'

Richard swallowed. 'I see.'

Elizabeth put her hand on his. 'It's all right. It's not your father.'

'There's been a fire,' Clive told him.

'Where?'

'At your father's house,' said Elizabeth.

'And?'

'As I said, your father's fine. There's nothing to worry about.'

'If there's nothing to worry about then why are you acting like someone's died?'

Elizabeth sighed. 'Someone has died.'

Richard lowered his eyes. 'You mean my stepmother.'

'Yes.' She moved even closer to him. 'I'm afraid so.'

Richard stared at the floor. 'She was pregnant,' he said suddenly. 'Did you know that?'

'No, I didn't.'

'Pregnant with my little brother or sister. She said we'd be a family when it was born.'

Something in Richard's tone worried Clive. He tried to catch Elizabeth's eye but she was too busy acting as comforter to notice. 'Oh Richard, I'm so sorry. Really I am.'

'How did the fire start?'

'Your parents had arranged to meet friends for dinner,' Clive told him. 'Your stepmother began to feel unwell so she went to bed instead. Your father wanted to cancel but she insisted that he go. Before he left he smoked a cigar in one of the downstairs rooms. It seems he didn't extinguish it properly. That's how the fire started.'

'Was my stepmother alone in the house?'

'Yes.'

'My father wasn't there?'

Clive shook his head. 'Richard I'm sorry you have to find out from us. As you can imagine your father is distraught. Your aunt and uncle haven't felt able to leave him since it happened. Your aunt asked if we would tell you. She would have asked your housemaster but she'd met and liked my wife and wanted us to be the people to do it. She'll come and see you as soon as she can.'

Suddenly a look of panic came into Richard's face. He turned to Elizabeth. 'You are telling me everything aren't you? My father is all right isn't he?'

'Of course he is Richard. Honestly.'

'I wouldn't have wanted anything to happen to him. I really wouldn't.'

'Of course you wouldn't,' said Elizabeth soothingly. She smiled at Clive. He smiled back, but again something in Richard's tone made him feel uneasy. There was a knock on the door. 'We're busy,' he cried.

The door opened a crack. The maid looked in. 'Sally!' exclaimed Elizabeth. 'I said we weren't to be disturbed.'

'I'm sorry Mrs Howard but Mrs Wheatley's on the phone. She wants to speak to you.'

'Oh God!' Elizabeth looked flustered. 'Sally please tell her I'll call as soon as I can.'

'It doesn't matter, Mrs Howard,' said Richard politely. 'You should go and speak to her.'

'No, it can wait. You've had a terrible shock. We need to talk some more.'

'Honestly, Mrs Howard, I'm all right.' Richard smiled at her. 'You've been very kind to me. Thank you.'

Elizabeth looked to Clive for guidance. He nodded. 'Very well. If you're sure. But Richard, we're both here for you whenever you need to talk. You know that, don't you?'

'Yes, I know that.'

She kissed his cheek. Then she rose and left the room, leaving him alone with Clive.

Clive struggled for more words of comfort but couldn't shake his sense of unease. 'I'm really very sorry, Richard,' he said lamely.

Richard hung his head. 'I wonder how my father must be feeling.'

'Yes indeed.'

'He must feel so guilty.'

'It was an accident.'

'I know. But it was his cigar. He must feel that it's all his fault.'

'Yes, I suppose he will. Poor man. What a terrible burden to carry.'

'Isn't it,' said Richard softly.

Then, suddenly, he began to laugh.

Clive felt himself grow cold.

'He'll have to live with the guilt for every second of every day for the rest of his life. From the moment he wakes up to the moment he goes to sleep. And even when he sleeps he won't be able to escape it because it'll be there in his dreams. Imagine having to live like that. Assuming you can even call it living.'

'Richard, you're upset. You don't know what you're saying.'

'Oh but you're mistaken, Mr Howard. I know exactly what I'm saying.'

Richard looked up. His eyes were pools of malevolence.

Clive's heart began to race. The old voices began to whisper in his head.

*This boy is dangerous.*

But now the words were even darker. More sinister.

*This boy is insane.*

'Richard, your stepmother is dead!'

'I know. She was my father's mistress for three years before they married. Did you know that? She was fucking my father while my mother was still alive.'

'She's dead! For God's sake, show some respect!'

'Respect? For some dirty whore?'

'That's enough!'

'I doubt her baby was even my father's. Probably got it from some pimp who paid her half a crown to fuck her in an alley.'

'THAT'S ENOUGH!'

Clives's face was crimson. He was shaking with fury.

'Get out of this room! You're ill! You're not right in the head! Maybe you can get help. I don't know. Frankly I don't care. The one thing I do know is that I won't have the other boys exposed to you for a moment longer! I'm going to speak to your father and have you removed from this school!'

'I wouldn't speak to him just now, sir. As you said yourself, he's distraught at the moment.'

'GET OUT! GET OUT NOW!'

Richard smiled. Slowly he rose to his feet and walked towards the door. Clive watched him go. 'There's another thing.'

'What?' said Richard without bothering to look round.

'You're to end your friendship with Palmer. You will stop all association with him. I don't want him infected with whatever sickness is in you.'

Richard turned back. He was no longer smiling. 'What did you say?'

'Your friendship with Palmer is over.'

'FUCK YOU!'

Clive rose to his feet. 'How dare you talk to me like that!'

Richard walked up to Clive and stared him straight in the eye. 'I dare sir because I'm upset. My darling stepmother and unborn sibling have been killed. Half my family has been wiped out. I'm devastated. I don't know what I'm saying.'

'You know exactly what you're saying!'

'You know that, sir. So do I. But who else is going to believe it?'

'What the hell is this?! Are you threatening me?!'

'I think you have that the wrong way round sir. You're the one talking about expulsion and separation from friends. I'd say you were the one who was making threats, not me.'

'You little bastard! I ought to . . .'

'Ought to what sir? Thrash me? I don't think so. That would be a very bad idea. Things aren't very good for you at the moment are they sir? Two dead boys in the same term. Hardly good publicity for the school is it? I wonder how many parents are considering removing their sons? Quite a few I'd expect. And when they hear that the headmaster has thrashed a boy and threatened him with expulsion only moments after telling him that half his family have been killed in a fire then I think there may well be quite a few more.'

Richard paused. He was breathing hard. His eyes were shining.

'So sir. Like I said. FUCK YOU!'

He turned and walked towards the door.

Clive made a final attempt to exert his authority. 'You'll be sorry for this behaviour, Rokeby. I promise you that.'

'No, sir. You're the one that's going to be sorry. REALLY sorry.'

He left the room, slamming the door behind him.

Clive's legs felt as if they would collapse beneath him. He sank down into his chair. He took slow, deep breaths, trying to calm himself while he decided what to do.

* * *

Later that evening the phone rang in the Ackerley house.

Marjorie was already in bed. She had retired early, pleading a headache. Both of them knew it was a lie, constructed to help them avoid the awkwardness of proximity.

Henry picked up the receiver. 'Hello?'

Silence, except for the faint sound of breathing. 'Hello. Is anyone there.'

Still nothing. 'Look I think you've got the wrong number. I'm going to hang up now.'

Then, in what was barely a whisper, a voice said, 'Shooters Lane. February 1948.'

The line went dead.

Slowly Henry put the receiver down. His hand was shaking so badly that it took him three attempts to return it to its holder.

# Chapter Two

Tuesday morning, fourth period. The day of respect was over. Routine returned to Kirkston Abbey.

Nicholas Scott sat alone in a double desk in Wellington classroom, trying to concentrate on the History book in front of him.

The class had finished the Civil War and now turned its collective attention to the restoration of the monarchy. As this was the first lesson on a new topic Nicholas had expected Mr Stewart to spend the lesson outlining the key events and trying to fire them with enthusiasm. Instead they had been told to read the relevant chapters and make notes.

Mr Stewart seemed preoccupied. A mountain of marking was piled in front of him but he paid it little attention. His features were drawn. He looked tired and anxious. Perhaps he was ill. Nicholas hoped not. He liked Mr Stewart.

The double desk at the back was empty. No George Turner and James Wheatley. The news on George was encouraging. The last operation appeared to have been successful. He was expected back next term. As for James . . .

But he didn't want to think about James.

He looked at the double desk by the window where Richard and Jonathan sat. Their heads were bowed together. They were whispering to each other. These days they were never seen apart.

People joked that they were joined at the hip. Nicholas didn't care. It meant nothing to him.

Richard turned to watch the groundsmen as they freshened the markings on the rugby pitch. Jonathan looked down at his book. He scratched his head, stifled what looked like a yawn and turned to observe the classroom. Casually his gaze fell on Nicholas. Their eyes locked.

Suddenly a look of absolute desperation flashed across Jonathan's face. A mute plea for help.

Then, as quickly as it had come, the look was gone. He turned back to Richard. Their heads bowed together. The whispering resumed.

Nicholas continued to watch them. He felt a warmth in the pit of his stomach. Then he remembered his last meeting with Richard.

The warmth vanished, replaced by scorn. So Jonathan was scared. Good. Jonathan had reason to be.

As did he.

*No! It wasn't my fault! Jonathan's the guilty one. He and Richard. They were the instigators, not me.*

Jonathan didn't deserve sympathy. He deserved everything he got.

He looked down at his book. He was still unable to concentrate.

The maid had left the morning post on a tray in the hall. Elizabeth Howard opened it in the drawing-room.

She was worrying about Marjorie Ackerley. She wanted to visit but there had not been a moment. Mrs Wheatley had phoned again this morning. She seemed to draw comfort from their conversations. Elizabeth was pleased by this, if a little baffled. All she could do was listen and sympathise. Perhaps that was all that Mrs Wheatley wanted; perhaps the rest of the family were too preoccupied with their own grief to listen to hers.

So she was pleased. But saddened too. The conversations

brought back memories of her dead brother that were still painful and she had been close to tears when finally she put the phone down. She was still upset as she began to work her way through the post. Nothing out of the ordinary. A dinner invitation. A circular about a book club. A telephone bill. And a single sheet of expensive writing paper, marked with three neatly printed sentences.

*Your husband is fucking your cousin. Any fool can see it. Why can't you?*

She stared at the note. The writing blurred before her eyes. Suddenly everything seemed out of focus. She reached for the envelope that had brought the note. There was no stamp or postmark; just the same neatly printed script.

*Mrs Howard — Personal.*

Who had done this? Who would do such a thing?
Who could think such a thing?
And what grounds could they have for thinking it?
'Lizzie.'
She jumped. Jennifer stood in the doorway. 'Sorry. Didn't mean to alarm you. How did it go?'
'Go?'
'With Mrs Wheatley. You were on for ages.'
'She's very upset, poor woman.'
Jennifer studied her closely. 'Are you all right?'
'Of course. Why shouldn't I be?'
'You look pale, that's all.'
'I'm fine. Just a headache.'
'What you need is a drink. I'll pour us both one. Anything interesting in the post?'
Elizabeth was startled. 'Why do you ask that?'

'That's what you're doing isn't it? Opening the post.'

'No. Nothing. Nothing at all.'

Jennifer walked towards the drinks cabinet. Elizabeth sat and watched her, the note still clasped in her hand.

Lunch was over. Games began in ten minutes. Jonathan was heading for the changing rooms when he heard someone call his name. It was Adam Fisher; one of the house prefects. 'Phone call for you.'

'Who is it?'

Adam shrugged. 'Some woman.'

'My mother?'

'I don't know. She just asked to speak to you.'

The phone was in a small booth near the prefects' studies. He picked up the receiver. 'Hello.'

'Jonathan?'

'Yes.'

It wasn't his mother. He didn't recognise the voice.

'It's Mrs Rokeby.'

'Mrs Rokeby!' He pulled the door shut and sat down on the battered chair. The booth smelt of chewing gum. Dozens of initials were scratched into the walls.

'I'm sorry to call you.'

'That's all right.' He tried not to panic. Why was she calling?

'I'm really sorry about what's happened.'

'That's kind of you, Jonathan. Thank you.' Her voice was tense, but warm as always.

'Do you want to speak to Richard?'

'No. I wanted to speak to you. I need to see you.'

'See me?' He struggled to keep the alarm out of his voice. 'Why?'

'I can't tell you. Not on the phone. Please Jonathan. It is important.'

He tried to think of an excuse but none would come. 'All right.'

'I can drive over this afternoon. I can't come to the school. I don't want Richard to know about this. I remember you said you had a bicycle. There's a village nearby called Bowerton. Do you know it?'

'Yes.'

'There's a pub in the village called The Fleece. There's a car park. Could you meet me there at four o'clock?'

'I've got games. We might not be finished.'

'Half past then. I know it's a half holiday. Please Jonathan.'

He swallowed. 'Very well.'

'Thank you. I'll be waiting.'

He put the phone down. His throat was dry. In the distance he could hear raised voices and the clatter of rugby boots on stone floors.

Marjorie Ackerley buttoned her coat. Henry watched her.

'Do you have to go?' he asked.

'There are things we need.'

'What if someone sees you like that?'

'Who do we know in Yarmouth?'

'Anyone could be there.'

'If you're so worried why don't you go yourself?'

'I'm ill. I told you.'

'You look well enough.'

'Appearances can be deceiving.'

She gestured to her face. 'Like mine perhaps.'

He hung his head. 'Go if you must.'

He heard the door open and close, then the sound of the car engine. Behind him he heard the phone. He let it ring.

Ten minutes later it rang again. This time he answered. As before, he heard nothing save the faint hiss of someone breathing.

'Who is this?' he whispered.

The same muffled voice. 'Shooters Lane. February 1948.'

Last night he had told himself that he had misheard. The effects of tiredness and too much drink. But there was no mistaking this.

'Who is this?! What do you want from me?!'

Soft laughter. 'The closet is opening. Soon all the skeletons will be free.'

Then silence.

Jonathan sat with Mrs Rokeby in her car.

The engine was running to power the heater. The inside of the car was oppressive. He wanted to open a window but didn't like to ask.

'Mr Howard called me last night,' she told him.

Jonathan, who had already heard about the confrontation, watched her warily. 'What did he say?'

'That he'd spoken to Richard; told him what had happened.' She began to twist her wedding ring. 'And?' prompted Jonathan.

'He was rather strange on the phone. He seemed to be suggesting that Richard might be happier at another school. That it wasn't good for him to be so isolated. That he needed to mix more with other boys and that he might be better able to do that somewhere else. I said it wasn't true. That Richard was mixing. That he'd made friends with you and that your friendship was a good thing. And it *is* a good thing. I know it is.'

'Did Mr Howard think it was a good thing?' he asked tentatively.

'He didn't say. He dropped the subject. He could tell that I wasn't willing to listen. He asked after Richard's father, said how sorry he was about what had happened.'

Jonathan swallowed. 'I'm sorry too.'

'I know you are. Bless you. You're a kind boy Jonathan. Richard is lucky to have a friend like you.' The affection in her eyes made him feel ashamed. He lowered his head. Outside it was starting to rain. He wished he was somewhere else.

'That's why I've come to ask for your help.'

'Help?'

She nodded, watching him anxiously.

'If I can. But how?'

'It's not for me. It's for Richard. He's the one who needs it.'

'Richard?! Richard doesn't need help from anyone.'

She smiled sadly. 'You think so, don't you? Everyone does. They take him at face value. They see the strength and the confidence and they think that's the whole story. But they're wrong.'

He was still confused. She took his hand. 'I'm going to tell you something now but before I do you must promise that you won't tell it to anyone else. Will you promise me that?'

He felt trapped. He wanted to climb out of the car and run away. But he knew he couldn't. Weakly he nodded.

'What has Richard told you about his mother?'

'Not much. He doesn't like to talk about her.'

'But he has told you something?'

'I know that he loved her very much. I know she died when he was nine.' He hesitated. 'And I know how she died.'

'What exactly did he tell you about that?'

'That she took an overdose. And that he was staying with you when it happened.'

'That's what he told you?'

'It's not true?'

She shook her head. 'I wish it was. Perhaps things would have been different if it had happened like that.'

Softly she began to cry. 'Please don't,' he said awkwardly. She squeezed his hand. She wiped her eyes, breathed deeply and began to speak.

'His mother's name was Madelaine. His father Malcolm met her at a party in London a few years before the war. She was an actress. Nothing grand you understand. She'd had small parts in films. She was very beautiful. The loveliest woman I ever saw. Richard gets his looks from her. You know that of course. You've seen the photographs.

'Malcolm fell in love with her almost on sight. He brought her to meet us. She was very shy and very sweet. We were all charmed by her. She was very young; only nineteen. Little more than a child really. She still lived at home with her father. Her mother had died some years earlier. She didn't like to talk about her mother.

'Malcolm proposed very quickly. She accepted, but on the condition that they live near her father in London. It seemed natural that she'd want to be close to him. She was an only child after all and her father was a widower with no other family. Within three months of meeting they were married.

'We didn't see much of them after that. They were in London. We were here in Norfolk. Occasionally they came to visit us. More often Malcolm came on his own. We didn't think anything of it. By then Madelaine was pregnant with Richard and we assumed that she didn't feel up to the journey. We offered to visit them but Malcolm was against it. He said that Madelaine was too tired for visitors. That things would be different when the baby was born.

'But they weren't. We saw her less not more. By then the war had started and travelling wasn't as easy so we still didn't think anything of it.

'Then one night Malcolm appeared on our doorstep. He was in a terrible state. He said he had to tell us something. That he would go mad if he didn't tell someone.'

She hesitated, staring at Jonathan. 'You do promise don't you? You won't tell anyone.' He wanted to refuse, to say that he didn't want to hear any more. But again he nodded.

'Malcolm told us that the day after they returned from honeymoon Madelaine's father came to see him. He said there were things Malcolm needed to know about Madelaine. And about her mother.

'He said that Madelaine's mother had been the most

charismatic woman he'd ever met. She had this energy about her; this inner strength. She was outspoken and confrontational. She was afraid of no one; was always looking to challenge authority. He said that it was this strength that he'd loved in her.

'But soon after Madelaine was born her behaviour became more extreme. It was as if she had this rage inside her that she couldn't control. She started to become abusive, then violent. He tried to keep it from everyone. Told himself he could cope. Then, one day, Madelaine broke a plate. Her mother went into a rage. She dragged Madelaine upstairs and tried to drown her in the bath. She would have succeeded too if Madelaine's father hadn't come home in time to stop her. After that he knew something had to be done so he had her committed. She spent the last ten years of her life in an asylum.

'He told Malcolm that Madelaine wasn't like her mother. That none of her mother's madness had been passed down to her. But it had had its effect. Ever since her mother's committal she had suffered from periods of depression during which she would retreat into her own little world. He said that it didn't have to be a problem. That all she needed was tenderness and understanding. He had always given her that. He had expected to go on doing so but had now discovered that he was ill and might not have much longer to live.

'He said that he knew he should have told Malcolm before the wedding, but that he had kept silent because he had wanted to make sure that there would be someone to take care of Madelaine when he was no longer able to do so.

'As you can imagine Malcolm was shocked. He told himself that it didn't matter. He adored his wife. He vowed to protect her and give her all the love she needed.

'But it wasn't that easy. Malcolm's a good man but he's not a patient one. He had never experienced anything like this before and try as he did he just couldn't cope with it. For months at a time Madelaine would be the sweet girl he had fallen in love with and then suddenly, without warning, she would withdraw into herself to a place where he couldn't reach her. No one could reach her except her father. And Richard.

'She adored Richard. She absolutely worshipped him. When he was a baby she used to sit and hold him and sing to him for hours and hours, and sometimes she'd cry because she'd remember what her own mother had done to her. She was obsessed with her mother. She was terrified of ending up like her.

'And Richard adored her too. He was such a beautiful child. I used to worry about him all the time. On the few occasions I saw him I always tried to get close to him but I never could. He had this strength in him that I'd never seen in any other child. I think he knew I wanted to protect him and he resented that. He didn't want protection. He wanted to be the protector. That was why he loved his mother so much, because he knew she needed him. He understood her illness better than Malcolm ever could. Almost from the moment he could speak he seemed to know what to do to reach her, to guide her out of the dark places she hid in and make her smile again. Just like her father.

'When Richard was five his grandfather died. After the funeral we all went back to the house. I remember Madelaine crying and Richard sitting beside her like a little man, telling her that she shouldn't be sad, that he would look after her and that everything would be all right. And I remember something else too. When Malcolm tried to comfort her Richard watched him with this look of hostility on his face. Now that his grandfather was dead I think he viewed his mother as belonging to him and he didn't want to share her with anyone. Not even Malcolm.

'By then Malcolm was spending less and less time at home. Madelaine's illness was becoming worse, her depressions more all-consuming, and he just wasn't able to cope. He hired a housekeeper and kept his distance. Richard's uncle and I told him that it wasn't right. That it wasn't fair to Madelaine or Richard, but it didn't make any difference. Things just went on as they were. They might have gone on like that for ever if he hadn't met Catherine.

'You met her didn't you? You know what she was like. She wasn't as beautiful as Madelaine, or as captivating. Nowhere near. But she was kind and she was warm and I think Malcolm saw in her the chance for the uncomplicated love that he needed and couldn't get from Madelaine. So he decided that he wanted a divorce and . . .'

She hesitated. 'Go on.' said Jonathan.

'And that he wanted custody of Richard.

'He went to tell Madelaine. I begged him not to. I said that Richard was everything to her. That the worst thing he could do was threaten to take her son away from her. Malcolm wouldn't listen. He said he owed it to Richard, that he had failed him as a father and wanted to make amends. He said that he would make sure Madelaine was looked after and received the care she needed. He said that it was for the best and that he could make Madelaine understand that.

'So he went to tell her. Of course she didn't understand. She was terrified. I think she thought he meant to have her locked up like her mother had been. She became hysterical. She begged him not to take Richard from her. And Richard said that he wouldn't go. He told Malcolm that he hated him, that they didn't need him. That he should go off with his new woman and leave them alone. Malcolm became angry. He told Madelaine that it was for the best and that it would happen whether she liked it or not. Then he left.

'The next morning Madelaine saw Richard off to school. Then she told the housekeeper that she had a headache, that she was going to lie down and was not to be disturbed.

'When Richard came back from school the housekeeper had tea ready for him. He said he was going upstairs to see his mother. The housekeeper tried to dissuade him; said his mother wasn't feeling well, but he insisted. He said she would want to see him. He said he'd only be a few minutes. But he didn't come down.

'Eventually the housekeeper started calling for him. She called and called but got no answer. So she went upstairs.

'He was with his mother, in her bathroom. She'd been dead for some hours. She'd slashed her wrists in the bath. Richard was sitting on the floor beside her, talking to her as if she were still alive, telling her what he'd done at school that day. He was in shock. He didn't seem to realise that the housekeeper was even there.

'Malcolm arrived at the house. So did the doctor, the ambulance and the police. They were all in one of the downstairs rooms. The housekeeper brought Richard in. He was still in shock. He didn't speak. His hands were clasped stiffly behind his back. Malcolm was crying. He told Richard that he loved him and that they would help each other through this. He held out his arms to him. Then Richard held out his own arms.

'He was holding a knife. He lunged at Malcolm. Malcolm put out an arm to shield himself and Richard stabbed him straight through the hand. Malcolm still has the scar. He always will. Richard was screaming that it was all Malcolm's fault, that he was a murderer and that he was going to kill him. It took three policemen to hold him down so the doctor could give him a sedative.

'Since then he's never let anyone get close to him. I've tried and tried but it's no good. He's built this fortress around himself and nobody is allowed in. For years it seemed the only emotions he was capable of were hatred for his father and contempt for everyone else. It might have stayed like that for ever if it hadn't been for you.

'You're the first person he's allowed to befriend him since his mother died. To you it's probably just another friendship. A boy like you must have many friends. But to Richard's uncle and me it's nothing short of a miracle. There's been so much pain in his life. So much anger and unhappiness. Now, in making friends with you, it's like he's trying to turn a corner and it gives us hope that some day soon he'll be able to make peace with his father and put all the hate behind him.

'That's why Mr Howard's call upset me so much. The last thing Richard needs now is to change schools. It would be the worst thing that could happen to him. You think he's so strong don't you? You think he doesn't need anyone. But it's not true. He needs you Jonathan. He needs your friendship. If he knows he can open up to you then perhaps he'll feel able to open up to others.

'And so I'm asking you to watch out for him. You know how headstrong and impulsive he can be. God knows it's got him into enough trouble in the past. I want you to try and stop him from doing anything that could give Mr Howard grounds to send him away. I don't know what it would do to Richard if the two of you were separated. I don't know what it would do to me either.'

She was still holding Jonathan's hand. He wanted to pull it away. He felt as if he were caught in quicksand.

'You do understand, don't you?'

He nodded.

He understood everything now.

Richard's mother had been haunted by fears of her own mother. She had been terrified that one day she might hurt her infant son just as her mother had hurt her. But her fears had been groundless. She had not inherited her mother's madness. It had skipped a generation to reappear in the little baby she had cradled so lovingly in her arms.

Her mother had been a psychopath. And so was Richard.

'You will help me won't you?'

He felt as if he were going mad himself. He wanted to jump out of the car and run away. To run from her desperation and his own fear.

But there was nowhere to go. This wasn't a nightmare that he could wake from. This was real and there was no escape.

He nodded.

'Thank you,' she whispered. Again she started to cry. So did he.

It was after six o'clock when he returned to his study. There was a note on his desk.

*Jon, Where are you? I've looked all over. Come and see me after supper. R.*

He crumpled the note into a ball and threw it on to the floor. He knew Richard would come searching for him. He tried to think of somewhere to hide until prep.

Elizabeth Howard ate supper with her husband and cousin.

What little conversation there was stemmed from Jennifer. Clive was preoccupied with the recent tragedy. He prodded unenthusiastically at his food. Elizabeth did likewise. She had her own preoccupations.

She studied her husband. He seemed uncomfortable. He always did when Jennifer was around. She knew he didn't like Jennifer. He had always made it quite obvious.

Too obvious?

'Well?' asked Jennifer.

She hadn't been listening. 'I'm sorry?'

'You were miles away.'

'I was thinking about Mrs Wheatley.'

'I thought we could go to Norwich tomorrow.'

Instinctively she shook her head. She felt a sudden aversion to being alone with Jennifer.

'Why not? You could do with getting away from here for a bit.'

'I don't know.'

'I'm sure Clive wouldn't mind. You don't mind do you, Clive? You can survive without your wife for a few hours, can't you?'

He looked up from his plate. 'Of course. You should go, Lizzie. Jennifer's right. It would do you good.'

'So that's settled then,' announced Jennifer. 'We'll go tomorrow afternoon.'

'Why not the whole day?' asked Clive.

'Good heavens no,' said Jennifer teasingly. 'I wouldn't dream of it. I know how the two of you can't bear to be parted for long.'

Clive shrugged. 'As you like.' He rolled his eyes at Elizabeth before turning his attention back to his food. Jennifer did likewise. Elizabeth watched them.

There were times when she was irritated by Jennifer's teasing. But she had been careful never to reveal her irritation. She knew that its source lay in envy at their happiness. She had always hoped that Jennifer would find some happiness herself.

Perhaps she had already.

No. It wasn't possible. Jennifer would never do that to her. Jennifer loved her.

She who had everything that Jennifer wanted.

This was insane! Even if Jennifer did feel something for Clive it would never be reciprocated. Clive adored her. He was always telling her how much he loved her. How his life would have no meaning without her.

Why did he tell her so often? Did he feel she needed reassurance?

Or was he trying to convince himself?

The note meant nothing. It was an act of malice. It had no basis in truth.

Jennifer smiled at her. She smiled back. The muscles in her face felt heavy. She reached for her glass. Her hand was shaking.

Prep had begun half an hour ago. Brian Harrington stood in the hall of Old School, putting up a notice about a forthcoming rugby match. In the distance he could hear footsteps. He assumed it was one of the masters making an inspection of the studies.

Richard Rokeby appeared from the corridor that linked Old School with Abbey House. He walked past Brian, heading towards the fourth-year studies.

'Where the hell d'you think you're going?!' bellowed Brian.

Richard ignored him.

'Hey, I'm talking to you!'

Richard turned and walked towards him. Brian glared at him. 'You'd better have a bloody good reason for marching around our House during prep!'

Richard slammed his elbow into Brian's nose. There was a crunching sound of breaking bone. Brian let out a cry and staggered backwards. Richard rammed his foot hard into Brian's balls. Brian collapsed in a heap. Richard walked round his prostrate body and kicked him in the head.

Brian lay groaning on the floor. Richard bent down and grabbed him by the hair, staring down into his face.

'When someone asks what happened tell them you fell down the stairs. Better that than admitting you were beaten up by a fourth year.'

He slammed Brian's head on the ground, then continued towards his destination.

Jonathan sat at his desk. His books remained closed. There was no point trying to work. He couldn't concentrate. He wondered if he would ever be able to concentrate again.

He couldn't go on like this. He had to do something. But what? He couldn't tell anyone. No one would believe him. They would react like Reverend Potter, saying that he was just being childish. If only it was true. He would give anything for it to be true.

And if they did believe him, what then? He could not hope for understanding or forgiveness. They would turn from him in revulsion; shun him as something monstrous. It was the price he had to pay for what he had done.

In this world at least.

The door flew open. Richard entered. The rage in his eyes was shocking. Jonathan felt as if he might lose control of himself.

'I waited. You didn't come. Where the hell were you?'

He swallowed. 'Nowhere.' In his head was the image of a mad woman trying to drown her daughter in the bath.

'Don't lie to me.'

'I went for a bicycle ride.'

'Why?'

'I wanted to think.'

'Liar.'

'I'm not.' He was starting to perspire.

'You were trying to hide from me.'

'I wasn't! I swear I wasn't. I was scared, that's all. I wanted to be on my own to think.'

'Why were you scared? I'll take care of you. You know that.'

'But ...'

'But what? Are you saying I can't?'

'No, of course not. I ...'

'I've done a good job so far. Remember what your life was like before I came along? How people like Wheatley and Ackerley used to shit all over you? I put a stop to that.'

'I know you did. I'm not saying ...'

'You can't survive on your own. You need me. Don't ever forget that.' Richard rubbed at his cheek. Jonathan stared at Richard's hand. 'There's blood on your fingers.'

Richard smiled. 'A disagreement with Brian Harrington. Don't worry. You should see the state he's in.'

'You had a fight with a prefect?!'

'He's not going to say anything. I saw to that.'

Another image. A small boy with a knife, lunging at

his father, his face contorted in murderous rage. He wanted to be sick.

'Richard, I am really frightened. I want to tell someone.'

'No way.'

'I can't cope with this any more. I need to tell someone.'

'The only person you need is me. Who are you going to tell? Your father?' Richard started to laugh. 'Do you really think he'd be interested?'

The words hurt more than any blow. 'Don't ...'

'He doesn't care about you. Why don't you just accept it.'

'Richard, please ...'

Jonathan's watch lay on the desk. Richard picked it up, rolling it over in his fingers, reading the inscription. 'You love your father, don't you?'

'You know I do.'

'Yes,' said Richard slowly. 'I do.'

He tossed the watch from one hand to the other. Jonathan sat and watched as if hypnotised.

'Do you love him more than you love me?'

Jonathan's throat was dry. He couldn't speak.

'I thought so,' said Richard quietly.

He let the watch fall to the ground. He crushed it under his foot. Then he leaned forward, pressing his face into Jonathan's.

'I can do that to your father any time I want. You know I can. You need me! You can't survive without me! I'm the most important person in your life and if you ever try and leave me then I swear to God I will!'

He turned and left the room, slamming the door behind him. The watch fragments scattered in the draught.

# Chapter Three

Morning chapel had just started. Abbey House was deserted. Alan Stewart sat in his study, staring at the note that had been pushed under his door during the night.

*It's only a matter of time. The police are on to you. Do you know what happens to perverts in prison? Take the easy way out. Kill yourself.*

It wasn't possible. They had been so careful. No one could know.

But someone did.

He had tried to convince himself that the first note had another meaning; that he stood accused of nothing more sinister than failing Paul Ellerson academically. He had been Paul's tutor after all, and a popular theory was that Paul's suicide had been prompted by fear over his forthcoming exams. He had known he was lying to himself but had hung on to his delusion. Now there could be no doubt.

The police didn't know. Not yet. Of that he was sure. Otherwise they would have visited him already. They wouldn't waste time in a case like this.

Could a prosecution succeed? There was no physical evidence. There had been no notes or letters, nothing in writing.

They had made sure of that. He could explain away the holiday. The two of them had been friends, nothing more. They might believe him. They might not. That didn't matter. What mattered was how much they could prove.

But there would be an investigation. His name would be spread across the papers. And everyone would know. His family. His friends. Mud would stick. He would never be able to teach again. His career would be destroyed. Who would want their son taught by a man accused of such an offence?

A voice in his head screamed for him to leave. Get out now while he had the chance. Go abroad. Go anywhere as long as it was far away from here. But to run would be an admission of the guilt that they might never be able to prove. And if he did run he would never be able to return. He would spend the rest of his life as a fugitive, always looking over his shoulder, waiting for the law to pounce.

And if he stayed, what then? He would be vulnerable to blackmail that might delay but would not stop the police being informed. He would always be watchful, always fearful, waiting for the shame to begin.

It was all over, whatever he did.

But in his heart he knew that it had been over since the first evening of the term when he broke with Paul, discarding the only true happiness he had ever known in his life for fear of what others might think.

Whatever happened to him, he deserved it. They couldn't despise him more than he despised himself.

In the distance he heard the sound of voices. Chapel was over, lessons due to begin. As if in a trance he rose to his feet and began to gather his books.

Marjorie Ackerley rose late. She had been plagued by headaches and had taken pills to help her sleep. As she made her way downstairs she assumed that Henry would already have left.

But she was wrong. He was sitting in the drawing-room. He

was still wearing his dressing gown. His face was grey from lack of sleep.

'Henry?'

No answer. He stared into space.

'What are you doing here? Are you ill?'

Still nothing. She began to be afraid. 'Henry please, what is it?'

'Someone knows.'

'Knows what?'

'Someone knows.'

His voice was hollow, like that of a ghost. Understanding came in a rush, accompanied by a wave of nausea. 'They can't!'

'They do.'

'It's not possible!'

'The calls we've been getting. That's what they are.'

She shook her head. 'No one could know.'

'Someone does I tell you. Do you think I'd invent something like this?'

Her legs threatened to collapse beneath her. She sat down. 'Who is it?' she asked him.

'I don't know.'

'What do they want? Money?'

'They haven't asked for any.'

'They will. What else could they want?'

'Justice.'

'Impossible. They can't prove anything.'

'What if they can?'

'They can't. We know that.'

'But what if they can?' He began to run his hands through his thinning hair. 'What then?'

She made her voice as soothing as possible. 'Henry, listen to me. They cannot know for sure. Otherwise they would have come forward at the time. Someone is trying to frighten us, that's all.'

'Us? It's me they want, not you.'

She lowered her eyes. 'They'd want me too,' she said softly, 'if they knew everything.'

He stared at her, his eyes wide with fear. 'But they can't, can they?'

She shook her head.

'I know they can't. It's impossible. Of course it is. But what if they do?' He began to rock back and forth in his seat. 'What if somehow they've found out? What are we going to do?'

'We'll manage.'

He wasn't listening to her; too wrapped up in his own panic. 'What if they do? Oh God, what will happen to me then? What will they do to me then?'

She stretched out her arm and put her hand on his. 'Nothing will happen, Henry. Not if we stand together. We did last time. We will now. We're strong together. You just have to trust me.'

He pulled his hand away as if she were diseased.

'Stand together?! Is that how you describe what we did?!'

'Now Henry . . .'

'It's not about standing together! It's about control!' He jumped to his feet. 'It's always been about control!'

'That's not true!'

'You're using this to manipulate me! Just like you did last time!'

She rose to her feet. 'Henry, we don't have time for this! Call it whatever you want but the only thing that matters now is that we need each other! We have to stand together. That's the only way we'll get through this.'

Suddenly the panic faded from his face, replaced by something that looked like regret.

'And if we do get through?' he asked her. 'What then?'

She said nothing. 'What then?' he asked again.

She shook her head. 'Don't. Not now.'

'I'm going for a walk. I need some air. I'll be back soon. We'll talk then. Decide what to do.'

He left the room. Slowly she sat down. Like him she began to rock back and forth in her chair.

The last period of the morning had ended. Boys filed out of their classrooms, swarming along the corridors towards the dining-hall.

Nicholas walked with the Perrimans. Michael was talking about the Geography test they'd just taken and which he was sure he'd failed. Stephen was trying to reassure him. Nicholas kept looking back towards the door of the class-room they'd just left, watching for Jonathan. He had sat alone today. Richard was absent, attending his stepmother's funeral.

Everyone had left now. There was still no sign of Jonathan. 'I've forgotten something,' he told them. 'Go on. I'll catch you up.'

He walked back to the classroom. Jonathan was sitting at his desk, arranging and then rearranging his books with a distant look on his face. It took him a while to realise that Nicholas was there.

They stared at each other awkwardly, like duellists, both reluctant to make the first move.

'How did you do?' asked Jonathan eventually.

'Do?'

'In the test.'

'Better than you. You spent the whole time staring into space.'

'Couldn't concentrate.'

'Expect not. Can't be easy when Richard's not here to hold your hand.'

Jonathan looked ashamed. Nicholas was glad. 'When you next see Richard tell him that my family send their regards.'

Jonathan hung his head.

'Tell him that my grandmother hasn't gassed herself yet but we live in hope. Tell him that yes, everyone would have been happier if I'd died instead of my brother but we're all making the best of a bad deal.'

'I'm sorry.'

'To hell with your apologies! I don't want them! I hate you for what you've done! I wish you were the one who was dead, not Wheatley!'

He turned to go. He knew he had hurt Jonathan. He told himself he was glad. He wanted so much to be glad. But in his head was an image of the two of them sitting astride a cannon on the hill overlooking Southwold beach, laughing together as his father took their picture. It had been a good time. There had been so many good times.

And he wanted them back.

He shut the door and turned back. A lump had come into his throat.

'Why did you do it?'

'Don't ...' began Jonathan.

'I trusted you. You were my best friend. How could you tell him?' Tears came into his eyes. 'You were the one person I trusted enough to tell. How could you do that to me?'

'I didn't do it to hurt you. You have to believe that.'

'I just want to understand.'

Jonathan shook his head.

'Please.'

'Richard hated you. He really did.'

Nicholas stared at him in disbelief. 'And that's why you told him?!'

'You don't understand!' Jonathan too was close to tears. 'You don't know what his hate is like. It's so intense. It scares me. He hated you being around. He used to go on about you all the time. I didn't want to lose you. I told him because I thought he'd feel sorry for you and that way he wouldn't hate you so much. But I was stupid! He doesn't ever feel pity. You tell him something painful and he just uses it to cause more pain.'

'You didn't laugh at me? You didn't think it was all a joke?'

'God no! How could I?!' He started to sob. 'I know how much it hurt you. I could never laugh about that. Just like you never laughed about my father and stepmother, about Paul Ellerson and about everything private I ever told you. We trusted each other and I betrayed you. You've got every right to hate me but you have to believe I didn't do it to hurt you. I did it because I wanted to keep you as a friend and I didn't think he was going to let me.'

A tear ran down Nicholas's cheek. He wiped it away. There was a sense of warmth, just as there had been when Jonathan had tried to catch his eye the previous day. But this time it was no illusion. It was the warmth of forgiveness and of finding something precious that he had feared lost for ever.

'I do believe you,' he said softly. 'And I do understand.'

He sat down beside Jonathan, struggling to keep the tremor out of his voice. 'Don't cry, Jon. It'll be all right.'

'How can it be? After what I've done?'

'You haven't done anything.'

'What about James Wheatley? What about Richard's step-mother?'

'It wasn't your fault.'

'Wasn't it?' Jonathan turned to look at him. 'You don't believe that any more than I do.'

They sat in silence for a time. 'Well if it is,' said Nicholas eventually, 'then it's my fault too.'

'You weren't there for all of it. Even when you were you didn't join in.'

'Maybe not, but I didn't try and stop you.'

'How could you? You couldn't have stopped Richard. No one could.'

Nicholas realised that Jonathan had started to tremble. 'Jon, what is it?'

'I keep telling myself that it's not my fault. That it was all just a stupid game. That it didn't mean anything. That all this mess will go away. But it won't go away. It just gets worse.'

Nicholas took a deep breath. 'How much worse?'

'I feel different inside now. Like there's something dark in me. Something that wasn't there before. Some power.' Jonathan swallowed. 'As if I can will things to happen without even needing the board.'

'But you're not going to do that, are you? You're a good person. You don't want to hurt anyone. Not deep down. That's Richard's way. It's not yours.'

Jonathan continued to tremble. 'There's more I haven't told you. I'm scared, Nick. I really am.'

'Tell me. You can trust me with anything. You know that.'

Jonathan managed a smile. 'Of course I do. You're the best friend I've ever had and I'm so sorry. I really am sorry . . .'

'Don't,' Nicholas told him. 'It's all in the past now. Just tell me what's been going on.'

Clive sat at his desk, working at his speech. He had called a school assembly for the following afternoon to speak about what had happened to James Wheatley. He read over what he had written and his heart sank. He had never cared for James Wheatley and undertones of that dislike came out in his words. He screwed the paper into a ball and threw it into the bin. He heard a floorboard creak. He looked up to see Jennifer standing in the doorway.

'I thought you were going to Norwich.'

'We are. Eventually. Lizzie has gone to visit that friend of hers. Marjorie what's her name. She'll be back in half an hour. We'll go then.'

'I see.' He reached for another piece of paper. She walked into the room, pushing the door shut behind her. He watched her warily. 'Was there something else?'

'Does there need to be?'

'I'm working.'

'As I see. So industrious all the time. Isn't my cousin a lucky woman?'

He felt anger rising up inside him. He tried to swallow it down. 'Don't start.'

'Me? As I remember you were the one who started things.'

'Nothing was ever started. Not between us.'

'Wasn't it?'

'You know it wasn't. I'm busy. I don't have time for this.'

'Don't have time for me you mean.'

He sensed the edge in her voice. He tried to ignore it. 'Take it however you want.'

'You had time once.'

He took a deep breath. 'Jennifer I think you should go.'

'I will. When Lizzie gets back.'

He put down his pen. 'I didn't mean that.'

'So what did you mean?'

'That you should leave here. That you should stop visiting. It's not doing either of us any good.'

'Not you perhaps. It does me a power of good.'

'This makes you happy?' He rose to his feet. 'Is your life really so empty that the only pleasure you have is in tormenting me?'

She flinched. Her eyes hardened. 'What do you know about my life?'

'That you seem determined to waste it. You have to stop this. For your own sake if not for mine. You're still young. You're intelligent, attractive. It's not too late to find happiness with someone.'

'Isn't it?'

Suddenly the edge vanished from her voice, revealing the pain that lay behind it. 'Look at me Clive. I'm not attractive. I'm not desirable. I never was. Do you think I don't know that? I have nothing in my life. Except the power to hurt.'

'But why must you hurt Lizzie?! What good will it do to tell her? She's devoted to you. She thinks the world of you. Hurt me if you must but why must you hurt her?'

'BECAUSE SHE'S EVERYTHING I WANT TO BE!'

Her eyes were flashing now. Her self-control was breaking down.

'Because she's attractive! Because she's popular! Because people are drawn to her like moths to a light! She is everything I ever wanted to be and I hate her for that!'

'Do you hate her enough to ruin all that she and I have together?'

'You think what you have is precious?' She started to laugh. 'So precious that the moment her back is turned you're making love to me!'

'Making love?! Is that what you call it?'

'And what would you call it? Making small talk?'

'I was lonely. She hadn't let me touch her in months.'

'So it was her fault was it? Her fault for being frigid!'

'She was ill! She'd had a serious miscarriage! She nearly died and then had to come to terms with the fact that she'd never have a child! She was distraught! She needed love and understanding.'

'And instead you betrayed her.'

His own eyes were flashing now. He was almost blind with rage. 'But I wasn't the only one was I?! You arrived on our doorstep overflowing with concern, saying how you wanted to help take care of her. It was all lies. You'd heard the state she was in and thought you'd take your chance to break us up! To have something of hers! You make this great show of caring and every minute you're brushing up against me and giving me those smiles and those looks and then one night when I'm so drunk I don't know what I'm doing you make your move. Oh Clive, I want you so much. I have done since we first met. Make love to me, Clive. Lizzie need never know.'

'And you did!'

'Yes I did. God help me I did! I was weak and I was lonely and I will always despise myself for that! But don't flatter it with the description of lovemaking. There was no love in it whatsoever. We had sex on a sofa. We were like animals fulfilling urges. And every time I kissed you I was thinking of her! Every second I was inside you I was dreaming of her! You were just a body I used to gain some sort of release! Nothing that happened was to do with us. Nothing!'

'BASTARD!' She raised her fist and tried to strike him. He caught her arms and held them.

'SO GO AHEAD AND TELL HER THEN!' he roared. 'Spread your poison if you must! But it won't just be my life you'll destroy! What about your own?! Oh she'll hate me when she finds out but how is she going to feel about you?! Do you think you'll still be welcome here when she finds out what you did when she was weak and needed you?! She'll never want to see you again! She's the only person in this world who really cares about you! You think your life is empty now?! What will it be like when you lose her?!'

'What indeed?' said a voice behind them.

Elizabeth stood in the doorway watching them both.

Clive released Jennifer's arms. The nightmare he had dreaded for so long had at last come true. He felt as if someone had kicked him between the legs.

'I didn't want to believe it,' said Elizabeth quietly. 'The two people I love most in the world. I told myself they couldn't do that to me.'

'But it wasn't my fault!' cried Jennifer. 'He forced himself on me! You have to believe that!'

Elizabeth shook her head. 'Oh Jennifer . . .'

Jennifer started to cry. 'He was drunk! You heard him say it! He raped me!'

'I think you should leave.' Elizabeth told her.

'He's an animal!'

'Jennifer, stop this please.'

'But it's true! I wanted to tell you but he said he'd kill me if I did! He's the one you should hate, not me! I wouldn't hurt you Lizzie! You know I wouldn't!'

Elizabeth stared at her in revulsion. 'I want you out of my house now!'

'Well damn you then!' cried Jennifer. 'Damn you and your happy marriage and your perfect life! You think it only happened once?! It happened hundreds of time! Hundreds! From before you got married right up to today! And when he wasn't doing it with me he was doing it with someone else! He was never yours! Never! Your whole life is a lie!' Sobbing she ran from the room.

Elizabeth turned to Clive. 'And what are you going to tell me? That she tied you down and made you do it?'

He shook his head.

'What then?'

'Nothing, except that I love you.'

Her face crumpled in pain. 'Don't. Please.'

'I have to. You are everything to me. All the joy I have comes from you. I would give my life for you. Without you I have no life at all.'

Tears came into her eyes. She covered her mouth with her hand. He held out his arms to her. She took a step forward. Then she stopped, shook her head. 'I can't. I'm sorry.' She left the room.


The bell rang, signalling the end of lunch period and the start of afternoon games. Nicholas and Jonathan still sat together in the empty classroom. They had been talking for over an hour.

'You have to talk to a priest,' said Nicholas finally. 'Someone who knows about these things.'

'It won't do any good,' Jonathan told him. 'Reverend Potter didn't believe me.'

'Of course he didn't. I like Reverend Potter but the only thing he believes in is a quiet life. He doesn't really believe in God or religion or good or evil.' Nicholas thought for a moment. 'But I know someone who does.'

'Who?'

'Mr Perriman. The twins' father.'

'Mr Perriman?! I couldn't talk to him.'

'Why not?'

'The twins hate me. They're not going to let me speak to him, are they?'

'They don't hate you. They're just scared and that's because of what their father's told them and that's good because it means he takes it seriously. He won't just dismiss what you say like Reverend Potter did. He'll believe you, and he'll be able to tell you what to do.'

Jonathan stared at him. 'Do you really think so?'

'Yes. Definitely. Does that mean you'll talk to him?'

Jonathan nodded.

'I'll speak to the twins tonight. They'll take some persuading but they'll come round. I know they will.'

Suddenly Jonathan's eyes widened with alarm. 'What about Richard? He comes back tomorrow night. What am I going to do?'

'You have to act as if nothing's changed. Don't talk to me. I'll pretend I still hate you. I'll make sure the twins do too. Richard mustn't find out about this.'

'But what if he does?' Jonathan began to tremble. 'Oh God, what will he do if he does?! And he will. I know he will. He looks at me sometimes and it's like he's reading my thoughts. I can't keep things from him.'

'You have to keep this from him,' Nicholas told him. 'You don't have any choice.'

'I know.' Jonathan took a deep breath. 'I will.'

'Of course you will. He won't find out anything. It's going to be all right Jon. You're not on your own any more. We'll work this out together, just you see.'

Jennifer's taxi had left fifteen minutes ago. Clive stood in the bedroom he shared with his wife, watching her fill a suitcase.

'Please don't do this,' he begged her.

'I have to.'

'No you don't.'

'Yes I do. Don't you see that?'

'I love you,' he told her. His voice was trembling. 'Please, Lizzie. We can get through this. I know we can.'

She closed the case and turned to face him. 'I wish we could. I really do. But how can we? You slept with Jennifer.'

He shook his head. 'It wasn't like that.'

'So what was it like?'

'It doesn't matter what it was like.'

'You're wrong, Clive. It does matter. It matters to me. You slept with my cousin. You betrayed me with her. I was ill. It was the worst time in my life and I needed you. I needed you both!'

'It was a mistake! A moment of madness! It meant nothing!'

Tears came into her eyes. 'It means everything! Don't you see?! Every time I look at you I'm going to picture the two of you together! The two people I love best in the world!' She started to cry. 'I'm sorry but I can't do that. That's why I have to go.'

She reached for the case. His heart ached as if someone had plunged a knife through it. He grabbed hold of her arm, pulling her towards him. He fell to his knees, threw his arms around her waist and buried his head in her skirt.

'Lizzie, I'm begging you, please don't leave me! Oh God, don't leave me! You're my reason for living. You're my whole world. I cannot live without you. Hate me, curse me, do anything you want to punish me but just don't leave me!'

He began to sob like a child crying for its mother. Her own tears were silent. Gently she began to stroke his hair. They remained like that for some time.

Eventually she moved away. He let her go. He knew that it was hopeless. He remained where he was, staring at the floor. He felt as if he were dying.

'Where will you go?' he asked her.

'I don't know yet.'

'Stay here. This is your home. I should be the one to go.'

'You're needed here. You have things to do.' She wiped at her eyes. 'I'm sorry it has to be like that. I love you and I don't want to hurt you, but I just can't stay. Please try and understand.'

She walked towards the door. He called her name. She turned towards him.

'Is there a chance, however faint, that one day you'll be able to forgive me?'

'Don't ask me that. Not now.'

'Please. I have to know. When you leave you take my life with you. I need something to hope for.'

'I love you,' she told him. 'I'm sorry.'

'When there's love there's always hope. That's right, isn't it? I have to believe that.'

'Believe it then,' she told him gently.

'I'll wait for you. For ever if needs be. I love you Lizzie. I'll never stop wanting you back.'

She left the room. He buried his head in his hands and wept.

'Absolutely not,' announced Stephen Perriman.

'He needs us!' cried Nicholas. 'We have to help him!'

Supper was over, prep period about to begin. The two of them stood facing each other in their study. Michael sat at his desk watching them both.

'I don't have to help him,' Stephen told Nicholas. 'Just like Jonathan didn't have to start messing around with things he shouldn't. I tried to warn him but he wouldn't listen. He's made his bed. He'll just have to lie in it.'

'But Stephen . . .' began Michael.

'Keep out of this,' Stephen told him before turning his attention back to Nicholas. 'Why are you so keen to help him anyway? He's no friend of yours. Don't you remember how he dumped you? How he and Rokeby laughed at you?'

'They didn't laugh at me. Anyway I don't care about that now. Jon needs our help.'

'He doesn't deserve help. What he did was evil.'

'He may have been stupid but he's not evil. He's just easily led. Rokeby's the evil one.'

'Poor little Jonathan,' sneered Stephen. 'Led astray by big bad Richard. Well that's shit and we both know it. No one makes someone do things they don't want to do. They're as bad as each other and they deserve everything they get!'

'How can you say that?!' cried Michael suddenly. 'You were the one who dragged me out of Richard's study that night! You were just as scared then as Jonathan is now!'

Stephen flushed. He turned towards his brother. 'That's rubbish!'

'No it's not! It's true!'

'I wasn't scared! I was just watching out for you, just like I always do because you're too dim to watch out for yourself! If it wasn't for me then you'd be the one sitting alone in the chapel, crying about what you'd done. You should be thanking me not trying to make me look stupid!'

Michael looked upset. 'I'm not!'

'Then keep your mouth shut!'

'I just don't see why we can't help him. He was our friend too. I miss him. Why can't we forgive him and go back to how things were?'

'Mike, just shut up. You don't understand.'

'But why not?!' Michael rose to his feet. 'You can't tell me what to do this time! We have to help him. It's what Dad would want. He's always talking about the importance of forgiveness and isn't that what this is all about? Nick has much more reason to hate Jon than we do. If he can forgive then why can't we?'

Stephen slapped his face.

Nicholas gasped. Michael cried out and covered his cheek. Stephen grabbed him by the hair and stared into his face.

'Don't you *ever* lecture me again! I spend my whole *fucking* life looking after you and what thanks do I get?! Well just remember that I'm the one who makes the decisions, not you, because I know what's best. And I have decided we are *not* going to involve Dad in this. It's not our problem and it's not his either.'

The bell rang for prep. Stephen released Michael and turned to Nicholas.

'I'm not going to speak to our father about Jonathan and neither is Michael. And if you want to stay friends with us then you'd better forget about helping him too.'

The three of them sat down at their desks. Stephen buried his head in a book. Michael was close to tears. He kept rubbing at his cheek. Nicholas stared at him. Their eyes met.

In the silence of the room a communication passed between them.

# Chapter Four

Dawn. 9th December 1954.

Marjorie Ackerley crouched at the top of the stairs.

The house was in darkness. Henry sat alone downstairs. He had been there all night. He had been drinking before she went to bed and would have continued long afterwards. She listened for the sound of snores but heard only silence. She was frightened. She could only guess at the dark journeys his mind would take when under the influence of alcohol and fear. She wanted to call out to him but dread paralysed her tongue. Safer to wait and say nothing.

It was cold in the house. She shivered. Wrapping her dressing-gown around her she continued her vigil.

Henry Ackerley sat staring at the framed photograph of his dead daughter.

She had been a beautiful child. Everyone had said so. She would bounce into a room full of strangers, all sunshine and laughter, captivating them all. One of the joys of his life had been to sit and watch the way people reacted to her. She would stand in the centre of the room, beaming at everyone, then her eyes would seek him out and they would exchange a special smile; hers the trust of a child in a father; his the intense love of a father whose dreams for his child's future now satisfied ambitions he had once harboured for himself.

He had always been ambitious; had always expected to make his mark in the world. It had seemed so easy when he was growing up. His family had been wealthy. He had enjoyed the best education money could buy, winning all the prizes available to him. As he finished his time at Oxford he had been offered a postgraduate position at Harvard. The cost was considerable but his father was proud of him and willing to finance the adventure. His future had seemed so dazzling then. He was determined to become one of the world's leading experts on the classical world. Perhaps he would have done too, if the invitation had not come.

His godparents were old friends of his mother's. They had always been fond of him and were proud of his achievements. They wanted him to spend the summer with them. They were the foremost family in their area; acknowledged leaders of local society. He had been quick to accept; keen to bask in their approval. He had strode around their huge house in Yorkshire, smiling graciously at everyone, enjoying the admiration of the younger maids as they whispered and giggled about this splendid visitor who would soon be leaving for America and a future of undoubted brilliance.

And as he revelled in their attention he noticed one who stood out from the rest; a girl of about eighteen with golden hair and a beauty that would have been the envy of many of the so-called belles that his godmother paraded before him. Each time their paths crossed he found he could not keep his eyes from her. He would watch the way she lowered her eyes as he approached, the way her hips swayed as she passed by, and the way she turned back and smiled invitingly at him before moving on. He would stand and watch her go; flattered by her infatuation and aware of his own desire.

One night his godparents had held a dinner party; their guests mostly middle-aged friends who applauded the brilliance of his conversation and toasted the brightness of his future. As he had made his way to bed, his head spinning from an excess of wine and admiration, he found her waiting at the top of the stairs. A look had passed between them and he had taken her hand and led her to his room.

There had been no words. It had been his first experience of physical love. He found it quick and easy; the satisfaction of a desire that was uncomplicated by emotional involvement. When it was over she slipped quietly away. In the days that followed his eyes were no longer drawn to her. It had been nothing to him. He assumed she felt the same. He did not give it another thought.

Two days before his departure he was summoned by his godfather. Another man was present; a rough, working man who reeked of liquour and heaped curses on him as the man who had ruined the life of his Marjorie. It took him some time to understand. He had never bothered to learn her name.

His godparents were sympathetic. It was a youthful indiscretion; nothing more. The father's anger was not so extreme that it could not be eased by a sum of money. That would be best. They could see that. They were sure that Henry's father would see it too.

But they misjudged him. He was appalled. He was a highly moral man who expected his family to live up to his own standards and had no sympathy for those who failed to do so. He told his son that he had wronged a girl and would now have to pay the price. He was withdrawing his financial support. A wedding must be arranged; all dreams of Harvard forgotten. Within weeks Henry found himself a married man with a pregnant wife to provide for.

He had taken a teaching job in London. The two of them had set up home in a tiny flat; people who had barely exchanged two words now forced into a relationship for which neither was prepared. He poured his energies into his work. She poured hers into trying to make him happy. Her life up to then had been harsh; her mother abandoning her as a child, leaving her to the mercy of a violent, alcoholic father. To her the marriage was a release and she was grateful and eager to please. She felt ashamed of her humble beginnings and tried to bury them beneath a veneer of sophistication. She took elocution lessons to soften her accent. She took care over her appearance; learning to dress well with little money. She had had little schooling but now read books to improve her mind and broaden her conversational range. Slowly, determinedly, she reinvented herself as a wife of whom any man would be proud.

The birth of their daughter acted as a bond between them. The intensity of his love for the child helped him to feel some form of affection for the mother. Little Sophie represented the best of them both; the golden haired beauty of her mother combined with the brilliant mind of her father. He would sit with her for hours at a time, teaching her the basics of literacy and numeracy; revelling in her thirst for knowledge and the speed with which her mind could absorb new ideas. Marjorie's charm had earned them many friends and he loved to parade Sophie's brilliance before them. He would sit her on his knee and give her mathematical problems that would cause her to frown and concentrate and then beam with pride when she gave the right answer. Everyone would applaud and he would wrap his arms around her and cover her in kisses. He would see Marjorie smiling at them both and he would smile back; telling himself that he could not curse a fate which had given him this adored child.

Death had come without warning. A child's winter cold that turned suddenly to pneumonia. Neither of them had realised the seriousness of her condition. Before leaving for work he had stopped to kiss her cheek and promise to bring her a present on the way home, and she had stared up at him with her hazel eyes and told him that when she was better she would learn to cook so she could help her mother make his favourite meals. He had left the house with a smile on his face. Early in the afternoon the message had come. He had run all the way home, racing upstairs to her bedroom to find Marjorie being comforted by friends and the doctor telling him that Sophie hadn't suffered and was now in a better place.

In those first days he was too numb to comprehend fully what he had lost. True understanding came on the day of the funeral; when he stood with Marjorie beside a tiny grave receiving the condolences of others. One mourner, trying in vain to cheer, said that at least they had each other for comfort and support in the dark days ahead.

At that moment he saw everything clearly; recognised the final ruination of all of his early ambitions. He understood that the love of his daughter had been the one thing to make his shabby life bearable. In her death he had lost the power to hope. Now he could only exist.

They moved away. He took a new job at a school in Berkshire. An attempt at a new start, doomed to failure before it had begun. Now that Sophie was gone the necessary courtesy that had governed their relationship began to break down. He hated his life and blamed her for it. He withdrew into himself; burying himself in his work and his memories; keeping her at a distance. She surrendered to her own demons. She knew there would be no more children. Her father was dead now. She had no other family and was plagued with a dread of growing old alone. The more he pulled away from her the more she tried to cling to him; a bizarre dance of revulsion and need that only added to the misery of each.

Until at last he realised that they could not continue. For both their sakes they had to part. He told Marjorie that they would divide what money they had and go their separate ways. She had wept, had said that he was all she had in the world and that she could not bear to lose him. They started to argue. She became hysterical. Feeling as if he were suffocating, he had run from her; driving for miles and miles; ending up at a country pub where no one knew him and where he proceeded to drown his misery in alcohol.

It was late evening when he drove home. Stormy too. The wind and rain buffeted the car which he was in no fit state to drive. He guided it homeward through country lanes; his reflexes sluggish, his eyelids weighted with lead. He did not see the girl until he was upon her; barely had time to register a pair of terrified eyes before he felt the thud.

Automatically he stopped the car. In the rear mirror he saw her lying motionless in the road. He knew that he should go back, try to find help. But with shock came clarity and the understanding that he could never turn himself in. With so much alcohol inside him he could not plead an accident. His only option was a lengthy prison sentence. So he had driven away; his heart pounding; his breath short and ragged; praying to whatever God was listening that the girl be dead and so unable to identify him.

In the privacy of his garage he inspected the car. Some small dents to the bumper. Unnoticeable unless a conscious effort was made to look. When he entered the house he found Marjorie waiting for him. He told her that he regretted what he had said; that he was sorry he had hurt her; that she should go to bed and that he would follow shortly. Instead he spent the rest of the night sitting downstairs; staring at the hands of the clock as they moved through the night and on until morning.

He made himself go to work; forced himself to behave as if everything was normal. Eavesdropping on conversations he learned that the body of a girl had been discovered in a remote lane some miles away; the victim of a hit and run driver. 'Terrible thing,' said one person. 'Poor girl was only seventeen. Her life had hardly started. Driver should be hung!' He knew then that all would be well. He allowed himself to breathe again. At the weekend he would take the car to a garage miles away; have the dents repaired. Cover his tracks completely.

Three days later the police came. It was early evening.

Marjorie showed them into the drawing-room. One was about forty; the other some years younger. He rose to his feet; trying to smile; fighting an urge to vomit.

They apologised for the intrusion, explained that there had been a witness to the accident; a poacher who had wanted to keep silent but now felt honour-bound to come forward. His evidence was limited; his view had been from a distance. He had not been able to see the face of the driver or make out the licence plate. All he could do was give the make of car and the information that the driver had been a man. They were now making inquiries of all known owners of the type of car in question. They shuffled awkwardly; again apologising for the intrusion, wondering if Henry could tell them what he had been doing on the evening in question.

He opened his mouth, trying to formulate a response, only for Marjorie to begin to speak. In her velvet voice she told them that she remembered that evening very well. Henry had spent the early part marking essays while she had prepared a supper of beef in a pepper sauce. She explained that this was a favourite dish of Henry's though the sauce was too spicy for her own taste. Both policemen nodded, agreeing that they too preferred plain food.

After supper, she told them, they had spent the rest of the evening sitting together in the living room, listening to a play on the wireless. She started to laugh; the sound like the chiming of bells; confessing that the play had been a romance that had bored Henry so much that he had fallen asleep within ten minutes. The policemen laughed too; both charmed by her. The elder one said that he was prone to do the same thing and that his own wife was far less understanding.

Marjorie apologised for not being able to remember the name of the play but said that she had made a note of it in her diary which was upstairs. She offered to go and fetch it. The elder policeman told her that it would not be necessary. Once again he said that Henry was lucky to have such an understanding wife.

Then, hesitantly, the younger one asked if, just for the sake of completeness, they could see the car.

At that moment he knew it was all over. He decided to confess, to finish it. But Marjorie was too quick for him. Still smiling she asked them to follow her, leading them to the garage and the car. He stood between the policemen, staring in disbelief. The dents were gone; the car as flawless as it had been before that evening.

'I'm sorry,' said the older policeman. 'But we had to ask. Formalities.'

Marjorie smiled. 'Of course. We understand, don't we Henry?' He nodded, too dazed to speak.

'Do you have any other leads?' she asked them.

Both shook their heads. 'We've phoned other police stations in the area,' said the younger man. 'Asked them to put out feelers. The only thing they've thrown up is some garage in Hornchurch which had a woman bring a car in for repair work yesterday. Nothing serious. They did it while she waited.'

Marjorie looked interested. 'Did they make a note of the licence plate?'

'No reason to,' said the elder man. 'Like Sergeant Wicks said, they did the work while she waited.'

'What about the woman? What was her name?'

'Cooper. At least that's what he thinks. He can't remember properly and she paid in cash so there's no receipt or anything. Said she wore loads of make up. Bit tarty. Strong accent too. Lancashire he thought, or Yorkshire. But that's it. Probably nothing anyway. We'd better be off Mrs Ackerley. Not take up any more of your time.'

Marjorie expressed sympathy at their having to work on such a cold evening. She offered them tea before they went. They refused, but reluctantly. The older man, staring at Henry with a look of unabashed envy, said that it had been a pleasure to meet them.

They stood on the doorstep together and watched the

policemen leave. Then they walked back into the house, shutting the door behind them. She stared at him. Her smile was gone: her expression an ugly mixture of triumph and self-disgust.

'It's dangerous for us to stay in this area,' she told him. 'We must move away as quickly as possible.' She turned, began to climb the stairs.

'There is no us,' he called after her. 'Don't you understand that?'

She turned back. 'Oh but there is Henry. There always will be. You'll never leave me now. Not after what I've done. Not after what I know.'

That had been six years ago; six years in which she had bound him to her with the fear of the harm she could do him if he tried to leave. He had escaped jail but he was not free. He was her captive, she his guard; their house a prison in which each circled the other warily whilst trying to deceive the world with a façade of normality.

And now someone knew.

But it wasn't possible. If someone knew then why not come forward at the time? If the motive was blackmail – which it surely was – then why wait six years before making contact? It didn't make sense.

Unless they had only just found out.

But how? Who could have told them? The one witness had not been able to identify him. The only people who knew the truth were Marjorie and himself. He had told no one. Marjorie would not have told anyone either.

Unless she had something to gain from doing so.

But that couldn't be? Her silence was her power. She would not jeopardise that by talking.

But what if she sensed that her power was failing? What if she suspected he might run the risk of breaking with her, leaving her alone as she had always feared?

No! It couldn't be!

But it would work! If he was frightened there was only one

person he could turn to. The only other person who knew. The person who had helped him before and would help him again.

He was vulnerable. He was dependent. She had control.

The blood was pounding in his temples. The pressure was so great he felt his head would explode.

BITCH!!

It was about control. It had always been about control.

BITCH! EVIL, MANIPULATIVE BITCH!

His fists were clenched so tightly that the nails cut into his skin. Blood began to flow between his fingers. In his head he was screaming.

First period had just ended. In the crowded corridor Jonathan felt something being pushed into the pocket of his jacket. Nicholas walked past him, talking to the twins, ignoring him completely.

He reached inside his pocket, found a folded piece of paper. He smoothed it out.

*Mike's agreed to help. Stephen doesn't know and must NOT find out. Don't try and talk to us. We'll come and see you straight after lunch. It's going to be all right. N.*

Nicholas turned slightly, caught his eye. Jonathan made no acknowledgement, just continued on his way as if nothing had happened.

Half past ten. Tentatively Marjorie Ackerley began to make her way downstairs. The house was still silent.

'Henry?'

No answer.

She called again. Still nothing. She entered the living room, pushing the door closed behind her. She expected to see him there but the room was empty. She heard footsteps drawing closer. She started to tremble.

'Henry?'

The footsteps stopped outside the door. She backed away, towards the window. 'Henry, we need to talk.'

The footsteps moved away. She heard the front door open then close. She sat in one of the chairs by the fireplace. On the carpet she saw spots of blood.

It was cold in the room. She built up the fire. Then, wrapping her arms around herself, she sat and waited.

Lunchtime. Alan Stewart sat at the desk in his study. The assembly for James Wheatley was in one hour's time.

He stared at the words he had written, then crumpled the page into a ball and threw it in to the fire. Another failed attempt. He couldn't find the right words. He wondered if he ever would. Could any words be appropriate for something like this?

He thought about James Wheatley; then of Jonathan Palmer and Richard Rokeby. Had they been involved in James's death? He told himself it was impossible. But some instinct said otherwise.

He would never discover the truth now. Perhaps no one would. Whatever had taken place had been well concealed. Better than his own secret had been.

Again he started to write. The words poured out; a flow of black ink that said nothing he intended. Another ball of paper went into the fire. He stared into the flames. Tears rolled down his face.

'I'm going to the San,' said Nicholas as they left the dining-room.

'Headache still bad?' asked Stephen.

Nicholas nodded. 'I can't face an afternoon assembly unless I've had some aspirin.'

He wobbled slightly on his feet, rubbing at his temples. Stephen and Michael exchanged looks. 'Are you sure you're all right?' asked Stephen.

'Just a bit dizzy.'

'Maybe one of us should go with you,' suggested Michael.

'There's no need.'

'Yes there is,' insisted Michael. 'I'll go.' He turned to Stephen. 'We'll see you in assembly hall.'

Stephen nodded. 'I'll save you seats.' He moved off in one direction; Nicholas and Michael in another; their pace quickening as the distance between them increased.

Jonathan sat at his desk. He had been waiting for half an hour. He had missed lunch. The mere thought of food made him nauseous.

He heard footsteps in the corridor outside. The door opened. He smiled in greeting.

Richard entered.

The smiled died on his face. He felt as if he had been kicked in the stomach. He couldn't breathe. Richard stared at him in alarm. 'God, are you all right?'

He managed to nod.

'You look terrible. Are you ill?'

'You're not supposed to be back.'

'Change of plan. What's the problem? Aren't you pleased to see me?'

'Of course I am.' He forced a smile which fell pitifully short of his eyes. 'How was it?'

'My father's a wreck. Keeps going on about how it's all his fault.' Richard started to laugh. 'Everyone's telling him he shouldn't blame himself but it doesn't do any good. He's going to crack up soon. You can see it in his eyes. Then they'll have to put him away, like he tried to do to my mother.'

Jonathan fought an urge to scream. Nicholas and Michael would be here any minute. As soon as he saw them Richard would know what he'd done and then God help them all. Richard was still laughing. If they heard the sound of laughter they'd know something was wrong; know to keep away. He joined in but the sound was forced. 'What's the matter with you?' demanded Richard.

'Nothing.'

'You're hiding something.'

He shook his head, like a child trying to convince a parent of a lie.

'What have you done?'

His heart was pounding. 'Nothing, Richard. I swear it.'

The eyes bored into him. In their pupils he saw the image of a mad woman trying to drown her daughter.

He managed to look away. His gaze fastened on a folded piece of paper on a pile of books. Nicholas's note.

He felt himself grow pale.

'What's this?' demanded Richard, reaching for the note.

He didn't answer. Just sat and watched as Richard read. His fear was so great that he didn't even notice the dampness spreading between his legs.

Jonathan's study was empty.

'Perhaps he's in the bog,' suggested Michael.

They heard footsteps behind them. William Abbott was walking towards his study. 'Have you seen Palmer?' asked Nicholas.

'Went off with Rokeby.'

'Rokeby!' Nicholas and Michael stared at each other. 'He's not due back till tonight.'

'It was definitely him.'

'Where did they go?' demanded Michael.

William shrugged.

Nicholas took a deep breath. 'I know where they've gone,' he said. 'Come on.'

Clive Howard stood at the window of his study, watching crowds of boys process towards the assembly hall. Soon he would have to make his way there himself.

He turned towards the mirror, studying his reflection; a tall, heavy man who seemed to have become old overnight. He looked a mess; suit creased, tie crooked, hair uncombed. Once upon a time Lizzie would never have allowed him to look so shabby, but his appearance was of no interest to her now.

She had been gone for less than twenty-four hours but it seemed like an eternity. His sense of loss was like a physical pain; as if a parasite was eating away at his heart. The prospect of a lifetime without her was too terrible to contemplate. He wanted to die but knew that in death he would lose for ever the hope that one day she would return.

Mechanically, as if in a trance, he began to run a comb through his hair.

Marjorie woke suddenly. The fire was out. The room was cold. She did not know how long she had been asleep.

Henry stood before her. He reeked of alcohol. His clothes were dishevelled. The look in his eyes turned her blood to ice.

'It was you,' he whispered.

Frightened, she tried to stand. He took a step towards her. She froze.

'It was you.'

'What are you saying?'

'It was you. You told them. You betrayed me.'

She shook her head. She had started to tremble.

'IT WAS YOU!'

She cowered in her chair. 'You're drunk. You don't know what you're saying.'

'DON'T LIE TO ME!'

'I'm not! I swear it!'

'LIAR!'

'Henry, on my life, I've told no one!'

'YOU CAN'T CONTROL ME!! I WON'T LET YOU CONTROL ME!!'

'Henry, this is madness! You can't mean this!'

But the look in his eyes told her that he did.

Her fear turned to terror. She knew she had to escape. She jumped to her feet, tried to push past him. He grabbed her, thrust her back into the chair. He loomed over her. His body was rigid.

'Well no more! NO MORE! Let them do what they want with me. I'm going to be free of you for ever.'

She started to whimper. 'Henry, please don't do this! For Sophie's sake!'

'Shut up!'

'You loved Sophie! Don't you remember how much?!'

'SHUT UP!!'

'You begged me to get rid of her! You pleaded with me! But I didn't! I kept her for you and you were glad of it! You told me that you loved her more than you'd ever loved anyone! Look at her picture! Remember how much she loved you! For her sake please don't do this!'

'SHUT UP!! SHUT UP!!'

He began pounding at his temples with his fist. A terrible groaning sound came from his lips. He collapsed to his knees.

'I want her back! Oh God I want her back! Why did she have to die?! She was only a baby. She had no life at all. She could have done anything she wanted. She had so much potential. A hundred times more than me.' He began to sob. 'I would have given my life to save hers! But I didn't get the chance. I didn't even get the chance to say goodbye!'

His head bowed, he whimpered like a wounded animal. She sat and watched him. Every instinct screamed for her to run now while she had the chance. Leave this house and never come back.

But there was nothing for her outside this house. He was all she had.

Tentatively she reached out a hand to touch his shoulder. 'I love you, Henry,' she whispered. 'We can get through this.'

Slowly he raised his head. She stared into the face of madness. She began to scream.

He jumped to his feet. He reached for the poker that lay by the fireplace. He was screaming too. Their screams merged together; rage mixing with fear to produce a hymn of destruction.

Nicholas ran into Abbey House, almost colliding with a group of boys who were rushing off towards the assembly hall. Michael followed behind him.

They climbed the stairs that led to the fourth-year studies. As they drew close they heard the sound of two voices, both raised. One was harsh and accusatory, the other defensive and fearful.

They reached the top corridor. The air was stale and heavy. The third door on the left was closed. The voices were clearer now. They stood and listened. Richard was screaming about loyalty. His words were jagged, incoherent. Jonathan was sobbing, saying over and over again that he hadn't meant to do it. That he had been afraid. There was the short crisp sound of a blow being struck, followed by a cry of pain. Nicholas saw Michael flinch. He had an overpowering urge to turn and run. This was nothing to do with him. It was between Jonathan and Richard. He was afraid of Richard. He was afraid of all of this.

But Jonathan needed him and Jonathan was his friend. He was not going to let him down.

He opened his mouth. His throat was dry.

'Jon?'

The shouting stopped, replaced by muffled whispers.

'Jon. It's Nick. I'm here with Michael.'

At first silence. Then the door opened. Richard and Jonathan stepped out into the corridor.

'Budge up,' said Henry Dalton.

'I can't,' Stephen told him. 'I'm keeping those seats.'

'Sod you then,' Henry told him, before sliding into a seat in the row behind. Stephen ignored him. His attention remained focused on the door, watching for the arrival of Michael and Nicholas.

'What the hell do you want?' demanded Richard.

His words were aimed at both of them but his eyes were fixed on Nicholas. Jonathan stood beside him. His lip was bleeding; his eyes wide and fearful. Nicholas was afraid too but stood his ground. 'We want to talk to Jon,' he announced.

'You can't.'

'That's for him to say. Not you.'

'He does what I tell him.'

'He's not your property. You can't tell him what to do.' Nicholas took a step forward. 'Jon, come on. Let's go.'

Richard grabbed Jonathan round the neck, pulling him close. 'He belongs to me! You keep away!' His eyes were wild. 'Nick,' cried Jonathan, 'do what he says.'

Nicholas took another step forward. 'I'm not scared.'

'You should be! Just go! Please!'

'You see?!' cried Richard. 'He doesn't need you! The only person he needs is me!'

Nicholas ignored him. 'Jon, come on. We can help you.'

Jonathan hung his head. 'You can't. No one can. Not after what I've done.'

'You made a mistake, that's all. It was a game. It wasn't supposed to be real. People will understand that.'

Richard started to laugh. 'It was never a game! We knew exactly what we were doing!'

'That's a lie!' cried Nicholas. 'Everything you say is a lie. Jon come on. It's not too late.' He took another step forward.

'MOVE ONE MORE INCH AND I'LL SHOW YOU WHAT SORT OF FUCKING GAME IT IS!!'

Richard was shaking with rage. His breath came in short bursts.

'No one fucks with us! If they do they get what's coming to them! Wheatley got what he deserved and so did Turner, Ackerley, Stewart, Howard, my murderer father and my whore stepmother! THEY ALL GOT WHAT THEY FUCKING DESERVED AND IF YOU TRY AND COME BETWEEN JON AND ME YOU'LL GET WHAT YOU DESERVE TOO!!'

'MAY GOD FORGIVE YOU!!' cried Michael.

He came to stand beside Nicholas. His face was flushed. He too was shaking.

'Your stepmother was going to have a baby! What did that baby ever do to you?! How can you call your father a murderer?! You're the murderer, not him!! You're a million times worse than him!!'

Richard released his hold on Jonathan.

He took a step forward. His face was very pale. 'What did you say?' he asked calmly.

'You heard!' cried Michael.

'I know,' said Richard, 'but I want to hear it again.'

Nicholas was really frightened now. He moved closer to Michael. 'Don't say anything,' he whispered.

But Michael ignored him. He too seemed unnaturally calm. 'I said that you were worse than your father. I don't care what he's supposed to have done. Even if he is a murderer he's not as bad as you. You disgust me. You're the one that should be dead.'

Richard took another step forward. Jonathan grabbed at his arm. 'Richard, he didn't mean it! He doesn't know what he's saying!' Richard shook him off. His eyes were fixed on Michael. 'You're going to regret that,' he said levelly.

'Richard!' cried Jonathan. 'Don't! Please!'

Richard continued to walk towards Michael. Nicholas moved between them. 'Leave him alone!' Richard threw him aside as if he were a doll and continued to advance on Michael.

'Mike! Run!' screamed Nicholas. Michael ignored him. His

eyes remained fixed on Richard. 'I'm not frightened of you!' he cried defiantly.

But as Richard continued to advance he began to back away.

The assembly hall was virtually full now. The air was thick with the sound of voices.

There was still no sign of Michael and Nicholas. There must be a queue at the San. That's what Stephen told himself, but for some reason he was becoming increasingly anxious.

'What's the matter?' said Henry Dalton sarcastically. 'Think Mikey-Wikey's got lost?'

'Piss off!' snapped Stephen.

'Bet he has. He's so feeble. He can't do anything without you.'

'He's not feeble! If you must know he's taken Scott to the San. Scott's our friend. You wouldn't know about friends would you?!'

'The San? Are you sure?' The comment came from Peter Craig; another fourth year who had just arrived

'What do you mean?'

'When I saw them they were rushing off towards Abbey House.'

Suddenly his anxiety had a focus. He jumped to his feet, moved to the end of the row. One of the prefects grabbed his arm. 'It's about to start! Where d'you think you're going?' He pushed him away. He ran up the aisle towards the door.

Michael had retreated as far as he could. His back was pressed against the banister. Richard stood ten feet from him. Their eyes were locked as if in an embrace. Nicholas and Jonathan stood together, watching. Both were too frightened to approach.

'He didn't mean what he said!' cried Jonathan. 'You don't have to hurt him!'

'I'm not going to,' said Richard slowly.

'I'm not afraid of you,' said Michael again. His words had no conviction now. He looked terrified.

'Richard please! Just let him go! You don't have to hurt him!'

'I told you,' said Richard slowly. 'I'm not going to.'

Suddenly his body went rigid. He lowered his head, as if praying. It seemed to Nicholas that the air was growing colder. In his head he heard Richard's last sentence repeated. This time he realised that emphasis had been placed on the first word.

Stephen tore out of the main school building and across the cloisters. He passed Old School and on towards Abbey House. In his head the same words kept repeating themselves over and over again like a mantra.

*let him be all right let him be all right oh god please let him be all right . . .*

The banister rail collapsed.

It had stood solid for fifty years. Now it fell apart like a house of cards.

Michael staggered backwards, his feet teetering at the end of the ledge. His arms flailed in a desperate attempt to keep his balance. He looked down and then back, his eyes wide with terror. He started to scream. He held out his hand. Nicholas ran towards him but again Richard blocked his path. All he could do was stand and watch as Michael vanished from sight, falling down the stairwell, his scream echoing up into the roof until, in one sickening thud, it was silenced.

Far below them a door opened and closed. There were footsteps, a howl of anguish and finally the sound of sobbing.

Clive Howard stood at the front of the stage, staring at the boys who sat in rows before him, waiting for him to speak.

His head ached. There was a tightness in his chest. He felt tired and ill. He didn't want to be here. He didn't want any of this. All he wanted was his wife. But she was not here. He had no choice but to go on.

'Please rise for the singing of the school song.'

Nicholas was crying. 'You bastard! You fucking bastard!' He ran towards Richard, his fists raised to strike. Richard grabbed his arms and sent him hurtling to one side. Nicholas cracked his head on the wall and collapsed in a heap on the floor. Jonathan rushed to help him. He was also in tears. The two of them clung to each other.

'Leave him,' instructed Richard.

'I won't!'

'You'll do what I tell you. Now leave him!'

'You can't do this!' cried Jonathan. 'It has to stop! Don't you understand that?!'

Nicholas buried his head against Jonathan's chest. He could still hear the sound of sobbing, and, from somewhere far away, the sound of singing.

'I can do anything I want. ANYTHING!! You talk about stopping?! I haven't even started!! I hate them all! Every fucking one of them! AND EVERY ONE OF THEM IS GOING TO PAY!!'

Once again he lowered his head. His body went rigid.

Nicholas knew then that it was all over. He closed his eyes and began to whisper the words of the Lord's prayer.

In the distance the singing stopped abruptly. At first there was silence.

Then the sound of uproar.

The song was nearly finished. Clive Howard mouthed the words. It seemed so close in the hall. The atmosphere was liquid. He felt as if he was suffocating.

Suddenly it was as if his chest was being squeezed in a vice. He couldn't breathe. He gasped for air but there was none. The pain was unbelievable. The blood was draining out of his face.

Surely he was dying. The boys in the front row fell silent, staring at him as if he were already a ghost.

He let out a cry and collapsed, rolling off the stage and on to the floor beneath.

Nicholas realised that the danger was over. Jonathan was still holding him. The air around them was fetid. He had soiled himself. He began to sob with a mixture of shame and relief.

'Now leave him!' ordered Richard.

Jonathan released Nicholas and rose to his feet. Nicholas grabbed hold of his arm. Richard walked towards them. Nicholas flinched. Richard laughed. 'You're so pathetic. You're nothing. You're not even worth hating.' He turned and walked towards his study.

Nicholas continued to hold onto Jonathan's arm. 'Jon, please don't go!'

'I have to,' Jonathan told him. 'I don't have any choice.'

'But I'm scared!'

'You don't have to be. Not if you go now.'

Tears were pouring down his face. 'But what about you? I can't leave you.'

Jonathan crouched down beside him. He was crying too. 'Yes, you can. You must. It doesn't matter about me. I know what I have to do now. This is my problem, not yours. I'm sorry I got you involved in this. You're the best friend I've ever had. Whatever they say about me always remember that and try not to hate me.'

Suddenly he threw his arms around Nicholas and hugged him. Then he moved away, following Richard into his study.

Slowly Nicholas climbed to his feet. He could hear Richard's voice raised in anger. He tried to concentrate on what was being said but his head ached and he felt dizzy. He leant against the wall, trying to regain his focus.

As he stood there he thought he felt the air moving around him. The shadows on the floor seemed to take on a life of their own, sliding past him to gather outside the study door where they twisted and turned, as if pulsing with dark light.

Fear overcame him. He turned and ran for the stairs.

Jonathan pulled the bolt shut and turned to face Richard. His breathing was slow, his heartbeat steady. At last he was done with fear. Now he felt calm.

'When are you going to face the truth?' he asked.

Richard stared at him. 'What do you mean?'

'You're so full of hate. Your whole life is about hate. You wear it like chainmail because you hope it's going to protect you.'

Richard looked as if he had been struck. 'What are you saying?!'

'But it's all lies. You don't really hate your father or anyone else. You just tell yourself you do because it's easier that way.'

Richard was starting to tremble. 'You'd better stop this!'

'You tell yourself you hate everyone but the truth is that the only person you really truly hate is your mother because you loved her and you needed her and then she went and left you! And now you try and hate everyone else because that way you never have to need anyone ever again!'

'I told you to stop!'

'Why?! It's true!! You should hate her! You think she loved you?! She didn't care about you! She didn't even love you enough to stay alive!!'

'SHUT UP!! SHUT UP!!'

'But the hate hasn't saved you has it?! You need me now just like you once needed her! And the thing that's driving you mad is the fact that I don't need you back! Not any more! I may have done once but that was only because I was too weak and too stupid to see you for what you really are! And now I do I hate you! I can't bear being around you! I'd do anything to get away from you! Even kill myself!'

Richard snapped.

He lunged at Jonathan, knocking him to the floor. He sat on his chest, pinning his arms beneath his legs, and put his hands around his throat. He began to squeeze, tighter and tighter, his knuckles turning white with effort.

Jonathan struggled to throw him off but wasn't strong enough. As the pressure in his head grew unbearable he stared up into Richard's eyes and again saw the image of the mad woman trying to drown her child.

His vision was blurring. In the final moments before losing consciousness his lips moved soundlessly. The ghost of a smile spread across his face, like that of a small child making a birthday wish.

Richard took his hands from Jonathan's throat.

He stared down at the body but did not see it. In his mind he was nine years old again and sitting beside the body of his mother. He let out a wail. He clenched his fists and began to pound Jonathan's chest. Tears were pouring down his face. His body shook with sobs. 'Why did you have to leave me?! I'd have done anything for you! How could you do this when I needed you!'

Then, suddenly, his back stiffened. The hairs on the back of his neck began to rise. Slowly he began to turn . . .

Nicholas had reached the bottom of the staircase when he heard the scream. The unspeakable terror it contained made his blood run cold. He couldn't tell whether it was Richard or Jonathan. He told himself to go back upstairs but he was too afraid.

He stood in the hallway. In front of him, surrounded by the wreckage of the banisters, Stephen cradled Michael's body in his arms. Helplessly he stared at them. He wiped the tears from his eyes. He did not know what to do.

He realised that he could hear music. Classical music, playing nearby. He began to follow the sound. It led him down a corridor towards a door. Mr Stewart's study. He hammered on the door.

No answer. 'Mr Stewart, you have to help me. Please I don't know what to do.'

Still no answer. He opened the door, stared at the body which hung limply in the air like a rag doll on a string.

The shock seemed to clear his mind. His eyes focused on the telephone on the desk. He picked up the receiver.

Constable John Blake stood outside the Ackerley house. Mrs Fleming, the next door neighbour, stood beside him.

'. . . terrible noise,' she was telling him. 'They've had their rows in the past, mind, but nothing like that. Both of them screaming at the same time. Sounded like wild animals. Quite put me off my lunch.'

'But you haven't heard anything since?'

'No. Like I said, it all went quiet. Too quiet if you ask me. Something's happened, I know it has.'

Mrs Fleming struck Blake as someone with far too much time on her hands. She should hear some of the rows his neighbours had! Still, he was here now and had better show willing. 'Let's find out what's been happening then,' he said cheerfully and knocked on the door.

There was no answer. He tried again. Still nothing. 'Are you sure they didn't go out?' he asked Mrs Fleming.

'No. I've heard nothing since that screaming.' Mrs Fleming began to rub her hands together. 'I tell you, something's wrong.'

He knocked a third time. Silence. He tried the door handle. It was not locked. He walked into the hall. 'Mr Ackerley? Mrs Ackerley? It's the police here.'

Still nothing. But now he could hear a noise. A faint rocking sound. It came from the second door on the right. He walked towards it, Mrs Fleming following like a terrier at his heels.

He knocked on the door. 'Mr Ackerley? I'm sorry but we've had complaints about a disturbance. May I come in sir?'

Silence. He opened the door and walked in.

A woman lay sprawled on the carpet. Her skull was beaten to a pulp. Her blood soaked the carpet, surrounding what remained of her head like a halo. A poker lay beside her.

A man sat in a wooden chair by the window, rocking backwards and forwards. His hands and clothes were stained with blood. His arms were wrapped around his chest, shielding a framed photograph of a beautiful child on a swing.

The man realised he was there. Slowly he looked up. Instinctively Blake took a step backwards. But the man's eyes were empty, all life drained out of them; the smashed headlights of a mind that had collapsed in upon itself.

'It's about control,' the man whispered, more to himself than to his horrified audience. 'It's always been about control.'

Mrs Fleming started screaming. Blake pushed past her, searching for a phone.


Twenty minutes later three police cars stood outside the Ackerley house. Blake stood in the doorway, talking to Chief Inspector Edwards who had just arrived.

'What a business,' said the Chief Inspector. 'Imagine how much resentment he must have been bottling up to do something like that.' Behind them they heard the telephone ring. 'Sheppard, can you get that please!'

'Have they got anything out of him yet?'

'Nothing. To be honest I don't think we will. Something's snapped inside his head. The ambulance will be here in a minute. They'll take care of him.'

Blake nodded. The Inspector stared at him. 'You look a bit green. Sure you're all right?'

'Just a bit shaken. You come expecting a standard domestic and walk in on that.'

Constable Peter Sheppard approached and whispered something in the Inspector's ear. 'Really?' said the Inspector. 'Well you'd better go and see what's happened.' He turned to Blake. 'Message from the station. They've just had a boy from the school on the phone, jabbering incoherently, asking us to come. It may be a hoax. Sheppard's going to have a look. Why don't you go with him?'

Grateful to have an excuse to leave, Blake made for his car.

Five minutes later he drove through the school gates. In the distance he could see the chapel and the school itself. He stared at the Victorian edifice. 'Bit severe isn't it?'

'Bloody grim,' said Peter Sheppard. 'Imagine forking out a fortune to send your kids somewhere like this.'

'Be worth it for a bit of peace and quiet.'

They both laughed. Blake steered the car up the path, taking the right turn and approaching the school buildings. In the distance he could see an ambulance with people milling around it. 'What's that doing there? It's come to the wrong place.'

'Look,' said Sheppard, pointing to some steps where a bespectacled boy of about fourteen was waving to them. Blake stopped the car and wound down his window. 'Are you the lad that telephoned?'

The boy nodded. Blake saw that his eyes were red. He smiled kindly as he climbed out of the car. 'Now then, what's been going on?'

The boy said nothing, just turned and walked into the building. Blake stared at Sheppard who shrugged. Together they followed the boy into the school.

They came into a hallway. There was no sound except a wireless playing somewhere in the distance. At the foot of a staircase, surrounded by what looked like broken banisters, knelt a boy, cradling the body of another in his arms.

'Jesus!' whispered Sheppard. 'Some hoax.'

'I didn't know what to do,' said the boy with glasses. His voice was blank. He was clearly in shock.

'That's all right,' said Blake gently. 'We know what to do.' He walked towards the boy at the foot of the stairs. He crouched down beside him. Only then did he realise that the body the boy was holding was that of his twin.

The realisation threw him completely. He took a deep breath, trying to regain his composure. 'Why don't you let me take him now,' he said, keeping his voice as gentle as he could.

The boy ignored him. He stretched out a hand.

'KEEP YOUR HANDS OFF HIM!!'

'Hey now . . .' began Blake.

'Go away! Leave us alone! We don't need you! We're going to stay here and he's going to be all right!' The boy began to cover his brother's face with kisses. 'You're going to be all right Mikey. Just you wait and see.'

Blake stood, turning towards Sheppard. 'You'd better fetch that ambulance over here.'

'I didn't know what to do,' repeated the boy with glasses.

'Of course you didn't,' Blake told him. 'No one would expect you to.'

The boy didn't seem to hear him. 'I thought Mr Stewart would help,' he continued. 'I went and asked him. But he couldn't do anything.'

'Who? What are you talking about?'

'He's in his study.' The boy pointed towards a corridor. 'That's his wireless playing.'

Blake and Sheppard exchanged looks. 'I'll go,' said Sheppard. 'You stay here.'

'Why don't you tell me how it happened?' said Blake to the boy.

'It was my fault. Michael shouldn't have come. I shouldn't have got him involved. Jonathan was my friend. It was my problem, not his.'

Blake was becoming increasingly confused. 'Hang on a minute. Who's Jonathan?' He gestured towards the boy on the stairs. 'Is that him?'

'No.'

'So where is he?'

'With Richard. They're upstairs.'

'Richard? Look, I'm sorry but you're going to have to start again.'

Sheppard appeared from the corridor and beckoned him over. His face was white. 'Well?' demanded Blake.

'There's a bloody suicide back there! Some bloke's hung himself! What the hell's been going on here?!'

Blake felt dizzy, as if he had walked into someone else's dream. 'God knows. This gets stranger and stranger. Apparently there are two other boys upstairs.'

'Do you think they pushed the other one?'

'Could have done. Perhaps they're hiding up there.' He turned to the boy with glasses. 'Exactly where are these two other lads?'

'In Richard's study.'

'Where's that?'

'It's on the top floor. The third door on the left.'

'What are they doing up there? Hiding?'

The boy shook his head.

'So what are they doing up there?'

'They're dead.'

'Dead!' His jaw dropped. 'But how?'

'I don't know.'

'You don't know?!'

'I haven't seen them.'

'So how do you know they're dead?!'

The boy's mind seemed to drift away. 'It's all my fault,' he said again. 'All of it.'

'I'm not going on with this,' announced Sheppard. 'I say we phone in. Get some reinforcements.'

'You can if you want,' said Blake. 'I'm going upstairs.'

'D'you think that's a good idea?'

Blake gave a hollow laugh 'After what I saw this lunchtime I don't think there's much that can shock me.'

He started up the stairs. After a moment's hesitation Sheppard began to follow.

They climbed up and up, eventually reaching the top floor. The ceiling was so low that Blake's head almost touched it. They knocked on the third door on the left. No answer. Blake tried the handle. It was locked. He rapped harder. 'This is the police. Open up now.'

'They might not be there,' said Sheppard.

'Of course they are. Door's bolted from the inside.' He raised his voice. 'Listen, either you open the door or we break it down. Do you understand?'

Still silence. Sheppard began to shiver. 'It's cold up here. Don't you think?'

Blake ignored him. 'I'm going to count to ten.'

He did so. The door remained closed. He pushed his shoulder against it, testing its strength. 'Stand back.' He pulled back his foot and kicked it open.

He had been right. Both boys were there. Both were dead.

One lay on his back; his eyes bulging, his tongue protruding from his lips. His neck wore the bruises of strangulation like a tartan scarf.

The other boy was pressed into the far corner of the room, his head tilted up towards the ceiling. His eyes were open. Frozen on his face was an expression of pure terror.

There was a smell in the room. A smell that Blake could not identify but one that he would never forget. The smell of something very dark and very cold. The smell of evil.

'God almighty!' breathed Sheppard.

Blake walked out into the corridor. He tried to open a window. It jammed. He smashed the glass with his fist, pushed his head through the pane and began to gulp down lungfuls of fresh winter air.

# PART FOUR

# Aftermath

# Article in the *Daily Mail*, 13th December 1954

### *Police Keep Silent on Norfolk Deaths*

*Norfolk Police have made no further statements regarding the deaths of three boys and a teacher at Kirkston Abbey School on 9th December.*

*The boys themselves are known to have been Jonathan Palmer and Michael Perriman (both 14) and Richard Rokeby (15). The teacher was Alan Stewart (29), head of the school's History department.*

*Mr Stewart hanged himself in his study. Michael Perriman died in a fall from an upstairs landing. The manner in which Jonathan Palmer and Richard Rokeby met their deaths however remains a mystery. When questioned by this reporter, Sergeant Hugh Collins of Norwich Police Department admitted that the deaths of all three boys were being treated as suspicious but would make no further comment.*

### *A Catalogue of Misfortune*

*Kirkston Abbey has had more than its fair share of misfortunes in recent months. In September it was rocked by the suicide of pupil Paul Ellerson (18). Two weeks ago another pupil, James Wheatley (14) was killed by a car while sleepwalking.*

*On 9th December itself two further tragedies took place. Henry Ackerley, head of the school's Classics department, beat his wife Marjorie to death in their home in Bowerton. It is believed that Mr Ackerley suffered some form of nervous breakdown which triggered the assault on his wife. He is now in a psychiatric institution. Headmaster Clive Howard suffered a near fatal heart attack during a school assembly. He is now recovering in hospital.*

### *Blackmailing Ring*

*The Police insist that the deaths of the three boys and the other tragedies are unrelated. However a source close to the Police and who did not wish to be named, said there was evidence of a blackmailing ring to which the dead boys belonged.*

*Investigation has revealed further links between the players in this unfortunate drama. James Wheatley, who was known to have been in a state of extreme mental distress in the days before his death, was a classmate of the dead boys. Jonathan Palmer and Richard Rokeby are also reported as having had a deep antipathy for Henry Ackerley.*

*The two boys (both 14) who were found at the scene continue to be questioned by the police. All developments in this disturbing case will be reported as they occur.*

In an interview room at Norwich police station Inspector Bradley stared across the table at Nicholas Scott.

'Let's start again. You say that Jonathan and Richard were both alive when you left them?'

'I've told you this ten times already!'

'And they were arguing.'

'Yes.'

'You didn't stay? Didn't try and stop them?'

'How could I? They'd locked themselves in Richard's study. Anyway I was scared. I knew something awful was going to happen.'

'Something awful had already happened. Or do you consider Michael Perriman's death as something trivial?'

'Of course I don't! How can you say that?!'

'I don't think that's an appropriate question,' snapped Nicholas's lawyer, Mr Clegg.

Inspector Bradley rubbed at his eyes. The room had no window and the overhead light was giving him a headache. He took a long drag on his cigarette. 'Let's move on then. You told Constable Blake that Richard and Jonathan were dead and yet you hadn't seen their bodies. So how did you know?'

'I've told you! I just knew! If you'd been there you'd have known too! Why are you being so stupid?!'

Inspector Bradley put down his cigarette and leant across the table. 'Let me remind you young man that you are in *very* serious trouble. We have three deaths, at least one of which was clearly murder, and all we get from you is nonsense about demonic powers.'

'It's not nonsense! Why won't you believe me?!'

'Because it's preposterous!'

'Richard made it happen! I saw him! He willed the banisters to collapse!'

'The banisters were rotten! They could have collapsed at any minute. All it needed was a good hard push. Did Richard push Michael?'

'No! He didn't have to!'

'This interview must stop,' announced Mr Clegg. 'My client is becoming distressed.'

'We'll stop in a minute,' said Inspector Bradley. 'I have one more question. What do you know about the death of Mr Stewart?'

'Nothing.'

Inspector Bradley reached inside his desk drawer and pulled out two sheets of paper. He handed them to Nicholas. 'Do you recognise these?'

Nicholas grew pale.

'They were found in Mr Stewart's desk. Do you know how they got there?'

Nicholas shook his head.

'I think you do.'

'My client has answered your question, Inspector.'

'You do know, don't you Nicholas?'

Slowly Nicholas nodded.

'Tell me.'

'Richard must have sent them.'

'Why would he do that?'

Nicholas stared at the floor. 'Well?' demanded Inspector Bradley.

'Mr Stewart and Paul Ellerson were lovers.'

'And what evidence do you have for this?'

'The picture.'

'What picture?'

'Jon saw a picture in Mr Stewart's study. It was a present from Paul. He and Richard worked it out from that.'

'What was this picture? Some dirty photograph?'

'No!' Nicholas ran his hands through his hair. 'You don't understand! Jon knew Paul really well. He'd fagged for him last year. He put the pieces together.'

Inspector Bradley took a deep breath. 'So who sent the notes?'

'Richard.'

'But not Jonathan?'

'No! Jon liked Mr Stewart. He wouldn't do something like that!'

'I think he would. After what you've told me about the things he and Richard are supposed to have done, I can imagine him capable of anything.'

'That's a lie! Richard did it! Richard hated Mr Stewart because he tried to break up their friendship! He hated anyone who tried to separate him from Jon!'

'And how did you know about Mr Stewart and Paul Ellerson?'

'Jon told me.'

'Jonathan seems to have told you an awful lot. Do you know what I think, Nicholas? I think that you and your friends decided that you were going to get some money out of Mr Stewart and cooked up a vicious little scam to do it.'

'That's not true!'

'That's enough!' cried Mr Clegg. 'I demand that this interview ends immediately.'

'Very well,' said Inspector Bradley. 'But we haven't finished with you yet Nicholas. Not by a long shot.'

As Nicholas was led from the interview room Chief Inspector Edwards appeared.

'Still sticking to his story?'

Inspector Bradley nodded. Chief Inspector Edwards sat down in the chair just vacated by Nicholas's lawyer. 'What about the notes?' he asked.

'As we suspected. He claims that Stewart and the Ellerson boy had some sort of relationship.'

'Is there any evidence?'

'He said something about a picture but I couldn't get much sense out of him after that. He says the Rokeby boy sent the notes. Insists that neither he nor the others had anything to do with it. Do you want us to keep exploring this?'

Chief Inspector Edwards shook his head. 'The Ellerson boy was only eighteen. His family are well connected. They've already had to cope with his suicide. How do you think they'll react if we brand him a pervert? They'll bring charges for defamation. Unless we turn up something conclusive we'd better let it drop.'

'What of the story he's telling about Ackerley?'

'There was a hit and run. Ackerley was questioned but no charges were brought. There was no evidence.'

'What about Ackerley himself?'

'I spoke to his doctors this morning. Catatonic state. Complete mental withdrawal. They doubt he'll ever come out of it.'

'And Howard?'

'He's stable now. One of our men is on his way to see him.'

'And I'm sending Hopkins and Meadows to talk to some of Palmer's classmates. I want them to find out about James Wheatley. His death is linked to this too. I know it is.'

Chief Inspector Edwards sighed. 'It still doesn't solve our problem though, does it?'

'Press still on your back?'

'Phone's ringing off the bloody hook. Have you seen today's paper? They've already got wind of the blackmail angle. God help us if they get wind of the rest.'

Silence descended on them. Chief Inspector Edwards leant back in his chair and stared up at the ceiling. He rubbed the back of his neck with his hand, trying to relieve tension. Inspector Bradley sat and watched him. 'Have you ever considered the possibility that he's telling the truth?' he said awkwardly.

'Of course not,' said Chief Inspector Edwards a little too quickly.

'Not even after seeing the expression on Rokeby's face?'

'Shock, that was all. About what he'd done.'

'His neck was snapped like you'd snap a pencil. It takes a lot of force to do that but there were no marks on him.'

'We'll find the marks.'

'We haven't found them yet.' Inspector Bradley's eyes remained fixed on his superior officer. 'And remember what Blake said. The smell in the room. The sense of evil.'

'He was confused. Overwrought. He'd already walked in on the mess at the Ackerleys.' Chief Inspector Edwards' tone was confident but he refused to meet his companion's gaze.

'Blake's a good man. That's what his superiors say. Level-headed. Not one to lose his head. Unless of course there's a bloody good reason to do so.'

Chief Inspector Edwards thumped the desk with his fist. 'I won't hear any more of this! Scott's story is pure fantasy. An attempt to exonerate himself. Well it's not going to work. I'm not going public with claims of demonic powers because there are no such things. We're going to keep a lid on this until we have a rational explanation for what happened in that room.'

'And if we never find one?' asked Inspector Bradley. 'What then?'

'Then God help us all,' said Chief Inspector Edwards.

Later that afternoon Inspector Bradley questioned Stephen Perriman.

He hated doing this. He had spoken in detail to Blake, had

heard about a boy sobbing over the body of his dead twin. He could not keep the image out of his head.

Stephen Perriman stared into space. His eyes were devoid of emotion. His lawyer, Mr Crowley, sat beside him. A motherly looking PC brought Stephen a cup of tea and then remained by the door, watching him anxiously.

'Are you ready, Stephen?' asked Inspector Bradley.

Stephen stared at the tea with his dead eyes, watching the steam rise from the cup. He nodded mechanically.

'How well did you know Richard Rokeby?'

'Well enough to hate him.'

'Why did you hate him?'

'Because he was evil.'

'Why do you say that?'

'Because it's true.'

'Nicholas has told us about the seances. Did you take part in those?'

Stephen shook his head.

'Nicholas says that you did attend one.'

'Nothing happened. It was a con. It worked on the others, not on me.'

'Why did it work on the others?'

'Because they were weak.'

'So Richard Rokeby didn't have any supernatural power then?'

'Of course not. His only power was that of a strong mind over weak ones.'

Inspector Bradley took a deep breath. 'Is that why it worked on your brother?'

At last Stephen's eyes came to life. 'It didn't work on my brother! I didn't let it!'

Inspector Bradley decided to change tack. 'What do you know about the death of Mrs Ackerley?'

'Nothing.'

'Are you sure?'

'Her husband bashed her brains in. So what?'

Inspector Bradley was taken aback. 'So what?!'

'Yes, so what?! So bloody what?! My brother's dead! That's the only thing that matters! He's dead and Richard, Jonathan and Nicholas are to blame! It's their fault! All of this is their fault!! I'm glad Richard and Jonathan are dead! They deserved what they got! Why are you questioning me?! Nicholas is the one you want! He's the murderer! I WISH HE WAS DEAD TOO!!'

He lashed out with his hand, knocking the teacup across the room. It smashed against the wall, sending steaming liquid trickling down to the floor. He buried his head in his hands. The woman PC rushed to comfort him. Inspector Bradley left the room.

Clive Howard sat in his hospital bed, his face ashen with exhaustion. He was answering the questions put to him by Sergeant Green.

'How well did you know Richard Rokeby?'

'Well enough to be frightened by him.'

'Why were you frightened?'

'Because he was dangerous. He was totally consumed by hate. He was the most destructive boy I ever met.'

'You're right there. He strangled the Palmer boy with his bare hands.'

'I know. Poor Jonathan. If only I'd intervened sooner.' Clive shook his head sadly.

'Why would you have done that? Were you concerned by the friendship?'

'I wasn't. Alan Stewart was. He was fond of Jonathan. He came to talk to me. He said he considered Richard a bad influence.'

Sergeant Green gave a hollow laugh. 'He got that right! There was madness in the family. Did you know that?'

'I did. Towards the end I began to think that Richard was mad himself.'

Sergeant Green was scrawling down notes. 'What of Jonathan Palmer?' he asked. 'What sort of boy was he?'

'Hardworking. Quiet. Blended into the crowd really. It's a tragedy what happened to him.'

'You don't think he brought it upon himself?'

'No, I don't. He was a decent boy. But vulnerable. Easily led. Richard was a very strong personality. He would have found it easy to dominate Jonathan. You must understand that whatever they did, they did because of Richard. He made the decisions. Jonathan did as he was told.'

'Nicholas Scott claims that they carried out seances. He says that they tapped into some sort of psychic power which they used against people.'

Clive nodded.

'You don't think it's a load of cobblers?'

Clive smiled wearily. 'There are more things in heaven and earth, Horatio . . .'

Sergeant Green looked up from his notebook. 'I'm sorry?'

'A quote from *Hamlet*.'

'You believe him then?'

'Do I think they tapped into some sort of dark power? No I don't. Do I think they believed they'd tapped into something? Yes I do. I think they believed it completely.'

A nurse put her head around the door. 'That's enough for today. Mr Howard needs to rest.'

Sergeant Green stood up. 'Thank you for your help. I may need to speak to you again.'

'Of course.' Clive gestured to his surroundings. 'I'm not going anywhere.'

He lay back and shut his eyes. He sank quickly into sleep. In his dreams he was confronted by Jonathan Palmer, his neck covered with bruises, his eyes huge and accusing. 'You should have expelled him when you had the chance. If you'd done that I might still be alive.'

When he woke he saw that he was not alone. Elizabeth sat in

a chair by his bedside. He stared at her in bewilderment, fearing she was just another part of his dream.

'They said I could come and sit with you while you slept.'

He stretched out his hand to her. She took it and held it to her cheek. He realised she was crying. 'Don't,' he said softly.

'When I heard the news I thought you were dead.'

He managed a smile. 'A little battered but still alive.'

'When I thought you were dead I wanted to die too. You told me once that you couldn't have a life without me. Now I know that I can't have a life without you.'

Tears came into his eyes. 'I didn't mean to do it. I was weak. It didn't mean anything ...'

'It doesn't matter. None of that matters now. I forgive you. I hope you can forgive me.'

He kissed her hand. He felt as if he had been reborn. 'You don't have to ask that,' he told her. 'Not ever.'

She smiled through her tears. He felt her tremble. 'What is it?'

'On the day it happened I had a feeling. I can't explain it. Just a sense that you were in danger. Now I don't feel it any more.'

'How could I be in danger? Now that you're here?'

Outside the sun was setting. The room was growing darker. They did not bother to turn on the light, just sat in silence, holding each other's hand.

'It's all finished at the school,' he said eventually. 'I can't stay as headmaster after something like this. I don't know whether the school will survive itself.'

'We'll survive. We have each other. What more do we need?'

They kissed each other in the dying shadows of the day.

Inspector Rothwell from Scotland Yard put down the photograph and shuddered. 'God, what an expression! What the hell happened to him?!'

'I don't know,' said Chief Inspector Edwards. 'We just can't explain it.'

'You have to make a statement soon. The press are going mad. Two boys dead and no details on how they died.'

'You don't need to tell me! Christ, I can't step outside without some bloody hack pouncing on me!'

'And the Scott boy won't change his story?'

'He won't budge.'

'What about the Perriman boy?'

'No good. Too distressed. He's been under sedation since his outburst yesterday.'

'Where is the Scott boy now?'

'With his parents. They're staying in a private house nearby. We're trying to keep his identity a secret but the press have already got wind of it. We can't risk them hearing what he's got to say. God, what a bloody mess!'

'Not necessarily,' said Inspector Rothwell suddenly. 'I have an idea.'

At ten o'clock that night Nicholas arrived back at the police station with his parents.

They were escorted through the rear entrance and into the same interview room where he had been questioned by Inspector Bradley. There was no Inspector Bradley this time. Instead he was greeted by Chief Inspector Edwards and two middle-aged men he didn't recognise. One was short and stocky with a full moustache; the other taller and thinner with kind eyes. He stared at them warily. 'Who are you?'

'This,' said Chief Inspector Edwards, pointing to the man with the moustache, 'is Inspector Rothwell from Scotland Yard. And this is Mr Blakiston, the Bishop of Norwich.'

Mrs Scott put her arm around her son. 'Nicholas has answered all your questions. He hasn't done anything wrong. Why can't you leave him alone?'

'I'm sorry, Mrs Scott,' said Inspector Rothwell, 'but

this is a very serious investigation and Nicholas is a key witness.'

'But I've told you everything!' cried Nicholas. 'Over and over!' His eyes filled with tears of frustration. He had hardly slept for days. He was exhausted.

'I know you have Nicholas,' continued Inspector Rothwell, 'but there's someone else we need you to talk to.'

'Who? Him?' He pointed at the Bishop. 'What's the point? You all think I'm a liar.'

'We don't think that,' said Chief Inspector Edwards. 'But we do think you might be a little confused as to what did take place.' He smiled reassuringly at Mr and Mrs Scott. 'It's understandable under the circumstances.'

'Now look here,' said Mr Scott. 'I've had just about enough of this. Either you charge my son or you let us take him home. This is pure harassment!'

Chief Inspector Edward's expression darkened. 'May I remind you Mr Scott that your son is heavily implicated in three deaths for which we do not yet have a satisfactory explanation. I would advise co-operation.'

'Are you threatening me?!'

'Not at all. I'm just advising you to think about what you're saying.'

As the arguing continued Nicholas stared at the Bishop and realised that his expression was sympathetic rather than accusatory. He was tired of being suspected. He wanted understanding. Suddenly he sensed that he might have found it. 'Very well. I'll talk to him. But alone.' He glared at the two Inspectors. 'I don't want either of you to be there.'

'Nicholas,' said his mother, 'you don't have to do this. Not if you don't want to.'

'It's all right, Mum. I do want to. Really.'

The room emptied. Nicholas sat down. The Bishop moved his chair so that the two of them sat side by side rather than at opposite ends of the table. He smiled kindly. 'Do you mind if I call you Nicholas?' His voice was soft and very soothing.

'No. What should I call you?'

'Why not Jeremy. That's my name.'

Nicholas blushed. 'I can't call you that.'

'Mr Blakiston then, if you'd be more comfortable with that. I don't mind.'

'All right. Mr Blakiston.'

'The dead boys were your friends weren't they?'

Nicholas nodded.

'I'm sorry. This must be very traumatic for you. Do you mind talking to me? We could wait a little while if you'd prefer?'

Nicholas shook his head. A constable entered, carrying a tray with two cups of tea and a plate of chocolate biscuits. The Bishop pushed the biscuits towards Nicholas. 'Why don't you have these.'

Nicholas took one. He bit down. Sweetness filled his mouth. He burst into tears.

The Bishop put an arm around him. 'Hush now,' he said gently. 'It's all right.'

Nicholas wiped his eyes. 'I'm just so tired of it. I keep telling them what happened and they don't believe me. They just look at me like I'm mad. They keep accusing me of terrible things and it's not true. No one believes me. I don't even think my parents do. They say they do but then sometimes I see them looking at me . . .'

The Bishop handed him a handkerchief. 'I'll believe you.'

Nicholas shook his head. The Bishop smiled encouragingly. 'Why shouldn't I?'

'How can you believe me? After they've all told you what a liar I am.'

'They haven't told me anything, Nicholas, really they haven't. Except that you're troubled and that it might help you to talk to me.'

'I'm not a liar. I am telling the truth. I swear it.'

'Then I swear that I'll believe you, provided that you do one thing for me.'

'Anything.'

'Do you believe in God?'

Nicholas nodded.

'And you know that it's wrong to lie. Especially about something as serious as this.'

'Yes.'

'Then I want you to promise me, solemnly, that what you tell me will be the complete truth. Will you do that for me?'

He swallowed. 'Yes.'

The Bishop smiled. 'Then I promise I will believe whatever you tell me. I'm not here to judge you, Nicholas. I just want to help you. Do you believe that?'

'Yes.'

'Good. Then why don't you start telling me about it.'

'Where shall I begin?'

'Why not tell me about Jonathan. Do you mind talking about him?'

'No.'

'Tell me how you became friends. You were best friends weren't you?'

Nicholas managed a smile. 'Since the first day at school.'

'Tell me about that day Nicholas. How did it all begin?'

Nicholas sipped from his tea and reached for another biscuit. Then he started to speak.

Four hours later. Nicholas had left with his parents; by the back entrance just as they had come.

The Bishop sat with the two inspectors. 'He is telling the truth,' he said for the third time.

'But that's not possible!' cried Chief Inspector Edwards. 'He's got to be lying!'

'He's not lying,' said the Bishop. He ran his hands through

his hair. His eyes were fixed on a photograph that lay on the desk before him. 'I wish to God that he was.'

'Then he's delusional. The fact that he believes it doesn't make it true!'

'He's not delusional,' said the Bishop. 'If it was just his word then perhaps I could have believed that he was. But there's Constable Blake's evidence too. What he felt in that room. If the poor boy is delusional then he's not the only one.'

'It's not possible!' cried Chief Inspector Edwards again.

'And what about this?' The Bishop pointed to the photograph. 'The body unmarked. The neck snapped. And the face . . .' He shuddered. 'I wish you hadn't shown me this.'

Suddenly he pushed the picture away as if it were contaminated. He turned to Chief Inspector Edwards. 'How else do you explain that?'

'I don't know!' wailed the Chief Inspector. He turned towards Inspector Rothwell. 'This wasn't supposed to happen! The whole point was to get him to change his story. To give us something we could use!'

'That's what I hoped,' said Inspector Rothwell.

'Well it hasn't bloody happened has it?! We're really in the shit now! What the hell are we going to tell the press?!'

'Nothing,' Inspector Rothwell told him.

'Nothing?! How's that going to look? There are enough rumours flying around as it is!'

Inspector Rothwell rose to his feet. 'I'm going to phone headquarters. We *cannot* let this story out. Imagine what the public reaction would be. We have to think of a way round this. I'm going to call now.' He left the room.

The Chief Inspector lit a cigarette. 'You must be pleased,' he said archly to the Bishop.

'Pleased?!' The Bishop stared at him in disbelief.

'Why not? You lot are always telling us that our souls are in danger. Most of us think it's rubbish.' He inhaled deeply and blew a cloud of smoke into the air. 'Now along comes proof that you're right and we're wrong.'

'I'm the one who's wrong,' whispered the Bishop.

Chief Inspector Edward eyes widened. 'What do you mean? You think he was lying?'

Up to now he had been too distressed at his own predicament to pay much attention to his companion. Now, at last, he gave him his full attention.

The man who faced him seemed to have aged ten years overnight. He looked exhausted; his shoulders sagged, there were bags under his eyes and his skin seemed as thin as paper. The Chief Inspector was concerned. 'You're in shock. I'll get you a drink. You need one.'

The Bishop shook his head.

'You do, believe me.' The Chief Inspector rose to his feet. 'It's nothing to be ashamed of. I know exactly how you feel.'

'No you don't.'

'This hasn't been easy for me either. I tell you, I've seen . . .'

The Bishop laughed. A hollow sound, devoid of mirth. 'Believe me, you don't know how I feel. Be grateful for that.'

The Chief Inspector sat down again. 'So how do you feel?'

'I've been in the Church for thirty years. I went in because I wanted to help people. I'm good at helping people. I understand that we all have our weaknesses, that we all make mistakes. I can listen and I don't judge. That's all most people really want from a so-called man of God. Not hell and heaven and thunderbolts and lightning. Just a sympathetic ear and the chance to try and make amends.

'I never believed in the forces of good and evil. I went through the motions of course in sermons, but I never believed it. When I was with friends I used to laugh about it; dismiss it as superstition. And when people came to me for help I used to tell them that God and the Devil did not exist as distinct beings. We all have the capacity for good and evil, and consequently God and the Devil are nothing more than separate parts of ourselves. I genuinely believed that, and I know that many people drew comfort from that idea too.

'And now I know that everything I mocked, everything that I sneered at, is true. People have spent the last thirty years coming to me for guidance and I've fed them lies. And if our souls are in the balance then what does that mean for mine?'

Chief Inspector Edwards didn't answer. He felt sick.

Nicholas sat at the interview table, with his parents. Inspector Rothwell and Chief Inspector Edwards stared coldly at him.

'We've completed our inquiries,' said Chief Inspector Edwards. 'We have no further need of you. You are free to go.'

Mrs Scott sighed with relief. 'We told you Nicholas hadn't done anything wrong. Didn't we always say ...'

'The fact that we are releasing your son does not mean that we are satisfied of his innocence,' said Chief Inspector Edwards forcefully. 'There are still a large number of questions to which his answers have proved far from satisfactory.'

'But I've told you the truth!' cried Nicholas. 'I told the Bishop too! He said he believed me! Why don't you?!'

'What the Bishop said and what he actually believes are two very separate matters,' said Inspector Rothwell sternly. 'You would do well to remember that.'

'But he said he believed me! He promised!'

'Enough of this,' said Chief Inspector Edwards. 'Like I said, you are free to go. But this is subject to one condition.'

Mr and Mrs Scott exchanged looks. 'What condition?' demanded Mr Scott.

'That your son make no further mention, to ANYONE, now or at any time in the future, about the seances. They never happened. Is that clear?'

'But they did! Ask the Bishop! He did believe me! I know he did!'

Inspector Rothwell addressed Mr and Mrs Scott. 'In one hour's time we are going to release a statement to this effect; Richard Rokeby pushed Michael Perriman down the stairs. He then strangled Jonathan Palmer. When he had finished he tripped and fell. He cracked his head on the wall. It was an unfortunate angle. His neck snapped. That is how he died.'

'But that's not true!' cried Nicholas.

'ENOUGH!' roared Chief Inspector Edwards. 'That is how it happened! Those are the facts that we are giving to the press. Those are the facts that will be given at the Inquest and those are the facts that everyone in this room is going to stick to. Is that understood?'

'But that's not what happened! That policeman knows! He'll tell!'

'Constable Blake will do no such thing,' said Inspector Rothwell firmly. 'He knows where his duty lies. As should you.'

'Nicholas,' said Mrs Scott. 'They're releasing you. That's all that matters now.'

'Well said, Mrs Scott,' said Inspector Rothwell. 'You should listen to your mother, Nicholas. She only has your best interests at heart. As do we all.'

'You're the liars! All of you!'

'Nicholas!' hissed Mr Scott.

Inspector Rothwell leant across the table, staring at Nicholas.

'That may be true,' he said slowly, 'but you would be wise to remember, Nicholas, that you have already spoken of harassment and of blackmail that appears to have resulted in the death of at least three people. If you should ever consider making any claims about seances, or indeed police cover-ups, then we will not hesitate to resurrect that evidence and use it against you.'

'But I wasn't involved in any of that! That's not how it happened!'

'Weren't you? We only have your word for that. There is no one to corroborate your story. And believe me we could make any case against you look very convincing.'

Chief Inspector Edwards joined in. 'And how,' he asked, 'do you think it's going to look if you start spreading your tales about demonic powers? Most people will think you're mad. We certainly will. You know where Mr Ackerley is now don't you? I'm sure you wouldn't want to join him.'

Mr Scott's jaw dropped. 'You can't threaten my son like that! How dare you ...'

'Oh but we can, Mr Scott,' said Inspector Rothwell. 'I've spoken to Scotland Yard and the Home Office and I have full authority to make whatever threats are necessary to ensure that your son's story remains secret. Do I make myself quite clear?'

The room seemed to spin before Nicholas's eyes. 'This isn't right! You can't do this!'

'Do I make myself clear?!'

He felt his parents eyes upon him. He knew he had no choice. He managed a nod.

'Then you may go. But remember what we've said today. These are not idle threats. If the need arises they will be acted upon.'

As they left the interview room Nicholas saw Stephen approaching, flanked by his parents.

Stephen walked slowly; his eyes empty. Each parent held one arm as if he could not stand unaided. Nicholas hadn't seen him since the police came to the school. He had heard that Stephen was under sedation. He looked like a zombie; someone who was dead but continued to go through the motions of living.

Mrs Perriman recognised him. She said something to her husband. Both tensed visibly. Nicholas sensed his own parents do the same.

The two families drew level. 'I'm so sorry for your loss,' said Mrs Scott. She held out her hand. It hung in the air like the branch of a tree. 'We don't want your sympathy,' said Mrs Perriman steadily. 'Stephen has told us everything. Michael would be alive today if it wasn't for your son.'

'I think you're being unfair,' said Mrs Scott gently.

'Leave it,' her husband told her. 'This isn't the time or place.'

Stephen seemed to become aware of his surroundings. He looked up at Nicholas. In his head Nicholas heard Michael's cry as he fell. His eyes filled with tears. 'I'm so sorry,' he said, his voice trembling. 'I really am. I didn't know it would be like that. I . . .'

Stephen spat in his face.

He heard his mother gasp. Mr Perriman tried to pull his son away. Stephen struggled to shake him off. His eyes remained fixed on Nicholas. 'Mikey would still be alive if it wasn't for you! Why couldn't you be the one to die?! Why did it have to be him?! I hate you! You're a murderer!! You and your friends! I HOPE YOU ALL BURN IN HELL FOR EVER!!'

The Perrimans dragged Stephen away. Nicholas stood and watched him go. His mother tried to wipe the spittle from his face. He pushed her away. He deserved it.

They left by the front entrance. Now he knew the terms of his release there was no need for secrecy. A car waited nearby, ready to take him home.

As they approached the doors he heard the sound of voices; of people pushing and shouting. He was afraid. He wanted to turn and run. But there was nowhere to go.

They walked through the doors. At once he was surrounded. A camera was pushed into his face. There was a flash of light. Momentarily he was blinded. He felt his parents' arms around him, guiding him towards the car and away from the hands that prodded him and the voices that screamed questions he couldn't answer.

'Is it true you were blackmailing Henry Ackerley?'

'How much money did you get out of him?'

'What happened to Richard and Jonathan? Did you kill them?'

'Did you do it? Have you struck a deal?'

'They should lock you up you vicious little sod!'

His parents pushed him into the car. His father started the engine, began to steer them though the crowd. Faces pushed against the window, hands pounded the glass. Eyes bored into him. Talk to us Nicholas, they screamed, tell us what happened, tell us what you did, tell us what it feels like to have got away with it.

He buried his head in his hands. He began to weep.

# Epilogue

## London, January 1999

———————————◣◦◦◦◣———————————

The tape recorder had been running for hours. Its gentle hiss had acted as background to the questions and answers that had crossed the room like shots in an endless tennis rally. Now at last it stopped.

Tim Webber lifted his hand from the controls and stared at Nicholas Scott.

'They really threatened you like that?'

Nicholas nodded.

'Jesus.'

'You have to understand that they were frightened. They'd never encountered anything like this before. Something that was not capable of rational explanation.'

'They could still have gone public.'

'No they couldn't. There would have been panic. I didn't understand that at the time, but I understand it now. Young boys tampering with forces they didn't really understand. Forces that most people don't believe exist.'

Tim's eyes were sparkling. 'Then they should know.'

Nicholas shook his head. 'You're wrong. You're like all journalists. You're obsessed with exposing the truth. You have no thought for the damage such exposure could do.'

'But people should know!'

'Why? What good would it do? I read once that one of the NASA expeditions discovered ruins on the dark side of the moon which could only have been created by intelligent life. There was panic in the White House and a decision was made that the truth be suppressed: that if conclusive evidence of extraterrestrial intelligence was revealed then everything that mankind holds sacred; its religion; its sense of itself, would be undermined, if not destroyed. Better to keep silent than risk that.'

Tim was pondering what had been said. The fire was dying. He put another log on. The heat wrapped itself around his face like a scarf.

'So they hung you out to dry,' he said slowly.

'Not exactly. They did their best. They made their statement and they stuck to it. They just wanted to bury it once and for all.

'But it didn't work. People weren't convinced. They suspected a cover-up. Rumours of blackmail had already leaked. Two and two was put together. So many of our so-called classmates rushing to join with the throng and enjoy their hour in the sun. They told of how Richard and Jonathan had hounded James. Poor James. Such a nice boy. Driven to his death by sadistic bullies. Then there was the landlady in Whitby. She read the articles and remembered two guests who'd fitted the description of Alan Stewart and Paul Ellerson. Two men who, in her tactful words, had seemed excessively fond of each other. Somehow the press heard about the notes in Alan's desk. They blamed us for Alan. They even blamed us for Paul. Said we hounded them both to death. God!' He leant back in his chair and stared up at the ceiling. 'They blamed Jonathan for Paul. Jonathan adored Paul! He was devastated when Paul died. He could no more have done anything to hurt him than he could have flown in the air.

'And the really terrible thing was that amongst all the hate letters I used to get there were some letters of support. People wrote saying that Alan and Paul were perverts. That they deserved to die. That we should be given medals, not condemned.

'In the end of course they turned us all into monsters. Cold-hearted monsters with no feelings whatsoever. Nobody was interested in us as people. We just became symbols for everyone's ignorance and fear.'

'Did you ever see Stephen Perriman again?'

'No.' He sighed. 'Poor Stephen. My life ended when the police came to Kirkston Abbey but Stephen's life ended with Michael's. I would never have believed it. He was always the strong one. Michael depended on him so much. It never occurred to me that underneath it all Stephen was just as dependent on him.'

'How did you feel when you heard about his death?'

'Nothing. That sounds terrible doesn't it. A youth of eighteen shoots himself and you feel nothing. But I didn't. I'd been expecting it. His mother wrote to me saying that I was responsible for his death, just as I'd been for Michael's.' Again he sighed. 'In a way she was right. I was responsible.'

A silence fell upon them. Nicholas stared into the flames; his eyes dark with the ghosts of a past that he had kept buried inside himself for over forty years. Tim sat and watched him. 'You never told me,' he said slowly, 'about what happened the first time you stayed behind in Richard's room. When the twins had left. When you were there alone with Richard and Jonathan. And the board.'

Nicholas didn't answer.

'Won't you tell me?'

'We continued with the game. A game in which we made wishes. That's all it was. Or at least that's what I told myself. And when it became really frightening that's what I kept telling myself. I chanted it over and over in my head like some sort of prayer. It's just a game, it's just a game, it's just a game ...'

'Why was it so frightening? Why were you so afraid? What happened ...'

'Enough,' said Nicholas suddenly. 'I've told you all I'm going to. There are some parts I don't want to remember. Even now.'

Again silence. Nicholas's eyes remained fixed upon the flames. Tim studied his face, searching for traces of the earnest, courageous, fourteen-year-old boy who had paid a terrible price for trying to hold on to the best friend he had ever had in his life. But there were none. That boy was lost for ever; buried beneath the combined weight of public condemnation and a lifetime of longing and regret.

'I'm sorry,' he said softly.

'What for?'

'For you. For what you've been through. You talked about being turned into monsters. It's true. I was scared before you arrived. Scared of meeting you. I suppose in my mind you're the monster the press made you out to be. Then I meet you and find out that you're just a person.'

'We were all just people,' Nicholas told him.

'How do you feel about the others now?'

'How should I feel? Should I hate them?'

Tim thought for a moment, then nodded.

'It's not that simple. I miss Jonathan. I dream about him sometimes. I dream about the happy times before Richard came and destroyed it all. Jonathan was a good person. His only fault was that he felt powerless. Richard made him feel strong.'

'And the others?'

'I feel bad about the twins. Stephen was right to hate me. I was responsible for Michael's death. I didn't plan it of course, but I was responsible. I persuaded him to defy Stephen and he died because of it.'

'And Richard? What about him?'

'I used to hate him. I don't now. Not now I've had time to stand back and look at his life and the demons that drove him. The demons inside his head. In this day and age he never would have developed as he did. He wouldn't have been allowed to.

After the death of his mother, and the way he reacted to it, people would have taken action. He would have received some form of help. It was so different fifty years ago. Anything bad was pushed under the table and ignored in the hope that it would go away. In Richard's case it festered and turned into something far worse.

'None of us were monsters. That was what so upset the police. They believed the story I'd told them but they didn't want to accept it. The implications were too awful. The fact that it could have occurred anywhere. It just happened to be us. Easier to believe us freaks or monsters. Easier that than admit the truth.'

'Which I now know,' said Tim slowly.

'I've never told anyone. Not since I spoke to the police. At first I was afraid to. And afterwards . . .'

He paused, rubbing the back of his neck. Tim picked up the pile of tapes and juggled them in his hand. 'It doesn't look much, does it?' he said. 'But it's going to make us a fortune.'

Nicholas shook his head.

'Of course it will. This is amazing! Demonic powers. A death that cannot be explained. A police cover-up. A Bishop who has a nervous breakdown. And a chance to understand the motivations of the boys who did it. It's a bloody goldmine!'

'I told you at the start; there would be no money.'

Tim stared at him as if he were mad. 'You don't think people will be interested?! You don't think they'll want to know this?!'

'Not at all. On the contrary I think they'd be very interested.'

'So what's the problem?'

'I've told you what really happened, as I agreed I would. But I won't tell it to anyone else and neither will you.'

'The police can't hurt you. Not after all this time. They're the ones who are going to be hurt, not you. You'll come out of this well. I promise. You didn't do anything wrong. You were just trying to watch out for a friend.'

Nicholas sighed. 'You haven't been listening. The story cannot be told. The police were right. It is too dangerous. How do you think people will react if they knew the truth? There are Richard Rokebys and Jonathan Palmers in schools across the country. What if some of them tried to harness the same power, knowing that there was a genuine power to be harnessed?'

'But they wouldn't! What happened to you would be warning enough.'

'You're not so naïve as to believe that. Joyriding is dangerous. People have been killed or maimed. That doesn't stop youngsters trying it. The same is true of drugs. The bigger the risk the greater the excitement.'

Tim shrugged. 'That's not my problem.'

'That's right. Your only concern is telling the truth and becoming a celebrity into the bargain.'

'Well what if it is?!' cried Tim indignantly. 'Like I said, it's not my problem.'

'This story cannot be told.'

'Do you think I give a damn about the consequences? This is my big chance and I am *not* going to blow it. And if you try and get in my way then you'll be sorry!!'

'Is that so?'

The voice was soft, but something in the tone stopped Tim in his tracks.

Nicholas leant forward in his chair. 'And how will you do that?' he asked.

His tired eyes had begun to shine. They held Tim. He reached for a response but found that he had none to give. His earlier confidence had evaporated. Suddenly he felt exposed and vulnerable.

'You don't want to threaten me Mr Webber.'

Tim gave a poor impersonation of scorn. 'Why not?'

'You know the answer to that already.'

He managed a sneer. 'Do I?'

'You would do, if you'd been paying attention.'

'What do you mean?'

'Did you believe my story? Do you think I've told you the truth?'

'Yes.'

'Then you know what I can do.'

The fire was still burning but Tim began to shiver.

'I was there. With Richard and Jonathan. I didn't participate. Not like they did. But I was there. And what seeped into them seeped into me.'

Tim swallowed. 'I don't believe you!'

'Then why are you trembling?'

'I'm not!'

'You know what I could do to you.'

'You wouldn't dare do anything to me!!'

'Without leaving a mark.'

Tim grew cold all over.

'I promised I'd tell you the truth. I've done that. But it was for my benefit. A chance to unburden myself after all these years. Now you have to promise me that it will remain our secret.'

'But I can't!' It came out as a wail.

'Yes, you can.'

'And what if I refuse?'

'Then you'll have to face the consequences.'

He took a deep breath. 'There won't be any!'

'If that's what you believe.' Nicholas rose to his feet. Tim panicked. 'What are you doing?'

'Thank you for your hospitality, Mr Webber. Now I must go.'

'But you can't go! Not yet!'

'Why not?'

'You can't do this to me!'

'You wanted fame. I've given you the chance of it. But the chance comes with a price. The question is, are you willing to pay it?'

'There won't be any price!'

'If that's what you believe.'

'You're sick! Just a twisted old man! I'm going to crucify you in my account! You think your life is bad now! You think your life is bad now! Just wait until my story hits the papers!'

'As you wish. Now you have a decision to make. Think carefully, Mr Webber. For your sake, try to make the right one.'

Nicholas Scott walked from the room. Tim remained where he was. His heart was pounding.

Two hours later. Tim still sat beside the fire.

Just the empty threats of a sad old man. It meant nothing. This was his ticket and he was going to use it!

And then what?

Nothing, except the success he had always dreamed of. The keys of the kingdom were his. All he had to do was turn the lock.

And then what?

Tim Webber, journalist of the year. Tim Webber media celebrity. Tim Webber star.

But for how long?

Publish and be damned.

He hurled the tapes into the fire. The brown thread began to twist and boil. The smell filled the room. He sat and watched his ambitions crumple and die.